# EASTERN PROMISE

## Peter Stafford-Bow

Cover design by Patrick Latimer Illustration
www.PatrickLatimer.co.za

www.PeterStaffordBow.com
@PonceDuVin

Printed and bound by CPI Group (UK) Ltd, Croydon, CR0 4YY

光復香港, 時代革命

# Chapter 1

## *En Magnum*

"Let no-one be in doubt," declared The Liar, "this vineyard was sown by the hand of God!"

The guests nodded. They knew.

As one, they swirled their glasses, sending the dark wine spinning. I followed. They bowed beneath the dimmed spotlights and inhaled. As did I. Eyes widened. Pulses rose. The guests straightened, transformed. Some sighed, others grinned. I smiled with them.

My neighbour gave me a conspiratorial smirk. "That's a bitchin' wine!"

Murmurs of agreement from our fellow guests. The man's judgment was sound.

"Pomerol is the motherlode of the Right Bank," continued The Liar, from the head of the table. He gestured at the empty magnums before him, then held his glass aloft like a flaming torch. "And Pétrus the jewel in its crown!"

As one, the guests imbibed. Some sucked air through the wine, as true connoisseurs do. The room filled with the sound of muted gurgling as black-stained gums were bathed, reverently, in the juice of one of Bordeaux's finest estates. I tilted my glass, trying to gauge the wine's colour in the restaurant's gloom.

"Gentlemen," purred The Liar, "I'll let the wine do the talking. You don't need me to tell you that 1990 was the finest vintage of the past half-century."

The assembled guests did not. No-one spending five thousand pounds on a fine wine tasting hosted by the sommeliers of Magnum Club Platine needed informing which vintages were the century's finest. And there were no round-bellied, red-nosed old soaks here either. My fellow afficionados were sharp, well-groomed, and immaculately moisturised. Apple watches and designer jeans. Two shirt buttons undone, sometimes three.

With a flick of my wrist, I sent the liquid spinning once more and brought it to my nose. Lifting my pencil, I added *'Bitchin...'* to my tasting note.

I watched The Liar from the corner of my eye. Strictly speaking, of course, he hadn't actually lied. Not out loud, at least. 1990 was, without doubt, an extremely fine vintage. By general consensus, one of the best ever. And Pomerol, that hump of gravel overlooking the last few miles of the fat, meandering Dordogne before it nudges its way into the Gironde estuary, might well be described as the motherlode. Neighbouring St-Emilion has the heritage and by far the prettier village, but from an auction price perspective, Pomerol was top dog. As to whether the good Lord had sown the clay soils of Pétrus's vineyards with His own hand, you'd have to ask a higher religious authority than myself. But I had no reason to doubt it.

So, you may well ask, what's your beef, Felix Hart? Why so judgmental?

The short answer, of course, is that it's my job. As Head of Alcoholic Beverages for the country's largest supermarket chain, judging the quality and value of the world's wines is the role for which I was placed upon this earth. The disappointed wrinkle of the nostril, the contemptuously expelled spurt of Cabernet, the dismissive wave of the goblet; these are the tools of my trade.

"More Pétrus, sir?"

The waiter's eyes flickered over my tasting sheet. I placed my arm across the paper.

"Please."

"You're making a lot of notes, sir," he said, delivering a stream of red from the decanter's spout to my razor-thin Zalto.

"Yes, I'm studying to be a waiter."

The waiter scowled and moved on to my neighbour.

Not that my fellow guests, nor The Liar hosting the event,

would have been aware of my day job. To them, I was Rupert Gastlington, Chief Marketing Officer of Throat, a new dating app designed to match lonely or promiscuous wine-lovers with similarly inclined partners, based on their palate compatibility. I'd come up with the cover story myself, just twenty-four hours earlier, and I was slightly taken aback by how many of my fellow attendees appeared genuinely keen on investing.

But the purpose of an evening at Magnum Club Platine wasn't to raise Series A funding for one's tech start-up – that was a mere side benefit. Magnum Club Platine described itself, in its Instagram bio, as a 'Gated Community for Serious People who love Serious Wine'. In plain English, a playground in which society's young winners could cartwheel through the finest beverages known to humanity without the buzz-killing presence of oiks on a budget. Membership of Magnum Club Platine was strictly invitation only and required a joining fee of ten thousand pounds. The monthly events – all of which were over-subscribed – each cost a further five grand. The evenings only ever featured top-end Bordeaux, Burgundy or a handful of New World icon wines, all served, as you may have guessed, *en magnum*. Tonight's theme was 'Premiership Pomerol'.

Again, you might ask, why was Felix Hart, wine democratiser and humble man of the people, attending such an event? Why would I hose thousands of pounds down the pan just to spend an evening in the private dining room of a ponce-infested Hoxton restaurant, surrounded by men gargling Chateau Le Pin and swooning over the disruptive potential of the Estonian fintech scene? Principally, I'm pleased to say, because someone else was paying.

"I don't bother with notes, man. It distracts from the sensory experience," said my neighbour, a three-buttons-undone man, watching the liquid creep up his glass. "It's all up here." He tapped the side of his head. "And here!" he added, tapping his trouser pocket, through which the outline of his wallet was visible. He barked with laughter.

I smiled. Glancing down, I moved my hand so I could re-read

my tasting note.

"What's the verdict then, Rupert?" asked Three-Buttons.

"Oh," I said. "Firm, generously bodied... plummy, overly forward fruit..."

"No, I mean what score have you given it?"

*Of course*, I thought. *It's all numbers with these boys.*

"Ninety-four," I said.

The man's face fell. "You're kidding me, man. This is a ninety-nine, at least. It's absolutely damn exquisite!"

"Parker gave it one hundred. That's good enough for me," said the stubble-bearded man sitting opposite. "Dude, this wine is better than getting laid!"

I allowed my eyes to wander down the table. They paused at a lanky, nervous-looking man fiddling with his wine glass. My partner in crime. *Pay attention, for God's sake, you dozy tool*, I thought. He glanced at me. I held his gaze for a second, then allowed my eyes to continue their journey to the end of the table.

"So, tell us," smirked Stubble-Beard. "If Petrus '90 doesn't make the grade, what wine *would* you give one hundred points?"

I was tempted to suggest that anyone who reduced a living wine – its relationship with its *terroir*, the stage of its development in its decades-long life, the conditions prevailing at the moment of its consumption, not to mention the company in which it was consumed – to a single numerical score, was a tedious, innumerate fool.

But I didn't. Partly because I was following precise orders and they didn't include provoking a fist fight in a darkened dining room. And partly because, not for the first time that evening, I'd become conscious that the guest a couple of places to Stubble-Beard's left was staring at me, quite brazenly.

I met his stare for a second, then returned to my notes. He was older than most of the attendees; probably in his late forties. East Asian, presumably Chinese. He wore a black fitted face mask over his mouth and nose, which he pulled down with one finger to allow himself a sip of wine, before letting the material spring back once he'd swallowed. One still saw the occasional international visitor wearing a mask at professional trade tastings, what with all the spitting and spraying, but it was unusual at a private consumer tasting like this. He was certainly the only person at Magnum Club Platine wearing a mask, apart from the large doorman guarding the entrance to our private dining room, and I suspected his was more about concealing his identity in the event of any rough and tumble, rather than preventing the propagation of respiratory disease. But why the hell was this Chinese man staring at me? And why was he being so unsubtle about it? Perhaps he was Magnum Club Platine management. My heart quickened. Was he on to me?

"Come on," said Stubble-Beard. "Name a wine that scores higher than Petrus '90. Don't you like claret?"

I did, as a matter of fact. And if I were the scoring type, I'm sure I would give that fabled vintage ninety-nine points. Hell, I might even give it one hundred. But this wasn't Pétrus 1990. It wasn't Pétrus 2000 either, or even Pétrus 2025.

"Oh, I'd give at least ninety-nine points to a top claret like that, for sure," I replied.

"Er, dude, Pétrus *is* a claret!" said Stubble-Beard, in a stage whisper.

Someone nearby gave a high-pitched laugh.

"I know it is," I said, lifting my glass and swirling the wine.

The room quietened a little. The guests either side of us had stopped their chatter and were watching me. The unsettling Chinese man continued to stare too. I stuck my nose into my glass and inhaled. Chateau Pétrus is a wine of immense power, particularly a superstar vintage like 1990, but it wears its power lightly, like a dandy knight, its chain mail hidden beneath folds of satin. The wine before me was a thug. Rich and intense, for sure, but more like a muscle-bound cage fighter rattling the bars as the audience bays.

"Then what are you talking about, man?" said Three-Buttons. He frowned and scratched the chest hair exposed by the crisp V of his shirt. "I don't get this guy," he said, to the room at large.

I set down my glass and slowly, casually, looked over to

my accomplice. He was tapping his fingers rapidly against his tasting sheet. Thank God the fool was watching this time. I placed my finger against my nose and held his gaze. The man's eyes widened, then he nodded, almost imperceptibly, and slipped his hand into his pocket.

"This isn't Pétrus," I said.

"Er, yes, it is, dude!" called Stubble-Beard.

The room had quietened enough for The Liar, chatting to the guest beside him, to realise something was up.

"He says this isn't Pétrus," called Stubble-Beard.

"Sorry, I've clearly missed something," said The Liar, still smiling. "Is there a problem...?" His eyes dropped to a sheet of paper on the table. "Mr Gastlington?"

The man with the high-pitched voice laughed again.

"There are two principal methods by which a fraudster fakes a wine," I said, bringing the glass back to my nose and inhaling.

The room was silent now, all eyes on me. All except the pair belonging to my nervous friend. His were focussed on his hands, which were fiddling rather unsubtly in his lap. He glanced up for a second to check he hadn't been spotted before returning to his furtive task, for it had been made very clear at the start of the tasting that the use of phones at Magnum Club Platine was strictly forbidden.

"The fraudster's first method," I continued, "is to substitute a cheaper wine from the same region, ideally from a similar vintage. The challenge, of course, is to find a wine good enough to pass, but cheap enough to make the fraud worthwhile."

I nosed my glass once more and glanced at my accomplice, who was now sitting watching me, mouth agape. I prayed to Bacchus he'd done his job properly.

"Pomerol, as you all know, is not exactly blessed with properties churning out bargain wines that can pass for Chateau Pétrus. You either get out your wallet or go home."

A few guests sniggered. Stubble-Beard nodded, approvingly. But the unsettling Chinese man didn't move, just continued to stare at me from behind his mask.

"I'm sorry, I'm afraid I must ask you to stop this nonsense," said The Liar, rising to his feet. He drew his gangling frame up to its full height and stared at me down the table. "There is nothing wrong with this wine. With the greatest of respect, Mr Gastlington, I think you'll find I've tasted rather more Chateau Pétrus than you."

I smiled. "Then you're a lucky man, sir. Because that means you have tasted a great deal of Pétrus indeed."

The Liar's face fell. I spotted my accomplice fiddling beneath the table once again. *Get on with it, man, for pity's sake!*

"The fraudster's second method," I continued, slightly louder, "is to substitute a cheaper wine from a different region, potentially not even using the same blend of grape varieties. The aim is simply to match the power of the original wine, to approximate the mouthfeel, the volume of fruit, the level of tannin and so on, without worrying too much about the finesse. Of course, this implies the victim of the fraud possesses a limited knowledge of the wine in question."

"Sorry, I don't buy it," said Three-Buttons. "I'm calling you out, bud. I know my wines. I drink a lot of serious wine."

There were murmurs of agreement from around the table.

"I think you've embarrassed yourself quite enough now, Mr Gastlington," said The Liar. "I'm afraid we must ask you to leave."

"You do know your wines," I said, turning to Three-Buttons. "You all do. What we have here, you see, is a combination of the two methods. Smell the bouquet."

I took a theatrical sniff. The room copied me. Even the Chinese man tugged the mask from his nose and leaned forward to smell his glass, though his eyes didn't break their stare.

"Pétrus is vinified nearly entirely from Merlot. Those of you who have tasted it previously may recall its intense black fruit, swathed in aromas of chocolate ganache and earthy mushroom. The very pinnacle of Merlot's expression, only achievable in Bordeaux's maritime climate."

I had the room's undivided attention now. Even The Liar

was impressed.

"But this wine has notes of prune and cherry. An absolute giveaway for warmer climate fruit. Gentlemen, you are smelling a Syrah blend. A good Syrah, mind you. Probably a decent Côte-Rôtie."

"Yeah, man. I can smell it now," said Three-Buttons. There were nods around the table.

"But there's Merlot and Cabernet Franc in there, too, as you'd expect in an old Pétrus," I continued. "That's where the first method comes in. It's just that the stuff they've mixed with the Côte-Rôtie is too thin. And too young. There's none of the perfume you'd find in a top Pomerol, is there? The wine's probably from the back slopes of Fronsac, a few miles away."

"Is this guy for real?" called a guest near the end of the table. "Is this wine fake?"

"Gentlemen, actually, now you mention it, the Pétrus might be slightly corked," said The Liar, twisting his head from side to side and inserting each nostril alternately into his glass.

"I don't think it's the cork that's rotten," I said.

The Liar's face reddened. "This is a one-off! The bottle's faulty. It happens."

"Shame about the rest of them," I said, pointing at the row of magnums before him.

"What do you mean?" said Three-Buttons.

"That's not Lafleur. That's not La Violette. That's not Le Pin. They're all dodgy. They're all cheap Bordeaux blended with premium Rhone, Languedoc, or Californian wine."

"Are you serious?" said Three-Buttons.

"Hey! You're not allowed to use a phone in here!" shouted The Liar, who'd spotted my accomplice dabbing at his groin.

"I'm not!" wailed the man, slapping his hands over his crotch, his face guiltier than a guide dog returning home without its master.

"Confiscate that phone!" ordered The Liar.

The waiter, who until now had been watching proceedings from the side of the room, strode over and lunged at my accomplice's lap.

I rose to my feet. "Well, it's been lovely, but I have to attend a blackcurrant liqueur tasting at the Polish embassy shortly. Farewell, gentlemen." I gathered my tasting notes and tucked them inside my jacket.

"No notes are permitted to leave the room," shouted The Liar, pointing at me. "Confiscate those papers."

The waiter stopped attempting to part my accomplice from his phone and advanced around the table. Unlike The Liar, he appeared quite a well-built chap. I turned on my heel and walked briskly around the table in the opposite direction.

"Get Igor," shouted The Liar. "Igor!"

The door opened assertively. Igor, clearly, was the mask-wearing bouncer employed to discourage riff-raff from entering our private dining room. It was also clear from his demeanour that his skill set included dealing with undesirables located within the room too. He stepped inside, closed the door behind him and approached me on the opposite side of the table to the waiter, leaving me caught in a rapidly closing pincer movement.

"No need for any trouble," I called, deciding the waiter would make the more manageable adversary. I trotted back towards him, my hands up, then lunged and grabbed his arms before he could lay a finger on me. I swung him round just as Igor caught up, pushed him into the masked bouncer and scurried in the direction of the door. Unfortunately, several of the attendees had become unsettled by the evening's sudden descent into light wrestling and jumped to their feet, cluttering my escape route with overturned seats and agitated guests. I hurdled the first couple of chairs only to collide with a small man who appeared to be having some kind of panic attack. He grabbed my sleeve and, despite my frantic karate chops to his arm, refused to let go. Igor, who turned out to be quite nimble, caught up with me and placed a large, pudgy hand around my throat.

"Take the tasting notes, they're in his jacket pocket!" shouted The Liar.

"Argh," I exclaimed, as Igor thrust his hand inside my jacket.

His grip was quite unpleasantly strong. I definitely couldn't breathe, and my head was beginning to feel rather hot.

The entire room was now on its feet. Most of the guests were barging for the door, some clambering over the table in an attempt to escape; the clatter of tumbling chairs interspersed with the tinkle of expensive wine glasses exploding against the floorboards.

"I think the police are here," called a voice.

My assailant turned his head towards the door. I was unable to do the same, due to the vice around my neck, but I spotted my moment. I reached out and pulled Igor's face mask up over his eyes. He released his grip and before he could tug down his blindfold, I took the opportunity to punch him as hard as I could on the nose. He grunted and took a heavy step back, raising his arms to parry the next blow. But there would be no need for further violence, not now the police were here. I glanced across the table to the doorway. Worryingly, there was no sign of flashing blue lights or a posse of hard-bitten detectives, just a handful of guests clustered around the exit, curious to see how our little tussle might play out.

"Where's the police?" I yelped.

The remaining guests shrugged their shoulders.

I turned back to Igor, who had ripped the mask from his face and appeared rather vexed. I noticed he had a small smear of blood beneath one nostril.

"Now look, no-one wants any trouble," I said.

Igor hurled himself at me. I leapt back, just avoiding his outstretched claws, and landed arse first on the table. I scrabbled backwards, but before I could propel myself out of reach the man grabbed my ankle, raised a fist, which I suspected was destined for a sensitive part of my body, and yanked me towards him with such force he pulled the shoe clean off my foot. As he staggered off-balance, fist and shoe waving wildly, I attempted to shuffle away again, but the discarded tasting sheets, spilt wine and my shoeless foot conspired to prevent me gaining any traction on the table, and the more frantically I flailed, the faster my hands and feet slipped on its wine-sodden surface.

"Police! Where the hell are the bloody police?" I shouted.

The doorman recovered his footing, threw my shoe aside and clambered onto the table. I kicked out at him with my single shoed foot, but I may as well have booted a half-ton sandbag for all the difference it made. Teeth bared, Igor raised his fists and prepared to pummel me through the tabletop.

"Somebody help, for God's sake!" I screamed.

I flung my arm back, desperately hoping I might grasp the far side of the table and somehow pull myself to safety, only for my knuckles to chime against something hard and smooth. I grabbed the object and, as the livid doorman fell upon me, swung it against his head with all my strength.

The magnum of Pétrus exploded with a quite spectacular bang. I'd already closed my eyes to avoid witnessing my imminent murder, which proved a very wise move as several shards of high velocity glass embedded themselves in my hand and face. The doorman, who turned out to be extremely heavy, collapsed on top of me and refused to move.

After a short while, once I was confident I was still alive, I levered the man's body aside, dragged myself off the table and attempted to shake the larger fragments of glass out of my hair and clothes. The excitement had clearly been too much for the remaining guests, including my so-called accomplice, for the only person remaining in the room was the Chinese man. He stepped over to the table, still wearing his mask, and peered at the comatose doorman.

"You have made a very big mess, Mr Hart."

I was about to protest that it was hardly my fault, when I realised the man had addressed me by my real name.

"And now, I suggest you leave very quickly, Mr Hart."

# Chapter 2

## Art and Antiques

"Well, Felix," said Sandra. "You cocked that one up, didn't you?"

"I think that's extremely unfair. How on earth was I supposed to behave while being subjected to a vicious attempted murder?"

Sandra rolled her eyes. I glanced at her colleague, my furtive accomplice from the previous evening. He appeared rather less nervous today, presumably because we were sitting in a bright, air-conditioned office in the London headquarters of his and Sandra's employer, Paris-Blois Brands International. The man's job title, Principal Legal Counsel, shone authoritatively from the nameplate attached to the office door. He frowned, in a lawyerly manner, and chimed his pen twice against the glass tabletop. It struck me that Paris-Blois was the type of corporation that liked to know what its employees were up to beneath their desks.

"What's the prognosis on the doorman?" asked Sandra.

"He'll live," replied the lawyer. "A fractured skull, severe concussion and multiple lacerations. He's lucky not to have brain damage." He looked at me disapprovingly.

"Oh, I hadn't realised you were a qualified doctor as well as a lawyer," I said. "How accomplished of you. Never mind his lacerations, look at mine!"

"Where?" said Sandra, leaning forward.

"There and there!" I said, pointing at my cheek and chin. It still gave me just the slightest frisson of excitement when she moved in close. How did she keep that skin so flawless? Vigorous scrubbing? A ruinously expensive elixir, applied nightly in the privacy of her bedroom?

"There's a miniscule scratch on your cheek," she said, sitting back. "I can't even see the other one."

"There were pieces of shrapnel literally hanging out of my face. It was like a charnel house."

"Yes, bit of a shame you destroyed the bottle," said the lawyer. "That might have been useful evidence."

"It's a bit of a shame you didn't alert your police friends before I was strangled half to death," I replied. "Where the hell were they? They were supposed to be on standby, ready to abseil through the windows."

"I don't recall the room having any windows, actually."

"Well, ready to knock the bloody door in, then! With one of those battering rams. Did you even send the message?"

"Yes, I sent the message following your signal, as agreed. The detective constable was waiting outside, as planned, and attended the premises."

"What, just one constable? And what do you mean, he *attended* the premises? What was he doing, asking the maître d' for a table with a better view of my murder?"

"I fear you have an overly optimistic expectation of the Metropolitan Police's Art and Antiques Unit," said the lawyer. "They only have two officers – one constable and a semi-retired sergeant."

"We're lucky they agreed to investigate at all," said Sandra. "They only bother looking into counterfeit wine because Paris-Blois pays them a grant to cover the department's staffing budget."

"The FBI once had a twenty-strong division devoted exclusively to wine fraud," said the lawyer, wistfully.

"So, where was this constable while I was being throttled? I definitely heard someone say the police had arrived."

"Yes, as I mentioned, the constable attended the premises. But, when he realised a violent altercation was underway, he retreated to the street to call for backup."

"Backup? Couldn't he have used his baton? Or fired a Taser?"

"It's the Art and Antiques Unit, Felix, not the Sweeney. Unfortunately, the constable in question has mobility issues. Walks with a stick. He's not really the type to leap around knocking people over the head."

"Jesus Christ. I'll sleep soundly in my bed tonight, then. Thank goodness the boys in blue are just a hobble and a crutch-swing away. I won't be volunteering for another job like this, I can tell you."

"You didn't actually volunteer though, did you Felix?" said Sandra. "I believe we funded a week-long, all-expenses-paid study trip to Siena for you to research the wines of Tuscany. Which, going by the amount of Brunello you drank, appears to have been a roaring academic success."

"You got a couple of Chianti listings out of it, I recall."

"We did, Felix, you're right. Very generous of you. All things considered, it might have been cheaper just donating the wines for you to put on Gatesave's shelves, but there we go."

"Look, I did what you asked. I identified last night's wines as fake and kept hold of my tasting notes as evidence. It's not my fault Paris-Blois don't employ anyone who can tell the difference between their top Bordeaux and a bottle of plonk."

"We employ plenty of people who can identify our luxury Bordeaux brands, Felix." Sandra ran her hands through her hair. "We just don't employ anyone who looks like the kind of over-entitled prick who'd spend ten grand joining Magnum Club Platine."

"Charming. Do it yourself next time, then."

"Let's get back to the point, shall we?" She turned to the lawyer. "Robert, are they going to arrest these people who've been merrily counterfeiting our wines for the past two years? Not to mention charging gullible bankers a fortune for the privilege of drinking Pinot Grigio mixed with food colouring?"

"Actually, the fakes were pretty well constructed," I said. "They definitely knew what they were doing."

"Shut up, Felix. I don't care how well constructed they were. Those fraudsters are stealing our bloody dinner. Robert, are the police going to press charges?"

"I'm afraid not. All the counterfeit wine appears to have been disposed of while the officer waited for backup. The suspects had disappeared by then, as had all the witnesses – except me, of course. The Art and Antiques Unit say they don't have enough evidence or resources to pursue a case. The police are interested, however, in speaking to the person who assaulted the doorman."

"That's outrageous!" I said. "He's the one who should be locked up."

"The man's lying unconscious in hospital with his head swaddled in bandages," said the lawyer. "So, you can understand why they might be taking an interest."

"To be honest, I'm quite tempted to grass you up myself, Felix, given last night's shambles," said Sandra. "Robert, I assume you hung around to give a statement to your police contact once his colleagues turned up? And I trust you didn't mention Felix's involvement?"

"No, it was not necessary to mention Felix. I explained to the police that it was I who had recognised the wines as fakes, and that I sent the waiting officer a text message, as arranged. I described how a Magnum Club Platine staff member spotted me using my phone, that he attempted, unsuccessfully, to confiscate it, and that following my manhandling I immediately left the premises. Thankfully, I was seated next to the exit and didn't witness the subsequent violence."

"Yes, thanks for the support," I said. "Much appreciated."

"So," said Sandra, folding her arms. "We've spent nearly fifty thousand pounds getting three people into Magnum Club Platine under pseudonyms which are now useless, blown our credibility with the Met's Art and Antiques Unit, and all we have to show for it is a doorman with a fractured skull."

"Yes, a pretty fair summary, I'm afraid," said the lawyer.

"What do you mean, three people?" I said.

Sandra didn't answer.

"You said you got three people into Magnum Club Platine. Me, our fearless legal eagle here, so who's the third?"

Another pause.

"Is he outside?" asked Sandra.

The lawyer nodded.

"Better get on with it, then."

# Chapter 3

## Inspector Ma

"I believe you've met Inspector Ma of the Hong Kong Police Force," said Sandra.

The man didn't offer his hand. In these germ-ravaged days, many didn't, of course. He sat down beside Sandra, placed his elbows on the table and stared at me over his clasped palms.

"Ah. It's you," I said. "Yes, the inspector and I share the same taste in wine. No mask today, then?"

Ma didn't respond, just continued to stare at me over his hands.

"Inspector Ma is on secondment to Paris-Blois Brands International," explained the lawyer, "to gather intelligence on the trade in counterfeit luxury goods."

"Just top Bordeaux? Or does he cover overpriced handbags too?"

"Our business is based on consumer trust in the integrity of our brands," said Sandra. "Whether they be fashion, perfume, spirits, fine wine or indeed, as your glib comment alludes, luxury leather goods. Unfortunately, as global demand for an aspirational lifestyle has increased so has the market for fakes."

"So, this chap's in charge of supressing Chinese knock-offs, is he? Big job, I imagine."

Ma's eyes narrowed slightly. *So you do have a pulse*, I thought.

"Our board has declared the trade in counterfeit Paris-Blois brands an existential threat to our business," said Sandra. "My CEO has placed me in charge of our efforts to suppress it."

"And is the inspector here working hand in hand with our

dynamic Arts and Antiques Unit?" I asked.

Sandra glanced at Ma.

"Regrettably, relations between the British authorities and the Hong Kong Police Force are no longer on such a friendly footing," said Ma. His voice was soft and precise. "Sometimes politics and law make uneasy bedfellows." He smiled.

The lawyer cleared his throat and pushed back his chair. "If you'll excuse me, I may be required to recuse myself." He rose and headed for the door. I noticed his nervous face of last night had returned. Once he'd shut the door behind him, Sandra continued.

"We need your help with another tasting, Felix."

"What, like last night's little soirée? No, thanks. I've had enough of being throttled half to death by psychotic doormen."

"I thought you were extremely effective, Mr Hart," said Ma.

Sandra raised her eyebrows.

"Thank you, Inspector. I'm glad somebody appreciates my efforts."

"Your description of the fake wine was very forensic. Most impressive."

"Well, of course, I'm trained in that kind of thing. I'm a qualified Minstrel of Wine, you see."

"So I understand. But what a shame you made a violent and unprovoked assault on that doorman."

"It was hardly unprovoked. The man was strangling me to death! You saw it!"

"Indeed, I was watching very closely. You hit the man when his guard was down. Not exactly Queensbury Rules, wouldn't you say? I'm sure the British police would be most interested to learn of your identity."

"What nonsense is this?" I said, looking at Sandra.

"Why don't you just help us, Felix?" she said.

"Or you'll dob me in? I don't think so. Your risk-averse legal colleague gave a dodgy statement to the police last night that omitted to mention I was working with him."

"So what?" said Sandra. "He didn't lie, not explicitly. And

I very much doubt the police are going to give Paris-Blois's Principal Legal Counsel a hard time, given that we pay their wages."

"They might when I tell them you bribed me to attend the tasting, so you could falsely claim the wines were fake."

"Here we go," said Sandra, folding her arms and rolling her eyes. "And why would we have done that?"

"Perhaps you had a commercial dispute with the organisers of Magnum Club Platine and were blackmailing them into a price increase, with help from a rogue Chinese policeman."

"Perhaps you're a horrible little thug who likes putting doormen in hospital," Sandra replied.

"I didn't even touch the man. It was him, I saw it." I pointed at Ma.

"I think you'll find there were many witnesses who would disagree, Mr Hart," said Ma, also folding his arms.

"Not that many. Most of the guests were attempting to flee the premises, just like Sandra's brave colleague. Difficult to tell who was doing what during all that chaos, I imagine."

"I'm sure enough of our fellow guests saw what happened."

"Well, good luck persuading any of those arrogant schmucks to admit they paid thousands of pounds for the privilege of discovering they can't tell the difference between First Growth Bordeaux and supermarket Côtes du Rhône."

That shut them up. Half a minute went by and no-one spoke. Ma stared at me without expression, Sandra with undisguised contempt. I didn't really mind. I'd given up attempting to insert myself into her good books years ago. To be honest, I should have stopped trying immediately after we first met. But we're all wiser with experience, aren't we?

"I give him his due, he thinks on his feet," said Ma, at last.

"I'll concede he has a certain peasant cunning," replied Sandra. "Though he's still a bloody liability."

"Hello?" I said. "I am actually here, you know. And, in case you hadn't quite got the message, I'm not participating in any more of your dodgy *dégustations*."

"Oh, I think you will, Mr Hart," said Ma.

I stood up.

"Do you now? Well, I'm afraid my day rate's just gone up, quite dramatically, and I suspect I may exceed Paris-Blois's expenses policy. Now, if you'll excuse me, I'm required back at Gatesave head office. I have a fascinating third-quarter budget meeting with my boss, and I'd hate to miss a moment of it."

"One million US dollars," said Ma.

I sat back down.

"On the other hand," I said, "I'm sure my boss can muddle through without me."

# Chapter 4

## Break Things

One million dollars to attend a wine tasting was a ludicrous offer, of course. I didn't believe it for a second. I won't deny that the inspector had piqued my interest, but I had plenty of experience of working with Paris-Blois over the past decade and there was always a highly unpleasant catch to any episode involving that fanatically ruthless corporation. I'd found myself impaled on the point of Sandra's stiletto too many times to count, and I had no intention of stumbling into another of her elephant traps.

I rested my hands on the table, determined not to be the one to break the silence. Ma sat unnaturally still, not even blinking, his eyes focussed rather unnervingly on my neck. Some kind of Chinese interrogation trick, no doubt. I transferred my gaze to Sandra. Cold blue eyes. Fair hair shining with blonde highlights. Cream, tailored shirt. Lower, through the glass tabletop, a short, dark skirt, crossed legs in sheer black tights. Low heels, one of which dangled tantalisingly from her toes. She stared back at me, lips pursed.

"Seriously, a million US dollars?" I said. "Where's the tasting?"

"We don't know," said Ma.

"Well, that's helpful. Do you intend to find out? Or am I to spend my evenings rummaging through the bins of Bishopsgate's more fashionable restaurants, looking for suspicious piles of empty Romanée-Conti?"

"You may have to travel further east than the City of London," said Ma.

"Hackney?"

"Hong Kong, Mr Hart."

"Ah, your own patch. What's the occasion? The Triads' Christmas party?"

Ma didn't smile.

"And, at the risk of sounding a touch mercenary, when might I see the money?"

Again, Ma chose not to respond.

"The Twelfth of Never, presumably?"

"The million-dollar fee is entirely genuine," said Sandra. "This is a matter of critical importance to every wine and spirits producer on the planet. Paris-Blois are just one of the contributors."

"Well, it all sounds unbelievably exciting. The trouble is, we have quite a lot of history, don't we, Sandra?"

Sandra's face hardened a little. "Work history, yes."

"A history of working together which often involves me being at a disadvantage. Life-threateningly so."

Ma glanced at Sandra.

"That's a rather silly exaggeration, Felix. And all water under the bridge, I'm sure."

"Sadly, much as I'd love to help, it all sounds a little too good to be true. I'll pass. Unless you're paying cash up front, of course."

I rose to my feet.

"We will see you tomorrow evening, Mr Hart," said Ma.

"Rather unlikely," I replied. "I already have an appointment with several very pleasant bottles of wine. Good luck with the rest of your secondment, Inspector."

\*\*\*

I hadn't been lying regarding my third-quarter budget meeting. My boss had looked moderately peeved as I sashayed into the meeting room halfway through his session, but I'd apologised profusely and he soon relented. You see, my star was riding high at Gatesave, thanks to the beverage department's consistently outstanding performance, which had been supercharged in recent years by the lockdowns, shutdowns and miscellaneous misery sweeping the land. In fact, it's fair to say that Gatesave Supermarkets as a whole had enjoyed a quite magnificent pandemic. As expected, I was given a ten per cent budget stretch, but I knew that wouldn't be too tricky to achieve so long as everyone kept drinking. And, given the year ahead's prognoses of pestilence, climate breakdown and nuclear Armageddon, that seemed like a damn good bet.

Gatesave Supermarkets had recently appointed a new CEO: a young thruster from the world of private equity by the name of Brad Schusselkind. The media called him 'Brad the Impaler' for his devotion to disruptive technology and his enthusiasm for dispensing with the more traditional aspects of human resources – that is to say, humans. Brad had embraced the pandemic's aftermath as an opportunity to revolutionise Gatesave and catapult it to the forefront of the artificial intelligence era. He had christened the new financial period Year Zero, declared that we were no longer managers but Change Agents, and fired all members of staff unable to generate one thousand new followers across their social media accounts within a week of his joining (a close shave – I managed to purchase several hundred aggressively pouting female Instagram followers from a Belarussian website just before the deadline).

Cometh the hour, cometh the man, and the markets adored Brad the Impaler. Gatesave's share price hit an all-time high and our crisis-swollen revenue streams were channelled into machine learning, large language models, robotic depots and an online-delivery drone fleet. All exciting, shiny stuff, I'm sure you'll agree, and our institutional investors were clearly dazzled. But for me, the jury was still out. Not least because every Wednesday, at six a.m., Brad hosted a ten-minute video conference call, named 'Break the Week', for his senior Change Agency Leadership team. Distressingly, this included me.

Brad was a big fan of rising before the sun. He called it Azimuthal Aspiration and it was one of the pillars of his personally crafted wellness regime, details of which were available in the link on his Instagram bio. Brad wasn't keen on alcohol, dairy products, or late-night gallivanting, which he termed 'sub-optimal lifestyle vectors'. I suppose that explained why Break the Week was a crack-of-dawn online conference call rather than a midnight fondue party in a beer cellar; though if I ever attain the heady heights of the C-suite, I'll be implementing the latter on day one, mark my words. Anyway, I digress. Gatesave's hundred-strong team of Change Agents were obliged, every week, to log into this six-a.m. video call with camera enabled. I had resorted to taping a couple of Six Sigma PowerPoint slides to my headboard, clipping my iPad to a carefully orientated music stand beside my bed and going to sleep in a work-appropriate shirt on Tuesday night. The moment my alarm sounded at one minute to six the following morning, all I had to do was struggle into a sitting position, open the video conferencing app, rap a stylus vigorously against my cheek, and I looked ready to gallop my cavalry across the corporate battlefield and take an enemy trench before breakfast.

"We are not living through one crisis, singular!" beamed Brad, teeth shining, from my iPad screen that morning. "We are living through multiple, simultaneous crises. Crises, plural. We are experiencing a Climacteric Matrix!"

Every few seconds, the video feed of four random Change Agents appeared in a row along the bottom of the screen. As each participant spotted that they were on air, they would suddenly lift their chin and begin nodding earnestly to Brad's inspirational brain dump.

"A Climacteric Matrix, people. Multiple, concurrent crises. Somebody, hit me, quick – what word's an anagram of crises?"

Silence.

"Guys, I need to hear you're ready to Break the Week! The week's half done already! *Tempus fugit*, people! I want to hear my Change Agents breaking things and re-forging them, faster, leaner, smarter!"

The four faces along the bottom of the screen furrowed their brows. They were replaced by another quartet, who stroked their chins and grimaced in intense thought.

"Felix Hart!" called Brad.

I nearly leapt out of bed. There I was, in the bottom left! I hadn't even recognised myself. Christ, I looked terrible; though in my defence, I had been drinking unfiltered orange wine at my local after-hours wine bar until two in the morning.

"Felix! Head of Beverages! Are you Breaking the Week with us, Felix? I want to hear an anagram of crises. Hit me! Go!"

"Oh, ah, erm… Christ, no, no, I mean, erm… Circus…? Crass…? Cress…? No, hang on."

"All wrong! It rhymes with prize!"

"Erm… Cries?"

"No! The answer is… Scries! Scries! Who knows the meaning of scries?"

No-one did.

"A person who scries is one who reads the future via a reflective surface," shone Brad. "Like a crystal ball. Or a mirror. Or…? Yes! A screen, like the device you're using right now! Change Agents, you are witnessing the future unfold before your eyes. But listen, I don't want witnesses. I want perpetrators. Do you understand?"

To my relief, my picture disappeared, to be replaced by Maria from Supply Chain halfway through inserting a spoon of muesli into an angry infant's mouth.

"I have great news, people. I'm using this call to introduce you to a group of really smart guys I've brought in to support Gatesave. They're from a West Coast consultancy called Fulmination Technologies. Everyone, say hi to Scott, Raj, Ed, and Zak. These guys are going to give you the rocket fuel you'll need to take this company orbital."

Maria, her muesli-rejecting infant, and the other Gatesave colleagues disappeared from the screen, to be replaced by four youths in t-shirts, none of whom looked old enough to buy fireworks unaccompanied, let alone procure rocket fuel.

"Hey," they said, in unison.

"Guys, I'm so stoked to be working with you again!" grinned Brad. "Ok, Change Agents, this week I need each of you to connect with your assigned partner at Fulmination Tech and develop a piece of creative disruption that takes this business up a level. I want to see your ideas by Friday."

The call ended and I crept to the toilet for a pee.

\*\*\*

I decided I'd base myself in the Gatesave office that afternoon. My physical presence wasn't required, but colleagues were obliged to spend at least eight hours every week working from company premises, presumably to discourage staff members from relocating permanently to Corfu. I had an evening appointment in the centre of town and it made sense to clock up a few old-fashioned office hours.

A while back, to avoid both the viral miasma of public transport and the physical misery of traditional cycling, I'd purchased a top-of-the-range electric scooter. Though technically illegal to ride on public highways, the machine was a godsend on the congested streets of London, despite the very real risk of a night-time pothole catapulting you into the path of a double-decker bus.

I steered my scooter off the Thames-side cycleway and accelerated up the footpath to Gatesave's great glass office. You were supposed to dismount once you were on campus, but the small army of security guards who once patrolled the paths and enforced that type of thing had been reduced to a solitary man sitting in a booth beside the service entrance on Fulham Palace Road. The rest of the human security team had been replaced by golf cart-sized robots, which hummed around the building's perimeter on rubber wheels, their dark glass domes concealing an array of cameras, sensors and, presumably, given our CEO's enthusiasm for radical forward compatibility, mountings for laser guns.

"Please alight from your transport, unless you have a mobility issue," called the nearest golf cart, in a friendly female voice, as I glided past.

"I'm disabled, I am," I called back, in an offensively poor Welsh accent.

"Please accept our apology for the challenge," replied the golf cart. "We're learning and we'll try to do better in future."

Frankly, there were so few people around that even if I'd been scooting blindfold, a collision would have been extremely unlikely. I parked my scooter in one of the bike cages, opened the head office app and held the phone against the ID panel beside the door. After a second's thought, the glass dividers parted, allowing me through to reception.

"Good afternoon, Felix," said a dome-headed wheelie bin. "Today your smart seat is on the second floor east."

"Top o' the morning to ya," I replied, in an accent that might have seen me reprimanded for cultural insensitivity if there'd been anyone around to care. I had no idea whether using different accents confused the security droids' voice-recognition software, but it was worth a try.

A few years ago, the interior of Gatesave's headquarters would have been fizzing like a beehive on speed. The eight panoramic elevators gliding up and down the building's façade in glass tubes would have been in constant use; those for the foot-soldiers stopping at every floor while the express lifts whisked the top nobs direct from ground to boardroom. At night, the block would have glittered silver and gold, its lights visible a mile downstream. But now, the top four floors were dark and the two beneath had been sub-let to an IT company for server space. Just a solitary elevator was in operation and it lifted me, silently and without needing to be instructed, to the second floor.

I nodded to the half-dozen colleagues on the second floor east, all sitting at separate banks of desks, and found the spot assigned by the app. I clipped the magnetic power cable to my laptop and opened the screen.

"Don't forget to sanitise!" said a soft female voice from beneath the desk.

I leaned over the arm of my chair towards the gel dispenser and held my hand beneath it. A blue light flashed on my palm once, twice, then the machine sounded a quiet raspberry and a curl of alcoholic paste fell into my palm.

"You weren't going to bother, were you, mucky pup?" said another female voice. A human one this time.

Marissa, Head of Product Integrity for canned and packaged goods, parked herself against the neighbouring desk and watched me rub the gel around my fingers. Her own hands were thrust deep in the pockets of a puffer jacket wrapped tight around her body. Since the move to home working, the comfort of Gatesave's network servers had taken precedence over that of the human employees, and the ambient temperature now hovered somewhere between tundra and Arctic.

"Hey, Marissa. How's it going?"

"I'm freezing. I ran in this morning."

Marissa's legs were sheathed in purple leggings, ending in multicoloured running shoes. She swung open her puffer jacket, hands still in pockets, to reveal her bare midriff beneath a purple sports bra, then wrapped it back round herself.

"Good to see you haven't let yourself go since last week."

"How long are you staying today? I think you should give me a lift home on that scooter of yours."

"I'd love to, but I'm catching up with a few winey friends tonight. Happy to give you a ride next week."

"I'm in the Maldives next week on business."

"It's a hard life, isn't it?"

"You can talk, mister, with a decade of fancy vineyard trips under your belt. I won't be going anywhere near a luxury stilt house, I can assure you. I'll be in Male, the capital, which is a hole."

"Problems in the world of tinned tuna?"

"Not for wider discussion, but it appears our supplier of ethically caught tuna has radically loosened his definition of ethical."

"He's being mean to the dolphins?"

"No complaints from the dolphins. It's the slaves shackled to his boats who are less happy."

"Oh dear."

"To make things even more interesting, our new friends from Fulmination Tech have declared this a glorious opportunity to radically remake the supply chain. They've suggested we buy a fishing fleet and operate it ourselves."

"That's a ludicrous idea."

"I know it is. But our CEO thinks it's a brilliant idea, so I've already been given the budget to lease a dozen boats and purchase the permits from the Maldivian Minister for Fisheries. Which I have to do in person."

"What, Gatesave's given you the money, just like that? It took me two years to get the budget for a dishwasher in the wine tasting room."

"This is the new world, Felix. Move fast and break things. Have you had your consultation with the Fulmination boys yet?"

"I'm speaking to them this afternoon."

"You'd better get your wish list polished, then. Anyway, enough chat. I have a video call with an Indian Ocean pirate captain in a few minutes. Not the kind of thing you have to deal with on your jaunts through Provence, I'm sure."

"Oh, the world of wine has its dirty little secrets, I promise you."

"Does it now?" Marissa took a step closer. "I'll be back the week after, so you'd better make yourself available for a night or two, ok? You can work from my place." She glanced around, slipped a hand from her pocket and ran it over the back of my neck.

Those of you familiar with modern workplace ethics might be shocked by this brazen invasion of my personal space. But, I don't mind admitting, it didn't bother me in the slightest. I'm not condoning such behaviour, of course; simply stating that a man of my presence and vitality should be prepared for, or even expect, such encounters. For in this brave new world, where confident, highly qualified women outnumber their male peers two-to-one, and intelligent, sensitive young men are more likely than not to be limp, lost and wracked with self-doubt, the presence of a male exuding animal magnetism like a bison on the sultry plains of Idaho is bound to induce recklessness on the part of many women (not to mention some men, too). It is the responsibility of such males to wear their power lightly: to display it respectfully but to deploy it, if unambiguously invited, with generosity and vigour.

Build it, as they say, and they will come.

"Hope you've sanitised, Marissa."

Marissa gently grasped a fistful of my hair.

"I'll block out the whole week, I promise. Don't get kidnapped by pirates."

# Chapter 5

## Summons

"Felix, hi! Great to talk. So, you're Gatesave's main wine guy?"

Scott, Raj, Ed and Zak, their heads each occupying one quarter of my screen, gazed at me rapturously.

"Yes, I suppose I am."

"So cool," said Zak, from the top right. "Look, I hope you don't mind but all four of us wanted to come on this call. Everyone at Fulmination Tech loves wine."

"Yeah, Zak has a cellar in Palo Alto with, like, a thousand bottles or something?" said Scott, from the top left.

"More like eight hundred, but yeah, that's my guy cave," smiled Zak.

"Very impressive," I said. "All local wines or are your tastes global?"

"Around three-quarters Californian, the rest is French. Pretty much all Burgundy."

"That'll be why I can't afford it anymore."

The four quarters of my screen laughed.

"Tell you what, if you're ever in San Fran, I'll take you to my private wine club. We meet every month and usually drink Screaming Eagle, Ridge, Harlan, you know the kind of thing. But my absolute favourite sessions are devoted to top Burgundy."

"That's a very kind offer. Bet you drink some special wines."

"We sure do. And I hear you're a Minstrel of Wine, right?" said Zak.

"Yes, I'm a fully signed-up member of the Worshipful Institute."

"There you go, Zak," said Raj, from the bottom right.

"Something for you to aspire to."

"Man, I would love to do the Minstrel of Wine exams," said Zak. "But I heard the final tasting exam is, like, insanely difficult. Some say it's the toughest exam in the world. Is that true?"

"Well, you're expected to have a pretty decent knowledge of the entire world of wine, not just top Napa and Burgundy."

"I guess you need a little more tasting practice, Zak," said Raj.

"Bud, you're so right. Felix, tell us about the exam. I heard you have to sing the tasting notes from a stage in front of all the Minstrels of Wine, or something?"

"Unfortunately, gentlemen, I'm not permitted to reveal the format of the final exam. The Institute is very strict about that. But, don't believe everything you read online. You don't have to be an opera singer to join the Minstrels of Wine, I promise."

"That's good, because Zak's singing really sucks," said Raj, and the four quarters of my screen guffawed once more.

"Hey, Felix," said Zak, "we're taking up your time with wine chat and we know you're busy. Look, I'm conscious Brad introduced us to the Gatesave team on this morning's call but, straight off, I just want to say Fulmination Tech are here to empower you, not to try to tell you what to do."

"That's good to hear."

"Otherwise you'd just be selling Californian wine," smirked Raj.

"There's nothing wrong with a bit of Zinfandel rosé," I said.

"Look, on behalf of all Americans, we apologise for White Zinfandel," said Zak. "The only rosé I drink is Krug."

"No need to apologise. Gatesave sell a million pounds of California blush every week."

"That is insane!" said Zak. "Hey, maybe that's where we should start. Is that your biggest selling wine?"

"No, we sell a lot more Italian Pinot Grigio and Prosecco. New Zealand Sauvignon, too. In fact, the cost of Kiwi Sauvignon is probably my biggest headache."

"Maybe Gatesave should contract directly with the grape

growers, then," suggested Zak, "instead of the wineries. Get closer to the cost driver. Tie them in to a long-term contract."

"Or just buy some vineyards," said Ed, from the bottom left. "Get yourself vertically integrated."

"And maybe take an equity stake in a UK bottling facility," added Raj. "So you have control over short-term demand volatility."

"All fantastic ideas," I said. "Though they all imply some pretty ambitious investment."

"Yeah," said Zak, "but interest rates are low and your cash flow is strong. We're recommending Gatesave make some big, strategic plays in the supply base. The past thirty years everyone's been divesting, contracting out, disaggregating their supply chains. But there's a new kid in town with a big, fat wallet, and he's sucking up all the resources. Unless you've built your motte-and-bailey, you're going to get wiped out."

I remained silent, hoping someone might explain what in God's name Zak was talking about.

"China, man," said Raj.

"Right," I said.

"Think on it tonight, then let us know tomorrow what kind of supply base assets you want to invest in," said Zak. "We'll help you run the slide-rule over them."

"Can't wait," I said.

\*\*\*

I steered my scooter off Victoria Embankment, increased my thumb's pressure on the accelerator and hummed up the rise towards Covent Garden. I skirted the market and Opera House, but instead of continuing on to Long Acre and approaching Minstrels Hall's magisterial front entrance, I pointed myself down one of the narrow medieval streets that burrow through the city like a secret warren. The sky, guillotined between the high, cold mansions, shrank to a ribbon of twilight. The smooth tarmac turned to cobblestone, shaking my body and turning my vision to a chaotic, vibrating blur. I lifted my thumb and freewheeled until the cobbles slowed me to a walking pace and I could see again. On my left sat a sign marked Minstrels Hall: Goods Entrance Only. I pointed my scooter down the ramp and ducked as I glided beneath the half-closed shutter.

"Minstrel Hart," nodded the guard seated inside the loading bay.

"Evening, Bob," I replied, skipping off the footplate and guiding the scooter to the bike rack. "Big session this evening so I'll probably leave it overnight, if that's ok?"

I reached for one of the coiled cables suspended from the wall and plugged it in to the scooter's charging port.

"We'll keep an eye on it," replied the guard. "Just slip us a decent bottle next time you're in. Have a good night."

I took the goods lift to the third floor and made my way to the grand balcony overlooking the ground-floor entrance hall. To my left lay the entrance to the Salon de Bordeaux, a rather grand restaurant and the only venue to which Minstrels were permitted to bring guests. To my right lay the Salon de Dijon, my favourite haunt, strictly for fully fledged Minstrels only. In contrast to the Salon de Bordeaux with its two hundred covers, the Salon de Dijon was a cheek-by-jowl kind of place; so small that on a busy Friday night, one could leap from the bar counter and rely on a dozen friendly pairs of hands to catch and transport you over the crowd to your seat, your future lover, or the exit, depending on your level of inebriation. I nodded to the guard leaning on his pinecone-topped staff, and spotted four of my closest Minstrel friends sitting at the corner table: Hugo, a young wine merchant in the midst of a post-graduate degree in ampelography – that's grapevine-gazing to you and me – Lily, a Pinot Noir fanatic and executive sommelier at one of London's most prestigious restaurant groups, Elmo, chief wine buyer at a Dutch supermarket chain, and Valentina, a globe-trotting consultant winemaker who'd chalked up a dozen tours of vinous duty over the past decade, from Mendoza to Marlborough by way of Beaune and Bad Kreuznach.

"Ah, here he is," called Valentina. "Come on, Feel, we've nearly finished the aperitif." She lifted the open bottle of Trousseau and directed a couple of inches into an empty Zalto.

I raised the glass. "To the Wines of Jura study group."

Four glasses were raised in reply and the Trousseau was soon finished. We exited the bar and bumped into a couple more study-minded Minstrels gossiping beside the balcony.

"Where's our lecture room then, Hugo?" I asked.

"I've secured a study area on floor minus two," replied Hugo, touching his pass against the elevator panel. I followed him to the lift.

"Minstrel Hart!" barked a stern, male voice.

The voice belonged to a guard holding his pinecone-topped staff diagonally across his body. That meant a summons from one of the Provosts. Not the type of request one should fob off.

"I'm just heading to a study group session, actually," I explained. "Could it wait until tomorrow?"

The guard took a step forward, reducing the distance between us to slightly less than the length of his staff.

"Right. It's important, is it?"

The guard tilted his head towards the entrance of the Salon de Bordeaux. That was strange. Generally, being summoned by a Provost implied a meeting in their chambers. Mind you, it was dinner time. Maybe I'd swing a free meal.

"Apologies, fellow students. Save the dregs for me, would you?"

"Looks like Feel's in hot water again," smiled Valentina. "Hope the Provost doesn't spank you too hard." My friends disappeared into the elevator, leaving me alone with the guard.

"Which House wants to see me? I assume it's Provost Jordaan?"

Jordaan was the head of my own House, the Terroirists. I had a minor role on a couple of House Terroirist committees and I guessed Jordaan required an update on something or other. Damn inconvenient timing, though. I'd been looking forward to that study session.

"Looks like more than one House wants to hear your pearls of wisdom, Minstrel Hart," replied the guard. "You've got a pair of Provosts waiting. So, I'd hurry up if I were you."

My bowels gave a faint churn of alarm. Two Provosts. There were only four Provosts in the entire Institute. And a meeting in the Salon de Bordeaux, too. That implied external guests. I crossed the hallway, the guard two steps behind. I tried to recall whether I'd committed any misdemeanours recently, particularly anything significant enough to bring the Minstrels of Wine into disrepute.

I stepped into the Salon de Bordeaux and scanned the tables. A party of Port shippers having a hearty business dinner recognised me and waved, but I saw no sign of any Provosts, let alone two.

The maître d' appeared noiselessly beside me. "They're in one of the private rooms, Minstrel Hart. Please follow me."

The maître d' led me to a doorway in the furthest corner of the restaurant, obscured behind a folded screen. I posted myself through a pair of heavy velvet curtains and emerged in a small, circular room. At the centre lay a round table illuminated by a low-hanging chandelier. Six chairs ringed the table, of which four were occupied.

"Good God!" I said.

# Chapter 6

## Le Cercle Chêne

"Sit down please, Minstrel Hart," said Provost Jordaan.

The silver hairs threaded through Jordaan's dreadlocks glittered in the chandelier's light. She patted the empty seat to her left and permitted me a brief smile, which I hoped meant I wasn't in immediate trouble. I stepped around the table and sat silently.

To Jordaan's right sat Provost Jägermeister, head of House Mercantilist, his purple gown linked at the neck by a silver chain. An unusual occurrence, for Provosts Jordaan and Jägermeister were known to dislike one another intensely. Partly this was due to a difference in ethos – Jordaan's House Terroirist championed the interests of smaller, artisanal wineries, while Jägermeister's House Mercantilist represented huge, multinational brand owners. But principally it was because Provost Jordaan was a decent, generous and supportive Head of House, while Provost Jägermeister was a dreadful, preening tit.

But it was the presence of the other two guests that had shocked me.

Inspector Ma stared at me, unsmiling, over clasped palms. And, opposite me, planted between Ma and Jägermeister, like a malevolent rose between two vicious thorns, sat Sandra, a smirk gracing her beautiful, spiteful face.

"Hello, Felix," she said.

"Yes, hello, Sandra," I replied, in a slightly deeper voice than I'd intended. "Nice to see you. I trust business is good at Paris-Blois?"

"No great change from yesterday when we last spoke, thank

you, Felix."

*Fine*, I thought. *No secrets here then, clearly.*

"I trust we didn't interrupt anything too important with our summons, Minstrel Hart?" said Provost Jordaan.

"No, nothing serious. Just a little Côtes du Jura study group. I'm sure I'll be able to catch up on anything I missed."

Jägermeister turned to his guests. "Apologies, I've been assured that Provost Rougegorgefils will be with us very shortly."

Inspector Ma gave a brief nod, Sandra a sympathetic smile.

*By the beard of Bacchus*, I thought. *Three Provosts at the same time. That's nearly a full house!* The only time I'd seen more than a pair of Provosts in the same room was in the Great Hall during *La Vendange*. That was the most important date in the Minstrels' calendar: the annual festival where the entire thousand-strong membership of the Institute came together to watch a clutch of hapless contenders attempt (and usually fail) to taste their way through the Minstrels of Wine's fiendishly difficult entrance examination. So, what the hell was important enough to bring three of them together at such short notice?

"Paris-Blois International have been extremely generous to the Institute this year," oiled Jägermeister to Jordaan. "As you know, several Paris-Blois employees are themselves senior members of House Mercantilist. Their employer has been benevolent enough to fund a new scholarship for promising young members of my House. Much to my embarrassment, Paris-Blois have *insisted* on christening it the Nathanial Jägermeister Scholarship!"

"How generous," said Jordaan. "And on what basis is the scholarship awarded? Most creative use of a Champagne cork?"

Sandra's smirk broadened, just for a second. Jägermeister's face reddened to match his cloak.

"It's a marketing scholarship to UC Davis, actually. Not the kind of thing to interest House Terroirist, I'm sure. Ah! Provost Rougegorgefils!"

A tall, birdlike woman slipped through the curtains and took the vacant seat beside me.

"Please do accept my apologies, Provosts and guests. I was

momentarily detained dealing with a group of Minstrels having a raucous and egregiously non-educational party on floor minus two, under the cynical cover of a Wines of Jura study group. They'll each be donating one hundred pounds to our House charity tomorrow."

Provosts Jordaan and Jägermeister glanced at me. I remained silent and focussed on the chandelier.

"I read your briefing note last week, Provost Jägermeister," continued Rougegorgefils. "It certainly sounded troubling but was rather light on detail. I assume we're here to be updated on the specifics of the matter?"

"Precisely," replied Jägermeister. "I'm sure it doesn't need to be said, but everything discussed from this moment forward is done so in the strictest confidence. I trust that's understood?" Jägermeister shot me a look. "Introductions first. Sandra Filton here is a senior director at Paris-Blois Brands International, a corporate friend of the Minstrels of Wine and a company whose global commercial interests are well known to all of us. Inspector Ma is with the Hong Kong Police and is helping Paris-Blois in their attempts to disrupt the trade in counterfeit branded goods, including fine wine."

"Ah. Very interesting," said Provost Rougegorgefils. She smiled at Inspector Ma, who managed to squeeze out a half-smile in return.

"Yes, Paris-Blois's interests align very neatly with our own," said Jägermeister.

Provost Jordaan gave the faintest of snorts, just loud enough to be heard by all, though too subtle to invite a challenge. Sandra's smirk hardened a little.

"For the benefit of our guests," continued Jägermeister, "Provost Rougegorgefils here is the head of House Archivist, one of the Minstrels of Wine's most venerable Houses. I asked her to join us today because she chairs the Institute's wine fraud action committee. House Archivist also manage the Institute's relationship with our foreign Chapters, not least our thriving outpost in Hong Kong."

At this, Jägermeister gave a snivelling little bow in the direction of Inspector Ma. The inspector remained expressionless.

"I have also asked Provost Jordaan, head of House Terroirist, to join us. House Terroirist concerns itself with the more esoteric end of viticulture and winemaking, which isn't really of interest to us today, but they do have some useful insights occasionally and, well, within their membership they have this… this Minstrel here. Minstrel Hart."

Everyone looked at me.

"Yes, hello. I think I know everyone."

"You do get around, don't you, Minstrel Hart?" said Provost Rougegorgefils, peering at me as if I were a provocatively off-route migratory bird.

"Yes," said Jägermeister, peevishly. "Paris-Blois have asked that we engage Minstrel Hart specifically in our joint anti-fraud project. I'm still not entirely sure why. In fact, Sandra, that is something I wanted to discuss–"

Sandra placed her hand on Jägermeister's arm and gave him a thousand-watt smile. "Nathanial, please allow me to provide some context."

Jägermeister's lips flapped like a trout having its tummy tickled. Sandra continued.

"Firstly, on behalf of Paris-Blois Brands International, I would like to thank the Worshipful Institute of the Minstrels of Wine for lending its support to this vital project."

"Vital to whom?" said Provost Jordaan.

"Vital to every single person on this planet who cares about the difference between genuine and counterfeit wine. My understanding is that your own House, Provost Jordaan, takes a particular interest in matters of wine provenance and authenticity."

"Your company is well informed," replied Jordaan.

"Thank you, Provost, it pays to be informed," said Sandra. "Now, you're all busy people so I will get to the point. Wine fraud is an activity as old as the wine trade itself. I have no doubt that Provost Rougegorgefils can attest to that."

"Oh, yes," agreed Rougegorgefils. "Our archives contain myriad documents detailing Roman, Greek, even Phoenician wine customers challenging their merchants on the provenance and composition of their shipments."

"And the more valuable the wine, of course, the greater the incentive to commit fraud," said Sandra. "You don't need me to tell you that over the past half-century Paris-Blois have acquired many of the most valuable vineyard properties in the world, from super-premium Californian estates to the *Grand Vins* of Champagne, Bordeaux, and Burgundy."

"No-one is doubting the muscularity of your brand portfolio or your ability to generate market-leading margins," said Jordaan. "My question is, why does a company as well-resourced as Paris-Blois require the help of the Minstrels of Wine?"

"A fair question, Provost Jordaan. Allow me to hand over to Inspector Ma."

"Thank you, Sandra," said Ma, mercifully shifting his stare from me to the wider group. "Three months ago, the Hong Kong Police Force received a complaint from a Mr Owen Farquhar, a Hong Kong resident. Mr Farquhar is a well-known wine merchant in the territory. He owns several upscale stores and a wine distribution business called Farquhar Fine and Rare, which has offices throughout East Asia."

"Yes, we know Mr Farquhar very well, Inspector," said Provost Rougegorgefils. "He is, after all, a Minstrel of Wine himself, not to mention a leading light in our Hong Kong Chapter."

"I am aware of that," replied Ma. "Earlier this year, Mr Farquhar attended a private wine tasting at the Burj Al Arab in Dubai. The guest list was extremely exclusive. CEOs, top financiers, members of the ruling family, and so on. Mr Farquhar himself was invited because his company had helped source some of the wines for the tasting."

"What wines were shown?" asked Jordaan.

"All top Burgundies, I believe," replied Ma.

"Of course they were," said Jordaan. "How original."

Provost Rougegorgefils placed the tips of her fingers together. "And the nature of Mr Farquhar's complaint, Inspector?"

"Mr Farquhar claimed that one of the wines was fake."

"As a result of tasting it?"

Ma opened a leather document bag, removed a transparent plastic folder and placed it before Provost Rougegorgefils. I could see it contained a thick, white menu card surrounded by a gold border, on which was printed a list of around a dozen wines. At the top, in fancy calligraphy, were the words *Le Cercle Chêne*.

"Wine number four is the one that raised the suspicions of Mr Farquhar," said Ma.

"Domaine Saint Hugues l'Etoille, Clos du Prieuré, 1947," read Rougegorgefils. "1947 was a good year for Burgundy. Very little of it left, I imagine."

"For that domaine, very little indeed," replied Ma. "Mr Farquhar informed me that they did not restart their post-war production until 1948."

"Well, that's rather a giveaway, then," said Rougegorgefils.

"Inspector," said Jordaan. "You won't find anyone around this table disagreeing that wine fraud is a troubling crime and a growing menace to the drinks trade. But dare I say, a single bottle of counterfeit Burgundy seems a rather trifling matter to concern a Hong Kong Police inspector. And you said the tasting took place in Dubai. That's quite some distance from your jurisdiction, is it not?"

Ma smiled. "It is indeed, Provost. The reason this is of interest to the Hong Kong Police is that the organiser of the event is a Chinese citizen, who conducts much of his business in Hong Kong."

"*Le Cercle Chêne*," said Rougegorgefils. "The Oak Circle? I haven't heard of it."

"Me neither," said Jägermeister, frowning.

"That is understandable," said Ma. "It is an extraordinarily exclusive club. The Chinese gentleman I refer to is an extremely wealthy and well-connected businessman. He uses *Le Cercle Chêne* solely for entertaining and influencing potential investors and politically influential stakeholders."

"*Guanxi*, I believe you Chinese call it – isn't that right, Inspector?" said Jägermeister.

Jordaan rolled her eyes.

"Yes, that is quite right, Provost," said Ma.

"Well, can you reveal who this person is, Inspector?" said Jägermeister. "He sounds like the kind of chap the Institute, and House Mercantilist in particular, should know about."

"If you will forgive me, Provost, I would prefer not to reveal his identity at this stage. He is an extremely influential man and walls have ears, as they say. I would not wish to put anyone in a potentially compromising position."

"I'm guessing this man also holds his *Le Cercle Chêne* tastings in Hong Kong, Inspector?" said Jordaan.

"That is correct. In Shanghai and Beijing too. You begin to understand the sensitivity of the situation, I think. The attendees of *Le Cercle Chêne* include political as well as business figures. Members of the Hong Kong Legislative Council, for example. The potential for embarrassment is significant."

"So, you need our help to ensure a bunch of Chinese politicians don't lose face?"

Ma smiled again. "No, Provost. That is merely a useful secondary consequence. We believe the operators of *Le Cercle Chêne* are using an extremely sophisticated counterfeiting method for their wines, undetectable by a professional taster."

"So sophisticated," added Sandra, "that it threatens the integrity of all fine wines and spirits, let alone the businesses that produce them."

"Provosts, allow me to spell out the seriousness of the situation," said Jägermeister. "This has the potential to plunge the entire fine wine ecosystem into extreme jeopardy! Not just the brand owners but the brokers, auction houses, the fine wine investment market, the prime vineyard real estate business, luxury retail…"

"All the sectors involved in margin inflation, speculation and price gouging, in fact. What a tragedy," said Jordaan.

"Let's just leave Marx and Mao at the door for once, shall we?" snapped Jägermeister.

"I'd love to get my hands on one of those fakes, Inspector," said Rougegorgefils. "You see, to counterfeit a wine, you have to do a lot more than just cook up a convincing blend. There's the bottle, label, cork, capsule – in fact, the liquid is arguably the most straightforward part of the fraud."

"Unfortunately, Provost, we do not have a sample. That is where we need your help." Ma transferred his attention to me, as did the rest of the table.

"Why are you looking at me?" I asked, in a small voice.

"We require someone to obtain a counterfeit wine bottle from the next *Le Cercle Chêne* tasting," said Sandra.

This didn't sound great. Didn't they cut people's hands off in Dubai for stealing?

"If I can interject here," said Jägermeister, his nose wrinkling, "I'm still not quite clear why the services of Minstrel Hart are necessary for the prosecution of this matter. I can think of several members of my own House who'd be far more suitable, whether in terms of fine wine experience, managerial credibility, familiarity with international commerce–" Jägermeister waggled his hand at me. "–not to mention emotional maturity and general conduct, too. No offence, Minstrel Hart."

"None taken," I replied. *You really are a self-righteous, arse-sniffing bollock frotterer.*

"Forgive me, Nathanial," said Sandra. "I understand your concerns, but Paris-Blois International have worked with Felix – Minstrel Hart – for many years now. He has valuable experience of these types of project, and he is known to and trusted by the very highest levels of my company. Only two days ago, he helped Paris-Blois and the authorities disrupt a criminal enterprise known as Magnum Club Platine, which, as I'm sure you're aware, has been fraudulently passing off plonk as fine wine for several years now."

"Oh. That was you, was it?" said Jägermeister, peering at me down his nose. "Didn't I read that someone ended up in hospital?"

"I understand a fight broke out later on," replied Sandra. "Nasty bunch. Nothing to do with our operation."

"I have also seen Mr Hart in action," said Inspector Ma. "I believe he has the very particular skill set we require for this project."

"Very well," sulked Jägermeister. "He's a member of House Terroirist, so it's up to Provost Jordaan to grant permission."

"If Minstrel Hart is confident that he can help, I'm willing to approve his participation in the project," said Jordaan.

"Thank you," said Sandra. "We've informed Felix that we're willing to pay reasonable expenses." She caught my eye and held it for a few seconds. I smiled back.

*You must take me for a right mug,* I thought. *How about you show me the bloody money?*

"Inspector, I'm terribly intrigued as to the identity of this character behind *Le Cercle Chêne*," said Rougegorgefils. "Their background may provide clues as to how the forgeries are constructed. However, I quite understand your reticence. After all, innocent until proven guilty."

"Thank you, Provost," said Ma. "We will, of course, share more information with you once we have obtained sufficient evidence."

"Why exactly do we have to take such a softly-softly approach, Inspector?" said Jägermeister. "I'm minded to give Minstrel Farquhar a ring and ask him what the devil's going on!"

"I regret to say that won't get you very far," replied Ma.

"Oh? And why is that?" said Jägermeister.

"Mr Farquhar fell overboard from the Cheung Chau ferry last week. His body was found washed up on a Lantau beach two days ago."

In the silence that followed, I became conscious of my lower intestines turning rather vigorous somersaults. Million dollars or not, the chances of me volunteering to go within a thousand miles of that festering pit of vipers had just shrunk from negligible to infinitesimal.

# Chapter 7

## Personal Banking

I woke to the sound of my phone vibrating against the empty wine glass on my bedside table. I opened one eye and peered at the screen to check it wasn't an incoming Gatesave video call, then answered.

"Good morning, Mr Hart. This is James from your Luxe Premier Team's Private Wealth Unit. How are you today?"

"Sorry, who? Calling from where?"

"James. From your Luxe Premier Banking Team. Is this a good time to talk? I wanted to run through some investment options for you. Unit Trusts, OEICs or ISAs, perhaps."

"Ah, yes. Now I understand. Don't tell me. You're a Nigerian princess and you need me to look after your inheritance for a few months."

"As a matter of fact, Mr Hart, my father is indeed Nigerian. Unfortunately, I have no royal connections. Not that I'm aware of, anyway. I think you may be alluding to the possibility that this is a fraudulent call, intended to misappropriate your funds."

"Yes, that was my first thought. It still is, frankly."

"Mr Hart. Do you have access to your banking app?"

"Would you like me to tell you the password?"

"No, Mr Hart, that would be extremely poor practice. Are you aware that the sum of seven hundred and eighty-two thousand pounds was deposited in your current account last night? That means your credit balance is just over seven hundred and eighty-one thousand pounds. You were slightly overdrawn until yesterday."

"Right. Pardon?"

"Yes, the payee was Paris-Blois East Asia Limited. The funds were transferred from the Causeway Bay branch of Standard Chartered Bank in Hong Kong. One million US dollars exactly, minus transaction and exchange rate fees. Do you recognise the payment, Mr Hart?"

I sat up, suddenly extremely awake.

"Oh, that payment. Yes, I do recognise it. Nothing to worry about."

"No, quite the opposite. A nice problem to have, I think. I'm calling because your current account only offers a zero point zero five per cent interest rate and your money should really be working a little harder than that. I'd like to invite you for a consultation at one of our Private Wealth boutiques. Our Mayfair branch is probably the closest."

"Yes, I suppose that would be sensible. When's the appointment?"

There was a short pause.

"You're a Luxe Premier Banking customer, Mr Hart. You tell us when the appointment is."

After the call, I opened my banking app and stared at the balance for several minutes. The figure looked surreal, not remotely like a sum of money. More like the serial number on a piece of computer hardware or the barcode digits on a tin of tomatoes. But then, as I continued to stare, a strange sense of dread crept over me, as if the figures were fake and the balance might decline before my very eyes; slowly at first, then faster and faster, like the stock market that day the Italian lockdowns were announced. I closed and re-opened the app several times and to my relief the digits remained reassuringly static. So, there I was. Officially, a dollar millionaire. I allowed my mind to wander: vintage Champagne *en magnum* at Michelin-starred restaurants, surrounded by beautiful, laughing women. Then an unwelcome image inserted itself: my bloated, shark-ravaged body being hauled out of the South China Sea in a trawlerman's net.

I visited James from the Private Wealth Unit that lunchtime, at his well-upholstered office near Berkeley Square. I was handed a glass of chilled Prosecco (God only knew how much money one needed to be served proper Champagne – a billion, presumably?) and he prattled on for a while about tax wrappers, setting up limited companies and treating my salary as dividends. When he'd finished this litany of dullness, he asked if I had any questions.

"I just wondered… Is there any way they can take the money back?"

James appeared nonplussed. "Take it back?"

"Yes, you know. Whisk it out of my account. Back to China."

"No, Mr Hart, I shouldn't think so. Unless they've transferred it to you by mistake, of course. In which case, I imagine their bank will be in touch with us fairly shortly. Have you any reason to believe this is a mistake?"

"No, no, of course not. It's a payment for some consulting work."

"Good. It's probably worth ensuring you have remittance advice or some other evidence to prove you were expecting the payment. Just in case you're subject to a money laundering check."

"Oh. Is that likely?"

"Not from us. Your payee is on our whitelist, they're a respected multinational corporation. We wouldn't have released the funds otherwise. But you may need proof of earnings if you wish to invest in UK property, for example."

"Right. I'll make sure I do that."

"Or you could let us take care of it, Mr Hart. Luxe Premier customers qualify for our Global Executive Assistant service. Unless you'd prefer your own PA to see to it?"

"Actually, my PA's pretty busy this week. Happy for you to take care of it."

***

As I hummed on to the Gatesave campus an hour later, three glasses of Prosecco down, my scooter felt as though it was gliding on air.

"Please alight from your transport, unless you have a mobility issue," trilled the dome-headed golf cart as I sped past.

"Mein artificial legs hef bin stollen!" I called, in an appalling German accent.

"Please accept our apology for the challenge," replied the golf cart. "We're learning and…"

But I was travelling at speed and the remainder of the droid's apology was lost on the wind. I stowed my scooter, scanned myself through the doors and ascended to my assigned seat. I was due another call with the boys from Fulmination Tech to discuss the New Zealand grape contracting proposal I'd sent through that morning. I hoped it wouldn't take too long because I had plans to meet Valentina at the new Champagne bar at the top of the Shard.

Bang on time, Zak and Raj appeared on my screen.

"Hey, Felix," said Zak. Raj raised a hand in greeting. Neither were smiling.

"Afternoon, guys. How's it going? Smashed any good Pinot since our last chat?"

"Er, we're being joined by Brad on this call, Felix."

"Brad?" I said. I tried to recall their two colleagues from yesterday. One was called Scott, was the other one Brad?

"Yeah, hey guys, I'm here, on audio," said Brad.

Holy shit, *that* Brad! Brad the Impaler! My own CEO.

"Oh, hello," I said, sitting up straight.

"Hey, Felix. Sorry I can't be on video, I'm in the airport lounge in Sao Paolo. Bandwidth here is a disaster. Really, really sucks. Anyway, look, you've been spitballing with the guys from Fultech, yeah?"

"Erm, yes, that's right. I've proposed we contract directly with some Sauvignon Blanc winegrowers in Marlborough, and–"

"Sounds a bit conventional, man."

"Oh. Does it? I mean, no retailers contract directly with grape growers at the moment. It's pretty innovative, financially. I think."

Zak and Raj remained po-faced.

"Look, I don't know if this really works for me, Felix, sorry," said Brad. "It's just... too incremental, you know what I'm saying? We need some different thinking, I mean, completely different, you know? How long have you been looking after wine at Gatesave?"

"Around ten years. Just under. Nine and a bit."

"Felix is a Minstrel of Wine," said Zak. "That's, like, super-specialist, right?"

"Yes, pretty specialist," I said, with a sinking feeling.

"Look, I'll be straight with you, Felix," said Brad's voice, "You're great, but you're too close to the subject. Much too close. I need someone with the cognitive distance to really recalibrate this business. Move tangentially, appreciate the parallax shift, you understand what I'm saying?"

"Yes, I think so."

"Great. So, let's disrupt things. I want to move the Head of Wet Fish into the wine role. Zak, Raj, I'll introduce you to them later."

"Cool," said Zak.

"Oh. Right," I said, miserably. "Does that mean I have to do Wet Fish?"

"I'll fess up. I don't know. We have a lot of vacancies in this business right now. I mean, a hell of a lot. You're a Change Agent, aren't you?"

"Yes."

"Let me hear it. Tell me you're a Change Agent."

"I'm a Change Agent."

"Yes, you are. So, take a look around. You can do anything you like, man. So long as it's different."

***

I didn't fancy checking out a rowdy new bar after that bombshell, but I definitely needed a drink. So, for the second evening in a row, I pointed my scooter towards Minstrels Hall. I won't deny that the thought of a million dollars nestling in my bank account took the edge off the guillotining of my wine career. But it was still a pretty sub-optimal development. Wine had been my entire vocation up until now and I had little desire to join any other sector of the food industry – whether it involved lines of moist-nosed Eastern Europeans miserably placing pepperoni slices on pizzas in a freezing warehouse just off the North Circular, tiptoeing through a crap-encrusted poultry shed, eyes smarting from the foetid smog of ammonia as ten thousand frenzied chickens pecked each other to death around my ankles, or hearing the hair-raisingly human screams of fattened pigs as they realised their journey up the slaughterhouse ramp was their last.

Call me Mr Picky, but I preferred the caress of the Mediterranean sun in an autumnal Languedoc vineyard, the aroma of gently fermenting grapes in a Spanish bodega and the pop of wanton Champagne corks in elegant Côte des Blancs chateaux. I'd dropped a note to the Head of People Needs asking for a list of buying vacancies and he'd replied with a long list of roles, the first three of which were Trading Manager for Tubers and Alliums, Category Lead for Rabbit, Rodent and Exotic Bird Accessories, and Interim Buyer of Detergents, Toilet Tissue and Moist Wipes. I'd stopped reading after that.

On arrival at Minstrels Hall, I took the lift up to the tenth floor and emerged on to the vast roof terrace, the home of La Terraza Asada, the Minstrels' open-air barbeque restaurant. It was a pleasantly mild spring evening and the restaurant was busy. Each of the terrace's four walls were dominated by a great charcoal grill, representing the four great barbequing nations of the world; Argentina, South Africa, Australia, and the United States. I strolled to the Argentinian *asada* and ordered a plate of lamb chops with chimichurri plus a fist-sized glass of Patagonian Pinot. Balancing my phone on my thigh and attempting to keep my little finger grease-free, I scrolled through the list of vacancies as I sucked the tender lamb off the bone. Despite there being dozens of vacant roles, none were really endearing themselves to me. The Head of Soft Drinks and Fruit Juice looked the most promising. Perhaps I could wangle a few buying trips to exotically located orchards. Florida, perhaps, or Cuba.

A message dropped into view at the top of the screen. From Sandra.

*Trust you haven't spent it all? We need to talk. Now.*

# Chapter 8

## Ground Rules

I was conscious, of course, that accepting a million dollars from a ruthless multinational corporation was likely to imply some sort of obligation on my side. And that Paris-Blois's expectation of services rendered might be more exacting than a PowerPoint presentation and a couple of well-formatted spreadsheets. But over the past few hours, I'd managed to nudge such inconvenient concerns towards the less visited recesses of my mind, particularly in the light of my recent career prang.

*Busy now but free later this week*, I replied.

*Don't piss me about. I see you. Book table for two at S de Bordeaux 9pm tonight.*

I looked up to check who might be spying on me. It wouldn't be Sandra herself, of course. La Terraza Asada was strictly Minstrels only and didn't permit guests. But the Institute contained several Paris-Blois employees within its ranks, and it was quite possible they'd been briefed to keep an eye out for me. I should have taken dinner in the Salon de Dijon, where it would have been easier to foil any malevolent surveillance.

I sent Sandra a thumbs-up emoji, then registered her as a guest and booked a table for two at the Salon de Bordeaux on the Minstrels Hall app. I scrolled through the remaining job vacancies, most of which were roles in Gatesave's clothing and general merchandise division. Head of Stationery and Back-to-School, Category Manager for Garden Accessories, Merchandise Lead for Women's Casual Bottoms. I shook my head. The only interesting aspect of the non-food roles was their location. All Gatesave's food positions were based in London, at the Hammersmith head office. But the general merchandise roles involved splitting your time between London and the company's network of global sourcing hubs. They looked like a gap-year planner's wet dream; textile buying in Dhaka and Phnom Penh, procurement in Jakarta and Ho Chi Minh City, merchandising in Karachi and Bangkok.

Ultimately, however, the thought of a career procuring garden gnomes from a Guangdong industrial estate didn't really do it for me. There was nothing for it but to resign. I wondered for how long I could remain on the run from Sandra and her multi-billion-pound corporation, given that I had the thick end of £800,000 in the bank. Most likely, she'd put a crack private detective on my tail and run me to ground within a week. Then, she'd probably hand me over to Inspector Ma and I'd find myself in a Xinjiang salt mine for the rest of my short life.

A ping from the Minstrels Hall app told me Sandra had arrived. I summoned the express lift and descended to Reception to meet her. I'd expected her to be wearing her usual office garb, but she was dressed casually in jeans and a loose linen shirt, a leather bag over her shoulder. A pair of male guests watched, a little enviously, as I nodded to the concierge and scanned her through the Strangers' Gate. We crossed the visitors' lounge, past the meetings rooms fitted with refrigerators and plumbed-in spittoons, and stepped into the guest elevator.

"We need to establish some ground rules now you've agreed to work for us," said Sandra, as the doors closed.

"I don't recall agreeing to anything."

"I have a contract here that says you do," she replied, tapping her bag. "Unless you'd like to pay back the money?"

I remained silent. The doors opened onto the third-floor balcony.

"I didn't think so," said Sandra. She stepped out.

We took our seats in the Salon de Bordeaux. Sandra ordered a sirloin, rare, with spring greens, *sans frites*. I explained that I'd already eaten and ordered a small cheese plate.

"Suit yourself. You're paying."

She caught my surprised expression and smiled.

"That came as a shock, didn't it! Become a little too used to supplier hospitality, have we? Oh yes, you're definitely paying, Felix." She caught a passing waiter's eye. "Two glasses of Krug, please."

I winced.

"Right. As I was saying, ground rules. Rule number one. In future, when I call, or message, or email, I need you to drop everything and respond immediately, understand?"

"I suppose so."

"Rule number two." Her voice dropped to a hiss. "If I call, message, email, or even send you a damn carrier pigeon, you drop everything and respond immediately. Do you understand?" She lifted her steak knife and pointed it at me.

"Ok, ok." I raised my hands. "I understand. I'm at your beck and call, promise."

"Good. Now sign and date this." She removed a document from her bag, folded it to the final page and dropped it in front of me.

"I think I should probably ask my lawyer to look over this first."

"Sign the document, Felix. Or we'll sue you for breach of contract."

"I haven't agreed to any contract!"

"Yes, you have. Last night, in front of me, Inspector Ma and Provost Jägermeister. All of whom dislike you and will testify to that effect. Plus, we've paid you and sent the remittance advice to your bank, at your request I believe. And, if we sue, we'll take back all the money we've just paid you, plus a very unpleasant chunk of compensation and legal fees."

I looked down at the paperwork.

"What does it say?"

"It says you'll do some consultancy work for us in exchange for some extremely generous remuneration. Just sign there. There's a copy for you underneath."

"There are quite a few pages. What's in the small print?"

"Just sign the bloody contract, Felix, if you want to keep the money."

I did as I was told.

"Thank you." Sandra slipped the signed copy into her bag. "That's your copy there. Now, I appreciate you have a fairly substantial day job running Gatesave's booze business, so I'm not expecting you to sprint out of any meetings, but I need to know you're on point, every waking hour, seven days a week, ok?"

"Yes, that won't be a problem," I said, leafing through the contract. I was pleased to note there was a paragraph titled Payments, which specified the figure of one million US dollars. Hopefully, the rest was in order too.

"In fact, one of the main reasons we've employed you at such a ludicrous cost is precisely because of your job role. It's how we're going to facilitate your invitation to the next *Cercle Chêne* tasting."

"Ah. I have a slight update for you regarding my employment status."

The waiter placed two flutes of Champagne on the table. Sandra's face darkened.

"Yes. You see, I've been kind of... moved on."

"What?"

I lifted the Champagne and took a sip while I worked out what to say next.

"What the hell do you mean you've been moved on?"

I noticed Sandra hadn't touched her own glass. There was no way I was letting that go to waste. Not if I was paying.

"Felix!"

"Sorry, yes. The CEO wants to move me to a different role. Another department."

"What kind of role? Still in wine?"

"No, I don't think so."

"Oh, Jesus wept. The whole point of employing you is to substitute you in place of the late Owen Farquhar, as one of the suppliers of fine wine to *Le Cercle Chêne*."

"Hang on, you want to set me up as the new bloated-body-washed-up-on-a beach guy? Sorry, I'm out. I don't think a willingness to be savagely murdered is a legitimate contractual obligation, frankly."

"Don't be so dramatic. No-one suggested he was murdered. Probably just fell off the ferry, drunk."

"Anyway, I don't understand. Gatesave's a supermarket chain. We sell a bit of premium stuff but we're not exactly a fine wine merchant."

"No, but your employer operates over one hundred superstores in China, which sell a lot of wine, and that would have given you a legitimate reason to travel to East Asia. Gatesave also have commercial relationships with companies who *do* produce fine wine, Paris-Blois included, so we could have set you up as a broker with preferential access to rare vintages – someone willing to do favours to important local individuals. Good *guanxi* for Gatesave. And you're a Minstrel of Wine, of course, which gives you extra credibility. Unless you're telling me you've just been expelled from this place too?"

"No, I'm still a Minstrel."

Sandra placed her hands at her temples and closed her eyes. "This is not great. At all. You've really messed things up."

I snatched up my copy of the contract, folded it and slipped it into my pocket. Sandra opened her eyes and scowled.

"I assume a deal's a deal, though," I said.

"Oh yes, Felix. A deal's very much a deal. You're not getting out of this. Tell me, what's your new job?"

"I'm not sure yet. There are quite a few vacancies. I can pretty much choose."

"Anything involving sourcing from East Asia? Dried noodles, green tea, that type of thing? Anything that might give you a credible reason to travel to China on business?"

"I'll have to check. There were several roles in homeware, textiles, that kind of thing. Most of it's manufactured in China."

"That might work."

"But I don't want to work in home accessories."

"I don't care. Get yourself a job, immediately, that gives you cover for frequent travel to Hong Kong. I want an update tomorrow morning, understood?"

Sandra stood up, downed the Krug in one go and banged her glass down before me.

"You need to recover this situation very quickly, Felix. I mean it. You really don't want to find yourself on the end of a Paris-Blois lawsuit. Being a declared bankrupt is a really poor lifestyle choice."

She stalked out of the restaurant. The waiter arrived with Sandra's steak and my cheese plate.

"Could you pop those into a takeaway box, please?" I said, miserably. "I'll have the bill too, thank you."

The waiter raised his eyebrows, turned on his heel and returned to the kitchen. The bill came to just over one hundred pounds, including my Minstrels discount, and I grumpily stabbed my pin into the machine. I wondered how long my cash would last if I had a steak and Champagne dinner every night. I did a quick calculation. Around twenty-two years. That cheered me up a bit.

# Chapter 9

## Operation Splashback

The next morning, I emailed the Head of People Needs stating that I wished to apply for the role of Senior Buyer, Kitchen and Bathroom Accessories. He responded with a one-word reply – *LOL* – obliging me to call him and explain that I was, in fact, deadly serious in my aspiration to immerse myself in bread bin, shower curtain and loo brush procurement, and that the purchasing of cut-price plastic tat from East Asian sweatshops was a meticulously planned, strategic step in my career development plan. Despite his protestations that the job was a grade below my current position, I insisted, and he only relented when I pointed out that Brad the Impaler himself had blessed me with permission to do whatever the hell I wanted.

I messaged Sandra with the news of my career handbrake turn. She phoned back immediately, telling me to apply for a mainland China business visa and to book a fully flexible business-class flight to Hong Kong, with the outbound leg scheduled for a month's time. I pointed out that Gatesave policy these days was economy only and that Paris-Blois might need to arrange the ticket for me.

"No, Felix. You're paying for the flight. Check your legal agreement. Your fee covers all travel expenses incurred in the course of your duties."

This struck me as a miserably penny-pinching arrangement, and I decided it might be time to seek some professional advice regarding my contract. I recalled that my Luxe Premier Banking status entitled me to use the services of the Private Wealth Unit's legal team. I called my Global Executive Assistant and asked them to arrange my Hong Kong flight, then scanned and sent them my Paris-Blois contract for some forensic legal analysis.

Next, I attended an e-meeting with my new Gatesave manager, Tabatha Shunt. She carried the exotic title of Director of Non-Food and, thankfully for people like me who prefer to work at arm's length from their bosses, she was based in Gatesave's Hong Kong global sourcing office.

"Aha! So, you're Felix Hart, are you?" shouted Tabatha, from my laptop screen.

Tabatha Shunt had a jet-black bob and wore extremely fierce eyeshadow. Her neck was adorned by a huge metal necklace that appeared to have been fabricated from pieces of scrap plumbing. Colleagues described Tabatha as a larger-than-life character, which was a euphemism for the fact that she was extraordinarily well-built and had a temper like a buffalo with distended testicles.

"You're in non-food now!" she snarled, moving to within six inches of her camera. "So, you'd better not swan around putting on airs."

I assured Tabatha that I considered kitchen and bathroom accessories the zenith of the buying universe and that I couldn't wait to get out to Hong Kong and start some rigorous procurement.

"In your dreams, lover boy," she growled. "Hong Kong's closed again to everyone except residents. You'll be doing your job from home, like everyone else, for the foreseeable future."

Anxious to show my enthusiasm, I enquired as to the key priorities in the world of kitchen and bathroom accessories. Tabatha stabbed a black-painted fingernail at me.

"Your number one, most urgent issue, by far, is to source a splashback-busting toilet seat."

"Toilet seat?" I said, aghast.

"Yes, toilet seat! You're in charge of bathroom accessories, sweet cheeks! Who the hell else is going to source them? The cushion and pouffe buyer?"

"Right. I hadn't appreciated that would be part of my portfolio. I'm assuming this is a special type of toilet seat?"

"It certainly is. An academic study was published last week on the dangers of viral contagion due to urinary aerosols and faecal splashback. Are you familiar with these issues?"

"I confess I am not."

"You'd better get up to speed then, bloody quick. Every wellness blogger in the metaverse is hyping the dangers of urinary aerosols. Faecal splashback is the top trending topic on Mumsnet. Even the *Daily Telegraph*'s running toxic-turd scare stories. Do some background reading and become a subject matter expert, like, tonight."

"Will do. Sounds like time is of the essence."

"Damn right. Every manufacturer of splash baffles and seat flanges sold out weeks ago. We need an all-singing, all-dancing, faeces-busting, piss-repelling, hermetically sealed lavatory seat in every Gatesave homeware aisle across the country. And we need it now!"

"I'll get right on it."

"You've got eight weeks to source, ship and launch the world's finest splashback-supressing toilet seat. And if you deliver me anything less than complete market dominance, your days in bathroom accessory procurement are done. Understood?"

Tabatha Shunt disappeared from my screen. Grand Cru Chablis it was not. But I had my orders.

\*\*\*

By the following morning, I had become a self-taught authority on urinary aerosols and faecal splashback, and a noxious evening of study it was, too. Ever since that day, I have closed the lavatory lid before flushing, and if you knew half of what I know of pathogen plume inhalation and splatter condensation, you'd damn well do the same.

Tabatha, I'm pleased to say, didn't completely abandon me to grope my clueless way through the Chinese lavatory seat sector. By way of guidance, she emailed a directory of manufacturers already active in the bathroom accessories market, and made it clear she expected a shortlist of the most promising candidates by Monday.

And thus, I spent the next forty-eight hours conducting conference calls with the export managers of Hangzhou East Sun Industrial Co., Foshan Yongbo Bathroom Products Co., Ningbo Hardware and Chromium Co., Xiamen Best Sanitaryware Co., and countless other entities specialising in the clean, practical, and comfortable facilitation of bathroom unmentionables. My brief was quite simple: namely, to find a toilet seat fitted with a snug, integral plastic seal which, when closed, prevented its passenger from being enveloped in a miasma of plague-carrying droplets, especially those users whose flushing technique tended toward the Niagaran.

After eliminating manufacturers who were either unwilling or unable to understand my requirements, and those who on closer questioning appeared to be chancers not in possession of an actual factory, I was left with a small handful of contenders. My favoured candidate was Mr Charles Fung, of Guangdong Intelligent Sanitary Co. Ltd. Gatesave already did a reasonable amount of business with Mr Fung, in the shape of liquid-soap dispensers and toilet roll holders, and he assured me that he was the largest exporter of lavatory seats to South Korea, which seemed a good sign. Mr Fung promised to send me some design drawings and preliminary costs and I agreed we would reconvene the next day when I had discussed his proposal with my superiors.

"Good!" declared Tabatha, on our next video call. "I hoped Charles would be on the shortlist. He's a reliable supplier."

"The preliminary landed cost looks sensible, the production timeline meets our target and I've shared the design drawings with the Hong Kong technical team."

"Right, what are you waiting for? I want to see samples before the end of the week. Tell Charles you'll throw in a few bottles of Cabernet if he knocks another ten cents off the unit price."

"He likes wine, does he?"

"Likes it? He adores it! He's an absolute wine nut. Runs a

wine appreciation society called the Pinot Pimpernels. They meet every month on his boat in Sai Kung. I've been a few times. Great excuse for a piss-up. He only drinks red, though, which I can't stand. I just stick to the G&Ts. Anyway, you should tell him about your old job in wine buying, he'll love that. It'll help with your *guanxi*."

Tabatha wasn't wrong about Charles Fung's enthusiasm for wine. On our video call a couple of hours later, my suggestion he offer a further discount in exchange for a case of wine was politely declined, but Fung appeared genuinely interested in my wine career, particularly my membership of the Worshipful Institute of the Minstrels of Wine. We were soon on first name terms.

"Felix, can you make me a Minstrel of Wine too?" he beamed, from my laptop screen.

"I would love to, Charles, but I'm afraid becoming a Minstrel involves a long and intense period of study, followed by a very challenging tasting exam at the Institute's headquarters in London. The Minstrels do maintain Chapters in several major cities, however, and I believe the Hong Kong Chapter is one of the largest. I'm sure they'd be delighted to provide details of how you can begin the study programme locally."

"Ah, thank you. Unfortunately, nearly all my time is taken up by travel and running my business, and this sounds very time-consuming. I thought perhaps it was easier, like joining my own wine club!"

"Or like *Le Cercle Chêne?*"

God only knew what possessed me to say that. A wish to impress Fung and appear important, perhaps? The thoughtless arrogance of a newly minted dollar millionaire? A deep-seated, tragically misplaced and utterly unrequited desire to prove myself to Sandra? Not that the callous vixen deserved it.

Charles Fung's eyes widened. He glanced left and right, as if to check he wasn't being observed.

"You know *Le Cercle Chêne?*"

My cheeks burned. I'd hit pay dirt. Was Mr Fung, toilet

accessories mogul, the mastermind behind the world's most sophisticated wine fraud? How the hell I was going to bluff my way through this one?

"Well, yes. I've heard about it from a fellow Minstrel of Wine. A member of the Hong Kong Chapter, in fact. I believe it's quite a famous wine club, isn't it?"

"Ah, no, not really," replied Fung. "Famous in a way, but not popular-famous. Quite secret, actually. How do you know about it?"

I pictured myself taking an involuntary midnight plunge into the South China Sea, a heavy-duty toilet bowl tied to my feet.

"Oh, the Minstrels of Wine know about most things going on in the world of wine," I replied, my heart pounding. "But they're very discreet."

"Like you, Felix."

What was that? A threat?

"Yes, very, very much so," I said. I clicked on the Wi-Fi menu and hovered the cursor over flight-safe mode. I could always pretend my internet connection had crashed.

"So, Felix, you know Joseph Lee?"

"Not terribly well, no," I replied, wondering who the hell Joseph Lee was and how the hell I might change the subject.

"Joseph Lee. Everyone knows Joseph Lee! Founder and CEO of Greater China Pharmco."

"Oh, yes, Joseph Lee. Of course!" I realised I had, in fact, vaguely heard of Joseph Lee. He was the richest man in China. Or one of the richest. "Yes, Joseph is a big wine man, I believe. Not that he likes to talk about it. Not widely, anyway. The Minstrels of Wine help to source some of the wines for *Le Cercle Chêne*, you see. That's where I've come across him. Not met him personally though."

"Ah, that is very interesting. So, as you may know, *Le Cercle Chêne* is a very exclusive club, for Mr Lee's close friends only."

"Only a matter of time before you're invited, Charles, I'm sure."

"Actually, it is very funny that you say that. This is very

confidential, but I have indeed just been invited to one of his tastings, in a month's time. I do a lot of business with some of Joseph Lee's companies, buying chemicals, paints, this kind of thing. I am very excited. He shows some incredible, rare wines at these tastings."

"Yes, so I've heard. Very old Burgundies, that kind of thing."

"Exactly," said Fung, eyes shining. "Sorry I can't take you, the invitation is for special guests only! And please, this is completely secret. I should not be telling you."

"Don't worry, Charles. I won't say a word. Just read your tasting notes to me afterwards, so I can imagine I was there."

Fung found this extremely amusing. A minute later, we agreed on a final price for one hundred thousand faecal splashback-busting toilet seats.

# Chapter 10

## Fully Flexible

"We need you in Hong Kong in two weeks' time."

Sandra glared at me over her glass of Sauternes. I glanced around, checking that no-one in the Salon de Bordeaux had drifted within earshot.

"I booked my flight, Sandra, as instructed. But I have bad news. Hong Kong is closed to non-residents. It looks like the whole thing's off, I'm afraid."

"Those quarantine rules are for ordinary punters. Give me your flight details and passport number and I'll send them to Inspector Ma. No-one will stop you at immigration."

"Oh. I didn't know that."

"There's a lot you don't know. All you need is a certificate showing you're negative. Get tested now, just in case, then arrive at the airport an hour early and they'll test you again in the business-class lounge. Until then, avoid travelling on rush-hour public transport and don't stick your tongue or anything else where it doesn't belong. We don't want you picking anything nasty up. If you jeopardise this trip, you can kiss goodbye to all that cash. And we'll sue you for damages on top, got it?"

"Fear not, I shall implement a personal *cordon sanitaire*. What am I supposed to do in Hong Kong?"

"The next *Cercle Chêne* tasting will take place at the Phantasos Hotel in Macau, two weeks on Saturday. We're attempting to arrange an invitation for you."

"How are you going to do that? I'm not exactly an associate of... I don't know, whatever bigwig it is who's running this circus."

I'd bitten my tongue, just in time. Much as I wanted to boast to Sandra that I knew the identity of *Le Cercle Chêne's* operator, something told me it might be better to keep my intel on Joseph Lee to myself. I wondered whether Charles Fung would be attending the same tasting. It seemed likely. He'd mentioned his invitation was less than a month away and I couldn't imagine Joseph Lee going to the trouble of hosting a *Cercle Chêne* tasting every week. How would I explain the coincidence to Fung? Poor chap would think I was stalking him.

"You recall Owen Farquhar?" said Sandra.

"The chap who attended a *Cercle Chêne* tasting one minute, then ended up a shark-nibbled corpse washed up on a deserted beach the next? Yes, I remember him well."

"His company, Farquhar Fine and Rare, is a supplier of wine to *Le Cercle Chêne,* including wine from estates owned by Paris-Blois. We do – or did – quite a lot of business with him, in fact."

"I don't understand. I thought *Le Cercle Chêne* showed fake wines, not genuine ones?"

"We're guessing they show genuine wines alongside the fakes, to make them harder to detect. Possibly, they only fake the really rare ones. We believe *Le Cercle Chêne* will still want to purchase wine from Farquhar Fine and Rare, given that the company has the sole importation rights into China for the most sought-after Burgundian estates."

"How does that get me invited to the tasting?"

"The organiser of *Le Cercle Chêne* likes to fly in winemakers from the top estates featured at the tastings, all under conditions of complete secrecy, of course. Trouble is, with the travel restrictions, it's near impossible for French vignerons to visit China. So, the organisers have had to fall back on inviting the local importers."

"Like Owen Farquhar."

"Exactly. Especially Owen Farquhar, in fact, given his stranglehold on the East Asian Burgundy market."

"But Mr Farquhar has splattered his last spittoon."

"Yes, quite," said Sandra. "The late Mr Farquhar's sales

director, a man named Adam Fromage, is now running Farquhar Fine and Rare. Fromage has been invited to the next *Cercle Chêne* tasting but, at our request, has agreed to declare a fever and persistent cough a couple of days before the tasting."

"That old chestnut."

"He made a bit of a fuss about it, clearly didn't want to miss out on the tasting. But we pointed out that Farquhar Fine and Rare owed its success to its exclusive and highly lucrative importation rights, and that certain Burgundian negociants might start looking for alternative distributors if cooperation wasn't forthcoming."

"So, this Fromage character will propose me as a substitute?"

"That's right. We're positioning you as a Paris-Blois brand ambassador, representing two of our super-premium estates in the Côte de Nuits. Fromage tells me that *Le Cercle Chêne* have placed an order for wines from both domaines."

"And what's the job description of a Paris-Blois brand ambassador?"

"There are three vintages from each estate in that box." Sandra indicated a heavily packaged parcel sitting beside her chair. "I suggest you taste them, commit them to memory, and become an authoritative and passionate evangelist for both domaines by the end of the week."

"I can do that. But what am I supposed to do at the actual tasting in Macau?"

"Don't worry about that. We'll let you know. Just concentrate on the wine for now. There's twelve thousand pounds' worth of fine Burgundy there, so don't bloody drop it or leave it on the bus."

"The bottles won't leave the building. I'll taste them right here with a few of my fellow Minstrels."

Sandra took a sip of Sauternes. "How's your new job working out? Your real one, at Gatesave."

"Fine, thanks. I can use my trip to Hong Kong to meet a few colleagues and home accessories suppliers."

"Good, sounds useful. Remember, you need to keep this

71

mission and your day job completely separate. Understand? So far as anyone else is concerned, including the Hong Kong Immigration Department, your trip is to conduct Gatesave business. Something important but not out of the ordinary. Sourcing personal protective equipment, perhaps. What kind of home accessories are you buying?"

"Oh, various things."

"Like what? Kitchen utensils? Coat hooks?"

"I'm currently working on a project to source a special type of toilet seat, actually. It's very hush-hush."

"A toilet seat? That's hilarious. And how very appropriate for you, Felix, given that you're so full of it. A special toilet seat. Wow. That's nearly cheered me up."

"I aim to please."

"I said *nearly*. This *Cercle Chêne* business is a bloody disaster. Our Chairman is having kittens over it." Sandra took an assertive sip of wine. "The board are panicking. They've decided to split up Paris-Blois International. They're spinning off the drinks brands, which they've decided are screwed, from the fashion and accessories brands. The wines and spirits will sit in a new company called Paris-Blois Beverages International. I've been told I'll be the acting CEO."

"Wow, CEO. Congratulations. What's the problem?"

"The problem, Felix, in case you haven't been paying attention, is that we have it on extremely good authority, from the Chinese security services no less, that some clever little bastard has found a way to counterfeit our fine wines and spirits to such a high standard that the fakes are, to all intents and purposes, indistinguishable from the real thing. Furthermore, we haven't got a clue how or where they're doing it, whether they intend to unleash these fakes on an unsuspecting world, or, when they do, how the hell we tell the shareholders of our new company that our brands are essentially worthless."

"Ok, yes, I see what you mean."

"Do you, Felix? Great, glad you've got the picture. Oh, and the cherry on the cake is that our only lead regarding the entire conspiracy involves sending a swaggering, drunken tit, who's just been demoted to toilet seat buyer, to try and outwit China's most brilliant business genius."

Sandra's eyes dropped to her glass. She'd let slip a little too much there.

"Joseph Lee," I said.

She looked up, astonished. Nice to be able to score one over her. It didn't happen often.

"How the hell do you know that?" she said, teeth clenched. "No-one at this Institute or in the wider wine world would know that. I doubt anyone in this country knows, except perhaps a couple of high-flying financiers. And I haven't told a soul."

"I've been doing a little networking. *Guanxi*, as they say."

Sandra stared at me a little longer, then knocked back the rest of her Sauternes.

"You know, it's possible, just possible, that I picked the right person for the job after all."

\*\*\*

"Hello, boys!" exclaimed Valentina, as I unveiled the six bottles of Burgundy in the Salon de Dijon later that evening.

It hadn't required much effort to persuade Hugo, Lily, and Valentina to join me for some expert and convivial *dégustation*. We seated ourselves around the square table near the rear of the bar and I began uncorking the bottles.

"My Provost tells me you're helping House Archivist on the wine fraud project," said Hugo.

"Oh, yes, very peripherally. I was asked to attend a couple of commercial tastings. One of the Institute's corporate sponsors suspected counterfeit wines were being poured there. All sorted now, I believe."

"Still doing mercenary work for Paris-Blois International, are we?" asked Lily. "Thought you might have learned your lesson by now."

"It's nothing compromising, my dear. Our own Provost

Jordaan is fully aware. And approves." Lily, like me, was a member of House Terroirist. On occasion a rather over-earnest member, in my private opinion.

"I hope you're not suggesting these are fakes," said Valentina. "Or is that why you've invited us here? To see if we can spot the dodgy ones?"

"No, no, these are definitely genuine," I said. "Well, I assume they are. I received them directly from the negociant."

"They're Paris-Blois wines, aren't they?" said Lily.

"Yes, I believe they own the domaines," I said, nonchalantly. "It doesn't make them bad wines, does it?"

"If they're made by bad people, you could argue they automatically qualify as bad wines," replied Lily.

"Well, let's put them on trial then," I said, as the barman lined up six glasses along each side of the table.

"Thanks, Petr," I said. "Grab another glass and have a taste yourself, if you like?" The barman beamed and sprang away, before returning with an empty Zalto.

"Right, let's taste the Grands-Echézeaux vintages first," I said, pouring everyone a measure from each of the three bottles. "Then we can move on to the Chambertin."

We started with the oldest vintage, a 1989. I nosed the glass, inhaled, and was immediately lost; the fruit more savoury than sweet, layers of leather and faint perfume weaving an ethereal dream of spice market melded with evening forest. Then, without pausing, I took a generous gulp. Silken fruit caressed my tongue. Rose petals and cedar wood, the texture firm but supple, like fine Darjeeling.

"That is quite stunning," said Valentina, who had taken a more professionally sized mouthful than me. She gazed at her glass in awe.

I glanced at Hugo, whose eyes were closed in rapture, then at Lily, who was staring back at me, her face a little flushed. Petr the barman held his wine in his mouth, lips pursed, and nodded like a sage.

"Perhaps amoral multinationals can make good wine, when

they put their mind to it," I said.

"I think Paris-Blois went on their domaine-buying spree in the mid-nineties, didn't they?" said Lily. "Which means this vintage is untainted."

"Well, then. Let's try the 2002," I said.

"You can try it later, Minstrel Hart," said a man's voice.

A guard, his pinecone-topped staff held diagonally across his body, stood in the doorway of the Salon de Dijon.

"Is it important?" I said, heart sinking.

"A summons from the Provost of House Archivist."

"Why is the Provost of my House summoning you, Felix?" said Hugo.

"It's this fraud thing, I expect," I said. "Just tying up a few loose ends." I rose to my feet. "I expressly forbid you from finishing any of these wines. There needs to be at least a quarter-bottle left in each by the time I return."

"Yeah, I'm sure there'll be plenty left, Feel," smiled Valentina.

"There better had be," I muttered.

The guard turned and I followed him to the elevator. We descended to floor minus three, the heart of House Archivist's realm. The guard escorted me down a long, wood-panelled corridor with doors every few yards either side. A few were ajar. As I passed, I glimpsed libraries lined with ancient books, storerooms piled high with wooden crates, and laboratories filled with glassware. The corridor ended in a tight, wooden spiral staircase.

"Down there," ordered the guard. "The Provost awaits."

# Chapter 11

## A Little Light Pilfering

I descended, slowly, into the gloom. The steps were steep and irregular, worn at their centre from decades of traffic. I kept a firm grasp on the handrail. The wooden wall panels, plain in the corridor above, were carved with vines, animals and woodland spirits, all intertwined. Every half-turn of the staircase, a bare lightbulb glowed inside a small recess, the polished panels reflecting the filament into multiple orange will-o'-the-wisps. Ancient soot coated each recess like black velvet, dark smoke marks spreading out and up towards the ceiling, while oilier stains, the residue from long-spent wax, drooled down into the low shadows.

After what seemed like a hundred turns, the stairs opened onto a hallway smelling of old paper and dust, dotted with archways leading God knew where. An ancient-looking painting of a vine-coated landscape under a stormy sky sat alone on the wall.

"Minstrel Hart!"

The high, clear voice of Provost Rougegorgefils. I followed the sound to one of the archways. This revealed a short corridor, at the end of which lay an open doorway and a well-lit room. I wondered if I'd ever find my way out. *I should have unwound a ball of wool as I came down*, I thought. I approached the doorway and knocked on the frame.

"Yes, come in, Minstrel Hart. You took your time!"

Provost Rougegorgefils was seated on a high, straight-backed chair which looked as if it belonged in a medieval banqueting hall. Before her lay an enormously wide desk, on which sat dozens of neatly bound bundles of paper, three laptops, a microscope and at least fifty bottles of wine, some empty, some sealed. One half of her face glowed blue in the light of a monitor set on a pile of leather-bound books. On the opposite side of the desk sat a woman in large round glasses examining a document through a magnifying glass.

"Apologies, Provost," I said. "The guard must have taken me on the scenic route."

The Provost raised her eyebrows.

"I sincerely hope not. The scenic route is reserved strictly for members of House Archivist."

"Oh, right. That was just a joke."

The Provost peered at me down her nose.

"This is not the time or place for jokes, Minstrel Hart. Allow me to introduce Minstrel Shuttlewort, my lead forensic investigator on the wine fraud action committee."

"Completely fraudulent," said the woman, without looking up from her magnifying glass.

"Hope you don't mean me," I said, with what I hoped was a winning smile.

"Is that another joke, Minstrel?" asked the Provost. "Or do you suffer from some sort of nervous condition that impels you to emit an inane comment every thirty seconds?"

"Apologies, Provost," I said. "The former."

"Amateurish, really," continued Minstrel Shuttlewort.

I remained silent.

"Ink-jet printer, modern paper stock. Destined for the naïve markets, no doubt."

"Very well," said Rougegorgefils. "Send a report to the brand owner, please. And place the retailer and importer on the database."

"Already done," said Shuttlewort. She straightened up, blinked a few times behind her glasses, and focussed on me. "And here's Minstrel Hart. How exciting!"

"Yes, our new helper," said Rougegorgefils. "You're off to Hong Kong and Macau shortly, I understand?"

"I believe so, Provost. Though I'm under the impression it's all rather confidential."

"Quite so, Minstrel," agreed Rougegorgefils. "The only people within the Worshipful Institute who know about this are the three of us, your own Provost Jordaan, and Provost Jägermeister. And you're to keep it that way, Minstrel Hart. So, I would strongly discourage you from dropping in on anyone you might know in our Hong Kong Chapter, for example. Outside the Institute, I believe the only others with full knowledge of the project are that glamorous young lady from Paris-Blois and her law enforcement colleague from Hong Kong."

"And there was poor Minstrel Farquhar," said Shuttlewort, blinking.

"Yes, the one who fell off the boat," I said. "Bit worrying, that."

"A terrible tragedy," agreed Rougegorgefils. "Minstrel Farquhar was the Minstrels' Head of Chapter in Hong Kong. A rather particular gentleman, but we all have our quirks."

"I understand you're going to steal a fake bottle from *Le Cercle Chêne* for us," said Shuttlewort, peering at me with excitement.

"Pardon? I'm doing what?"

"Minstrel Hart hasn't been briefed yet," smiled Rougegorgefils.

"Oops, sorry!" said Shuttlewort, putting her hand to her mouth.

"Wonderful," I said. "Always fun to be the last to know. Could you possibly give me a hint as to when I might receive a briefing? If it's not too much trouble?"

"This is your briefing, Minstrel Hart," said Rougegorgefils, tapping her keyboard and pursing her lips at the monitor. "Now, listen. You are due to travel to Hong Kong in two weeks' time and make contact with a gentleman called Adam Fromage. He is currently acting CEO of Farquhar Fine and Rare following the tragic death of Minstrel Farquhar himself. Mr Fromage was invited to attend the next *Le Cercle Chêne* but you will attend the tasting in his place, acting as brand ambassador for two of Paris-Blois's Burgundian domaines. This much you know already, I believe?"

"Yes, more or less."

"Mr Fromage has supplied us with the tasting menu for the event in Macau. He really is being extremely cooperative."

*I bet he is*, I thought, picturing Sandra turning the screws on the hapless wine merchant.

"There are twelve wines on the list. We don't know how many are counterfeit, of course. The only wines we know to be genuine with any confidence are the two Paris-Blois wines, supplied via Farquhar Fine and Rare, which, of course, you will be representing."

"Am I expected to deduce which of the other wines are fakes?"

Provost Rougegorgefils gave a little snort. "You're a competent taster, Minstrel Hart, but we believe we are up against a fraudster of quite exceptional abilities. I fear you will not be able to distinguish the fakes by sensory analysis alone."

"So, what am I even doing there?"

Rougegorgefils glanced at Shuttlewort and nodded.

"You are our Raffles, Minstrel," said Shuttlewort, gleefully. "Our gentleman thief."

My bowels began to churn, as they often do when someone suggests I put my life in peril for the sake of the common good. What was the penalty for theft in Macau? Something combining suspension from a meat hook and the mains power supply, no doubt.

"We have suspicions regarding at least two of the wines," said Shuttlewort, holding her magnifying glass before her face, which had the unsettling effect of expanding her left eye to several times its normal size. "Wine number eleven, for example." Shuttlewort lifted a piece of paper and tapped it with her magnifying glass. "A 1978 Musigny Grand Cru. Vanishingly rare. No stock at any of the reputable French, British, or American merchants, and no full cases have passed through the major auction houses for over two years. Doesn't mean it's not kosher, of course. It could have been sold by a private collector or via a small broker, but it's a big red flag."

"Tell Minstrel Hart about the final wine on the list," said Rougegorgefils.

"Let's just say you can glue a horn to my forehead and go fetch the blacksmith!" declared Shuttlewort.

"I'm sorry, glue what?" I began to wonder whether Shuttlewort had made an early start on the grappa.

"A unicorn, my dear poacher. Wine number twelve is a 1921 Richebourg."

"Blimey," I said. "Over a century old."

"The wine is described as Les Richebourg 1921, Charles Viénot," said Shuttlewort. "If it's counterfeit, the fraudster has at least made some effort to research pre-*appellation* historical vineyard ownership."

"So, is it a fake or not?"

"We have no idea!" said Shuttlewort, cheerfully. "But it's just the kind of wine that greedy fraudsters use to reel in their credulous victims. Mr Fromage, incidentally, is certain it's a fake. He says Farquhar Fine and Rare sourced a similar bottle at a Paris auction five years ago on behalf of a Chinese client. By way of thanks, the client then invited Minstrel Farquhar to the private dinner where the wine was opened and consumed."

"Minstrel Shuttlewort verified his story, of course," added Rougegorgefils.

"Yes. The wine was listed in Artcurial's auction catalogue that year and the buyer was indeed Farquhar Fine and Rare. It was the only bottle offered for sale and the provenance was sound. And that's the last time that vintage was offered for sale at a major auction house."

"So, the chances of another bottle suddenly popping up are pretty slim?" I said.

"They're called unicorns for good reason, Minstrel Hart," said Shuttlewort.

"And who was the Chinese client who bought the original

bottle? The one that Farquhar helped demolish," I asked.

"Bravo, my muscular Poirot!" exclaimed Shuttlewort, in what I felt was a borderline inappropriate tone. "That's exactly the question we asked. But Mr Fromage claimed client confidentiality."

"I'm sure Sandra could help loosen his tongue."

"We did ask, but she appeared unwilling to push Fromage on that particular issue," said Shuttlewort.

"We understand some matters may be a little sensitive at this stage, so we left it at that," said Rougegorgefils. She fixed me with an expression that suggested I should avoid tugging too many tiger tails myself. "Now, you might find this useful." Rougegorgefils pushed a weighty hardback across the desk towards me. "Jasper Morris's *Inside Burgundy*. You'll be familiar with the first edition, no doubt." I nodded, respectfully. The book was considered the definitive guide to the wines and vineyards of that hallowed French region. All dedicated Burgundy enthusiasts possessed a well-thumbed copy, though I confess I hadn't quite got round to ploughing through it myself. "The author was kind enough to send House Archivist a few copies of the second edition when it was released. You can take that one, if you don't possess it already."

"Thank you. I'm sure that will further buttress my authority. But please can you explain exactly what I'm expected to do at this tasting?"

"We need to get our hands on one of those fake bottles," said Rougegorgefils.

"I don't think Mr... Big, whoever he is, will be too chuffed if I trouser his bottle of '21 Richebourg, will he? Unless he's knocked off a whole case and won't miss one."

"We suggest you procure an empty bottle of the Musigny '78," said Rougegorgefils. "Given that its provenance is also suspect. Mr Fromage tells us that the organiser of the tasting procures six bottles of each wine, wherever possible. Pilfering the single bottle of Richebourg, even if it's empty, might be a challenge too far."

"Even for a man of your legendary talents," added Shuttlewort.

"I see. And how am I supposed to execute this pilfering expedition, exactly, without getting caught and strung up?"

Rougegorgefils frowned, giving her the appearance of an inconvenienced owl.

"We've been led to believe *you're* the expert at that sort of thing, Minstrel Hart," she said. "One assumes that's why you were recruited for the job in the first place!"

# Chapter 12

## Fragrant Harbour

"Is your flight sorted, Felix? And you tested negative?"

Sandra sliced a strip of steak from her fillet and speared it with her fork.

"Yes. I used that clinic you mentioned. All clear."

I took a mouthful of roast potato and steamed wild garlic. Delicious. Another all-expenses-paid dinner at the Salon de Bordeaux, courtesy of exploited sugar daddy Felix Hart.

"Actually, Sandra, the airline really shafted me for changing the dates. Don't suppose I can claim the penalty charge back from Paris-Blois, can I?"

"No, I don't suppose you can. Why didn't you book a fully flexible ticket, like I told you to?"

"I was looking after the pennies."

Sandra rolled her eyes and cut another slice of steak.

"My PA has sent you some attachments with technical information on the wines you're representing. Vineyard yields, volatile acidity, all the geeky stuff. Study it and make sure you know what you're talking about before next week."

"Will do."

"You need to arrange a meeting with Fromage as soon as you arrive in Hong Kong. I understand you've been briefed by your Minstrel colleagues on what's expected of you." Sandra pointed her fork at me, on which was impaled a gobbet of meat. "So, I hope everything is clear?"

"Not really, no. Apparently, I'm supposed to thieve an empty bottle of Burgundy from the tasting and deliver it to Provost Rougegorgefils so her team can determine its authenticity."

"Exactly. Sounds like everything is clear, then."

"Yes, but how am I supposed to actually do it? Without being beheaded by the Triads, that is. Or the Communists, or the Worshipful Company of Roulette Wheel Spinners, or whoever the hell runs Macau these days."

"Fromage has attended one of these tastings before. He can advise you on the best approach. I'm sure you'll work something out." Sandra pushed her half-eaten steak aside. "Book yourself into the Shangri-La in Kowloon. Not the one on Hong Kong Island, understood? Better if you keep your head down." She dabbed her lips with her napkin and stood up.

"Shangri-La, Kowloon, got it. Just wondering, do I have to pay for the hotel myself?"

Sandra dropped her napkin on the table and slung her bag over her shoulder. "Thanks for dinner, Felix." She nodded to the waiter and breezed to the door.

"I'll finish that, if you don't mind," I said, impaling her still-warm steak and transferring it to my plate before the waiter could whisk it away.

"Would you like to finish her wine, too?" he suggested.

I poured Sandra's half-full glass into my own while the waiter curled his lip.

"Good call," I said. "And I'll have another glass of Saint-Émilion while you're at it, thank you."

I considered spending the evening at a sweaty dive bar in the hope I might contract something problematic that would invalidate my entry to Hong Kong. But Sandra's warning of legal action and bankruptcy was ringing in my ears and, besides, I'd started making serious investment plans for my little nest egg. On Saturday I kept myself busy, helped by the fact that Tabatha Shunt and her Hong Kong team worked a six-day week and had been bombarding me with toilet seat-related emails all morning. Things quietened down by midday, once the Hong Kong office had departed for evening beers and noodles, and I thanked my lucky stars that I hadn't ended up based permanently in one of the East Asia sourcing offices. A two-day weekend was short enough, in my opinion. To lose your Saturday, too, struck me as slave labour.

I headed to Heathrow nice and early on Sunday afternoon. The woman at the check-in desk had frowned as I handed over my UK passport, demanding proof of my Hong Kong residency. But when I presented the Hong Kong Immigration derogation letter which Inspector Ma had arranged, her expression changed and after a few rattles on her keyboard I was waved towards departures, boarding pass in hand. I booked myself a test at the little pop-up clinic in the business-class lounge and waited for my result with a plate of dim sum and a handsome glass of Mosel Riesling.

A couple of hours later, a negative test result nestling in my inbox, I settled into my business-class seat, Champagne in hand. I was one of only three passengers in the entire cabin and there can't have been more than a dozen back in economy either, going by the thin line of travellers at the gate. I tapped out an email to Adam Fromage, suggesting we meet at the offices of Farquhar Fine and Rare the day after tomorrow, and sent another to Tabatha Shunt, informing her of my imminent arrival in Hong Kong. Finally, I sent a gushing note to Charles Fung, confirming my excitement at the forthcoming visit to his toilet seat factory over the border in Guangzhou. As soon as we were properly airborne, and conscious of the horrors of jet lag, I cajoled my seat into its best impression of a bed, necked a third anaesthetising glass of Champagne, and settled down for an early night.

As Sandra had promised, immigration was swift and painless. In most countries, the opportunity to brighten one's day by interrogating a lone foreigner would be too tempting for any self-respecting official to miss, but the Hong Kong Immigration Department barely raised an eyebrow and with a thump of rubber on passport, I was waved through. Hong Kong's Chek Lap Kok airport was an enormous building – the largest in the world, somebody once told me, until the Chinese built another ten airports that were even bigger. Walking through its deserted vastness made me feel like the last man on Earth, the only sounds the whirr of my wheeled hand luggage and a faint echo of piped music. I emerged into the arrivals hall to find my suitcase riding the carousel alone, like an unloved sushi dish on a restaurant conveyer belt.

I found my near-solitary arrival in Hong Kong rather unsettling. Not least because I was no stranger to the city – quite the opposite. On my first ever trip Down Under (a scholarship prize awarded by the Australian High Commission for outstanding entrepreneurship during an Aussie wine sales incentive), I found myself on a twenty-hour layover in Hong Kong. I still remember the shock of stepping from the cool, air-conditioned MTR station – itself preceded by the smooth, air-conditioned train, and before that the air-conditioned airport, not to mention the frostbite-inducing climate inside the aircraft itself, all the way back to the start of my journey in very much un-air-conditioned but miserably bracing Britain – only to be mugged by a wave of hot humidity as I passed through the sliding doors that divided cool, dry, indoor Hong Kong from its sticky, wet and wild exterior. That sensational, shocking change seemed bizarre and temporary, as though a practical joker had assaulted me simultaneously with a hairdryer and a tropical plant-mister, and once you'd swatted them aside the ambient temperature and humidity would revert to normal. But, of course, there was no reversion to normality. And then it had struck me, with slowly dawning pleasure, that this warm, moist embrace was a permanent thing; that there was no need for jackets, coats, gloves, bobble hats or anything heavy, woollen and oppressive at all, and that you could wander the streets in a t-shirt and shorts, swigging cold beer and singing to the moon until the first faint stirrings of dawn, without suffering so much as a solitary goosebump.

Some people, of course, specifically a certain type of Westerner, find such a climate uncomfortable and bothersome, and don't mind telling you so. In my humble opinion, such people deserve to be stripped to their yellowing underwear and chained to the railings of an out-of-town Midlands shopping centre, where they can be left to enjoy the British weather in all its drizzling, frigid glory, out of earshot of the rest of us.

Anyway, I digress. I was, as I mentioned earlier, somewhat unsettled. I had worried, as I caught the deserted airport express to Kowloon, that Hong Kong itself might be silent and still, its roads deserted, the shopfronts shuttered, the restaurants dark, the market stalls stripped and bare. But thirty seconds after my lonely taxi pulled away from the rank beneath Kowloon station, we emerged onto Austin Road and with a rush of relief I saw the city I remembered: the late-afternoon streets frantic with traffic, delivery trucks competing for space with stately, yellow double-decker buses, mopeds taking their life in their hands, and every second vehicle an enthusiastic red taxi, switching lanes just a little too frequently, each driver determined to squeeze as many fares into their shift as day and night permitted.

We passed the warehouses blocking the view of Victoria Harbour and all at once the Hong Kong skyline blazed into view; mirrored towers of silver and steel, the aggressive angles of the Bank of China, the porthole-studded façade of Jardine House, the glittering, cloud-scraping, nostril trimmer of the International Financial Centre. And, behind them, the dark, steeply wooded slopes of The Peak, its summit shrouded in mist.

I know of no other city that greets the visitor quite like Hong Kong. Other cities approach you slowly, gradually. Even if they're high rise, like New York or Tokyo, you see them coming. But with Hong Kong, it's suddenly there, with a bang, right in front of you, and you're forced to dive right in. It took my breath away all those years ago on that one-night layover, and I vowed at the time that I would pay a visit every time I travelled East – a promise I've kept.

I stepped out of the air-conditioned taxi and stood for a moment, soaking up the warm, late-afternoon air, the humidity tinged with that unique Hong Kong scent of cooking oil, traffic fumes, incense, and gently fermenting rubbish. You may think I sound judgemental, but the smell isn't offensive unless you find yourself down a particularly ripe back alley. Rather, it's the smell of a living city, of the unapologetic consumption of food, of commerce, the busy pursuit of success.

A hotel porter, mistaking my reverie for disability, idiocy, or simply spotting an opportunity for a tip, ripped my bag from my grasp and disappeared into Reception. In contrast with the bustling streets, the hotel was distinctly un-busy, and the staff were clearly surprised, not to mention suspicious, at encountering a non-resident Westerner. Sandra had instructed me to inform any overly inquisitive personnel that I was on a UK government-approved visit to source a vast quantity of personal protective equipment. If I continued to experience problems at the hands of any awkward hotel managers, immigration officials, policemen or general busybodies, I was to present them with a Hong Kong Immigration Department letter, supplied by Inspector Ma, inviting any over-zealous interrogator to phone an official number – on the other end of which, I suspected, would be a person happy to offer the caller an all-expenses paid, one-way trip to a Xinjiang garment factory.

Happily for all concerned, the hotel staff accepted my explanation for visiting the territory and I retired to my room to run through the week's agenda. What remained of the day was my own, with the exception of a video call from my bank's legal services team following their review of my Paris-Blois contract. Tomorrow, however, was rather busier. I had an afternoon appointment with Mr Fromage at the offices of Farquhar Fine and Rare, where, I hoped, I would receive more clarity on how to pilfer a fraudulent wine bottle from the forthcoming *Le Cercle Chêne* tasting without being publicly guillotined. I also had a dinner date with Tabatha Shunt, who was demanding an update on my splashback-busting bathroom accessories project. On Wednesday, I was due to catch a ferry upriver to China proper, specifically to the manufacturing district of Foshan, to visit Charles Fung's factory. There, I would finalise any outstanding piss-proof loo seat logistics and, with a bit of luck, gain some subtle intel on Mr Lee and *Le Cercle Chêne*. I then had a couple of days' grace before Saturday, the night of the *Le Cercle*

*Chêne* tasting. On Sunday, if things didn't quite go to plan, my bloated corpse would be fished from a paddy field irrigation ditch somewhere up the Pearl River Delta, and by Monday, all going well, I'd be back in Britain, awaiting my own post-mortem. Assuming, that is, there was enough of my cadaver left to examine once the flesh-eating wildlife of Guangdong had finished with it.

My phone alarm sounded. Seven p.m. Hong Kong time, midday in London. I opened my laptop and clicked on the Zoom link from Luxe Premier Banking. Within seconds, an extremely attractive woman was smiling back at me.

"Hello, Mr Hart. My name's Amrita. I'm a client legal advisor with your Luxe Premier Banking team. How are you?"

"Oh, hello. I'm fine, thank you." I turned my laptop a few degrees, so the background captured the view of Hong Kong's skyline through my window, rather than the bed and my open suitcase full of un-ironed boxer shorts. "Please, call me Felix."

"That's a great view," said Amrita. "Is it real or one of those backgrounds?"

"Oh, it's very much real," I said breezily. "Just arrived for a few days' business."

"I didn't think anyone was allowed entry to Hong Kong at the moment. We have an office in Central but everyone's working from home. There are no international clients in town."

"It depends what line of work you're in," I said, in a tone both modestly humanitarian and assertively go-getting. "I'm on government-sanctioned business, sourcing PPE for the health service."

"Oh. I thought you were some kind of wine taster," said Amrita, lifting a piece of paper and frowning at it.

My cheeks flushed a little. "Yes, that too. I take it you've reviewed my contract?"

"Yes, I have. Let's kick off, then. The first thing to make clear is that you shouldn't, under any circumstances, sign this contract."

I let out an involuntary and quite audible groan.

"Are you all right, Felix?"

"Yes, fine, thank you," I lied. "Sorry, do carry on."

"You haven't signed the contract, have you?"

"No," I lied, helplessly. "But why? I mean, what's wrong with it?"

"Oh, it's just completely one-sided. Have you read it?"

"Yes. Well, I've scanned it," I lied, miserably, for the third time in under half a minute.

"Essentially, you'd be accepting an open-ended obligation to Paris-Blois International. They would have complete discretion to decide whether you'd discharged your obligations under the contract or not. There are no objective or measurable deliverables, just their opinion as to whether you've completed the project to their satisfaction. It's not even clear what the project actually is. Just some generic statements around attending certain events and resolving any subsequent legal and contractual matters that arise from said events."

"Right. But apart from that, it's ok, is it? I mean, the money side of it?"

"Well, the obligation on their side is relatively clear, namely the payment to you of one million US dollars, after currency and bank charges. But they can withhold payment or demand repayment if you don't complete the project to their satisfaction, which, as I've mentioned, isn't at all fair on you. There's also a section that obliges you to cover a very broad set of expenses, which looks extremely one-sided. You'd be completely exposed there, so that definitely needs tightening up."

"Right. Well, thanks very much. I'll bear that in mind."

"There's also a very onerous NDA attached. A non-disclosure agreement. It means, for example, that you wouldn't be allowed to discuss this project with anyone. Which would strike me as a disadvantage if you're pitching for similar work, wouldn't you say?"

"Yes, I suppose so."

"So, I strongly suggest we redraft the agreement. Then we can send it back to Paris-Blois for revision."

"Oh, yes. That's a good idea. Thanks."

"No problem. I'll need some information from you around what the deliverables should be, so we can write them into the agreement. Are you able to articulate any of those right now?"

*Oh, yes, Amrita, very much so*, I thought, bitterly. The main deliverable would be the retention of my head and its continued attachment to my torso. The same regarding all other limbs and fleshy appendages of note. Absolutely no beatings whatsoever, whether by fist, bamboo cane, barbed wire-wrapped club, bicycle chain or cat-o-nine tails. I would add a sub-clause insisting on a complete absence of electrical shocks to my body, particularly to the genitals. And finally, the total number of stabbings, gougings, animal savagings, and impalings inflicted on my person should not, under any circumstance, exceed zero.

"I'll send you an email," I said.

"Wonderful," said Amrita. "Well, I hope everything goes well for you in Hong Kong. Stay safe."

I gave a rictus grin until Amrita's beautiful face disappeared from my screen. Then, as my grin faded to a grimace, I opened the minibar, unscrewed a half-bottle of mid-market claret and downed it in one.

# Chapter 13

## Farquhar Fine and Rare

"Felix, old chap! Come in, please. May I call you Felix? Forgive my informality."

Fromage strode across the carpet and pumped my hand. Strong grip. I guessed he was in his early fifties. Tanned, fit, a regular on the tennis courts of Happy Valley, no doubt. Dapper, too, a triangle of red silk erupting from the breast of his pale linen jacket.

"Tea, please, Connie, thank you," he called through the door. "I assume you Brits do still drink tea?" He winked.

"Tea would be perfect, thank you, Mr Fromage. Are you not British yourself?"

"Firstly," said Fromage, directing me to a leather chair, "it's From-*idge*, not From-*arge*. Secondly, please call me Adam, if only to avoid further embarrassment. And thirdly, no, I certainly am not British. I'm a Hong Konger. The real McCoy. Great-grandfather was French. Big wallah in the tea trade, upriver in Canton. We've been here ever since."

"Apologies, Mr Fromidge. Adam, I mean. I've clearly been misadvised."

"Sounds like you have been, rather. Never mind. When did you get in?"

"Yesterday evening. I set my alarm for midday. I'm feeling a little jaded, to be honest."

After my inconvenient legal consultation, I'd headed out for a few courses of dim sum at a nearby restaurant, washed down with half-a-dozen bottles of Tsingtao beer. With a touch more assistance from the minibar, my plan was to have passed out by two a.m., but I hadn't succeeded in dropping off until gone six.

"Poor chap. Jetlag's a pig. Never mind, the tea will sort you out."

A young Chinese woman entered carrying a silver tray. Upon it sat a black, cast-iron teapot decorated with the initials FFR, two cups and saucers, and a matching milk jug and sugar bowl, complete with miniature tongs. She placed the tray on Fromage's desk and lifted the teapot.

"Don't worry about that, Connie, I'll be mother. I'm sure Felix doesn't need waiting on."

"As you wish," said Connie, replacing the teapot and adjusting it so the handle faced Fromage. Then, instead of heading for the door, she approached the armchair where I had comfortably sunk myself and, to my mild alarm, leaned over me, placing a hand on each of the armrests.

"Is there anything else I can get for you, Mr Hart? Some water, perhaps?"

"No, I'm fine with just the tea, I think," I said, feeling rather like an invalid being interrogated by the duty nurse. I attempted to wriggle into a more elegant, upright position, but without the use of the armrests, which were occupied by Connie's slender hands, I wasn't able to do more than writhe ineffectually from side to side.

"You will be dehydrated after your flight," said Connie, smiling. I nodded up at her, ensuring my eyes remained respectfully focussed on her rather attractive face. I was conscious that the top of her white satin blouse had fallen away from her neck a couple of inches, and that my ungentlemanly peripheral vision was recommending a furtive peep.

*Discipline, Hart,* I thought, focussing precisely on the spot where the fringe of her black bob met her flawless forehead. But the combination of jetlag and minibar abuse was weakening my resolve, allowing some devilish section of my brain to describe the view beneath the saintly Connie's shirt; two milky half-moons delicately encased in sheer white cotton, a slender strap of lace running up to each shoulder.

I blinked and Connie's face moved even closer. I was surprised and somewhat delighted to find she appeared to be undoing my shirt.

"Good Lord, has he actually passed out?" I heard Fromage say.

I became conscious of Fromage's head alongside Connie's, and that it was he who was undoing my shirt.

"No need for that," I slurred, swatting his hand aside and attempting to thrust myself out of the depths of the armchair.

"Ah, you're back. Connie, get him some water, would you? Make it a pint."

"I feel a bit groggy," I said.

"Stop talking and drink this. The whole lot. Thanks, Connie."

Fromage thrust a glass into my hand. I drank it down.

"Good. Now for some sweet tea. Stay there, don't want you fainting again."

He returned to the desk and shovelled a load of sugar into a cup. He topped it up with tea and gave it a vigorous stir.

"Drink that."

The tea was sickly sweet, but I could feel it doing the trick.

"Back with the living now, are we?"

"Yes, I think so. Sorry about that." I finished the cup and grimaced as a slurry of undissolved sugar poured into my mouth.

"Don't worry. Happens to the best of us. Here, have a refill." Fromage retrieved the teapot from the desk. "Haven't got the shakes, have you? Don't want to scald you." He took my cup, refilled it and returned to his seat. Fromage poured himself a cup, took a sip and leaned back.

"Anyway. So, you're the chap who's stolen my place at the *Le Cercle Chêne* on Saturday."

"Yes, I think that's the idea. Hope it hasn't caused you too much trouble."

"Bit of a bloody pain, actually, but there we go."

"Oh. Why's that?"

"Well, in case you hadn't noticed, my business is selling fine wine. And *Le Cercle Chêne* is a rather good place to meet people who like buying it."

"I see. Sorry. I'm not sure how I can–"

"Never mind. Can't be helped." Fromage took another sip of tea. "I know which side my bread's buttered." He gave a thin smile.

"I'm not quite sure what you mean."

"Come on, Felix. You're associated with that appalling little policeman, Inspector Ma, aren't you?"

"I've very briefly met the inspector, yes," I said, warily.

"And that bitch who works for Paris-Blois?"

*Oh dear*, I thought. *Doesn't exactly sound like we're one big happy family.*

"Sandra, you mean?"

"San-dra, yes." Fromage drawled the name, making it sound like some kind of tropical disease. "Friend of yours, is she?"

"Not a friend, as such. Business acquaintance."

"Yes, it's all business with people like that, mark my words." Fromage took another sip. "So, what's persuaded a nice chap like you to get tangled up with people like that? Blackmail? Violence? Sex?"

I had a flashback to my last meal with Sandra at the Salon de Bordeaux. She'd worn tight leather trousers paired with a loose, blue shirt, the top buttons left not-so-carelessly undone, just enough to permit a glimpse of black lingerie. Not for my benefit, sadly. Our meeting was a mere *amuse-bouche*. She'd been off to some Paris-Blois junket at a recently reopened celebrity restaurant in Fitzrovia, to which I was very much not invited.

"Or just money?" asked Fromage.

"I'm being paid expenses, if that's what you mean."

"Money it is, then. What was it Sun Tzu said about spies? 'None should be more liberally rewarded.' I trust Sandra is rewarding you liberally?"

"Can we talk about the tasting, please?"

"Whatever you say, old chap. What do you want to know?"

"I'm supposed to steal one of these fake wines."

"Yes. An empty bottle, I believe. So your boffins at the

Minstrels of Wine can have it checked out."

"Exactly. I was hoping you could tell me how I'm supposed to do it."

"How the hell should I know? You're the Minstrels' bagman, not me."

"I'm not a bag anything, thank you," I snapped, flushing a little. I was starting to go off Mr Fromage, even if he had just saved me from death by dehydration.

Fromage raised his hands.

"All right. Apologies, old chap. I didn't mean it. I'm just a little sore that I've been bumped from one of Farquhar Fine and Rare's most lucrative sales gigs. It's not been a great couple of years, what with the hotels empty and the airports deserted half the time. Not to mention the death of our founder."

"No offence taken. And I'm sorry for your loss. I was just hoping for a little help, that's all."

"Look, I've been to a couple of these tastings, one in Beijing and one in KL. They're pretty formal events, but it's not like being in a museum. There'll be around thirty attendees, plus a similar number of staff. Once they're poured, the empty bottles are lined up for the guests to inspect and pass around. That's where you'll get your chance. They'll search you on the way in to check you're not carrying any listening devices or secret phones. Or weapons, for that matter. But I doubt they'll search you on the way out. The attendees are all bankers, billionaires or politicos, the last thing they're worried about is someone stealing the cutlery."

The mention of weapons lowered my spirits a little.

"Is it dangerous? What if I'm caught?"

"It's a wine tasting in a luxury hotel, old chap. Not a Somalian arms bazaar."

"But Mr Lee's a crook, isn't he? That's why we're investigating him."

Fromage's face hardened a little. He rose and walked to the door, which was still ajar. He glanced through, then closed it quietly.

"Mr Lee," said Fromage, once he had retaken his seat, "is China's fourth-richest man. Soon to be third richest, I'm told. Now, you're a man of the world, Felix, so you know that money is power. But in China, you see, there is only one permissible source of power. The Party. Everything is subservient to the Party, and all power flows from it. The courts, the police, the military, the clergy, the food hygiene inspectorate, the pensioner in a peaked cap who cleans the pigeon shit off the swings in Victoria Park, all have their authority bestowed upon them by the Party. And that includes the captains of industry, too. The oligarchs, the big crocs, whatever you want to call them."

"So, is Lee dodgy or not?"

"My point is that he's only dodgy when the Party decides he's dodgy. And if they haven't, then he isn't. So, I would be extremely careful what you say when you're in China. That includes Hong Kong, too, by the way, especially these days."

"Fine. Let me ask a more specific question. Is Lee making fake wine?"

"I don't know, old chap. Probably."

"And what makes you think that?"

"You've seen the tasting list for Saturday's *Le Cercle Chêne*, I assume? The one I was very politely asked by your friend Sandra to share with your accomplices."

"The one with the '21 Richebourg?"

"Exactly. Farquhar Fine and Rare sold a bottle of '21 Richebourg to Mr Lee a few years ago. Mr Farquhar himself supervised the decanting and was even permitted to enjoy a half-glass alongside Lee and his friends."

"Couldn't Lee have procured another one?"

"Well, anything's possible. But I doubt it. I'm quite jealous you're getting the chance to taste it, to be honest. Interesting to know whether he's done a good job faking it."

"And there's a 1978 Musigny Grand Cru in the line-up."

"Yes," said Fromage. "That's pretty suspect too. I've not heard of any significant quantity surfacing on the legitimate market for a long time."

"So, some of the wines are real, including the two you're supplying and which I'm representing as brand ambassador, but some are fake. Why would he do that? He's a billionaire, isn't he?"

"I have absolutely no idea, old chap. For kicks? Because he can?"

"And how's he doing it? Are you telling me he's creating extremely expensive fake wines by blending together extremely expensive genuine wines? I know billionaires can be eccentric, but that strikes me as a very tedious hobby."

"I've told you, I don't know. I think that's what your boffins back at Minstrels HQ are supposed to be working out, isn't it?"

"There's something you're not telling me," I said. "Frankly, I'm beginning to get rather cold feet. I only agreed to do this in the first place because I'm public-spirited." I recalled the legal advice I'd received regarding Sandra's contract and a feeling of gloom descended upon me.

Fromage sighed and rubbed his forehead.

"Right. You did not, under any circumstances, hear this from me, understood? And you'd better not, for your own sake, repeat this to anyone. Not while you're here in China, anyway."

"You can trust me."

"Lee is Greater China Pharmco, yes? One of the largest pharmaceutical businesses in China, with subsidiaries in over a hundred countries. He founded it, he's the sole shareholder, and he grew it from a manufacturer of scalpels on the outskirts of Shanghai to an empire that spans medical devices, chemical manufacturing, generic drugs, vaccines, gene therapy, all that biotech stuff, the lot."

"I've read his Wikipedia page, yes."

"Then you'll know he's a mathematics genius too. His current focus is the application of data science to create new drugs faster than anyone else. Don't ask me how he does it, it's not exactly my field. But it's pretty much the sole topic of conversation at the *Cercle Chêne* tastings, apart from the wine. He uses the tastings for networking. The guests are potential investors, top financiers, local Party bosses, anyone with a vested interest in Greater China Pharmco."

"So... what are you suggesting? Is he cooking up the wines in his labs, or something?"

"I don't know. But then I'm just a humble wine merchant, not a maths genius running a multinational biotech firm. I have no idea what these companies are capable of. They can create a vaccine from scratch in a few months, so why shouldn't they be able to conjure up a gallon of fake Romanée-Conti?"

"I think this might be why some of my Minstrel colleagues are a little concerned," I said. I recalled Provost Jägermeister dancing his jig of angst back at Minstrels Hall, and Sandra's grim face as she briefed me at the Salon de Bordeaux.

"Oh, it's got the potential to be an absolute shitshow, old chap. I mean, Lafite and DRC at the touch of a button? Rare Scotch, Bourbon, and Cognac, too? It'd be curtains for me, the fine wine market and the whole bloody shooting match. That's why I've agreed to help you and your rather questionable friends."

It occurred to me that my career move into bathroom accessories might have been rather prescient.

"And you're sure I can just pick up an empty and walk out with it?"

"I reckon so. There'll be six bottles of the suspect Musigny '78 at the tasting, so I suggest you target one of the empties and, when no-one's looking, secrete it about your person."

"Where exactly am I going to hide a wine bottle?"

"Look, old chap, I don't know. Put it in your bag or something. I told you, they're not going to search you on the way out. Do you have a bag? A decent one?"

"Not really. I've got my laptop bag. Or I could buy something at the market in Mong Kok tonight."

"Good God, man. You're the brand ambassador for two of Paris-Blois's most prestigious domaines. You'll need to do better than a nylon rucksack sewn together by some poor devil in a Gansu prison camp. Here, let me find you something."

Fromage spun his chair round and opened a filing cabinet. He rummaged around for a few seconds, grunted, pushed it shut and opened the drawer beneath.

"There," he said, tossing a vintage leather satchel on the desk. He stood, ran his finger down a stack of books piled on top of the cabinet and extracted a thin volume. He waved it at me and slid it into the satchel.

"A 1960s vineyard atlas of the Côte d'Or. Look after it, please, I'd quite like it back." Fromage showed me the inside of the satchel. "You see, still plenty of room in there for a bottle. Try not to stain everything with the dregs."

*Or with my blood*, I thought, miserably.

"You do appreciate you're representing Farquhar Fine and Rare, as well as the two Paris-Blois domaines at this event, don't you? After all, I'm the one who's supposedly recommended you."

"You needn't worry on that account. I'm a Minstrel of Wine."

"It's not your ability to wax lyrical about the fruit of the Grands-Echézeaux that concerns me, old chap. It's you putting your foot in it, culturally speaking."

I decided that henceforth I would pronounce Fromage to rhyme very firmly with the French *homage*. If he wanted to be a Fromidge he could change the bloody spelling.

"I know how to behave culturally, thank you."

"Well, just remember, wine talk only. Nothing about Taiwan, Tibet, Xinjiang, Ai Weiwei, the Cultural Revolution, burning down the Summer Palace, the Wuhan Flu, Chairman Mao's bowel movements or the resemblance of the current Emperor to Winnie the Pooh, got it?"

"Got it."

"And I appreciate things might hit the fan fairly soon, but if you're going to burn the world down, please could you wait until you're back in Britain before you do it? I want as much distance between you and Farquhar Fine and Rare as possible before the shooting starts, ok?"

"Who said anything about shooting?" I said, my stomach lurching.

"It's a metaphor, old chap. Do calm down."

The subject of violence reminded me that I hadn't asked about Fromage's ex-boss.

"So, what happened to Mr Farquhar? He was the one who raised the alarm about Lee in the first place, wasn't he? I heard someone killed him."

Fromage sighed and looked at the ceiling. "Nobody killed Mr Farquhar."

"Seems a bit of a coincidence that he fell off the Cheung Chau ferry straight after raising the alarm about Mr Lee, doesn't it?"

"Mr Farquhar," said Fromage, "was a raging alcoholic, who by the time of his death could barely tell the end of a corkscrew from his own arsehole. He fell off the Cheung Chau ferry because he was as pissed as a priest at Christmas, and he failed to climb back on to the Cheung Chau ferry because he weighed twenty-two stone and probably thought he'd fallen into his gin and tonic."

Fromage gestured at a point high on the wall behind me. A vast portrait of a bearded man wielding a decanter scowled down at the room. It was clear from the picture that the late Mr Farquhar was indeed a large unit.

"The only mystery about the demise of the blessed bloody Mr Farquhar, peace be upon him," continued Fromage, "is that when he fell overboard he didn't capsize the Cheung Chau ferry and every other vessel in the South China Sea."

I suspected that employee relations might have been a little tense under the late Mr Farquhar.

"Right," I said, after a respectful pause. "Thanks for clearing that up. And thank you for the tea. I'll let myself out."

# Chapter 14

## Tabatha Shunt

"Felix, gorgeous!" boomed Tabatha Shunt from her corner table. "Darlings, meet Felix, my latest slave!"

The waiters either side of Tabatha glanced up before returning to the job of attaching a napkin the size of a small tablecloth to the front of her body. Their task was complicated by the presence of her astonishing necklace which, for reasons that only a true fashionista could explain, consisted of a loop of spiked fencing chain to which someone had welded several brightly coloured croquet balls. After a series of careful tucks and folds, the waiters attached the top corner of the napkin to Tabatha's lapel with a silver clasp and stepped back. Tabatha drained the remainder of her rosé and grinned.

"And another bottle of Rock Angel, darlings, *tout suite!*"

The waiters gave a little bow and disappeared.

"Felix, welcome to Felix!"

The restaurant at the summit of the Peninsula Hotel was indeed named Felix. Tabatha had been quick to clarify that she dined there every Tuesday night and any coincidence was entirely that, rather than an attempt to flatter.

"The best view in Hong Kong. Just look at it!"

I turned to take in the evening skyline glittering across the waters of Victoria Harbour. Impressive, without a doubt, though a touch marred by the clutter of cranes and the ever-multiplying hotels, museums and shopping centres sprouting from the harbour front. The view from Aqua Bar at the top of nearby One Peking was definitely superior, I decided.

"Or maybe the second-best view, eh, sweet cheeks?"

I was about to enquire whether Tabatha shared my opinion of Aqua Bar's superior vista, when I realised she'd been addressing my buttocks.

"I suppose it depends where you're seated, madam."

Tabatha's lips curled in delight and she made a sound that I can only describe as wild boar unearthing record-breaking truffle.

"Well, then, my little gym bunny, get yourself seated right there," she ordered, indicating the chair opposite.

I did as I was told.

"And talking of sitting, first things first. Where are my splashback-proof toilet seats?"

"All on schedule, Tabatha. I'm meeting Charles Fung at his factory tomorrow, to observe the final production run."

"Tomorrow? Those seats should have been shipped last week!"

"They've just completed testing on the hinges. Production starts tomorrow and they're shipping on Friday. I'll bring a gold seal sample back with me."

"Slower than I wanted. I'll have a word with Charles when I next see him. Ah, thank you, gorgeous."

This final comment to the young waiter who had glided in with a bottle of chilled Provençal rosé. He peeled away the foil, removed the cork and, as Tabatha rotated her forefinger, filled her glass until the wine was a quarter-inch from the rim. The man stepped around the table and moved to fill my glass.

"I don't suppose you have a decent, light Pinot Noir? Or a Beaujolais Cru, perhaps?" I asked.

The waiter paused and looked at Tabatha.

"If it's good enough for me, darling, it's bloody well good enough for you! You might be a buff little soldier, but it doesn't mean you get to order your own wine!"

"Apologies, rosé it is. I'm very partial to Provençal wines, actually."

"Oh, yes. I'd forgotten you were some sort of wine expert. Perhaps you should come round to my place for a little educational tasting."

*I'd rather smear my naked body in zebra fat and sprint through a hyena enclosure,* I thought.

"I'd be delighted," I said.

"No red wine, though. I'm allergic to red. Gives me a splitting headache. Tastes disgusting, anyway."

"You must have a particularly sensitive palate."

"Rosé all the way for me." Tabatha drove home her point by decanting a third of the wine down her throat. She replaced her glass and rapped her knuckles approvingly against the table. "Actually, I might have a use for you and that magic tongue of yours."

I remained silent and steeled myself for whatever horrifically inappropriate task Tabatha might have in mind.

"We're opening a new flagship store in Shenzhen next month. You could do a wine tasting for some of the local influencers. Showcase our range. I'll have a word with the agency that runs our local PR. Reckon you could get back out here in five weeks' time? I'll tell the retail division to cover your expenses. Damned if it's coming out of my travel budget."

"Yes, that might be possible."

"Good. Now, I have a question for you. How come you're able to breeze your way in and out of Hong Kong when you're not even a resident? The only people I know who can do that are top politicians and multinational CEOs."

"Oh, I belong to an international wine organisation – the Minstrels of Wine. They have a Chapter here and I've been asked to deliver some new vintage samples. Quite valuable. French."

It was a pretty feeble story, but I couldn't think of anything better. Strictly speaking, I shouldn't have mentioned the Minstrels at all, but I could hardly brandish Inspector Ma's letter at Tabatha and claim I had a side hustle procuring PPE for His Majesty's Government.

"Why don't they just DHL them like everyone else?"

"They're very valuable. Unique. And fragile. Temperature sensitive. They refuse to allow them out of a trained Minstrel of

Wine's sight."

"Last time I checked, you weren't allowed to take bottles of wine on a flight."

"They're specially sealed, with a special security seal," I gabbled. "They inspect them at security and they get a special seal." My cheeks began to burn.

"Sounds like a load of bollocks," said Tabatha.

"Yes, I know. Bit annoying, really, having to travel all this way just to courier a couple of bottles. One of the duties of being a Minstrel of Wine, you see."

"And these Minstrels are covering your flight and accommodation, are they? For an entire week? Because I know we haven't paid for it. Must be costing a fortune."

"Yes, it's all covered by the Minstrels of Wine. But the flights were cheap and it's budget accommodation."

"Sounds a bit funny to me. You are aware your Gatesave contract forbids other employment without the permission of the business, aren't you?" She narrowed her eyes. "You'd better not be moonlighting!"

"I'm not! Not at all," I squeaked. "It's unpaid, they just cover my expenses. It was cheaper to book the return flight a week later."

"Where are you staying?"

"Chungking Mansions."

"Good God! Well, don't come any closer to me. I recommend you boil your clothes when you get home. Better still, burn them."

"Right, will do."

"In all seriousness, you should buy a new outfit, keep it in a sealed bag, then change at the airport. Discard your old clothes, take a shower there and really scrub yourself clean. Maybe even shave your body hair. In fact, I know a place on Staunton Street where you can get a full body wax. All the young gay guys go there. You should do that before you leave."

"I'll definitely bear that in mind."

"So, what are you doing for these Wine Minstrel people? I'm

not happy that you're messing around doing work for someone else, frankly. Not happy at all."

"Honestly, I'm not doing any work for anyone else. I just thought it was a great opportunity to come out and see Charles Fung's factory and meet you and the Hong Kong sourcing team properly. I've already dropped the wine samples off at the Minstrels' Chapter in Wan Chai. That's it. All done."

"It better bloody have been. You work for me, and only me, understood?"

"I'm all yours, I promise."

This appeared to satisfy Tabatha. She sat back and sluiced the rest of the rosé down her gullet. Then she jabbed a ring-encrusted finger at me.

"Do you think I'm stupid?"

"No! I don't! Definitely not."

"I know why you're here."

My heart stopped.

"Oh. Do you?" Christ, was she having me followed?

"Yes, I do. Let's drop the pretence, shall we?" Tabatha pointed at her glass and a waiter swooped in to refill it.

Unable to think of anything to say, I lifted my glass and took a long, slow sip. I wondered whether I could ask Inspector Ma to threaten Tabatha with imprisonment in Shek Pik.

Tabatha slapped her palm on the table, making me jump and causing Provençal rosé to slosh over my nose and chin.

"You're here on a jolly, Felix Hart!" she grinned, like a hungry ogre catching sight of the dessert trolley. "Soon as you're done here, I bet you're headed straight to Lan Kwai Fong. You'll be shirtless, covered in beer, dancing on a table and sucking some girl's face by midnight. Am I right or am I right?"

"Oh, God, you're absolutely right," I said, as my sweaty, rosé-misted face cooled beneath the aggressive air-con. "Guilty as charged!"

# Chapter 15

## Light Manufacturing

You'll be disappointed to hear that I did not take a taxi that evening to Lan Kwai Fong, the legendary ex-pat drinking district, and offer my gyrating torso for the delectation of any lascivious, cocktail swilling young ladies. Instead, I headed straight back to my hotel and was in bed by midnight in a futile effort to recalibrate my biorhythms to East Asia time. I finally dropped off after subjecting myself to a CNN documentary on female entrepreneurship in Saudi Arabia, and when my alarm sounded at seven a.m., I felt like a drugged bear hauled from the depths of a mid-winter hibernation.

A brisk, twenty-minute walk across the tip of Kowloon to the China Ferry Terminal did little to lift my brain fog. I waved my passport and Inspector Ma's letter at immigration, boarded the ferry, settled into my window seat and promptly fell fast asleep. I woke two hours later on the deserted passenger deck to find an elderly man in a grubby face mask poking my thigh with a litter picker.

"You go!" he explained, waving his refuse bag in the direction of the exit.

I climbed the metal gantry, bleary and sweating in the sub-tropical heat, and stepped into the blissfully cool arrivals lounge of Shunde Ferry Port. My driver, who had sensibly deduced that the dopey-looking, sole Westerner in the terminal was his client, bustled over and held up a laminated sheet of paper stating, 'Guangdong Intelligent Sanitary Co Ltd welcomes Mr Hart!'

"Hello. You come with me," he ordered through his mask, and led me to the car park, where I was waved into the back of an immaculate, air-conditioned people carrier stocked with chilled mineral water and disposable face masks. "Forty minute," he declared, and the sliding door hummed shut.

We accelerated out of the ferry terminal car park and merged with a three-lane motorway built high above the soggy farmlands of the Pearl River Delta. A patchwork of murky green reservoirs, divided into neat rectangles by mud embankments, stretched into the distance either side of the road. Every so often, one of the river's oozing tendrils would interrupt the man-made geometry, forcing its way through the landscape towards the open sea.

After a while, the watery vista began to break up and farmland gave way to warehouses and lorry parks. Other highways joined and diverged from our own, overhead signs advertising the routes to huge, unknown conurbations; Dongguan, Panyu, Guicheng, Zhongcun. Then the warehouses also thinned out, replaced by thousands upon thousands of low-rise apartment buildings built right up to the edge of the road, the exteriors clad in identical cream tiles. It began to rain. Scattered, heavy drops at first, tapping on the vehicle's roof, then a deluge. The road was transformed into a dancing, translucent sheet, thousands of spouts of rainwater pouring from the balconies either side of us, splattering onto the pavements beneath. All I could see, for mile after mile, was white ceramic tiles, cascading water and spray. I felt for all the world like a waterlogged beetle or soggy cigarette end being hosed down a vast urinal by a line of lager-addled giants.

I dismissed my mood as temporary nausea, brought on by jetlag and the driver's habit of pulsing the gas pedal in time to the stereo's Cantopop. The rain eased and we turned off the motorway, passing a series of building sites constructing more low-rise, white-tiled apartment blocks, before entering an industrial district. I spotted a sign helpfully pointing the way, in both English and Chinese, to the 'Artificial Christmas Tree Zone', another to the 'Garden Accessories and Tiny Statues Zone'. Every hundred yards, we passed a factory entrance guarded by a metal gate and a ten-foot-high perimeter wall displaying the name of the company in English and Chinese; Zhenbei Best Hotel Furniture Co. Ltd, Pengda Scrubbing and Toothbrush Co. Ltd, Qiandeng Nozzle and Suction Co. Ltd.

The driver slowed. He turned into a driveway and nosed his way to within touching distance of the entrance gate. A masked guard marched up to the driver's window, peered into the back, and returned to his hut without a word. The gate trundled open and once a sufficient gap had presented itself, we accelerated on to the premises of Guangdong Intelligent Sanitary Co. Ltd.

Charles Fung was waiting for me in Reception. He seemed extraordinarily pleased to see me. Even through his face mask, I could see he was beaming as he pumped my hand. He pressed an ice-cold bottle of mineral water on me and hustled me into his highly polished office.

"Welcome, Felix. So good you could come. I am so happy," he declared, tossing his face mask on the table. "How was your journey?"

"Fine, thank you, Charles. Still a bit jetlagged though."

"Oh dear. But I hope you enjoyed the river journey? It used to be quicker to drive from Hong Kong but there are big delays at the border these days."

"The ferry was very pleasant. I slept most of the way."

"Ah, very good. And you have special dispensation to cross the border? Not many people have this right now."

"Yes, they're letting a few people through. If you're on important business."

"Ah, good. In fact, this is very unusual. Even I had some trouble travelling to Hong Kong recently. So this is very good that they are relaxing things for foreigners."

I smiled and remained silent in the hope that he'd change the subject.

"So, I will give you a tour of the factory and the showrooms. Even the dormitories, if you like. You will want to see the final production of your splashback-proof seats, I think?"

"Yes, please, Charles. I'll need to take a gold seal sample

back to the office in Hong Kong. And, I have a gift for you, too."

Charles Fung beamed. "Really? For me?"

Following my meeting with Fromage, I'd purchased a rather good Saint-Émilion from the Wan Chai branch of Farquhar Fine and Rare. I extracted the bottle from my bag and placed it on the desk.

Fung beamed even wider. "Felix, this is very kind of you! I am embarrassed. You are my customer, I should be buying gifts for you!"

"No gifts necessary," I said, hoping Fung might feel forced to reciprocate with something wildly expensive next time we met. "All I expect from you is the world's finest splashback-proof lavatory seat."

"You will have it," declared Fung, stroking the Saint-Émilion label. "Now, let me take you on a tour of my factory."

We proceeded to an oven-like changing room, where one of Fung's foremen provided me with a disposable boiler suit. I climbed into it and zipped it up. Warm sweat trickled down my back.

"And you must wear a N95," said Fung. "There will be some fumes if they are spraying."

The foreman passed each of us an industrial-grade respirator with built-in chemical filter. I fastened the strap around the back of my head and, as I inhaled, the mask moulded itself snugly around my nose and mouth. I felt a moustache of perspiration building on my top lip. The foreman attached his own mask, handed me a pair of goggles, and we followed him to the factory floor.

I'm not sure what I had been expecting from a toilet seat factory. Machines, I suppose. Something similar to a winery bottling line, perhaps, but calibrated for laminated lavatory accessories rather than glass, labels, and cork. Bright lights, whirring conveyor belts, mechanical arms stamping and welding, sparks flying, the occasional white-coated operative checking a display panel. Perhaps even a robot, pivoting back and forth on its turntable, lifting and palletising finished goods.

But there were no robots, no mechanical arms and no white coats. And there were no bright lights, either. Instead, I found myself in a dim, clatteringly loud, low-ceilinged warehouse the size of a football field, filled with perhaps one thousand men and women, all toiling away in the dark, dust and fumes. I felt a hand on my shoulder.

"The parts come in there," shouted Fung, through his mask.

He pointed to a garage door-sized entrance in the corner, the only source of natural light and air to the factory, so far as I could see. A posse of men unwrapped pallets of short, curved wooden planks and carried them to a long bank of workstations, where lines of women armed with glue guns and rubber mallets assembled them into recognisably buttock-hugging ring shapes. A pair of men took the completed seats and hung them, one by one, on a slowly moving cable festooned with hooks, which rose from a trapdoor in the floor like some medieval torture device. The cable ascended to the low roof, clanked over a pulley, then travelled half the length of the factory ceiling, hundreds of toilet seats dangling just inches above the heads of the workers. The cable and its lavatorial passengers passed through a curtain of fabric strips on the opposite side of the factory and disappeared from view.

Swap the Chinese for a crowd of grimy northern Englishmen and I suspected the scene wouldn't have been dissimilar to a mill in 18th-century Manchester.

"Through there is where we spray," shouted Fung, indicating the vanishing procession of toilet seats.

I followed Fung and the foreman to the curtain of fabric, behind which a cacophony of hissing could be heard.

"Put up your hood," shouted Fung, tugging at the back of my boiler suit, "and pull the strings tight."

I did as I was told. The hood drew taut against my damp hair and goggles. The foreman opened a door next to the curtain and we passed into the spray-painting room. Above us, the cable and its dangling loo seats nosed their way in from the factory floor, soon lost from view in the swirling grey mist ahead of us. I followed Fung and the foreman into the fog and saw what I assumed were robotic arms fitted with paint nozzles weaving between the seats, coating each in brilliant white in a matter of seconds. I marvelled at the machines' dexterity and was about to ask Fung how much they cost, when one of them suddenly moved out of position. What I'd assumed was a machine was actually a man swathed in overalls, a paint-splattered piece of fabric tied around his mouth and nose.

"These are the most skilled workers in the factory," shouted Fung, next to my ear.

I noticed that the man was wearing a paint-caked baseball cap and a pair of swimming goggles. The exposed skin on his upper cheeks and the tufts of hair poking from the sides of his cap were frosted with gloss paint.

"Why aren't they wearing protective equipment?" I shouted.

"They take very regular breaks," Fung shouted back. "They are used to it."

I began to feel rather light-headed. Drops of sweat tickled their way down my nose and crept, hot and salty, between my lips.

The foreman waved us on. We passed into a drying room, where furnace-heated air roared over the gleaming white rings, baking the paint hard. Beneath my boiler suit, my shirt clung hot and wet against my skin. Thankfully, before I fainted, we moved on to the final section of the factory, where a man on a raised platform removed the painted seats from the cable hooks and sent them sliding down a chute to a foam-covered workbench. A group of men retrieved the white rings, paired each with a white oval disc from a pile, and then distributed them to a long counter staffed by drill-wielding women whose job was to join them with a silver hinge. The conjoined seats were moved to another long workstation where a line of men added the securing bolts, then a third area, where a group of women fitted the faecal splashback seal.

"Here is the secret stage!" shouted Fung, as the women stuffed a ridged silicone ring, looking for all the world like a giant troll's contraceptive device, into a slot running around the inside perimeter of the toilet seat.

The finished splashback-busting seats were then placed in a plastic bag, slotted into a box, taped shut, and placed into a cardboard outer of twelve. The outers were stacked on a pallet, the pallet wrapped in clingfilm, and the whole lot hauled to the loading bay on a pump truck, each stage performed by an exclusively single-sex group.

"Here is your gold seal sample," shouted Fung.

The foreman handed me an unsealed box branded 'Gatesave Home' and sporting the official product description, 'Splashback-proof hygienic lavatory seat'. Beneath a picture of a relieved woman flushing a loo equipped with my turd-baffling triumph was a series of bullet points explaining that this purchase would protect your family from urinary aerosols, faecal splashback, rectal plume inhalation and colonic splatter.

"You are doing God's work, Felix," said Fung, clapping me on the shoulder.

We left the factory floor and with delight I shed my mask, goggles and boiler suit. The foreman handed me a wad of paper towels to mop my sweat-drenched face, and we headed to Fung's product showroom.

"Did you enjoy the tour, Felix?" asked Fung, as we passed through a series of rooms filled with every bathroom accessory a soiled family could dream of.

"Yes, thank you. Though it was a little more manual than I expected." I perused a plinth running the length of the room, on which were displayed several hundred models of toilet brush, including one in the shape of a lightsaber.

"If you pay me more money for your toilet seats, I will buy some machines!" chuckled Fung.

I lifted the lightsaber toilet brush and slid forward the switch in the handle. With a hum, the shaft illuminated red.

"Do you like it? It makes an authentic sound as you move it."

"But wouldn't it be cheaper in the long run, investing in automation?" I waved the brush from side to side, slowly at first, then faster, and the hum rose in volume with each swipe.

"To be honest, Felix, yes it would. But the local authorities will be very upset if I make too many people redundant. So, we keep things as they are. Actually, I am building a new factory in Hanoi, which is far more automated. When it is completed, we will move some of our production there."

"And your local authorities will be happy with that?" I struck the end of the brush against the plinth. It hummed and crackled loudly.

"I will find a way to keep the authorities happy," smiled Fung.

I turned off the lightsaber and returned the brush to its stand. We passed through a room full of soap dishes and toilet roll holders, then another festooned with shower curtain rings and towel rails.

"The chrome and plastic products are fabricated at a different site, in Jiangsu," said Fung, rapping his knuckles against a heated towel bar.

I decided to try my luck.

"I'm guessing that's one of the sites that does business with Joseph Lee?" I said, nonchalantly examining a purple curtain ring. "He's big in the chemicals business, I believe."

"Er, yes, that is correct, Felix. But what is your interest in Mr Lee?"

"Oh, I forgot to mention," I said, tapping the curtain ring against a frosted tooth-mug holder, "I'm attending the *Le Cercle Chêne* tasting on Saturday, in Macau."

"You?" said Fung. "That is a very enormous surprise. You are not, forgive me Felix, the type of businessman Joseph Lee would usually invite to his tastings."

"No, of course, I realise that," I said. "I'm a mere supermarket buyer, not a big-shot industrialist. But I happen to be the brand ambassador for two Burgundian estates that Mr Lee intends to show at his next tasting. I've been invited to talk about the wines."

While Fung absorbed this, I strolled over to a table displaying a collection of strange contraptions, each consisting of a small, transparent box at the end of a long shaft.

"But this is absolutely incredible, Felix! You will be in Macau on Saturday? At *Le Cercle Chêne*? I cannot believe this!"

"Yes, at the Phantasos Hotel, I believe. A nice venue." I lifted one of the contraptions. At the end of the shaft sat a handle and small lever, rather like a litter-picker.

"It is, yes, an extremely nice venue. It is just called Phantasos, actually. Not Phantasos Hotel. Mr Lee owns an entire floor."

"Phantasos. Right. It sounds very exclusive." I squeezed the lever and a trapdoor opened in the transparent box at the opposite end. "What's this for? Retrieving goldfish from your toilet bowl?"

"No, it is for catching, er..." Fung paused and grimaced.

"Catching stray turds?" I asked, genuinely astonished.

"No, no, no!" exclaimed Fung. "Sorry, I do not like to say the word. The horrible, creepy-crawly things." He held out a hand and, turning his head away, pointed his fingers down and wiggled them.

"What, spiders?"

"Urgh!" exclaimed Fung, and visibly juddered. "Even the word I find very horrible, Felix."

"Oh, I see. Fair enough. Lots of people hate spi–, sorry, I mean, hate those creepy-crawly things."

"They are the most disgusting, horrible things on Earth." Fung closed his eyes and hugged himself.

"Right. Just as well you manufacture a range of state-of-the-art creepy-crawly catchers then."

"It is my mission to create the world's best creepy-crawly catcher, Felix. Look, this is my latest model."

Fung grasped the end of a gently curving, two-metre-long, telescopic rod, at the end of which sat a transparent hemisphere the size of a halved football. Fung squeezed the handle and a portion of the hemisphere's base slid open.

"This has a very long handle so you can stay at a safe distance from the creature."

He tossed a screwed-up fragment of paper on the floor.

"You place the catcher over it, like so. And the base slowly closes. You see, the trapdoor is slightly lower than the outer ring of the base, so the creature is not squashed. I do not want to deal with squashed creepy-crawlies."

"Ingenious," I said.

"It also has lights, in case you are in a dark room, at night, in the countryside." Fung shivered and clicked a button in the handle. A dozen tiny lights lit up the rim of the hemisphere.

"Look at that! It's like a spider disco!" I said.

Fund dropped the device and shuddered. "Please! Don't use that word!"

"Sorry, sorry, I do apologise." I stooped to retrieve Fung's spider catcher.

"With this model, the creature can be removed by a staff member and taken far away – to the next village, for example," said Fung, keeping his eye on the screwed-up piece of paper, lest it metamorphose into a tarantula.

"Very practical," I said. "Perhaps we should stock these at Gatesave. I don't think we need the two-metre handle and the lights, but... that one perhaps?" I lifted a more modest model with an arm-length handle and a neat, transparent pyramid at the base.

"You have spiders in England, but only very small ones, I think," said Fung.

"That's right. Nothing huge, like that," I said, wiggling my hand.

Fung jumped and took a step back.

"Sorry," I said. "Nothing that big."

"How big?"

"Oh, maximum two or three inches, I would say. Maybe like that." I held up my thumb and forefinger, trying not to make any overtly spidery movements. "That's leg-tip to leg-tip, by the way, not the body size."

Fung looked horrified. "I did not know that! That is still very big."

"Well, they're not poisonous or anything. They're completely harmless. Mind you, they can really move. If you disturb one, they absolutely leg it across the floor!" I swept my hand towards Fung to indicate the sprinting speed of the common British house spider.

Fung screamed.

"Jesus, Charles, I'm sorry! I didn't mean to scare you."

"I did not know this about England," said Fung, quaking. "I did not know you had big, running creepy-crawlies. Where do they live? Just in the wild areas with no people, like Scotland?"

"Well, they live all over, really. They're called house spiders, so they live in houses, mainly."

"In houses?" shouted Fung, twitching. "I am travelling to England in two months' time and staying in a friend's house! Will he have these creatures in his house?"

"Well, I couldn't really tell you," I said, wishing I could change the subject back to sociopathic Chinese billionaire wine fraudsters. "Does he live in a big, old house with a large garden?"

"Yes!" squealed Fung. "Very big and very old, with huge gardens!"

"Right. You might want to stay in a hotel in the centre of town, then. Something modern with minimalist décor."

I apologised again for unsettling Fung and reassured him that he was extremely unlikely to encounter any large creepy-crawlies in England. I gave a verbal commitment to purchase three thousand spider catchers, which cheered him up a little, he thanked me again for my wine gift, and we concluded our visit on good terms. Fung's driver transported me back to Shunde Port, accompanied by a medium-sized spider catcher and the production sample of my splashback-proof loo seat, and the afternoon catamaran was soon carving its way down the Pearl River Delta to Hong Kong.

# Chapter 16

## Macau

The next morning, I rose at nine and felt for the first time that I had turned the tide of battle against my jet lag. I strolled to the Gatesave global sourcing office, which was as sparsely populated as its London equivalent, and dropped off the splashback-proof lavatory seat and the spider catcher for the technical department to examine. I settled into a window seat at the end of an empty bank of desks, which boasted a fabulous view north over Kowloon to the rolling hills of the New Territories, and composed a highly creative press release to accompany the launch of my innovative bathroom accessory. I dispatched it to the PR team for vetting, then dealt with a few outstanding emails; principally the delivery address confirmation for a rather ambitious fine wine order I'd placed with Berry Bros. in London, and some administration regarding the second deposit due on a small ski chalet purchase in Cervinia. The latter transaction had seemed like a very good idea two weeks ago, but since my legal advice from the beautiful Amrita, I'd started to wonder whether I'd been just a tiny bit hasty.

I left work early and caught the Star Ferry across the harbour to Central. My trip to Macau was less than twenty-four hours away and I needed some time to formulate a plan for the big gig. Walking slowly to avoid marinading myself in sweat, I meandered through the sharply scented neighbourhood of Sheung Wan, passing shopfronts piled high with medicinal fungi, edible bird's nests, bags of sun-dried shark fins, and crispy crucified geckos. Resisting the temptation to invest in a multipack of desiccated seahorses, I turned inland and, as gently as I could, began to climb the streets to Mid-Levels, emerging on Hollywood Road close to the Man Mo temple. I paused in the shadow of a huge gatepost and peered across the courtyard into the gloom beyond the temple door. At first, the interior appeared black. Then, I began to discern shapes: the giant incense coils hanging from the ceiling, brass pots studded with smoking joss-sticks, the movement of worshippers bowing to their ancestors. A whisper of breeze sent a fug of sweet jasmine across the courtyard, masking the background scent of drains and market tables. I pushed on. A short climb further and I was among the bars and restaurants of Elgin Street. I stepped into a branch of Farquhar Fine and Rare and purchased a splendid-looking Adelaide Hills Chardonnay. A minute or so later, I reached my final destination, Chong Qin, one of my favourite Sichuan restaurants, whose proprietor practiced a very civilised bring-your-own-bottle policy. A couple of glasses later, accompanied by a dish of exquisite steamed jade vegetables, I considered my predicament.

*Perhaps I've been overthinking things*, I mused. All I had to do was swan into *Le Cercle Chêne,* give a decent spiel on the Paris-Blois Burgundies, be generally charming and witty and not overly upset anyone, then slip an empty bottle of Musigny '78 into my bag. If Fromage was right and no-one paid much attention to what the guests got up to, it should be a doddle. I could position the unzipped satchel beneath my chair, pretend to examine one of the empties and just drop it in when no-one was looking, possibly using Fromage's old guide to the vineyards of the Côte d'Or as cover. Then it would be *zàijiàn* everybody, toodle pip, lovely to meet you, sorry to rush but I simply have to be up early for church tomorrow. I'd catch the night ferry back to Hong Kong, my flight to London the next morning, deliver the empty bottle to Provost Rougegorgefils at Minstrels Hall, confirm that my contract with Sandra and Paris-Blois had been fulfilled to everyone's satisfaction, and hallelujah, Felix saves the world again.

As my taxi glided through the harbour tunnel later that evening, my belly full of Sichuan beef and superlative Chardonnay, I felt more confident than I had in quite a while. I still had the fat end of half a million in my bank account and it struck me that it might be sensible to invest in a Mediterranean property sooner rather than later, before the market fully recovered. The only question was, should I choose Provence, Le Marche, or Corfu?

***

The Turbojet ferry powered out of Victoria Harbour and with a slowly rising growl accelerated past the southern coast of Lantau. Wreathed in morning cloud, the island's forested peaks drifted by, the occasional orange-tiled temple winking from the carpet of green. Within minutes, the outlying islands were behind us and we hit choppier waters where the Pearl River's monstrous mouth met the open ocean. The Turbojet's engines now rose to a roar. The cabin walls and seats vibrated faster, the waves slammed more angrily against the bow until, just as the vessel seemed ready to tear itself apart, the hydrofoils lifted the hull clear of the water. The vibrations ceased, the waves fell silent beneath us and we sliced like a silver blade across the South China Sea to Macau.

Despite my intention to flee Macau immediately after the tasting, I had decided it would be wise to reserve a hotel room as a base or potential safe house. I'd chosen the Notting Hill Resort Hotel, principally because it was located close to Phantasos, though I won't deny that the London-themed name felt like a good omen. I cleared immigration at the Macau Ferry Terminal, jumped in a taxi and directed the driver to Cotai, the vast pleasure district that barely a century ago was a pair of damp little islands populated only by pirates and salt miners.

My taxi glided across the two-mile-long, near-empty Amizade Bridge and we were soon among the towering casinos of the Cotai strip. My driver explained with pride that such is the Chinese appetite for gambling, Macau now boasted ten times the gambling revenue of Las Vegas, though the quiet streets suggested recent events might have knocked the shine off his figures. He pulled off the main drag and proceeded up the dual carriageway drive of the Notting Hill Resort Hotel, which to my surprise turned out to be quarter of a mile wide and thirty storeys high. I was fairly sure, in fact, that the hotel was larger than Notting Hill itself. Of even greater surprise was the presence of a man-made lake in front of it, out of which rose a full-scale version of Big Ben's clock tower, significantly shinier and more golden than the original. A cascade of dyed-blue water poured from the tower's summit and, just in case any unworldly visitors had failed to recognise the cultural reference, an enormous, illuminated sign emerging from the lake made clear the body of water represented the 'London Thames River'. Two Chinese Beefeaters stood guard either side of the hotel entrance and as I approached, they bowed and touched their hands to their bearskins. I returned their salute and passed through the automatic doors.

The centre of the lobby was dominated, intriguingly, with a red, open-topped, double-decker bus. Inside it, pressed against the windows, sat a variety of grinning waxworks, most of whom appeared to be members of the royal family or the Beatles, though on closer inspection I spotted Margaret Thatcher, Sherlock Holmes and a Peaky Blinder leering recklessly from the top deck. The driver's seat was occupied by a wild-eyed Boris Johnson, one hand making a thumbs-up sign, the other brandishing an antique pistol. Several blond waxwork children sat in Johnson's lap, fighting over the steering wheel. Further inside the lobby, a black cab, driven by a psychotic-looking waxwork punk with a green Mohican, was embedded artfully in the Reception desk. To emphasise the violence of the impact, the shattered counter and surrounding floor were sprinkled liberally with fibreglass bricks. A waxwork Metropolitan Police constable stood nearby, smiling benignly at the punk and his misjudged ram raid.

"All right, mate?" said a young Chinese woman, as I

approached the section of the counter not hosting a drug-induced traffic incident. She appeared to be dressed as some kind of pre-war domestic servant.

"Yes, thank you, I'm absolutely fine," I replied. "Checking in for two nights. The name's Hart. Felix Hart."

"All right, mate?" repeated the woman, less confidently.

"Er, yes. All good here." I peered a little closer, wondering if she was some kind of automaton. The woman took a step back.

A man dressed as a Victorian chimney sweep popped up from behind the counter. "Good afternoon, sir. How are you? I speak English."

"Oh, jolly good. *Nǐ hǎo.* I'm checking in."

The chimney sweep looked blankly at me. I handed over my passport. With visible relief he opened it and began tapping at a keyboard beneath the counter.

"You stay in Stonehenge wing, floor seventeen." The chimney sweep handed me a key-card. "No smoking."

"Not even in the fireplace?" I joked, gesturing at his costume. The sweep's face fell.

"Never mind," I said. "Thank you for your help."

"Very welcome, sir!" said the sweep, cheering up. He looked at the woman and nudged her.

"All right, mate?" she said, quietly.

"Yes, still absolutely fine, thank you."

Once in my room, which was bereft of any England-themed décor bar a framed painting of a castle surrounded by a murderous-looking gang of cows, I hung up my suit and checked my equipment: Fromage's leather satchel, his 1960's guide to the Côte d'Or vineyards, the copy of Jasper Morris's *Inside Burgundy*, second edition, provided by Provost Rougegorgefils, the tasting notes folder and domaine information supplied by Sandra, my phone loaded with return ferry e-tickets, a pack of luxury paper napkins to mop up wine dregs and conceal the theft of bottles, a short bungee cord with hooks should I need to escape from a hotel balcony, and a corkscrew with a particularly sharp foil-cutter, in case I found myself involuntarily tied up or threatened by bandits. I checked my wallet. A decent wad of Macanese patacas, Hong Kong dollars and US dollars. A few large denomination notes for serious bribes and plenty of small ones for tips, taxis and miscellaneous palm-greasing.

There would be no need to ask for directions. I could see Phantasos from the window, looming out of the overcast sky. In fact, I'd spotted it a mile away as my taxi approached Cotai over the Amizade Bridge, even before my driver began gesturing excitedly through his windscreen. For Phantasos was a genuinely eye-popping sight. In contrast to the brutal, box-like design of the Notting Hill Resort, Phantasos was a futuristic wedge of black glass reaching towards the clouds, its centre punctured by huge, irregular holes, like craters in the crust of an incompetently prepared soufflé. The building's exterior was imprisoned within an exoskeleton of huge iron straps, giving the structure the appearance of a colossal robot in kinky bondage gear who'd lost a fight with a soldering iron.

I could also see from my seventeenth-floor perch that the few hundred yards separating me from Phantasos was obstructed by high walls and a six-lane highway. It was clear my approach and departure would have to be vehicular. I glanced at my watch. Sunset was still an hour away. Then an hour more before *Le Cercle Chêne* commenced. Tall, grey clouds were pushing in from the ocean and a faint whistling sound had risen outside the window. I ordered a plate of steamed dim sum from room service and read through my Paris-Blois wine notes a final time, opening a large bottle of Tsingtao beer for Dutch courage.

As I leafed through Fromage's old guide to the vineyards of Burgundy, I realised the room had darkened to such a degree I could no longer distinguish the contours of the maps. I rose to switch on the light and was shocked to see the sky behind Phantasos roiling with black thunderclouds. I hadn't bothered to check the forecast but a glance at my weather app suggested an extremely moist night ahead. I decided to make a move before all the taxis were taken. I ran an iron over my shirt, dressed, and packed my satchel. Notes, books, escape equipment, weapons, all present and correct. I placed the rest of my belongings in my open suitcase and headed down to the lobby.

"Very London weather!" said the bowler-hatted man at Reception. "Fog city!"

"Touch damp tonight, is it?" I replied.

The man frowned. "Black rain. Be careful." He pointed to the television screen behind the counter. A couple, sitting in a lavishly decorated dining room, appeared to be having a heated argument in Korean with Chinese subtitles. Spotting my confusion, the bowler-hatted man stepped closer to the screen and pointed at the corner, which was occupied by an angry-looking weather symbol.

"Black rain, sir."

"Ah, I see. That's very public service orientated. They don't tell you the weather on British television. Unless it's the weather forecast, of course. Even then, it's more of an educated guess, really, rather than the actual weather."

"Black rain," repeated the man.

I thanked him and crossed the lobby towards the main entrance. I'd noticed the sound of background static as I stepped out of the lift and had assumed it emanated from the television or the lobby speakers. But as I neared the front doors, I realised the noise was caused by the torrential rain scouring the driveway outside. I paused to button my jacket, then approached the automatic doors. They parted and I was immediately enveloped in a warm, angry mist. A man dressed as a 19th-century stockbroker, both hands clinging to the rim of his enormous top hat, enquired whether I might need a taxi.

"Very wet, sir," added the stockbroker, dipping his top hat in the direction of the storm.

I looked out at Big Ben. The clock tower was indistinct, only visible as a shimmering yellow wand rising from the seething lake. The wind howled around the tower, whipping its blue cascading waters into furious whorls that danced and merged with the downpour. The two Beefeaters huddled beside the doorway, their bearskins damp and decidedly limp.

"So it would appear," I said. "Phantasos, please."

The stockbroker pressed a button on a post and a pair of headlights shone dimly at the end of the drive. Slowly they approached and the diffuse shape of a vehicle appeared, its wheels leaving white trails in the frothing surface water. The cab reached the shelter of the hotel's canopy and sluiced its way into the pickup bay, windscreen wipers flapping like beached salmon.

"You lucky, nearly all taxis stay home," explained the stockbroker as he opened the cab's rear door, nearly losing his top hat to the storm in the process. "Phantasos, *tèjià*," he shouted to the driver.

The car smelt of new vinyl and wet dog. As we left the canopy's protection, the rain hammered against the vehicle's roof like lead shot. God alone knew how the driver knew where he was going. The view through the windscreen looked like a conceptual art installation, as if some lunatic had applied a propeller to a fish tank full of black dye and multicoloured fairy lights. I averted my eyes and prayed that my driver possessed some kind of bat-like navigational super sense. To take my mind off the road conditions, I unzipped my satchel and checked the contents once more. Back at the hotel, I had opened the pack of napkins and removed one. This now nestled in the satchel's inner sanctum, delicately refolded and held together with a tab of tape. I extracted it, removed the tape and slid it carefully into my jacket pocket.

"Phantasos," announced the driver as we bumped on to the hotel's driveway.

I squinted through the window, but only the base of the building's exoskeleton was visible in the hurling rain, dull and wet.

"I'm in one of the private residences," I called, over the drumming rain.

"Wha?" he shouted.

"The event, it's taking place on one of the residential floors."

"Wha?"

The hammering stopped as we passed beneath the porte-cochère.

"The residential floors. Never mind, let me ask one of the staff."

I lowered the window and presented my phone to the approaching concierge. The man, dressed in a sharp satin suit, took my phone and read the email from *Le Cercle Chêne* forwarded to me by Fromage. He touched his earpiece, observed me for a few seconds, then smiled.

"Welcome to Phantasos, Mr Hart."

The concierge gave some complicated-sounding instructions to my driver and pointed back the way we'd come. An unmarked road blocked by a gate was just visible through the curtain of rain. I extracted a ten patacas note but the man pressed his hands together and stepped back.

"Thank you, but that is not required, Mr Hart."

We left the protection of the porte-cochère and the rain resumed its punishment of the cab's roof. As we reached the private road, the gate slid open to reveal a guardhouse with mirrored windows. The drumming on the roof grew irregular and I realised we were passing beneath mature trees. Uplights buried in the grass verge cast a flickering glow against the dark, glistening bark. I wondered, idly, how one populated a resort with half-century-old trees when just two decades earlier the land we were driving on was wild, open sea.

"Very nice. Very rich," called the driver.

"That's how I roll," I replied, peeling off a few notes.

A minute later, a guard in a waterproof poncho appeared out of the rain. He directed us towards an open-sided carport and we pulled up beside a row of limousines. A group of uniformed chauffeurs, surrounded by a haze of cigarette smoke, looked up from their phones and stared as I counted damp fifty-patacas notes into my driver's hand. My cab reversed back into the frenzied rain, executed a slow U-turn and vanished into the deluge.

# Chapter 17

## Phantasos

The guard directed me to a plush foyer, dotted with bottles of cologne and huge coffee table books on inspirational architecture. I was greeted by a young, face-masked woman bearing a neatly folded towel.

"Thank you," I said, taking the towel and dabbing my moist hair.

The woman giggled in embarrassment. "No, for your feet!"

"Oh, I see," I said. I bent over and rubbed my shoes.

"No, not like that!" said the woman, looking mortified.

"Apologies," I said, handing the towel back.

"No!" she said, shrinking away.

"Sorry. What exactly is it you want me to do?"

"Please go." The woman pointed to an elevator door tastefully integrated into the space between two bookcases.

I deposited my towel in a wicker basket and approached the elevator. The door slid open noiselessly. Floor number fifty-three, the only available button aside from floor one, was already illuminated. As the door slid shut, I saw the woman, now wearing disposable gloves, carrying the basket from the room at arm's length.

The elevator slowed as it reached its destination and the lights dimmed to a more sensual level. I was disgorged into a large, silent room with floor-to-ceiling panoramic windows. The view on a normal evening would have been fantastic, no doubt, but tonight all was obscured by the torrential rain hurling itself silently against the glass.

"Good evening, Mr Hart," said a face-masked flunky. "I do

hope the weather has not inconvenienced you. Please, follow me."

The man led me to the corner of the room where an alcove revealed itself, cleverly concealed through some trick of the décor. Inside it, in the semi-dark, sat a security guard at a small table, his scowling face illuminated by the glow of a laptop.

"Please step inside, Mr Hart."

I did so. The scowling man rattled a few keys on his laptop, glanced at me, then returned to his screen. He muttered to the first man in Mandarin.

"You have a phone in your jacket pocket and some items in your bag, Mr Hart. We are required to keep those safe for the duration of the evening, please, if you don't mind."

I glanced at the archway I'd just passed through. There were no signs of wires or winking lights. I wondered what might happen if I said I did mind and that I'd be keeping hold of my phone and other possessions, thank you very much. But, mindful of my mission, I chose the path of compliance and placed my handset in the felt-lined tray beside the guard's laptop.

"I do apologise, Mr Hart. Please could you also place the contents of your bag on the table? The scan showed up some items we need to check. It's for your own safety, of course."

I removed my tasting notes folder, the Burgundy guides and the napkins, followed by my corkscrew and the bungee cord. The man inspected the corkscrew, extending first the metal screw, then the viciously sharpened foil-cutter.

"You will not need your own bottle opener tonight, that will all be taken care of." He clicked the blade home and placed the corkscrew in the tray. "And this item...?" The man lifted the bungee cord and inspected the hooked ends. "Is it a medical device?"

"No, I just use it to attach the bag to my bike," I said, reddening slightly.

"Well, you will not require a bicycle tonight, Mr Hart, so we can look after this. I'm sure you understand. Please, let me help you with your papers."

The man handed back my books and tasting notes and, after a brief inspection, my paper napkins. I slid them into my satchel.

"It is time to join the other guests. Mr Lee asks that you do not shake hands or touch the other guests, for hygiene reasons."

"Is that rule just for me, or for everyone?"

"For everyone, of course, Mr Hart."

We passed through a leather-bound door. The cold silence of the reception room was replaced, quite suddenly, by the buzz of conversation. I found myself in a huge dining room, its centre dominated by a long, dark, marble-topped table lined either side with antique chairs. Groups of well-dressed men and women stood chatting around the edge of the room, Champagne glasses in hand. A handful wore masks. One side of the room was glazed from floor to ceiling in tinted glass but, as in the previous room, the storm obliterated any view of the city below, instead transforming the window into a rippling translucent sheet pulled relentlessly earthwards.

"Salon, Mr Hart?" murmured a face-masked waiter.

I took a glass of Champagne from his tray, wondering if it was fake. It certainly tasted real. I began a slow circuit of the room, attempting to eavesdrop on my fellow guests. I picked up a few snatches of accented English here and there alongside the high, musical tones of Mandarin and the more guttural, slurred cadences of Cantonese. So far as I could tell, most people were discussing the weather. A couple of guests stood alone, reading their phones. I wondered why mine had been confiscated. One rule for the nobs, another for the plebs, clearly.

"Mr Hart, allow me to show you to your seat."

Yet another flunky who knew my name. Perhaps there was a picture of me taped to the wall of the staff toilet. I followed him to the far end of the table. Each place setting consisted of an immaculately folded square of white linen behind which sat a row of razor-thin wine glasses. Between each setting lay a vase-shaped spittoon made of hammered brass, which glittered beneath the ceiling spotlights as I passed.

"Our trade guests will sit at this end of the table. You may leave your bag here."

Sure enough, a gold-lettered place card stating 'Mr Felix Hart' winked back at me from the final place setting. I glanced at the card to my right, but it was in Chinese. To my left was some empty space and then the end of the table. I was pleased to see that I would have only one immediate neighbour. Hopefully, that might grant me more opportunity to slip a bottle into my satchel unseen.

"Will I be sitting next to Mr Lee?" I said, indicating the place card next to mine.

The flunky gave a delicate smile and his eyes travelled to the far end of the table. "Your host, Mr Lee, will be seated at the head of the table."

A transparent screen, several feet high, separated Mr Lee's place setting from his immediate neighbours.

"Am I right in thinking Mr Lee's not keen on germs?"

The flunky glided off without answering. I slid my satchel beneath my chair and counted the place settings. Fifteen either side, plus Mr Lee's at the far end. I rounded my end of the table and peered at the place card opposite. The gold lettering announced a Ms Kaia Lafleur.

"Felix, hello!" called a familiar voice. Charles Fung, looking very dapper in a three-piece suit, propelled himself across the room, his beaming smile visible beneath a silk mask.

"Charles! Hello there."

Fung thrust out a hand, then remembered himself and snatched it back, before bringing his palms together. I did the same and gave a little bow.

"Did you know, we are sitting next to each other! Actually, I asked for this, I hope you do not mind?"

"So this is you?" I pointed across the table to the place setting beside mine.

"Yes, that is my name in Chinese, very formal. Usually, everyone wants to sit near Mr Lee, but this way I can ask you questions about wine, which is much more interesting. I hope you will forgive me?"

"No problem at all. I'd rather sit next to you than anyone else, Charles."

Fung beamed even wider.

"There are some very rare wines being tasted tonight, Felix. Nobody knows what, but we have been promised a real treat."

I was tempted to reveal that I'd seen the order of service already, but I didn't want to spoil Fung's excitement. There would be plenty of opportunity to show off during the tasting.

"Well, I am aware of two of the wines, Charles, and I can assure you that they're superb vintages from excellent domaines. But I'm sure Mr Lee has all sorts of other surprises in store."

"Yes, of course, you told me you represent two of the wines, Felix. You know, I was thinking, this is such an incredible coincidence. That we do business together on bathroom accessories and then we find ourselves here at Mr Lee's tasting. Very strange, wouldn't you say?"

My stomach gave a little twinge. What was that, a warning? Was Fung keeping an eye on me? Sandra had explicitly ordered me to keep my Gatesave cover separate to my Minstrels and Paris-Blois work, only for me to merrily mix the whole lot up with Fung before I'd even started.

"Yes, it's an amazingly small world," I said.

"Not too small for you to find your own seat, I hope?" said a woman's voice, so close that I could feel her breath against the back of my neck. I turned to find a striking woman smiling at me; all dark eyes, freckles and cascading black hair. She wore a powder-blue dress studded with gold buttons, which ended some way above the knee.

"It's Balmain," she said, extending a hand.

"Felix Hart," I replied, shaking it gently.

"I mean," she paused, smirking, "the dress is Balmain. You seem very interested in it."

"Oh, Balmain, yes, of course. That's what I thought." My cheeks began to burn. "It's a beautiful dress."

"Thank you. So, what are you wearing, since we're talking fashion?"

She looked me up and down, considerably more thoroughly than the glance I'd given her.

"Oh, the suit's Ted Baker, I think."

"Wow, that's quite a statement!" she laughed. "You didn't want to overdress at the world's most exclusive wine tasting, then?"

"Well, we're not all millionaires, you know," I said, remembering a second too late that I actually was a millionaire, or reasonably close, at least. *Perhaps I should invest in a new wardrobe*, I mused.

"I'm only teasing. You wear Ted Baker very well. Perhaps they should use you as a fit model."

She looked me up and down again. *This seems to be going well*, I thought.

"I'm guessing you're Kaia Lafleur," I said, once she was looking me in the eye again.

"An inspired guess, Felix Hart. Well done."

"And I'm Charles Fung," said Fung, bobbing out from behind me.

"Ah, yes – sorry, Charles, I should have introduced you sooner. Charles is a business acquaintance of mine." I bit my tongue, too late.

"Oh, really?" said Kaia, frowning. "But you're with Farquhar Fine and Rare, aren't you? I thought we were the only two trade people here. What do you do, Charles?"

"Oh, no, I'm not in the wine business!" chuckled Fung. "But I would love to be! Actually, I am a guest of Mr Lee. But Felix and I know each other through mutual business interests."

*For Christ's sake, Hart, you idiot, you complete and utter bloody idiot*, I thought. I wondered whether it mattered that I'd just doused my cover story in petrol in front of one of Joseph Lee's trade guests and was now cartwheeling cheerfully through the flames. *Perhaps I should just climb on the table and shout my life story to the assembled guests. Then challenge Lee's army of henchmen to a punch-up.*

"Oh, I see," said Kaia. "I'm with Wooston Swire. We

represent a lot of Grand Crus across East Asia and Australia. Mainly Bordeaux. Felix's colleagues at Farquhar Fine and Rare have most of the decent Burgundy estates already sewn up, of course, don't you?"

"Yes, I suppose we do."

"I will leave you two to talk," said Fung. "See you when the tasting begins. How lucky that I am sitting near two wine experts. Now I can get the real inside story!" Fung gave me a knowing smile.

My bowels gave another little lurch. The real inside story? A coded threat, if ever I heard one.

I lunged for a glass of Salon from a passing tray carrier, then, remembering my manners, grabbed a second.

"That's sweet of you, Felix, but I don't drink on duty."

"Don't tell me you'll be spitting everything out? At a tasting like this?" I took an assertive swig of Champagne.

"I might make an exception for a couple of the really special wines. But I have to sing for my supper, and I can't do that if I've downed half a dozen glasses of fizz. I'm not as big as you."

"Fair enough. So, which wines are you representing? You said your company mainly deals in Bordeaux, but this tasting's all Burgundy."

"I'm not representing anything tonight. I'm just here to dispense expert advice, if Joseph Lee or anyone else calls for it. I'm based in Macau, so I'm a useful fall-back for when they can't fly in the vignerons or estate owners themselves. Which, obviously, they can't at the moment."

"I see. So, you know what's being shown?"

"Yes, Lee's people showed me the line-up yesterday so I could do a bit of homework. But I think tonight's guests are going to have more on their mind than fine Burgundy."

"Really? What are they going to talk about? The weather?"

"You are kidding me, right? You know Greater China Pharmco has its IPO in, like, three months' time? Joseph Lee's taking his company public in Hong Kong and New York. It's the biggest listing of the year. These tastings are basically part of the marketing. Most of the people here are potential investors."

"So, I'm a sideshow."

"Sorry to burst your bubble, Felix, but yes. A pretty little sideshow."

# Chapter 18

## Jeopardy

Our conversation was interrupted by a high-pitched, tinkling chime. A masked flunky, almost delirious with self-importance, was circling the room, ringing a small handbell.

"Ladies and gentlemen, please take your seats."

The instruction was issued in Mandarin, followed by English, then Cantonese.

The guests moved swiftly to their assigned places; Kaia and I opposite one another, me with my back to the storm-lashed window, while Charles Fung plopped himself down beside me. I'm not a furniture historian, so I have no idea whether the chairs were genuine antiques or Shenzhen knock-offs, but they were certainly magnificently buttock-caressing. I patted the curved, gilt-covered armrests feeling as decadent as old Louis XVI himself.

I placed Fromage's vineyard guide, my copy of *Inside Burgundy* and my folder of notes from Sandra beside my spittoon, in the hope they'd project a vaguely authoritative air. Kaia lounged in her chair watching me, her arms draped louchely over the armrests. She smiled at my little pile of books and paperwork, giving me the unfamiliar and rather unsettling sensation of being the class swot.

A Chinese man took the seat opposite Fung, his disappointment at being placed at the tradesmen's end of the table vanishing as he realised he would be spending the evening beside Kaia. As she leaned over to greet the man, complimenting him on his expensive suit, I casually propped my satchel, flap open and unzipped, against the leg of my chair on the blind side of the table.

Fung removed his mask and rubbed his hands. "What do you think the first wine will be, Felix? I hope we get to taste lots of DRC. I expect they will pour the younger vintages first, do you agree?"

"Yes, younger wines first, I'm sure. And I'll wager there'll be plenty of DRC, Charles."

But would it be genuine Domaine de la Romanée-Conti? Or something cooked up with a little help from Mr Lee's chemistry set?

More musical chimes from the handbell wrangler. The conversation quietened. I realised that Kaia had been talking to her neighbour in fluent Mandarin.

"Ladies and gentlemen. Your host, Mr Joseph Lee."

All eyes turned to the head of the table. The transparent glass screen, which I had assumed was to protect Mr Lee from stray sneezes, turned a translucent, milky white. I spotted three projector lights shining from the wall behind Lee's empty chair. The screen turned black, flickered for a second, then the head of a young, intense-looking Chinese man with close-cropped hair filled the screen. Behind him lay a suspiciously un-rainy Hong Kong skyline.

"Oh!" whispered Fung. "He is not here!"

"Good evening and welcome to *Le Cercle Chêne*," said Lee. The sound was crisp and assertively loud. No-one would be talking over our host tonight. "My sincere apologies, but my helicopter has not been granted clearance to fly from Hong Kong this evening due to the weather." Chinese subtitles appeared across the bottom of the screen, giving Lee's head a strangely disembodied appearance. "So, I am very disappointed to inform you that it will not be possible to join you in person."

A chorus of sighs ran around the table.

"Yes, it is a most frustrating situation. Greater China Pharmco can do many things, but we cannot yet control the weather. Though we do, of course, have a three-year plan to address that challenge."

The audience tittered politely. The floating head narrowed its eyes and gave a mirthless smile, which I suspected was the closest Mr Lee ever came to come to guffawing and punching his neighbour's arm.

"More seriously, I do not think the future investors in Greater China Pharmco would be impressed if their CEO took a life-jeopardising risk just seventy-two days from the biggest IPO of the decade."

The faces round the table weren't laughing now. I became conscious that there was something rather curious about Lee's face. He didn't appear to be actually on the screen, more hovering somewhere just behind it, as though he was actually present and just pretending to be virtual. I moved my head from side to side and realised I could see slightly more of his left ear, then more of his right ear as I shifted my viewpoint.

"Yes, it's a 3D TV," whispered Kaia.

I glanced at her. She opened her mouth in mock surprise, mouthed a "Wow", then grinned. Sarcastic little cow. I wondered if I was starting to fall in love with her.

"I guarantee, however, that I shall be here with you, virtually, for the whole evening. I know many of you have questions regarding the GCP prospectus and I will be delighted to discuss any aspect of our business with you, particularly Project Athena."

At this, a buzz rose around the room.

"My comms team will now distribute headsets, so you may ask questions privately, if you wish."

Two flunkies were already working their way down the table, placing wireless headphones beside each guest's spittoon. They didn't, however, leave one for me or Kaia.

"The most disappointing aspect of being unable to join you tonight is that the best of my wine collection is on floor fifty-three of Phantasos, with you, while I remain stranded in Hong Kong."

More laughs from the table and a thin smile from the screen.

"I have procured, however, a little something that will permit my participation in this evening's programme, even if I am obliged to do so at arm's length."

The camera panned down to reveal a side table, on which sat a bottle of La Tâche Grand Cru, already open, and a glass containing an inch of wine.

"DRC!" exclaimed Fung.

"Naturally, I apply the same ethos to *Le Cercle Chêne* as I do to everything in life. Begin with absolute excellence and ascend without deviation."

Lee surveyed his guests, rather unsettlingly. When his eyes reached me, they stopped.

"As is customary at *Le Cercle Chêne,* we are joined tonight by two authorities from the world of wine. Their knowledge and experience are at your disposal. Please welcome Kaia Lafleur, the top sommelier in Macau, and Felix Hate of Farquhar Fine and Rare. I hope I have pronounced that correctly?"

"Well, actually, it's–"

"Perfectly, thank you, Mr Lee," smiled Kaia, cutting across me.

"It's Felix Hart," I said, but Lee had begun speaking in Mandarin and my pathetic protest was lost beneath the room's powerful audio.

*Felix Hate? What the hell was that all about? Was it deliberate? Or just a typo on his briefing document?*

"Look, Felix, they're serving the DRC!" exclaimed Fung.

Sure enough, a pair of white-gloved staff were approaching our end of the table with open bottles of Domaine de la Romanée-Conti, La Tâche Grand Cru. The vintage was 2002, a pretty damn fine one. One waiter poured me a small measure, the other did the same for Kaia. The guests turned to watch.

"We're quality control, then, are we?" I said.

Kaia lifted her glass, swirled and sniffed it, then nodded. I did the same and took a sip, just to be sure. The wine was magnificent. The waiters moved down the table, pouring a half-glass for each guest, Fung clapping his hands with joy as his was filled. Another pair of staff stepped forward with identical bottles and the process was repeated. Again, we declared the wines good. The second pair of waiters proceeded to the far end of the table and poured for the guests beside Lee's floating head, then worked their way back to the middle. When all the attendees had received their rations, the waiters returned to our end of the table, filled Kaia's and my glasses and placed the bottles, each of which still contained a couple of inches of wine, beside me in a neat line.

I silently raised thanks to Bacchus. It looked as though my end of the table was to be the spent-bottle graveyard. There was a good chunk of parking space for all the empties and I guessed each wine would be lined up, in turn, as the evening progressed. I was in the perfect position to swipe the bottle I needed and drop it into my satchel, provided no-one was looking. I casually lifted one of the bottles of La Tâche, examined the label, then slowly poured myself an extra half-inch, to see whether it raised any cries of alarm. Sure enough, out of the corner of my eye, I spotted the purposeful stride of a flunky, heading straight towards me. Still holding the bottle, I innocently raised my glass to my nose and inhaled, expecting him to snatch the La Tâche from my grip.

But the flunky simply placed two more bottles, sealed this time, behind the four open ones. I recalled Farquhar mentioning that *Le Cercle Chêne* purchased six of each wine, in case of spoilage. I couldn't believe my luck. The unopened samples were slightly out of reach, right at the end of the table, but with a suitable distraction I wondered whether I'd be able to filch a full bottle instead of an empty. That would get me some serious Brownie points from Sandra. Maybe she'd even award me a performance bonus.

"Making a night of it, are we?" asked Kaia, eyeing my glass.

"Just checking it's not oxidising," I replied, swigging back a proper mouthful. God, it was good.

I noticed that the flunky remained nearby, his eye not-so-nonchalantly observing the bottle in my hand. I placed it back down beside the others and he stepped forward, adjusting its position so it was precisely lined up, its label, like all the others, facing up the table towards Mr Lee's floating head.

"I will not say *gānbēi*, ladies and gentlemen, because these are wines to be savoured," declared Lee, lifting his glass. "But I shall raise a toast to your health and prosperity. Both of which we take extremely seriously at Greater China Pharmco."

"Health and prosperity," replied the guests.

Lee's disembodied head took a precise sip. His eyes fluttered for a second, as if some internal supercomputer were analysing the wine's chemical composition, then he nodded.

"I find perfection a quality in disappointingly short supply," said Lee, surveying his guests. "Few even understand the meaning of the word. But the six-point-zero-six hectares of this Grand Cru are very much an exception." He paused and nosed his glass. "Ripe but not over-extracted. Elegant but never trivial. Precise but not... mechanical."

Lee's words hung in the air, the marble tabletop and the vast window adding a hard edge to the acoustics.

*Mechanical*, I thought. *Is that a secret joke?*

I took another sip of the wine. Christ, if this was a fake, it was a bloody good one. I took a closer look at the bottle. The label looked authentic, though Lee was hardly likely to have printed one off the internet. At a push, the wine might have been from a different domaine in Vosne-Romanée, but it would still have to be from one of the greats, the wine was just too good. Then I remembered that Lee was allegedly cooking these up from scratch in his mum's garage, or wherever the hell a billionaire hangs out when he's planning to shaft the world.

"Perhaps our expert from Europe could give us his opinion," said Mr Lee.

Kaia cleared her throat. With a shock I realised he meant me.

"Yes," I declared, rising to my feet. "Our host has articulated it better than I ever could. This is not the output of a factory or a production line. It is a work of art. The creation of a virtuoso."

I raised the glass in Lee's direction. He held my gaze.

*What do you make of that, then, smart arse?* I thought, before wondering whether a little more subtlety might be in order. Had

Lee's expression hardened just a touch? Perhaps, as Kaia had suggested, I had indeed downed a couple too many glasses of Salon.

"But what can you taste, Mr Hart? Other than art and virtuosity and other assorted clichés."

Kaia gave a tiny snort. I glanced down at her. *You may be Macau's top sommelier*, I thought. *And, though it's unfashionable to say such things aloud these days, quite possibly the most attractive woman east of Suez, particularly in that dress. But Yours Truly hasn't reached the dizzying summit of the international wine trade without the ability to turn the bullshit-ometer up to eleven when the occasion demands it.*

I raised my glass and addressed the wine directly.

"I taste fruit. But fruit so dark, so deep, that it merges into savoury, into sweet game and blood and the sap of ancient spice. I taste leather, but the texture of satin, a liquid silk that caresses like perfumed skin against hot flesh. And I taste the earth, humus and mineral, the living soil of Vosne-Romanée, that unforgettable, divine *terroir* where stone and oak and sun dance outside the realm of men and conjure forth… perfection."

The room was silent. Lee's head stared at me, his palms pressed together before his mouth. My Burgundian soliloquy had, quite clearly, inspired him to prayer.

"Very, very good!" declared Fung, clapping his hands. "I can definitely taste spice and silk. And earth. A very good description!"

The rest of the table joined in the applause, slightly uncertainly at first, a few guests keeping an eye on Lee's disembodied head.

"A most unexpectedly poetic tasting note, Mr Hart. Please, do sit."

I bowed towards the screen and gave Kaia a wink as I retook my seat. She shook her head, but I could tell she was impressed.

The guests gargled their La Tâche and the buzz around the table grew. Fung chatted away in Mandarin to the guest opposite, breaking off briefly to introduce me. The man appeared to be some sort of underwriter at a Beijing bank. Unfortunately, or perhaps thankfully, he didn't speak much English, so I was unable to contribute to their discussion of the Chinese IPO regulatory regime, the desperate shortage of piano teachers in Chaoyang, or whatever the hell they were chirping on about. Kaia, rather rudely I felt, ignored me and listened in, nodding and agreeing whenever her neighbour finished a particularly long sentence. I left the three of them to it and enjoyed my La Tâche while I waited for the next wine.

Soon enough, a pair of waiters entered the room bearing new bottles. The chatter subsided. They poured Kaia and me a small sample, before taking a step back and presenting the label for our inspection. A Bonnes-Mares Grand Cru, 2002. Same vintage as the previous wine. I swirled, took a professional sniff, then tipped the whole lot into my mouth. The wine was absolutely incredible. A little lighter than the DRC, for sure, but to my mind just as polished.

Kaia and I nodded, and the wine began its journey down the table. We approved the second pair of bottles and they, too, were poured. Once my own glass and Kaia's had been properly topped up, the second set of bottles was lined up, very precisely, alongside those of the first. Again, they were joined by two unopened ones right at the end of the table. I tested the staff's tolerance a little further by messing around with a couple of the empties, lifting one, then another, peering at each of the labels in turn. A server, standing sentry-like against the wall, took a couple of steps forward. I turned to him and smiled. The man gave a tiny bow and smiled back, his eyes on the bottle in my hand. I replaced it carefully and he stepped up to the table, giving each bottle I'd touched a microscopic adjustment. Filching a sample, it appeared, might be more of a challenge than I'd assumed.

A few more words from Lee, in Mandarin this time, then more chat around the table. The third wine arrived; a Mazoyères-Chambertin Grand Cru from a venerable domaine. A 1999, that superb Burgundian vintage that drew the 20th-century so magnificently to a close. Kaia and I tasted the wines, which were exquisite, and waved them on.

The fourth, then the fifth wines arrived, triumphs of autumn bramble, dew-kissed meadow and truffle-scented Oolong. But at the sixth wine, a Romanée St Vivant Grand Cru from the '93 vintage, the rhythm of the evening changed. I tasted my sample, a symphony of delicately charred duck, winter violets and ripe cherry, which nearly brought tears to my eyes. I smiled happily at the waiter and waved my glass down the table.

"No," said Kaia.

She was frowning. She took another sniff, shook her head, and placed the glass aside. I took in the bouquet of my own glass once more, but the wine was immaculate. Mine had been poured from a different bottle, of course.

"May I try?" I called, but the waiter had lifted Kaia's glass and was already striding to the exit with both goblet and bottle.

"It happens," declared Lee. "But we plan for such eventualities at *Le Cercle Chêne*, just as we plan for all contingencies at Greater China Pharmco. Thank you Ms Lafleur for spotting the fault. A one-off, I trust, given that Mr Hart appears to have approved his sample."

I inhaled my glass a third time, slowly. Was there an underlying taint or not? Once a thought like that becomes lodged in your head, it's hard to shake. They train you at the Worshipful Institute to resist outside influences, to immerse yourself entirely in the wine before you, for even the most skilled taster can be led astray by tricks and fancies. Who could forget the flower, fruit, leaf, and twig fallacy – a theory that infected the more suggestable wing of the biodynamic community a decade or two ago, and which declared the flavour intensity of a wine waxed and waned with the cycles of the moon? Or the cult of the mushroom, which insisted that the aromatic signature of a wine could be correlated with the plumpness of the fruiting body of any nearby indigenous fungi? Even the steeliest sniffer, the true soldier of empiricism, can succumb to pulmonary infection; find their precious senses battered and scattered to the four winds, their favourite, most vivacious wines struck dumb. And for the serious wine aficionado, the most frightening malady of all still lingers, weakened but undefeated, in the sweaty corners of wet markets, hospitals, aeroplanes and changing rooms. That accursed virus, whose name I shall not speak, which inflicts the noble taster with parosmia, the transmutation of alluring smells and flavours to foulness – proof, if anyone doubted it, that the gods love to vex the proud.

*Focus, Felix*. I finished the tasting sample. Definitely not corked, I would swear to it. The wine was astonishing: delicate perfume and muscular fruit in absolutely perfect harmony. Was it too good, in fact? Could a wine be too perfect? Had Lee identified and assembled the precise ingredients that make a great Romanée St Vivant and discarded anything that might detract from the ultimate expression of Grand Cru Burgundy, even the tiny flaws that impart authenticity; those stray hints of hamster cage, sweaty linen or vinegary volatility? But what about Kaia's corked wine? Had he faked a tainted wine too? Any tasting involving forty-eight bottles closed with natural cork is bound to throw up one or two dodgy specimens. Rather suspicious, in fact, if none were corked at all. I glanced up the table at Mr Lee's floating head. Was he watching me? Or was that just the effect of the 3D screen? *You clever, clever bastard*, I thought.

A waiter poured Kaia a sample from a new bottle. She sniffed and smiled. The wine, plus my earlier approved bottle, made their way up the table.

"What is your favourite so far, Felix?" asked Fung.

I noticed that he'd left a small measure of wine in each glass. The Beijing underwriter, by contrast, had barely touched his. *What a bloody waste of an invitation*, I thought, before recalling Kaia's warning that tonight's guests might be more interested in Lee's IPO than fine Burgundy.

"I think this latest wine is the best so far, Charles. How about you?"

"Ah, for me it has to be the DRC," beamed Fung.

"Perhaps they'll serve another. Maybe even Romanée-Conti Grand Cru itself."

"That would be incredible. What vintage will they serve, do you think?"

I'd seen the list, of course, so I knew they'd be pouring the 1985. I was conscious Kaia was watching me.

"1990, perhaps. What do you think, Kaia?"

"I'm surprised you didn't say your own wines were your favourite. That's what you're supposed to say, isn't it? As a brand ambassador?"

"Charles asked me my favourite so far, not my favourite from the whole line-up," I replied.

"Oh, yes, you're so right. My mistake." Kaia smiled, then turned away and began a conversation with the Beijing underwriter.

The rhythm of the tasting changed again with the next wine. This was one of mine. Or, more precisely, a Paris-Blois wine imported by Farquhar Fine and Rare. But instead of being presented with a bottle of Grands-Echézeaux 1989, the waiter poured me a sample from a decanter. A second waiter did the same for Kaia.

"What's this?" I said. "Where's the bottle?"

"We took the liberty of decanting your wines, Mr Hart, to allow them to breathe."

"It's good," said Kaia, placing her glass down.

"Hang on, I want to see the bottle. And the cork," I said.

"Just taste the wine, you silly Minstrel," whispered Kaia.

"What's the matter, Felix," asked Fung. "Is there something wrong?"

"No, I just wanted to see the original bottle," I said, suddenly conscious that the entire room was watching.

I nosed the wine. The 1989 was one of the vintages Sandra had given me back at Minstrels Hall and which I'd sampled with my friends around the table at the Salon de Dijon. The wine smelled correct. By which, I mean it smelled incredible, astonishing. The near-savoury bouquet, the gentle aroma of leather, the lick of spice. I threw the sample back and there it was, that weepingly beautiful fruit melded with perfumed wood, subtle at first then powerful beneath, and a seemingly never-ending finish; the tumble of fruits and herbs morphing into new flavours as each second passed, like a spice box through a kaleidoscope, until you were left with a whisper of a thousand different wines, each grander than the last.

"Does Mr Hart recognise his wine?" said Lee's voice.

"Yes," I said, quietly.

"Then, assuming he is happy, may we all be permitted to try it?"

# Chapter 19

## Magician

A few giggles rose around the table. So, not only tricked but ridiculed too. It was pretty clear Lee was up to all sorts of shenanigans. But, by substituting my wines for his own fakes so blatantly, was he going a step further? Making it obvious he knew that I knew? Making it clear he was untouchable – that he didn't give a damn whether I knew? I recalled Fromage's warning that all power came from the Party. How many Party members, I wondered, were sat around this very table?

"Yes, I'm happy with it. I just wanted to see the bottle," I muttered.

The waiters proceeded down the table with their decanters and were replaced by two more, who poured a pair of identically magnificent samples.

"The wine's pretty damn good. What's the matter?" said Kaia.

"Why is mine decanted while all the others were poured from the bottle?"

"Perhaps Mr Lee is being respectful. Or perhaps he felt they needed decanting."

"What, he can smell them from Hong Kong?"

Lee's voice sounded from the end of the table. "Mr Hart, would you be kind enough to tell us a little about your wines?"

"Of course," I said, feeling suddenly rather unconfident. I recalled, vaguely, that famous art heist; the one where the thieves replaced all the paintings with such brilliant replicas it took the gallery a year to realise they'd been burgled.

"We shall serve your second wine right now, so you can

educate us regarding both domaines."

Another pair of decanter-wielding waiters stepped up. Again, no sign of the original bottles. I was poured a sample of what was supposed to be my Chambertin Grand Cru '85. I smelled and tasted it and found myself unable to fault the wine in any way at all. It may as well have been the finest Burgundy I'd tasted in my life.

Before the waiter could move on, I caught his arm.

"Fill me up properly, would you? My throat's a touch dry."

He did as I asked. I downed half the glass, which warmed my chest and served to wash away any festering scruples. I placed my hands on the table and launched myself to my feet.

"Unmistakable!" I declared to the room. "Absolutely unmistakable!"

Five minutes later, I retook my seat to the roar of applause. Though I say so myself, it was one of my finer educational speeches, and I'm sure the dozen glasses of Champagne and alleged Grand Cru Burgundy only added gravitas to my oration. The *pièce de résistance* was the story of a visit with my dear father, at the tender age of fourteen, to the slopes of Le Chambertin Grand Cru where he permitted me a taste of the nectar conjured from that hallowed site, my first encounter with the wines of Burgundy and a moment seared upon my young mind. Then, a dozen years later, the same trip, alone this time, to sprinkle his ashes between the vines by the light of a cold harvest moon. The story brought tears to a few eyes, not least Charles Fung, who wept so freely over his glass that I feared he might dilute his Grand Cru into Beaujolais Nouveau.

"That was really nice, actually," said Kaia.

I gave her a proud yet vulnerable smile in return, the type one might see on the face of a medal-festooned war veteran easing into his wheelchair after a tour of some long grassed-over battlefield.

It would have spoiled things to reveal that my first taste of Grand Cru Burgundy was actually a bottle appropriated from the off-licence I'd worked in shortly after my expulsion from school. Or that my father had abandoned me and my mother while I was still a babe-in-arms, and I'd no more scattered his ashes on the rolling hills of Burgundy than I'd chiselled him a cliff-top grave on the north face of the Eiger.

As I poured myself another well-deserved glass of Chambertin 2.0, a suited flunky accompanied by a waiter appeared at the end of the table.

"You wished to see the original bottles, Mr Hart," said one.

Sure enough, the waiter presented me with two empty bottles: a Grands-Echézeaux '89 and a Chambertin Grand Cru '85.

"Thank you. Better late than never."

I took the Grands-Echézeaux and held it up to the light. It was completely empty, not even a dribble in the base. On the back was a small label stating, 'Imported by Farquhar Fine & Rare, Wan Chai, Hong Kong SAR.'

"Would you leave them here, please?"

A flash of panic passed across the waiter's face, but the suited flunky nodded, and the empty Chambertin was placed beside my spittoon.

"Would you like to inspect the other bottles, too, Mr Hart?"

"Yes, please," I said, brightly. The flunky's face stiffened a touch. "I hope that's not too inconvenient?"

"It is no trouble. It is just that the bottles are stored in another part of the hotel, so it may take some time."

"Oh, that's strange," I said. "Why weren't they kept with all the others?"

"We wanted to give these wines special treatment, Mr Hart. To decant them, by way of thanks for the honour you have bestowed upon us by attending our tasting. Mr Lee insisted on it."

"Did he now?" I said, stung by the painful thought that someone at this very moment might be frantically pouring the genuine wines down the sink.

"You've done a wonderful job," said Kaia to the pair. "I'm sure Mr Hart doesn't really need to see all the bottles. Particularly given how busy you are."

"It is absolutely no trouble," said the flunky. He turned and strode away, the waiter scurrying after him.

"What's that all about?" said Kaia.

"I don't like being taken for a fool," I replied.

A stupid, reckless comment, and I regretted it immediately. Kaia, stung by my change of tone, turned to the Beijing underwriter and began another conversation in Mandarin. Had I spoilt my chances? Was I ever in with a chance? Had I drunk too much wine? A possible yes to all three, I decided.

The next wine arrived. La Romanée-Conti 1985, the wine that Charles Fung had been dreaming about. As the bottle hove into view, Fung squealed with delight, gripping my arm as I approved the sample, nearly causing me to slop the wine down my jacket. Then, when Fung's own sample was poured he became very serious, lifting the glass to his nose with both hands and giving the wine the briefest of swirls before closing his eyes and inhaling for an entire minute.

I won't bore the oenophobes among you by waxing too lyrical, but the wine, suffice to say, was bed-wettingly beautiful. I've tasted La Romanée-Conti a few times in my privileged life and there wasn't a chance in hell I'd have called out the sample before me as a fake. The Romanée-Conti was followed by the tenth wine, a Clos de la Roche Grand Cru from the fabled '82 vintage. The wine was so exquisite that when Kaia and I tasted the samples our eyes met and I knew my behaviour had been forgiven, washed into the forgotten past by the sheer sensuality of the liquid bathing our palates. The empty bottles were joined by those of my own wines, finally retrieved from some distant storeroom and placed in two neat rows beside the others. By now, our end of the table was occupied by a regiment of glass in perfect parade-ground formation, the ceiling spotlights peppering the bottles with green pinpoint stars.

"Might you invest in the IPO, Felix?" asked Fung.

He had brought his glass of DRC to the centre of his place setting and was resting the forefinger of each hand on the base, as if he didn't quite trust his glass not to leap spontaneously into the air and hurl its contents over the tabletop.

"I assumed the flotation would only be open to institutional investors, Charles. Are keen amateurs able to participate?"

"Oh, yes. Not the Hong Kong listing, that is for big institutions only. But this is a dual listing, so you could apply for shares through the New York Stock Exchange."

"Well, perhaps I shall. I'm looking to invest at the moment. No point in having money sitting idle in the bank."

"Who still has money sitting in the bank?" laughed an American-accented woman the other side of Fung. She repeated the question in Mandarin for the benefit of the Beijing underwriter, who smiled.

"Oh, I've just received a few dividends," I replied, casually swirling my Clos de la Roche '82. "I was going to re-invest in a couple of fintech flotations."

"Forget fintech," said the woman. "You need to invest in sectors that are solving problems."

"Not causing them," said the Indian man sitting the other side of the underwriter.

"Biotech," said the woman.

"Biotech, biotech, biotech," added the man.

"Right," I said. "Biotech it is. Thanks for the advice. Sounds like I should go all in with Mr Lee, then."

"If you're smart, you would," said the Chinese–American woman.

"Excuse my ignorance, but what is it Mr Lee can do that other biotech firms can't?"

But no-one chose to answer my question. There was no embarrassment, no disapproval, simply silence.

"I do apologise," I said. "I didn't mean to ask an inappropriate question. I shall stick to subjects I understand, like fine wine." I raised my glass to my lips and glanced at Kaia. She was studying me, a faint, quizzical leer on her face. I sipped my wine and smiled back. What were my odds? Slightly better than evens, I fancied.

"No need to apologise, Felix," said Fung.

"Mr Lee is a genius," said the Indian man. "He is a generation ahead of anyone in understanding how artificial intelligence can be applied to biochemical polymerisation. Hence, Project Athena."

"Right," I said.

"He makes things," said the Chinese–American woman. "Like, fundamentally, *makes* things."

"Oh. What kind of things?" My eyes were drawn to the mostly empty wine glasses before me and I had to make a concerted effort to tear them away.

"Anything, Felix!" said Fung.

"Anything where there's value-add," said the Indian man. "Hypercomplex nano-pharmaceuticals, obviously."

"Obviously," I said.

I was saved by the arrival of the next wine.

"Good God!" I said, as the bottle was presented, loudly enough to turn the heads of the nearest guests.

"This is a good wine, Felix?" asked Fung.

"Yes, erm, yes, it should be very good," I stuttered, blushing like a thief caught prising open the children's cancer charity collection box.

For the wine, of course, was the Musigny '78 – the almost certain fake, the bottle I was supposed to steal. I took a deep breath and a gulp from my water glass.

"Are you all right?" asked Kaia. "That's the first time I've seen you drink water all evening."

"Fine, thank you," I replied. "Let's taste it, shall we?"

It's not often that one samples a half-century-old Grand Cru Burgundy, even if there is a murky cloud over its provenance. The wine was beyond astonishing, somehow melding a magisterial and venerable authority without surrendering the beauty of its youth, a melting, velvet savouriness wrapped in vibrant fruit; a siren inviting vinous sailors to drown gladly, even euphorically, in its depths.

"Does my Musigny Grand Cru meet with our guests' approval?" intoned Lee's floating head.

"It's quite incredible," I said.

Kaia rose to her feet and raised her glass. "I'm sure I speak for everyone here when I say it has been an honour to drink these wines at your table, Mr Lee. Even as a wine professional, I am truly humbled by the sensory feast you've laid on for us this evening."

Lee smiled and, unless it was the drink, I swear his floating head glowed a little brighter. And who could blame him? Unless Lee was a machine himself, he could not have failed to notice the brevity of Kaia's dress. What a shame he had to observe it via a video screen rather than in real life.

"Thank you for your kind words, Ms Lafleur," said Lee. "It has been a pleasure. And I am delighted to tell you there is still one wine to taste, a very special bottle indeed. But for the moment, I shall take questions from my guests."

As the guests donned their headphones, the four empty bottles of Musigny '78 joined the earlier wines in a precise row, two unopened samples completing the half-dozen right at the end of the table. Frustratingly, the wines had been lined up in order of serving, with the row of La Tâche '02, the first wine, right beside me, and each subsequent wine slightly further away. The final wine, the Musigny '78, sat right across the table on Kaia's side. I couldn't exactly stand, lean over the table, pluck an empty and slide it into my bag.

"May I look at the last bottle, please?"

Kaia stood and passed an empty over the table. "I won't give you a full one, in case you drop it."

"Very wise," I replied.

I turned the bottle, examining the label beneath the spotlights. Nothing looked remiss, of course. Lee would hardly have written over the label with correction fluid and a Sharpie. I glanced down at my open satchel propped against the chair leg. Kaia was watching me, chin resting on her clasped hands. I was in the full view of Fung, too, his chair half-turned towards me as he sipped his DRC. Even the Beijing underwriter kept a lazy eye on me as he listened to Lee's Q&A. This was going to be much trickier than I'd thought.

"What floor are you staying on?" said Kaia, softly.

It may sound a touch presumptuous, but her question sounded far more like an invitation than a query. An immature boor might have quipped back 'same floor as you', but the teenage Felix Hart was a decade gone, and the mature Felix, empathetic and sensitive, was an altogether different beast.

"My invitation was rather last-minute and all the rooms were taken," I replied. "But if there's a vacancy, I'll stay on whichever floor I'm told."

Kaia frowned for a second. "Oh, I assumed you were at Phantasos. Where are you staying, then?"

"Oh, what's it called? The Notting Hill."

Kaia laughed. "The Notting Hill Resort Hotel! Oh, my God, that's hilarious. That's such a dump."

"Well, that's as far as Farquhar Fine and Rare's budget would stretch, so I guess I'm slumming it," I said.

"And good luck getting back through that," said Kaia, nodding at the vast window behind me.

I turned and, sure enough, the floor-to-ceiling glass still shimmered with light refracted through the silent, torrential rain. As I turned back, a waiter swooped in and the empty bottle of Musigny, which I'd foolishly released from my grasp, was whisked away and replaced precisely in line beside Kaia. I swore, silently.

My despondency, however, was interrupted by the arrival of a unicorn.

# Chapter 20

## The Unicorn

A suited, white-gloved flunky stepped into the room, flanked by two waiters. He held an open bottle before him, one hand on its neck, the other beneath its base, the constipated expression on his face giving the impression less of a sommelier and more of a bomb disposal operative carrying a recently unearthed and irregularly ticking artillery shell.

"Ladies and gentlemen," called Lee's floating head. "Thank you for your questions regarding our placement and, of course, Project Athena. And now, by way of gratitude, something very special indeed."

The flunky and his waiter outriders proceeded across the floor at a comically slow pace, finally coming to a stop before Kaia. One of the waiters placed an empty glass upon the table, the other stood ready with a cloth to soak up any misdirected drips. The flunky leaned over and directed a measure of light, tawny liquid into Kaia's glass. She smelled the wine, tasted it and nodded.

"A 1921 Richebourg," declared Lee's floating head. "Probably the twentieth-century's finest pre-war vintage."

The wine made its way to the top of the table then back down. For a moment I thought Fung had received the final few drops, but the flunky knew his job and I received the same half-inch measure as the rest of the guests. The sole empty Richebourg was placed in the middle of the table before the massed ranks of bottles, like a regimental sergeant major.

I smelled then tasted the wine. To be honest, it wasn't that great. Not faulty, just rather knackered. Every wine develops in the bottle and fine wines certainly improve for years, even decades. But all peak at some point before decline sets in. The finest wines may remain interesting as they decay, they may even exhibit new dimensions invisible at their peak. But oxygen, present at the time of bottling and diffusing in minute quantities through the cork, never stops its destructive work; tearing complex molecules apart and spoiling alcohol into vinegar. And this one's glory days were well and truly behind it.

"Incredible," muttered a voice further down the table.

"Just magnificent," agreed another.

"Excuse me," whispered Fung. He rose to his feet and waddled to an artfully concealed doorway in the corner of the room. However proudly you trumpet your heritage, however beautifully you package your product, however glamorous your brand ambassadors, even Domaine de la Romanée-Conti ends its days in the great democracy of the municipal sewer system.

Now, I wouldn't want you to think that Felix Hart had strolled into the lair of an international criminal mastermind without at least some kind of plan, beyond attempting to slip an empty wine bottle into his codpiece. It had become clear from the get-go that I'd have to create some kind of diversion in order to filch the dodgy Musigny '78 and spirit it back to Minstrels Hall. The issue was how to do so undetected. The obvious option, of course, was explosives. Fireworks, despite being illegal in Hong Kong, are relatively easy to procure, not to mention spectacularly diverting compared to their feeble Western counterparts. But I knew I'd be searched on entry, so had reluctantly rejected the idea of stitching a bandolier of firecrackers inside my boxer shorts. There was also the risk of causing an actual fire and either being arrested by the authorities, executed by Lee's henchmen, or perishing in my own self-inflicted penthouse conflagration.

For similar reasons, I'd disregarded smuggling in a smoke grenade or igniting the soft furnishings with the aid of an accelerant. Simply setting off the fire alarm manually might have been an option, but even if I'd managed that undetected, I suspected Lee's staff would be ushering the guests to the nearest fire exit before I could so much as retake my seat, let alone purloin the target bottle. I had tinkered with the idea of an olfactory diversion: rotten eggs, fermented sea cucumber or, most potent of all, mashed durian. But, again, the difficulty of smuggling in the required volume of foetid material had put paid to that idea. Inducing some kind of medical emergency (in another guest, not myself, obviously) was a possibility, as was spiking someone's drink with amphetamines or hallucinogens, but the difficulty in administering such a dose, not to mention the risk of ending up on trial for murder or hurled from the top of Phantasos by a psychotic flunky, had obliged me to dismiss such pharmaceutical options. Causing a flood by blocking sinks or toilets might have worked, but my early reconnaissance visit to Lee's orchid and frankincense-strewn guest bathrooms had put paid to that idea, too, for the lavatories were staffed by a squad of exquisitely polite attendants who would doubtless have addressed any plumbing mischief within seconds. An audible commotion courtesy of a discreetly hidden mobile phone might have worked, but the irritatingly efficient security staff had already relieved me of my handset. A more technologically savvy operator might have introduced a Trojan horse to the building's nerve centre by way of a devilishly deployed thumb drive or longer-range infiltration, but such techniques were outside my area of expertise. At the more low-tech, kinetic end of the scale, an area in which I generally excel, I was disadvantaged by the confiscation of my sharpened corkscrew and bungee cord. And, in any case, I had quickly discounted any plan involving attempting to break the inches-thick windows or balancing something clattering atop a door, for the venue was saturated with attentive doormen, waiters and miscellaneous flunkies.

Nevertheless, I still had one final reserve plan. It had involved smuggling in an item, true, but one easily concealed and inobtrusive enough to escape even a rigorous pat-down. This item was invisible to scanners, metal detectors and X-ray machines, impervious to the attentions of sniffer dogs, and emitted no odours or chemical fumes. Most importantly, it was non-toxic, incapable of causing injury and completely legal.

It was Charles Fung himself who had given me the idea. And as my amiable, lavatorial business partner retook his seat, his bladder liberated of the filtered produce of Burgundy's finest *terroirs*, I confess I felt a tiny twinge of guilt for what I had done.

"I have left the DRC until last, Felix," smiled Fung, rubbing his hands.

"I wonder if Mr Lee might let us open another bottle," I replied. I eased my chair back a few inches and rested my hands lightly upon the table. Ready for action.

Fung chuckled and moved aside his napkin, lying untidily before his crescent of glasses.

But it wasn't Fung's napkin.

It was mine.

While Fung had been relieving himself in Lee's exquisite bathroom, I had very casually risen to my feet, napkin in hand, and wandered to the window, apparently to observe the black rain still raging impotently against the glass. Then, with Kaia chatting to her neighbour and most of the other guests distracted on their headphones by Lee's pearls of IPO-related wisdom, I had wandered oh-so nonchalantly back to the table, only to accidentally drop my napkin on the floor. Silly me. Crouching between my own seat and Fung's, and sheltered from view, I had freed my little helper from the envelope of tissue inside my jacket pocket. Placing my napkin upon it, I had risen to my feet and coolly deposited the linen on Fung's place setting, while simultaneously deploying the card sharp's old distraction technique of raising a wine glass with my other hand and observing it thoughtfully. The final step was to claim Fung's original napkin as my own and retake my seat.

I make it sound easy, of course. But by this point my heart was pounding like a Thoroughbred's hooves. Hand shaking ever so slightly, I raised my glass to my lips and surveyed my fellow guests, ending with Kaia. Sickeningly, I realised she'd finished her conversation with the Beijing underwriter and was staring right at me.

"What are you up to?" she said.

My heart stopped.

"The same as you, I imagine. Just enjoying the wine."

"You've lifted that glass three times, inhaled it, then scowled like an apprentice somm."

The shirt beneath my armpits felt distinctly damp. Sodden, in fact.

"You've been watching me, have you?"

"Maybe I have." She smiled, which jump-started my heart, thank God, and dare I say even sent a little rush of blood to the peripheries.

Then Fung had returned to his seat, conveyed his delight at returning to his beloved Romanée-Conti, and moved aside my strategically placed napkin.

Steeled for action I may have been, but I was utterly unprepared for what happened next.

Fung emitted a noise so remarkable that I assumed it had been generated by some kind of vintage mechanical device concealed beneath his chair, possibly operated by a muscular and highly trained monkey. It began with a bass-level hum, rising and falling in pitch like a hand-cranked air-raid siren, before climbing to the timbre of a professional tenor belting out a particularly anguished bit of Wagner. As headphones were removed from disbelieving ears, and widening eyes turned to observe him, I placed a protective finger in my right ear, for Fung was now broadcasting his distress at a volume that would not have disgraced the great Pavarotti himself. Even Lee's head, floating malevolently at the end of the table, was aware that the evening's agenda had taken a rather sub-optimal turn.

Fung's eyes were rooted on the table before him. More precisely, of course, on the item that I had hidden beneath his napkin. For at six inches across, its chicken nugget-sized body coated in smooth brown fur and its front killing legs angled like those of a demented crab, the huntsman spider is a very unpleasant-looking beast indeed, even for the non-arachnophobe. And Charles Fung, it was fair to say, was very much an arachnophobe.

The sound emitted by the traumatised Fung rose higher, to a soprano wail. I could faintly hear Lee's voice barking in Mandarin, presumably demanding to know what the dickens was going on. His staff, though, remained rooted to the spot, unclear as to how one should tackle a hysterical bathroom accessories mogul in the midst of an invertebrate-induced nervous breakdown.

"Fear not," I said, rising to my feet and preparing to throw my napkin over the dead spider.

For, of course, that particular huntsman was very much an ex-spider. I had purchased it from a pet shop in Sheung Wan the previous day and had dispatched it back in my hotel room that evening. The challenge had been to keep the eight-legged fellow in reasonable shape, so he (or maybe she) was able to put on a good performance post-mortem. I had come up with a humane, respectful and possibly even enjoyable slaughter method involving pouring most of a bottle of baijiu spirit into the spider's tank and waiting for the creature to expire of alcohol poisoning. I don't know if you've ever tried to murder a huntsman spider with cheap baijiu but it's not the easiest task. For one thing, huntsman spiders are shockingly fast runners and this one appeared to have mastered cartwheels, too, so it was a hell of a job to prevent it leaping out of the tank as I attempted to pour in sufficient liquor to send the little bastard to sleep.

In the end, I managed it, ensuring the creature remained marinaded in the spirit overnight for preservation purposes. Not my finest hour, I know, and heartfelt apologies to any animal lovers out there, but sometimes one has to sacrifice oneself for a greater calling, and I like to think that particular arachnid would have been able to hold its head high as it joined its friends in invertebrate heaven.

Holding a corner of my napkin in each hand, I stepped forward, intending to drape the square of linen over the huntsman. My fellow guests, utterly transfixed by Fung's vocal gymnastics, appeared not to have spotted the creature, camouflaged as it was against the dark tabletop.

"I've got this, Charles!" I declared, not that he or anyone else could hear me over his ear-splitting shrieks.

And then, to my absolute horror, the creature somewhat unsteadily raised its two front legs and waved them at Fung. And it wasn't a friendly wave.

"Jesus wept!" I shouted, dropping the napkin.

Fung took this development extremely badly. His shrieking abruptly ceased, to be replaced by a kind of horrified wheeze. I've never actually heard a death rattle before, but this sounded ominously like one and it occurred to me that my half-baked attempt to steal an empty bottle of Lee's dodgy Burgundy, not to mention the opportunity to land a multi-million-pound toilet seat contract, might be expiring before my very eyes.

The huntsman fixed Fung with all eight of its eyes and took two steps forward.

Fung began to judder like a badly maintained vintage car.

"Nobody panic!" I shouted.

I'll be honest, I was a little shaken myself. The thought that a live, hungover huntsman had been nestling next to my bosom for several hours was not a pleasant one. Huntsman spiders can deliver a nasty bite and I thanked the gods that the supermarket baijiu had been sufficiently potent to keep the creature comatose for the day. Looking around frantically for some kind of weapon, I spotted my copy of Jasper Morris's *Inside Burgundy.* Quick as a flash, I grabbed it and with a battle cry of "Die, you bastard!" I hurled the volume down upon the hapless arachnid.

But the little monster had regained its fighting spirit. It scuttled out of the way, leapt on to Fung's hand and galloped up his arm.

Fung emitted a noise like a distressed steam kettle.

"Stay completely still!" I ordered, retrieving my napkin. "I'll knock it off."

But the creature had already cartwheeled over Fung's shoulder and was making its way down the back of his chair. I snapped my napkin at it, but those eight eyes saw me coming a mile off.

It flung itself from the chair, executed a mid-air 360-degree spin and landed on the ground before hurtling away along the floor.

"I've got it!" I shouted, sprinting after the critter and attempting to stamp on it. But the tricky little beast ran in a most un-sportsman-like zig-zag and whenever I thought I was close enough to bring my foot down and end the little bugger's shenanigans once and for all, the blighter changed direction and accelerated away even faster.

I collided, rather heavily, with a flunky.

"What are you doing, sir?" he asked.

"I'm attempting to detain the spider that just attacked one of your guests," I replied, suddenly aware of how quiet the room had become.

"There is no spider, sir."

"Of course there is!" I spluttered, pointing at the floor.

But the man was right. The devilish creature had made good its escape.

"Did nobody see it?" I said, looking to the guests.

The silence suggested that if any of Lee's guests had spotted an acrobatic arachnid at the world's most exclusive Pinot Noir tasting, this wasn't the moment to mention it.

"Well, you might want to check your pest control procedures," I said.

The room watched me return to my seat, cheeks burning.

"Christ, Charles, did you see that little bugger move?" I whispered, clapping Fung on the shoulder. "Anyway, no harm done."

I glanced at Fung and took a shocked step back, for his face was as white as chalk.

"Is everything all right, Charles?" I asked, quietly.

For a second, I thought Fung was dead. Then, he screamed like a prize piglet at a fiesta and, to my astonishment, leapt clean out of his chair. He didn't just jump a few inches, or spring to a standing position, he actually propelled himself several feet into the air in a manoeuvre that would have made a human cannonball proud. The end point of Fung's trajectory, I realised, would be the very spot on which I was standing, a fact which caused me a split-second of dismay, for though Fung had not launched himself at me in anger, several decades of fried dim sum and expensive red wine had taken their toll and it was fair to describe his build as uncompromisingly chunky.

Thankfully, my shoulders are broad and my reflexes sharp. As Fung descended into my outstretched arms like a catapulted manatee, it struck me that my distraction plan had played out pretty poorly. Not only was every pair of eyes in the room upon us, from the humblest waiter to Lee himself, but as I staggered backwards Fung insisted on flinging his arms around my head and hooting hysterically in my ear, rendering me blind, deaf and borderline concussed.

Perhaps if I'd had sufficient space I might have regained my balance. But some malevolent bastard chose that moment to grab my ankle and that was it, I tripped and tumbled hopelessly backwards. In a final act of reflexive self-preservation, I managed to hurl Charles Fung on to the table as I fell, saving myself from being pinned and, quite possibly, crushed to death beneath his plumpness. My final recollection of the whole unhappy episode was Lee's exquisitely sprung floorboards cracking spitefully against the back of my head.

# Chapter 21

## Tactical Withdrawal

I'm not sure for how long I blacked out. Possibly just a few seconds. But after what had seemed like an eternity of Fung bleating, wailing or screeching just inches from my ears, it was rather a relief to be reminded there were other noises in the world. The sound of smashing glass, for example, or wine bottles skidding across marble tabletops. Or, for that matter, chairs tumbling, spittoons clanging, guests squealing and an entire choir of flunkies babbling.

For it was against this cacophony that I regained consciousness. I opened my eyes and found myself lying on the floor, the ceiling spotlights in my face. A dark, straight-edged shadow obscured half my view and it took me a moment to realise it was the underside of the table. My foot appeared to be tangled in the strap of my satchel, while all around me lay bottles of wine, many of them broken. Every second, more bottles rolled from the table and landed on the floor, which was doing a pretty thorough job of separating them from their contents. An empty spittoon glanced off my shoulder and chimed against the boards. I took cover further beneath the table.

There was clearly an almighty brouhaha underway. I could hear Fung still hooting, while staff and guests yelled in English, Mandarin, and Cantonese. A dozen pairs of legs were crowded around the end of the table and I spotted Kaia's among them as she shouted to give Fung some space. Her advice didn't appear to be helping, for Fung erupted into another paroxysm of wailing, hammering his feet against the tabletop and sending another tranche of bottles tumbling to the floor. A full one smashed and

164

threw a sheet of ruby across the boards. The panic grew louder and the air was filled with the aroma of the planet's finest fake Pinot. I winced at the waste.

Slightly offended that no-one had seen fit to check whether I was all right, I untangled the satchel from my foot and pushed aside the slew of empties that had joined me beneath the table. Labels winked up at me as the bottles rolled over; Romanée St Vivant, La Tâche, Clos de la Roche. Then, the Musigny '78. The one I was supposed to steal. I lifted the bottle. It was a full one! I ran my fingers around it, checking for cracks. It didn't appear to be damaged. I lifted the flap of my satchel and had just slipped the bottle inside when another label caught my eye. Old-fashioned, cursive lettering and a slightly odd, broad-shouldered bottle. It was the Richebourg '21.

Good God. The unicorn. I turned it over carefully and gazed at the label.

"Are you ok, sir?" called a voice.

A pair of legs ending in polished shoes appeared beside my chair. The owner of the legs dropped to a crouch and peered beneath the table. A suited flunky. I froze, my fingers still resting on the bottle.

"Fine, thank you. Just taking cover. Sounds a bit lively up there. Everything all right?"

"You are hurt?"

The man waddled forward and ducked his head beneath the table, surveying my bottle-strewn lair.

"No, I'm absolutely fine, thank you. Be careful, there's broken glass there."

The man winced. He snatched his hand up and bumped his head against the underside of the table.

"Oops!" I said.

The man frowned and examined his finger. I spotted a drop of blood.

"You should wash that out. Make sure there's no glass in it."

The man recognised good medical advice when he heard it. Nursing his finger, he withdrew from beneath the table and disappeared.

Seizing my chance, I laid the sole empty Richebourg '21 beside the full bottle of Musigny '78 in my satchel. Aiming to avoid the fate of the injured flunky, I edged backwards, away from the more excitable end of the table with its spilt wine and broken glass, emerging between the empty chairs of Fung and his Chinese–American neighbour. I stowed the satchel beneath Fung's chair and peered over the tabletop.

The scene before me could only be described as a spectacular shambles. All the guests were crowded around the end of the table, which was littered with upset bottles. A tide of spilt Burgundy had stained the nearby linen crimson, while broken bottles and splintered wine glasses glittered beneath the spotlights. Mortified waiters, their hands wrapped in wine-soaked fabric, were frantically pushing these hazards further up the table before they caused anyone a mortal injury, while others attempted to intercept rolling bottles in danger of liberating themselves from the tabletop. Charles Fung himself was stretched out in the midst of the carnage, still convulsing and occasionally emitting a goose-like honk. Various flunkies were pinning down his legs in a vain attempt to prevent him kicking further bottles across the room, while the Chinese–American woman and the Indian banker were attempting to secure Fung's flailing arms. Kaia was undoing the top buttons of his shirt, which made me momentarily jealous, and the air was thick with contradictory medical advice shouted in a variety of languages.

I rose to my feet and strolled a little closer to the action, just in time to catch a bottle struck by Fung's elbow from spinning wildly off the table. I nodded to a nearby waiter in a comradely way, but the poor man, already clutching several broken samples in his napkin-wrapped hands, appeared on the edge of tears.

"I need some help!" called the Indian banker, as he wrestled with Fung's increasingly assertive left arm. Before anyone could come to his aid, Fung landed a meaty slap on the man's face. "How the hell did this happen?" the Indian banker shouted. "What caused this?"

"I couldn't see," called the Chinese–American woman. "But something spooked him. Where's that wine guy?"

It occurred to me the party might have run its course and that now was the time for a quiet exit. With a shock, I realised I'd forgotten about Joseph Lee. I spun around, expecting to see his glowing, floating head staring right at me, but the far end of the table was dark, only Lee's empty chair visible through the transparent screen.

I glanced back at Kaia, but she was busy wafting a damp napkin over Fung's face. A shame to leave without saying goodbye, not to mention asking for her number, but I've always been pretty good with priorities and I suspected immediate flight might be the best course of action. I placed the bottle I'd caught back on the table and retrieved my satchel from beneath Fung's chair.

"Sir, wait there, please."

But I didn't want to wait. I marched swiftly to the leather-bound door, turned the handle and gave it a push. It didn't budge.

"Stop, sir, please," called the voice.

I began to sweat. I gave the door a more assertive shove, but nothing budged. I stepped back a couple of paces and gave the door a proper shoulder barge. The bloody thing didn't even make a sound, let alone move. An electromagnetic lock, presumably. I looked around for a release button, but the wall was smooth either side. I broke into a mild panic. Of course I wasn't going to get out. I was in the private apartments of a genius criminal mastermind. Every entrance and exit was probably controlled by Lee himself from his Hong Kong lair. I grabbed the handle and twisted it violently from side to side, giving the door a kick for good measure. Nothing moved a millimetre except the bottles in my satchel, which gave a quiet clink of complaint.

"Sir!" called the voice, louder now.

There had to be a back exit. I'd have to fight my way out. I tore my sweaty palm from the door handle and to my astonishment the door followed, nosing towards me a couple of inches and bumping against my foot.

*Christ man, pull yourself together!* I yanked the door open and sped across the silent reception room to the security alcove. I'd been fretting over how difficult it might be to retrieve my possessions, particularly my phone, but there they were on the table, arranged neatly in the velvet-lined tray. The security man, his face bathed in the soft light from his laptop, glanced at me before returning to his screen.

"I'll just take these, then," I said, lunging at the tray.

The man ignored me. I pocketed my phone and stuffed the bungee cord and corkscrew in my satchel.

"Same way out, I assume?"

The lift door was open. I could see the illuminated green button winking at me from across the room. I didn't wait for an answer. I jogged towards it, praying to the gods to keep it open.

"Mr Hart, one minute please." The flunky had followed me through the leather-bound door.

"Back in a second," I called.

I hurdled a small table in my path, dived into the lift and stabbed at the green button. The lift door remained entirely stationary. The flunky, by contrast, began striding at an assertive pace across the room. He seemed rather larger than the average flunky and as he caught my eye I saw he wore a quite unpleasantly determined expression. I turned back to the control panel. Just three buttons: the green one marked with a one, floor number fifty-three, and an alarm. Nothing to make the bloody doors close faster. I stabbed the green button a few times more, to absolutely no effect.

"Stop!" ordered the flunky.

The security man now emerged from his alcove, frowning. I considered attempting to physically pull the lift door closed, but it was flush with the body of the elevator, the gap between them seamless. I shrank into the corner and fumbled in my satchel for the corkscrew. Would a ruthless billionaire's security detail be discouraged by a one-inch, semi-sharp, foil-cutting blade? It seemed unlikely.

My fingers brushed against the bottles. Probably a better

weapon than a miniscule knife blade, especially if I lamped the flunky with the full one. But what a waste after all I'd gone through. My fingers found the corkscrew. Hopefully, if I just waved it at him, he might stand back long enough for the world's most relaxed lift doors to close. I stabbed the green button a few more times.

My pursuer was now a dozen feet away, and mere seconds from entering the lift and closing his hands around my throat. The only obstacle between us was a pair of chairs and the little table that I'd hurdled a moment earlier. For a second, I thought he might do the same, but something in the flunky code of conduct must have forbidden such indecorous behaviour and the man took a detour around the furniture. Pressed into the back corner, I withdrew the corkscrew from my satchel and, hands shaking, unsheathed the tiny foil-cutter.

"I'll use it!" I shouted as the flunky reached the lift. I brandished the miniscule blade at him and the man took a step back, clearly surprised by my defiance. His hand moved to his inside jacket pocket, presumably to withdraw his own weapon. A machete, perhaps, or a silenced pistol.

And then, to my astonishment, the lift door began to close. I have made a point ever since of observing the closure speed of elevator doors, from the gleaming glass cylinders that ascend the super-high hotels of Abu Dhabi, to the battered, garbage-scented goods lifts servicing the loading bays of food factories, but I'm damned if I've ever seen an elevator door close as slowly as that one did on that God-forsaken night on the fifty-third floor of Phantasos.

The flunky's eyes moved from the tip of my corkscrew blade to the closing door. I resisted the urge to stab again at the ground-floor button, in case the door interpreted it as a desire to remain on the fifty-third floor after all, and idly retraced its route to a fully open position. The man withdrew his hand from his jacket, adopted a vicious karate-chopping stance and made to intercept the closing door with his palm. Fortunately, I had anticipated the flunky's move. I jabbed the corkscrew blade in the direction of his fingers and the man snatched his hand away before he was able to molest the door. He gave me a look that suggested I was being less than sporting, then his eyes slid to a point beside the lift at around waist height. With a sickening feeling I realised it was the call button. As the gap between the lift door and frame narrowed, agonisingly slowly, to its final few inches, the man lunged for the wall panel. His face was replaced by my own as the mirrored door eased closed and I heard the click-click-click as his fingers stabbed repeatedly at the button.

The lift remained completely still. I felt like vomiting. In a second, the doors would re-open, this time no doubt at super-fast speed, and there would be the flunky, machete raised, while his security colleague trained a machine gun on me. I pointed my corkscrew blade at the door and raised a prayer to Bacchus.

And then, a euphoric moment of weightlessness as the elevator began its descent. I was filled with a desire to shout 'Praise the Lord!', but I made do with a prayer of thanks to the Swiss lift manufacturer instead, whose name and address adorned a small plaque beside the control panel. I pledged to thank the company board in person if I ever found myself in Basel with an hour to spare, albeit accompanied by some earnest feedback on the need to improve this particular model's door closure velocity.

But seconds later, as gravity reasserted itself with the slowing of the lift, my relief turned to dread. What faced me in the ground-floor foyer? Another gang of armed flunkies? I raised my corkscrew once more and prepared to plunge the foil-cutter into the first thug standing in my way. With a bit of luck, I'd surprise them and in the general chaos make a break for the exit.

The doors opened and I found myself face to face with the shy young woman who had offered me a towel earlier that evening. Misinterpreting my outstretched foil-cutter as a hostile act, she screamed.

"I'm terribly sorry! I was just checking my corkscrew was still in working order. And look, it is, so I can put it away. There. No harm done. And honestly, no need to keep screaming."

But the woman remained resolutely un-reassured by my

calming words and continued to raise merry hell, at which point a uniformed security guard appeared from some unseen doorway. It would have been defeatist to surrender after I'd come this far, so after glancing at the security guard's hips and feeling reasonably confident that he wasn't heavily armed, I decided the best policy was to run away as fast as I could.

I charged a pair of fire doors, praying they weren't double-locked. The security guard yelled. I've no idea what he yelled, because as the doors gave way and I leapt for freedom, his words were lost in a roar of wind and I was hit by what felt like a water cannon. I staggered backwards, the assault nearly flinging me back inside the building, and buried my face in my arms to protect it from the stinging spray. Crouching and peering through my fingers, I saw the slanting rain frothing against the concrete, the palm trees' slick leaves flailing like whips against the black sky. It dawned on me that I wasn't under attack from a sadistic division of the Macau Police, but that I'd plunged once more into the rainstorm still raging over the city.

I considered retreating to the shelter of the foyer, but a glance over my shoulder revealed that the security guard had been joined by two colleagues, all of whom appeared to be shouting at me. I turned back and charged into the storm, heading for a dimly lit shelter a few dozen yards ahead. The wind barged me left and right and the ground was one continuous, dancing puddle. Within seconds, my shoes were full of water, my socks squelching revoltingly every time I made contact with the tarmac. I recognised my destination as the carport where I'd been dropped some hours ago, and as I splashed my way out of the driving rain, soaked to the skin, it became clear I presented an even more fascinating spectacle to the knot of smoking chauffeurs than I had when I arrived.

"Taxi?" I shouted, more in hope than expectation.

This provoked a fair degree of mirth from the unhelpful drivers that only increased when I extracted a damp five hundred-patacas note from my wallet. Eventually, one of their number indicated a white parked car just visible through the rain, a thirty-second dash away. Taking a deep breath and clutching my satchel to my side, I threw myself back into the storm. I was within touching distance of the vehicle before I realised the writing along the side, straddled by Chinese characters, stated Polícia, and that the For Hire sign on the vehicle's roof was, in fact, a red-and-blue lightbar.

Even in the dark, torrential rain, I was close enough to catch the attention of the vehicle's uniformed occupants. More worryingly, they quickly decided that a bedraggled Westerner cantering through a black rainstorm carrying a suspiciously bulging satchel might be worthy of further investigation. The car turned on its headlights and a loudspeaker shouted something harsh in, I assume, the local dialect. Unable to think of a credible explanation as to why I was carrying two rare wine bottles, whose ownership was likely to be disputed within a minute or so by a posse of pursuing security guards and assorted flunkies, I decided once again that flight was the most sensible policy.

# Chapter 22

## Pursuit

My only option was to race back to Phantasos. If I attempted to run along the driveway or into the open night, I'd be overtaken in no time. As I sprinted away, the car's engine fired up and its siren emitted a bone-tingling shriek. I skirted the carport and its gang of malevolent chauffeurs, passed through the line of palm trees that ran parallel to Phantasos, and raced along the footpath at its base, hoping I might spot another way into the hotel. But the only entrances I found as I tore past the great struts of the building's exoskeleton were windowless utility doors, all sealed tight against the storm.

The weather, I could swear, was worsening. As if the screaming rain wasn't enough, every few seconds a torrent of cold water cascading from the building above would sluice over me like a punishment from a sadistic gym teacher. But it barely mattered, I was already as saturated as if I'd swum in from Hong Kong. Behind me, beyond the row of palm trees, the police car hunted its prey, the rain diffusing its red-and-blue beacons into vast, fuzzy-edged spheres that coloured the sky. The tops of the palm trees, silhouetted before the lights, thrashed in the gale like a line of frenzied witches. I prayed I had enough of a head start to be invisible through the downpour. With a bit of luck, I could sprint all the way round the hotel and bribe a cab to whisk me off the premises.

The paved walkway suddenly ended and I was running on grass. Not the nice, soft grass of home but that hard, spiky stuff you find in less gentle climes, that at a distance pretends to be a nice expanse of turf, but turns out to be half thistle, half bogbrush. The blades were soon catching at my ankles and elevating my suffering to a whole new level of unpleasantness. But, as it happens, that vicious lawn proved my saviour, for I'd slowed down sufficiently to spot through the sodden gloom a six-foot-high wall built right across my path. Without a doubt, I would have hospitalised myself if I'd hit it at full pelt, but just in time I was able to fling out my arms and spare myself any serious injury. My satchel, though, swung hard against the brickwork and for a sickening moment I thought I'd smashed the bottles. Panicking, I felt inside the bag and to my enormous relief found both were still intact.

I glanced back at the flickering red-and-blue halo from the police car's beacons. The car's headlights were visible now through the row of palm trees, each surrounded by a hazy ring. I could tell the vehicle was gaining on me, but the floodlights on Phantasos pointed outwards and I was in deep shadow. However, I had a new problem. The wall I'd slapped up against was joined to the hotel and ran perpendicular from it into the wild darkness as far as my eyes could see. Iron railings sprouted from the top of the wall, rising at least another six feet, and the wet shine of a floodlight revealed that they were crowned with fearsome fleur-de-lys spikes.

I was trapped. If I moved away from Phantasos along the line of the wall, I'd be lit up by the advancing police car as soon as I passed through the row of palm trees. If I headed back the way I'd come, I'd pass perilously close to the vehicle as it crawled by, and once I was back at my start point I would be doubtless be intercepted by a squad of enraged security guards, sommeliers and assorted flunkies. The only option was to tackle the obstacle. I reached up, grabbed a railing in each hand and pulled myself up until my elbows rested on top of the wall. Complete darkness the other side, except for a smear of light in the distance. I appeared to be at the corner of Phantasos. Above me, a pair of the building's vast metal struts plunged into the darkness beyond. If I wanted to continue my journey round the hotel and reach the front, I'd have to go over the top.

The railings were too narrow to squeeze between. They were wide enough, however, to allow my satchel through. I removed the paper napkins, which I stuffed down my pants for extra protection, then looped the bungee cord through the satchel's handle. I latched the metal hooks around the railings, then carefully posted the satchel between the bars and played out the cord until the elastic took the strain and the bag hung suspended on the far side of the wall.

Now it was my turn. Glancing back, I saw there was no time to waste. The police car had moved much closer, its headlights casting creeping palm tree shadows on the wall. The railings were slick with rain so I used the old cat burglar's trick, spitting on my palms and rubbing them together for extra grip. I hauled myself up until my feet found the top of the brickwork. The storm seemed louder up here; the snare drum of rain now a deeper, more full-throated roar. Wrapping an arm around a railing, I wiped away the water running into my eyes and tried to perceive what lay on the other side. But all I could see was darkness. It was possible, of course, that there was a horrible drop the other side. I felt for the phone in my jacket pocket, which I'd wrapped inside a handkerchief in a pathetic attempt to keep it dry. After a few fumbles I managed to activate the torch. I shone it into the darkness, but all I could see was a chaos of raindrops shooting past like tracer fire.

I replaced the phone and plunged my hand down the front of my pants, extracting one of the luxury paper napkins. Within seconds it was disintegrating in the scything rain, but I tossed it through the railings and, head pressed against the bars, watched as it was battered to the ground. And there it lay, just visible six feet or so down, a faint, ghostly shred. The ground was the same height the far side of the wall.

The fleur-de-lys spikes, now catching the flickering red and blue of the police car's beacon, looked damn intimidating. I prayed their design was more ornamental than military. A supporting rail ran helpfully along the top of the bars just beneath each fleur-de-lys, so a quick scrabble and a chin-up brought my head level with the spikes. Holding tight to the rail, I examined one with my spare hand. As I'd hoped, they were blunt and rounded. Not the kind of thing you'd want to fling yourself on from a great height, but benign enough to climb over, provided you avoided entanglement with any soft fleshy areas. The wad of paper napkins bulged proudly against the front of my trousers like a papier-mâché codpiece and I prayed they'd fulfil their duty before they dissolved in the sodden swamp of my crotch.

I've never compared myself to a teenage Russian gymnast (unless you class counterfeit Burgundy as a performance-enhancing substance) but I've scaled enough walls, fences, and drainpipes in my time to make short work of obstacles that would deter lesser mortals. I swapped my grip on the rail to palms-out, jammed my feet in the gaps between the railings and thrust myself upwards. A second later, I'd swung my legs clear over the fleur-de-lys, my feet planted once again upon the top of the wall, and I was looking back through the railings in the direction I'd come. In the meantime, the police car had also reached the wall, just the other side of the line of palm trees. Had they spotted my acrobatics? Possibly, but good luck catching me now. I shinned down the wall and dropped to the ground.

I stumbled as I landed. The ground was firm, tarmac or stone of some sort, but set at a peculiar angle. The roar of the storm was even louder this side of the wall, and the rain more vicious, too. Rather than slicing down from above, it seemed conjured from the very air, assaulting me from all sides. I peered up at Phantasos, its exoskeleton girders black against the dim smudge of windows many storeys above. The structure must have sheltered me as I sprinted along the pathway earlier but now I was facing right into the storm. For the first time, I felt cold. Unsurprising perhaps, given that I'd been soaked to the skin for God knew how long, but now that I'd stopped running I began to shiver. A squall came out of nowhere and hit me full in the face, a savage, cold slap that made my eyes sting. I had to get moving. I stood and edged forward, only to stumble again. The ground was irregular, like broken paving. I reached out for the wall and my palm found the wet leather of my satchel, swaying on its elasticated bungee. I took a slow, careful step forward only to bump my shin against something hard. Was I on a flight of steps? No, the object before me was too high. Curse this darkness! I groped forward with my other hand and made contact with wet stone. Where the hell was I? I opened my eyes wider, attempting to pierce the darkness, and for my trouble received another slap of spray across my face. This one really hurt. I crouched against the wall and pressed my hand over my stinging eyes. There was water up my nose and in my mouth. As I spat, I realised I could taste salt.

Something was very wrong. I felt the obstacle beside me with both hands. Cold, wet stone, irregularly shaped, rough edges. The ground beneath me was similar. Abrasive rock, not smooth paving. Hands shaking, I fished in my pocket for my phone, my numb fingers taking an age to free it from the sodden handkerchief. I turned on the torch and the air before me erupted with dazzling shooting stars. I pointed the light at the ground a couple of feet before me, cupping my free hand over the phone to keep the rain off. Slowly, the terrain revealed itself.

I was perched upon a boulder the size of a large car, its edges angular and unnatural. It was only by good fortune that I had landed on a vaguely horizontal surface; to my right and before me the boulder's edges slipped down into the dark. To my left, against which I had knocked my shin, loomed a similar rock, partly resting upon my own, as if tossed there by some careless giant. And there was something else, too, out in the darkness. Something moving in the black space just beyond the point where the boulder's surface slipped down into the gloom. Something ghostly and unfocussed. What the hell was it? A ribbon of faint, white silk, just for a second, then nothing. I craned my neck and held the phone at arm's length. There it was again, a pale wraith, swaying and tumbling over itself. And then, with a roar, a great battering of cold, salty water struck me full in the face and my heart nearly stopped. For I realised I was perched right on the edge of Macau's harbour defences, daring a Force 12 typhoon to sweep me into the raging South China Sea.

"NO SELFIE!" screamed a Chinese voice somewhere above me.

Suddenly, I was bathed in a circle of yellow light.

"NO SELFIE! NO SELFIE!"

Through the railings, a few yards down, I spotted a peaked cap silhouetted against a backdrop of flickering red and blue. An arm, ending in a powerful flashlight, reached through the bars.

"NO SELFIE!"

"I'm not taking a selfie," I shouted.

"NO SELFIE! YOU MAD! STUPID! YOU COME BACK!"

"Yes, yes, I know. I am coming back. I took a wrong turning."

Shivering, I stood and reached up, grasping the railings. I attempted to hoist myself back up the wall, but my strength had left me. The metal bars slipped through my hands and my shoes scrabbled uselessly against the brickwork. I spat on my palms, flexed my fingers to warm them up and tried again, this time just managing to get my feet atop the wall. With a fair degree of effort, I pulled myself to a standing position.

The police car had been parked right alongside the wall, and the officer with the flashlight was standing on the vehicle's roof. His partner had taken up position at the spot where I had scaled the railings. He scowled up at me, rain dripping from his cap.

"Hello, officer. Sorry for the trouble."

"You come over now!" ordered the policeman beneath me.

"Yes, that's the idea. Just gathering my strength."

I shinned up one of the vertical bars and got my hands over the horizontal rail, but I could feel my muscles threatening to cramp. I managed to swing first one foot, then the other, up between two of the fleur-de-lys spikes but was forced to pause for a moment and hang there while I summoned my strength, like a sloth negotiating a tricky bit of rainforest. I took a deep breath and gave a mighty heave, just as I had a few minutes earlier in the other direction, but the cold and the wet and, frankly, the buttock-clenching fear had taken their toll and I failed to clear the tips of the spikes. One fleur-de-lys raked its way painfully across my chest and tore open my shirt, while the other, to my horror, chose to tangle with my padded codpiece, snagging the flap of my flies. The result was that rather than swinging cleanly over, my groin area became impaled on one of the spikes and I was left hanging by my hands and crotch, my feet flailing pathetically in mid-air.

The sensitive souls among you, I'm sure, will by now be weeping in empathy at my predicament. The more anatomically minded may even be fearing the unthinkable. But I'm delighted to report that a combination of my strategically placed paper napkin padding and the robustness of Ted Baker's tailoring served to maintain my bodily integrity. I was, however, completely stuck. Despite my best efforts, principally a series of ever-more frantic hip thrusts, I couldn't for the life of me free myself from the crotch-molesting fleur-de-lys.

"You come down now!" shouted the policeman beneath me.

"I'm bloody trying!" I called, into the rain-lashed sky.

I attempted to wrench the trouser fabric free with one hand while clinging for dear life to the rail with the other. I was acutely conscious that if the material suddenly gave way, I might not have sufficient strength in that single, cold, numb hand to prevent me from plunging to the ground ten feet below. So, it was with unalloyed horror that I felt two gloved hands suddenly grasp my forearm and attempt to wrench my grip from the railing.

"What the hell are you doing?" I screamed.

"You come now!" repeated the policeman, from somewhere behind my right ear. The psychopath must have climbed on top of the wall alongside me while I was struggling like a wild boar on a hunter's spear. But rather than helpfully aiding me in the release of my trousers, the lunatic was attempting to tear me down without the slightest care as to how I might land.

"YOU COME NOW!" yelled the policeman one final time, and with that he leapt from the wall, still grasping my forearm. I didn't have a hope in hell of supporting half my own weight plus the entirety of a crazed Macau law enforcement officer, and my hand was torn from the rail, leaving my crotch as the sole suspension point of our combined weight. And, robust tailoring or not, this was a bridge too far for Ted Baker's stitching. With a great, shrieking tear, the material parted and I began to descend towards the ground. As my trouser seams were rendered asunder, I felt the rain splattering against an increasingly large expanse of my inside thigh, and I had the sense to grab the railings with both hands to brake my descent. Then, with a snap, the fabric parted completely, and I tumbled the final few feet to the earth.

Mercifully, my impact was cushioned by the body of the unhelpful policeman, whose face became intimate for several seconds with my unsheathed buttocks. I claim no expertise in Chinese expletives, but I could tell from the officer's tone that he was exceedingly displeased by this outcome. I, however, could summon not a shred of sympathy for the man. His actions had been needlessly reckless – it was only thanks to the quality of my suit and my own cat-like reflexes that my fall hadn't been heavier. If we had shared a common language, I would have told him as much but, given the circumstances, I remained silent as I was dragged to the police vehicle and shoved, quite unprofessionally, into the back.

On the face of it, detention by an unfriendly police force was a tactical disaster. But the back seat of the vehicle was warm and comfortably upholstered and I was relieved to be out of the rain. The car proceeded slowly through the dark, the rain drumming on the roof and the writhing palm trees flashing red and blue in tandem with the roof beacons. Then, we stopped. Through the metal grille separating me from the front, I spotted the little guardhouse that I'd passed in the taxi on the way in. And there, just ahead, was the sliding gate, shining wetly in the headlights. My spirits rose. It looked like I might at least escape the clutches of Lee's flunkies. Perhaps the police would be kind enough to drop me at my hotel. After all, I hadn't actually committed any crime, unless you counted sitting pant-less, without consent, on a policeman's face.

I became conscious of a knot of people glowering at the car beneath dark, Phantasos-branded umbrellas. The policeman in the driver's seat lowered his window and a man in a waterproof fleece stepped forward. My blood froze. It was the large flunky who'd attempted to intercept me as I fled the tasting. He spoke to the policeman for a minute or so, then my own window was lowered an inch and the flunky peered in. He gave a monosyllabic acknowledgement, there was a metallic click and the door opened.

"You will come with me, please, Mr Hart."

# Chapter 23

## Detention

I followed the flunky to the guardhouse, leaving a large pool of water on the police car's rear seat. A dozen or so staff, mainly security guards plus a sprinkling of chauffeurs and minor flunkies, watched me, open-mouthed. I briefly considered doing another runner. Perhaps with a run-up I could scale the gate and dash for a taxi before the police vehicle followed me through. But in my weakened state I doubted I'd be able to pull it off. My ragged shirt and trousers flapped cold and wet against my skin, and my ribs ached from where the fleur-de-lys had raked my chest.

The flunky waved me through the door. I stepped inside, fists clenched, expecting to be set upon by a gang of vicious goons. To my astonishment, the only person inside the guardhouse was Kaia, leaning against the wall, arms folded.

"Oh, my God, Felix! What the hell have you been doing?"

"I must have taken a wrong turn," I said, waving a nonchalant arm.

"A wrong turn? You're absolutely soaked. And what the hell happened to your clothes? You look like you've been attacked by dogs."

"I was being pursued by this unsavoury character," I said, as the flunky stepped inside and closed the door against the howling wind.

"You were running away from Anton?" said Kaia.

"Anton, is it? Well, that's nice. You're all friends, then?"

"You left your book behind, Mr Hart," said the flunky. He pointed to a small table in the corner of the guardhouse, on which sat Jasper Morris's *Inside Burgundy*, second edition. "I was trying to return it to you."

"Right. So, I did."

"The police said that Mr Hart was taking selfies on the sea wall in the storm," said the flunky.

"What?" said Kaia. "How drunk are you?"

"I wasn't actually doing that, exactly."

"Mr Hart was in very, very great danger."

"I was fine, I just got a little lost. The lighting was very poor."

"Jesus," said Kaia, staring at my trousers. "I can literally see your genitals."

I glanced down. Sure enough, my trousers and underclothing had been ripped apart so comprehensively that an embarrassingly significant acreage of flesh was exposed. I turned away and attempted to gather up the sodden, ragged flaps of fabric, but there appeared to be a lot less material available than required to preserve my modesty. I suspected that several square inches of crotch fabric might still be flying from the top of the fleur-de-lys, like a wind-shredded flag marking the high point of a doomed mountaineering expedition. I tried tying a couple of the longer strips of material into a knot, in a miserably unsuccessful attempt to preserve my modesty.

"That's not working," said Kaia. "I can still see, like, a significant proportion of your genitals. What are all those lumps of wet tissue? Were you attempting to take a dump in the sea or something?"

"Look, this is all an unfortunate accident, ok?" I placed my open hands strategically in front of the area most poorly served by the remaining trouser fabric.

"Do you know how many times men have exposed themselves to me and claimed it's an accident?"

"Not too often, I hope."

"Very often, actually. Tiresomely often. On the street, on public transport, in restaurants, elevators, taxis, business meetings, you name it. When you tell other men, they never really believe it. Unless they're the type who make a habit of exposing themselves to women, of course."

"I really do apologise. This is definitely an accident," I said, cheeks burning.

"You know, on this occasion, astonishingly, I actually believe you. Congratulations. This may genuinely be the first time in my life, and no doubt the last, that a man has full-frontal flashed at me, entirely accidentally. What a moment."

I glanced down to check my hands were sufficiently guarding my dignity. I noticed I was standing in a slowly growing puddle dotted with lumps of luxury paper napkin.

"Anton, are the police ok?"

"They are not happy, but I talked to them and everything will be ok."

Kaia observed my trousers a few seconds more.

"But those clothes are definitely not ok, are they? The police won't let him wander around like that."

"No. The police will definitely arrest Mr Hart, for indecency. His trousers are very indecent."

"Right, I'll take care of this. Felix, you need to come with me. My car and driver are outside. You can come to my suite and we'll order up some new clothes."

"Thanks, but that won't be necessary," I said. "If you could just drop me off at my hotel, that will be fine."

"No, it's not fine. You're not on a bachelor weekend in Prague. If you return to your hotel looking like that, flashing out of the storm with your wet meat and veg swinging, they'll call the paramilitary police. And while I don't really care whether you end up in a Macau jail cell or not, I definitely don't want the authorities linking you with this evening's tasting. It would reflect very badly on me, and possibly even Joseph Lee, which would be most unwise. So, it would be great if you could just help me out and do what you're told, ok?"

"Ok."

"Good. Don't forget your book. And didn't you have a bag when you arrived this evening?"

"No, don't think so."

"Yes, you did. You had a nice, vintage leather bag over your shoulder. I remember seeing it."

"Oh, that bag. I've lost it."

"What do you mean? Where have you lost it? Did you leave it at Phantasos?"

"I don't know. That why it's lost."

"Are you suffering from some kind of brain injury, Felix?"

"Mr Hart had his bag with him when he left the building," said the flunky, unhelpfully.

"So, you've dropped it outside somewhere? It'll be ruined."

"I will ask the staff to look for it in the morning," said the flunky.

"I remember now. I left it in the carport with the drivers."

"We will make enquiries with the chauffeurs and find the bag," stated the flunky.

*Good*, I thought. *Hopefully, they'll all have the soles of their feet beaten vigorously by the authorities. That'll teach them to be such spiteful bastards.*

Using Jasper Morris's *Inside Burgundy* to hide my shame, I was escorted underneath an umbrella to Kaia's car. I was observed silently by the group of Phantasos employees, which had grown significantly since my arrival, and by the scowling policemen, who had parked their vehicle across the exit gate. Kaia climbed in the front beside the driver. I was pleased to see that the large flunky didn't join us, but I was dismayed to find us heading away from the gate, back the way I'd come.

"Where are we going? I thought you were staying in the hotel."

"I am. We're taking the back door, via the private foyer. The hotel has a dress code and I believe there's a rule suggesting men don't wander through the communal areas with their tackle hanging out. Fussy, I know, but there you go."

I was pretty sure I was heading into a trap. But why had they left the large flunky behind? The driver seemed quite a diminutive chap, not the fighting type at all, and I couldn't see Kaia pursuing me for long in that dress and heels – though I confess I found the thought of that unsettlingly exciting. But if I leapt out and did a runner, how the hell would I get past the police car at the gate?

"So, what happened to your friend?" asked Kaia.

"My friend? Who's that?" I said, genuinely confused.

"The guy you were sitting next to. Charles something. You said the two of you did business together?"

"Oh, yes. Charles Fung. I don't really know him very well. We've only met a couple of times."

"Quite a coincidence that you ended up sitting next to each other at a *Cercle Chêne* tasting, then?"

"Yes."

I supressed the urge to keep explaining. I knew I'd only end up saying something stupid or compromising.

"Well, didn't you see? The poor guy had some sort of fit. Do you know what brought it on?"

"He mentioned something about a spider."

"And what were you doing slamming that book down and dancing around? Looked like you'd lost your marbles."

"I was trying to scare the spider away."

"Sounds like you made it worse. Didn't you want to check he was ok?"

"He'd pretty much calmed down by the time I left."

"He didn't calm down for a long time. Mr Lee's team moved him to the medical centre and gave him a sedative. The staff thought it was epilepsy at first, but it sounds more like a panic attack."

"Poor chap."

Again, it seemed wise to close down the conversation. Presumably, Kaia already thought I was an idiot, so staying dumb seemed much the best policy. We passed the carport, which was now deserted, and stopped before the entrance to the foyer. The housekeeper I'd traumatised earlier with my corkscrew was busy mopping the patch of floor in front of the fire doors. When she spotted me emerging from the car, Jasper Morris's *Inside Burgundy* positioned politely in front of my ragged trousers, she dropped her mop and scurried into the back. I strongly considered doing a vanishing act myself. That lift in the corner only had one destination – floor fifty-three – and I suspected Lee's security guards were already polishing their fingernail pliers.

"Relax, we're not going back up there," said Kaia, from beneath her umbrella. The rain, I noticed, had begun to ease. "This way."

I followed her into the foyer. She tossed the umbrella aside, still open, and led me to a different lift. As the doors opened I was relieved to see it boasted two-dozen illuminated buttons, all much lower than the number fifty-three. Kaia touched a card to the panel and we ascended. A minute later, she swiped us into a living room furnished in crystal, gold, and black velvet.

"Good God, this room's enormous," I said. "This is where they've put you up?"

"It's a suite, actually. Office through there. Second bathroom opposite. And the balcony's very cool, you should check it out once the rain's stopped." She touched my wet sleeve and grimaced. "You're going to catch hyperthermia in this air-con." She plucked a tissue from a golden dispenser and dried her fingers. "You should get out of those wet clothes and under a shower, like right now. Use that bathroom."

I shed my sodden, ruined clothes, dumped them in the bathtub, then stepped into the vast monsoon shower. As the hot, steaming spray enveloped my body, I let out a long, involuntary bleat, like a lamb returning to a sunlit meadow after a lost winter in the mountains. Half an hour later, my skin tingling from the application of luxury exfoliating shower scrub and my perfumed body wrapped in a soft white robe, I poked my head around the bathroom door, determined not to expose myself a second time to my host.

"That was rather revitalising, thank you. Has my change of clothes arrived?"

"They'll send them up in the morning," said Kaia, as she perused a huge tabletop book featuring pictures of modernist furniture.

"Ah, ok. I assume there's a second bedroom?"

"No, only one." She rose to her feet. "It's through here. And no red-blooded man should be caught dead in a fluffy bathrobe. Remove it immediately."

# Chapter 24

## Liberation

Kaia hadn't been lying about the balcony. We ate a brunch of eggs benedict overlooking the South China Sea, the thick, humid air the only reminder of last night's storm. Ten storeys below, the Macau traffic honked and revved, while private jets descended to the international airport marooned off the coast, a mile-long strip of grey surrounded by brown, brooding ocean.

"Anton has spoken to all the drivers but none of them have your bag."

"Well, one of them is lying. But don't worry about it. There was nothing valuable in it."

"He's asked security to review the CCTV. We'll find it."

"It's no bother, but thanks."

"You look good in the new clothes, by the way. Sharper."

"They're nice. You need to tell me how much I owe you. I'll ping you the cash." A designer label, procured at a five-star resort. Millionaire or not, I dreaded to think how much they'd cost.

For a moment I thought she was going to wave the suggestion away. "I'll send the invoice to Farquhar Fine and Rare, if you like?"

"Perfect, that's much easier," I said, my spirits rising. If Fromage complained, I'd tell him to forward the bill to Paris-Blois.

"I'd love to spend the day with you, Felix, but I have to go to work. I'm representing some of our agencies at a big lunchtime junket at the Wynn Palace."

We left the balcony's fuzzy warmth for the frigid dryness of the suite. Kaia swapped her shorts and t-shirt for a smart, figure-hugging suit while I dropped a capsule into the coffee machine and buzzed myself another espresso.

"Look what Anton dropped round for me this morning," she said, placing a wooden wine case on the coffee table. "Some souvenirs, as a thank you. He's so sweet."

She opened the box, removed three empty wine bottles and placed them on the table. I nearly choked on my espresso. All three were from the previous night's tasting. A Romanée Conti '85, a Clos de la Roche '82, and only a bloody Musigny '78, the very wine I'd slipped into my satchel.

"I've got this room for the whole day, so I'm leaving my stuff here while I do the tasting at the Wynn. You don't have to go straight away if you don't want to. Order something to eat from room service, if you like. It's on my corporate account."

"That's nice of you," I said, slightly stunned. The bottles winked at me from the coffee table.

"Yes, I am nice, aren't I? I won't be back until gone six, so I'm guessing you'll have headed back to Hong Kong by then. I'll be in touch. I want to do this again. Not the wine tasting, the bedroom stuff."

"Me too," I said.

"Here, take this, in case you want to check out the resort and let yourself back in. I'll get another from Reception."

She tucked her room card into my breast pocket and kissed me.

And with that, I was left alone with three empty bottles of Burgundy, one of which I'd spent an entire night and damn-near killed myself trying to steal. At least I'd managed to pilfer a full bottle. For the purposes of my mission, it would be far better to return with that, not to mention the bonus empty Richebourg '21 I'd manged to filch. And it would be better not to steal Kaia's souvenir bottle, if I could help it. I suspected she'd be less likely to want another hook-up if she felt I was the kind of person who stole the cutlery at dinner parties. Question is, could I retrieve my satchel? Might it be waterlogged after a night in the storm, the contents saturated with brine and ruined? Or, more likely, dashed to pieces by the waves, the bottles now a thousand glittering fragments at the bottom of the South China Sea? And had Anton, the well-built, yet ever-so-sweet flunky, checked the CCTV, located my satchel's hiding place, and decided to crouch in the shadows beside the sea wall with a claw hammer, waiting to bludgeon me to death the second I attempted to retrieve it?

In the end, the thought of my million-dollar consultancy fee swung it for me. I waited a few minutes, then, not forgetting my copy of Jasper Morris's *Inside Burgundy*, I slipped out and retraced my steps, taking the lift down to the private apartments' foyer. I took a deep breath and marched confidently through the room, weaving between the low coffee tables sporting their bottles of designer cologne, and praying I wouldn't encounter the sensitive housekeeper. To my relief, a different woman was on duty. With a cheery wave I strode outside and picked up the footpath running around the perimeter of the building. Everything looked smaller in the sunlight; the carport, the now motionless palm trees, even the great black struts of Phantasos's exoskeleton, plunging into their concrete anchors. At the point where the path ended, I stopped and checked I wasn't being followed. But I was at the far corner of the hotel grounds, on the back side of the hotel, and I appeared to be alone. The railing-topped wall lay a few dozen yards ahead. The grass glistened beneath the morning sun and the air was heavy with the fug of damp clay. As I stepped on to the spiky blades, the earth squelched underfoot.

I approached the wall slowly, conscious a cosh-wielding flunky might be hiding behind one of Phantasos's struts. The railings and their fleur-de-lys spikes looked much less intimidating in the sunlight, barely half the height they'd appeared last night. I felt along the top of the wall where the railings met the brickwork. There they were, the two little bungee hooks, still pressed tight to the metal.

On tiptoes, I reached both arms over the wall and grasped the cord. To my relief, it was still taut. I reeled it in slowly, pulling the cord up hand-over-hand, the laden satchel bouncing lazily at the end of the elasticated rope. The bag's handle nuzzled into my palm and I eased it through the railings. But as I lifted it down, my heart missed a beat; for the bag in my hands was not the satchel I'd left behind. I whirled round, assuming some joker had substituted a fake and that I'd walked into an ambush. Yet the path behind me was empty. I examined the satchel. The exterior was coated in a flaky grey crust and streaked with silver lines like a white tiger. I lifted the flap, the leather creaking in complaint, unzipped the pouch and peered inside. From the satchel's depths, the two bottles winked back at me, reflecting strange, shrunken copies of the Macau sun high above.

It was my satchel, after all. The bag had not fared well after its night of punishment at the hands of the storm-lashed sea. Its seams were swollen and tide marks of dirty salt scarred the leather. Mr Fromage, I guessed, would not be best pleased. But the bag had retained its structural integrity. So far as I could tell, neither rain nor sea spray had penetrated the inner sanctum and the bottles remained unsullied. I slid my copy of *Inside Burgundy* into it, returned along the path to the private apartments' foyer and slipped back into the lift, Kaia's card whisking me back up to her floor. I followed the signs to the Phantasos resort, passing through smoke-filled casinos full of unsmiling baccarat players, past Michelin-starred dim sum restaurants, and all-you-can-eat surf and turf buffets, eventually emerging in the vast main Reception. I marched at speed, head down, past the concierge desks, desperately avoiding the gaze of anyone in uniform, blasted through the front doors, and jumped into a taxi. To my enormous relief, the driver responded to my request for the Notting Hill Resort Hotel, though I still fretted all the way back, fearing that I'd be pulled over any second by Lee's friends in the Macanese Police.

I dashed into my hotel, retrieved my luggage, then summoned another taxi to the ferry port. It was only when the Turbojet opened its throttle and we were skimming our way back across the South China Sea that I felt I could breathe again. Even then, I kept glancing back, half-expecting to see a pursuing powerboat gaining on us, the bow packed with fist-waving flunkies. But Macau's skyscrapers were soon no more than blurred smudges fading into the ochre haze and the only vessels to be seen were fishermen's sampans bobbing in the steel-grey sea.

# Chapter 25

## Herr Krupp

"Clever Minstrel Hart! Clever, clever, clever!"

Minstrel Shuttlewort beamed at me through her vast round glasses and returned her gaze to the two bottles on the bench before her.

Provost Rougegorgefils nodded. "Yes, we certainly didn't expect you to pilfer a full bottle of the '78 Musigny. Nor an empty bottle of '21 Richebourg, for that matter!"

"Well, I aim to please."

I gazed at the framed periodic table hanging high on the wall. It kindled vague memories of incomprehensible science lessons and dismal examination results.

"Why the frown, Minstrel Hart? Don't tell me this is the first time you've been inside a chemistry laboratory?"

"No, Provost, of course not. Though this is, by some distance, the most impressive one I've seen."

"Thank you. We consider this one of House Archivist's Rolls Royce assets. One could hardly expect us to conduct gold-standard research without such a facility, of course."

I surveyed the shelves lined with glassware of every shape and size, from tiny teardrop pipettes to round-bottomed flasks the size of a cauldron. Atop the gleaming white counters sat all manner of equipment; centrifuges, hotplates, furnaces, and water baths, not to mention an array of electronic devices with screens, dials and trailing leads, the purpose of which I would be at a loss to tell you, given my premature and quite unjust ejection some years ago from the world of secondary education.

"How did you manage to swipe them?" asked Shuttlewort.

She wore a white lab coat festooned with pockets. "Did you slip them down your trousers?"

"I'm not at liberty to divulge my methods, I'm afraid."

"Was there any rough stuff?" Shuttlewort's voice dropped to a whisper.

"A little."

Shuttlewort inhaled sharply and shut her eyes.

"Let's not ask too many questions of Minstrel Hart," said Provost Rougegorgefils. "We don't want him incriminating himself, do we?"

Rougegorgefils gave her wireless mouse a shake and her laptop glowed into life.

"Now then. To business. Since yesterday, when you were kind enough to provide us with these excellent samples, we've conducted a preliminary analysis of the labels. Minstrel Shuttlewort, please share your findings with Minstrel Hart."

Shuttlewort addressed the bottle of Musigny '78 directly.

"Executive summary: a complete fraud."

"Oh, wow," I said. "Sorry I didn't spot it."

"No need to apologise. I'll credit it as a reasonably competent fraud. The label copy and design, for example, are spot on. No spelling mistakes, no missing detail on the illustration, no silly omissions or additions. More impressively, the domaine individually numbers its bottles and the number used on this fake label is a credible one. We've cross-referenced it against the major auctioneer databases and it doesn't appear in any of them, so they haven't just copied it from a catalogue. We've also checked with the domaine themselves and it's a legitimate number. It's not higher than the domaine's total 1978 production, for example."

"So, how do you know it's fake?"

"Quite simple," sighed Shuttlewort. "It's screen printed. A genuine fine wine label of that vintage would be produced the old-fashioned way, on a plate press. At least they went to a bit of effort. They could have just used an inkjet. That would have been really insulting."

"Right. So, it's definitely fake?"

"Without a doubt. You can spot the colour separation under a decent magnifying glass. And, once you get this cheeky little felon beneath a microscope, the real crime scene emerges. You can see their amateur attempts to age the paper stock. There's superficial thermal damage, caused by baking the paper to make it look yellowed. And abrasions, caused by rubbing with steel wool. You can even see tiny, broken-off fragments of steel embedded in the paper. And don't get me started on the glue."

"I won't."

"Let's just say the chromatogram didn't exactly evoke the *Sounds of the 70s*."

"I'm guessing you mean they used a modern glue, not a vintage glue?"

"Precisely, my dear footpad!"

"Wonderful!" I said.

Rougegorgefils looked up from her laptop and frowned.

"I mean, wonderful that you've done the analysis so quickly and thoroughly," I added, attempting to look grave.

What I'd meant, of course, is that it was utterly wonderful that my work was now done. I'd be back in Sandra's good books, she could sign off on my consultancy contract, and I would be the toast of Minstrels Hall. And, most importantly, I would be free to get on with the serious business of spending my million dollars. I might even be awarded a medal by Inspector Ma.

"And this one's dodgy too, I assume?" I gestured at the empty bottle of '21 Richebourg.

"Actually, this one is more interesting," said Rougegorgefils.

"Indeed," agreed Shuttlewort. "So far, I can't fault the label. No mistakes that I can spot and definitely printed on a plate press this time. The paper stock is almost certainly pre-1950s. No signs of artificial ageing. I checked it under blue light and it doesn't fluoresce. Glue isn't modern, either. So, they've made a real effort with this one."

"We know it's a fake, though, don't we? Fromage said they'd sold the bottle five years ago and the dearly departed Mr Farquhar is on record as having drunk it with Joseph Lee himself. Do you think they saved the bottle and recycled it?"

"Did they open the bottle in front of you, Minstrel Hart?" asked Rougegorgefils.

"No, it was brought in already open. In fact, none of the wines were opened in front of us."

"What a surprise," said Shuttlewort, winking through her enormous glasses like a disturbingly lewd owl. "However, fear not. I've only had my hands on this chappie for twenty-four hours. We still have a few tricks up our sleeves."

"Time to call upon the services of Herr Krupp," said Rougegorgefils.

"Ready and waiting," replied Shuttlewort. She approached a large floor-to-ceiling cupboard and opened the doors. "*Guten Tag,* Herr Krupp!"

The cupboard contained an enormous and ancient-looking metal safe.

"Please tell me you haven't imprisoned a small German man in there," I said.

"Still with the jokes I see, Minstrel Hart," said Rougegorgefils, tapping at her laptop.

"I wasn't joking. Who and where is Herr Krupp?"

"This is Herr Krupp!" declared Shuttlewort, giving the safe an affectionate knock.

"Right. A safe?"

"Not just any safe. Herr Krupp was the captain's safe on board the *Friedrich der Grosse*, a dreadnought battleship, Kaiser class, of the German Imperial Navy," explained Shuttlewort.

The safe's door, I could see, was indeed embossed with the word Krupp. "Ok. I'm sure that's relevant, but you may need to elaborate a touch."

"The *Friedrich der Grosse* surrendered to the Royal Navy following the capitulation of Germany in 1918," sighed Shuttlewort. "She and her crew were interned in Scapa Flow in the Orkneys, along with much of the German fleet. But the German crews scuttled their warships and sent them to the bottom rather than allow them to be absorbed into the Royal Navy. Now, that's a lot of steel to leave lying around on the ocean floor. So, in 1936, the *Friedrich der Grosse* was raised and broken up for scrap. The ship's safe was kept by the Admiralty, and House Archivist purchased it in the 1960s."

"Well, that's a fascinating story," I said. "But I do feel we're drifting a little off topic."

With a mighty clank, Shuttlewort turned the safe's handle.

"I shall explain further. But first, I require the help of a strapping young man."

At Shuttlewort's direction, and with a fair degree of effort, I swung open the door. Inside sat a small, modern-looking machine, the size of a shoebox. A pencil-shaped probe lay beside it, attached to the machine by a coiled wire. Shuttlewort returned to the workbench, retrieved the empty bottle of '21 Richebourg and placed it upright inside the safe. She took the probe and lowered it into the bottle, until its nose rested in the base.

"Now, if you'd be kind enough to close Herr Krupp, please."

I put my shoulder against the door and heaved it shut. Shuttlewort returned the handle to the locked position and turned her attention to a panel on the side of the safe.

"The safe is airtight. We've attached a pump so we can evacuate the interior atmosphere."

The machine began to emit a low hum.

"It took two weeks of drilling with a diamond-tipped mining drill to make a hole in the side. They broke over a hundred drill bits before they got through. They don't build them like that anymore."

"I'm sure they don't. Now, I know it's a silly question, but why have we just locked an empty bottle of '21 Richebourg in a safe salvaged from a First World War German battleship?"

"There's little danger of mistaking you for a man of science, is there Minstrel Hart?" said Rougegorgefils.

"I confess I'm more on the arts and humanities side, academically speaking, Provost."

"Are you? To be honest, Minstrel Hart, I'd be surprised to

discover you on any side, academically speaking."

"We're checking the bottle for radioactivity," said Shuttlewort. "There's a crust of sediment in the base, so we're testing that too. We'll need to leave it for a few days."

I glanced back at the safe.

"Low-background steel," said Shuttlewort. "In 1945, the first atomic bomb was tested, shortly followed by their use in anger. Then, for the next twenty years, the world's nuclear-armed countries conducted atmospheric nuclear testing, until it dawned on them that it was a bad idea. The upshot is that the Earth's entire atmosphere is now contaminated with low-level radioactivity, which was not present before 1945. And anything that uses oxygen, whether plant, animal or industrial process, is contaminated too."

"Like grapes," I said. "And glass."

Shuttlewort smiled and nodded at the safe.

"Oh. And steel."

"By Jove, he's got it," said Rougegorgefils.

"Exactly," said Shuttlewort. "The only place on Earth where we can conduct this type of measurement is underground, inside an airless box with six-inch-thick metal walls made from steel manufactured before the atomic era. If we detect background radiation from the sample, it means the wine or the bottle are post-1945 and definitely fake. If we don't detect radioactivity, it doesn't mean the sample is genuine, but it does at least suggest it's pre-Second World War. *Danke schön*, Herr Krupp."

A low, warbling noise interrupted our geo-political discussion. For a second, I thought the sound was emanating from Provost Rougegorgefils, until she stood and answered an old-fashioned office phone attached to the wall.

"Very good. Please bring Monsieur Laflamme to Analysis Lab Alpha, thank you."

"Oh, good!" exclaimed Shuttlewort. "He's still in London."

"Yes. If anyone can help us with the '78 Musigny, it's Monsieur Laflamme."

"May I ask who, or what, is Monsieur Laflamme? Some

type of Napoleonic flamethrower, perhaps, to boil the wine into revealing its secrets?"

"Do try to supress your idiocy for a little while longer, Minstrel Hart," said Rougegorgefils.

"Denis Laflamme is the owner of the domaine that makes that wine," said Shuttlewort, pointing at the bottle of Musigny. "Or rather, he's the owner of the domaine that definitely didn't make that wine."

"He's not terribly pleased about the whole situation," muttered Rougegorgefils.

"Surely, he should be flattered," I said. "Imitation being the sincerest form, and all that?"

Rougegorgefils shut her laptop and placed the mouse on top. "I advise you not to venture that opinion within earshot of Monsieur Laflamme. In fact, I advise you not to venture any opinion at all, unless directly instructed, and even then I recommend you write it down first and submit it to me for vetting."

The door opened and a staff-wielding guard showed Monsieur Laflamme into the room. Provost Rougegorgefils rose and directed two air-kisses either side of his face.

"*Bonjour Denis, ça va?*"

"*Madame*, you are the only thing in this savage city that makes it bearable."

Laflamme was a tall man with a neatly clipped white moustache, giving him the air of a recently retired fascist general. He peered briefly at Shuttlewort, shook his head in bewilderment, then turned his attention to me.

"Is this the boy you sent to steal the fakes?"

"That's really supposed to be a secret, actually," I began, but a stare from Rougegorgefils shut me up.

"A secret?" barked Laflamme, moustache quivering. "A secret that I am being robbed and raped in public? I wish it were a secret, boy! A secret dead and buried."

I opened my mouth, intending to provide a conciliatory response, but Rougegorgefils continued to stare at me, quite fiercely, and I closed it.

"Is this it? The pirate juice, the filth, that humiliates eight generations of Laflamme? That urinates without shame upon the *terroir* of *Bourgogne*?"

Laflamme strode over to the bench and snatched up the bottle. Shuttlewort bobbed around wringing her hands and, I must say, it looked odds-on that he was going to hurl the sample across the room. Laflamme scowled at the label and turned puce.

"Devilry!" he shouted, in my direction. It wasn't clear whether I was included in this description, but Rougegorgefils's face made it clear that inviting clarification would be ill-advised.

"Denis, it is beyond generous of you to help us in this matter. We are working closely with the authorities on two continents to identify the counterfeiting ring behind this crime, and we have made excellent progress."

"*Un scandale,*" muttered Laflamme.

"Minstrel Shuttlewort would like to open the bottle so we can analyse the cork. We will carry out an analysis of the wine itself, of course, so we can compare it against a genuine bottle from your domaine."

"Very well. Let your housekeeper open the wine."

"I think that means you," I whispered to Shuttlewort.

"I may only smell it," continued Laflamme. "I'm not sure I can bear to taste it, in case it fouls my throat."

Shuttlewort fetched four sample glasses, then she tugged off the foil capsule and inspected it.

"That came off a little more easily than I expected. Though it doesn't have the creases you find on capsules that have been carelessly removed then replaced. It would be very useful to compare it against an original."

She handed the capsule to Laflamme, who peered at it, shrugged, and tossed it on the bench. Shuttlewort retrieved it and slipped it into a pocket on her lab coat. Then she moved a plate-sized magnifying glass, clamped to the bench via a flexible arm, over the bottle. A ring of tiny bulbs set into the lens's frame suddenly illuminated, flooding the specimen with white light. Shuttlewort peered down through the magnifying glass at the top of the cork.

"No sign of abrasion to the rim of the bottle. Cork is suspiciously clean. No wine egress, which, of course, might just mean it's been well stored. But very little muck or bloom either, which you definitely would expect after all this time. And, wait… yes, there's an indentation near the centre. Very narrow. Too narrow to be caused by a conventional corkscrew. More like a needle."

"An air pressure opener?" asked Rougegorgefils.

"Possibly. Hell of a reckless way to open a bottle like this. Though, silly me, this wouldn't be the bottle they'd opened, of course. But it looks too small for an air pressure device. More like a Coravan." Shuttlewort adjusted the glass slightly. "Aha. Gotcha. Looks like this cork has suffered the attentions of a twin-blade."

"Will we ever taste the wine?" sighed Laflamme.

"Yes, of course," said Shuttlewort. "Just channelling Doctor Locard."

She moved the magnifying glass aside and carefully twisted a waiter's friend into the cork.

"Who's Doctor Locard?" I asked, quietly.

Shuttlewort shook her head. "Never mind. Forensic geek joke."

Very slowly, she levered out the cork.

"Well, they've certainly used a decent quality closure. I can't tell whether it's from '78 without a comparison sample but it's definitely not a new cork."

Shuttlewort positioned the magnifying glass at an angle and slowly rotated the impaled cork.

"There we go. You can just see the indentations on either side of the cork. It's been extracted previously using a twin-blade. There's some printing on the side. *Mise en bouteille au domaine.* Does this look genuine, Monsieur Laflamme?"

Shuttlewort passed the cork and corkscrew to Laflamme, who squinted at it and shook his head.

"Not my cork," he said, and tossed it on the bench.

"Shall I pour?" I asked.

Rougegorgefils nodded. I could sense Laflamme's moustache quivering at me from the other side of the bench. I deposited an inch of red into each of the tasting glasses, slid two of them a little closer to Laflamme and Rougegorgefils, then withdrew.

"Have you ever tasted a genuine '76 from the domaine?" said Laflamme, staring at me.

"No, sir, I have not," I said.

This appeared to please Laflamme. He and Rougegorgefils each lifted their glasses and Shuttlewort and I stepped forward and took the other two. I swirled the glass and inhaled.

Even under the bright, sterile lights of the lab and the utterly non-convivial atmosphere, the wine's aroma transported me back to the tasting at Phantasos. I took a small mouthful and there it was, that melding of power, age, and the sweet memory of youth, perfectly integrated like a sweeping orchestral score.

I watched Laflamme, who was standing completely still, eyes wide open. Only his mouth moved as it interrogated the wine. I took another sip, a larger one. I wondered if they'd let me take the bottle up to the Salon de Dijon when we were done, before remembering that this whole fiasco was supposed to be a secret.

"Well, I think it's still pretty good," I muttered, forgetting that I wasn't supposed to speak.

I glanced at Rougegorgefils, but she and Shuttlewort were transfixed by Laflamme. I followed their gaze and was shocked to see tears running down his cheeks. His glass was empty and he just stared into it, shaking his head. Then, by the movement of his moustache, I realised he was whispering something. The same phrase, over and over.

"*C'est impossible. C'est impossible. C'est impossible.*"

# Chapter 26

# Full House

A working dinner, the guards had called it. That was a complete lie. There were some olives and cornichons in little bowls right at the start, but they were whisked away before I'd consumed half a dozen of each. If I'd known, I'd have ordered an early supper, or at least smuggled in a sourdough bap and a side of wagyu biltong.

The venue was the same small, round room off the Salon de Bordeaux to which I had been summoned by the Provosts a month earlier. The attendees were nearly identical too. Sandra, stern but glowing, as though lit from within by some sensual fire, her hair loosely tied, her suit chic and effortlessly tailored. Quite how I was able to restrain my male gaze from straying into ungallant staring, I cannot say. Sheer, steely willpower, I suppose. Of less visual interest, but greater political importance, were the three Provosts. Each wore their purple cloak, implying a matter of official Institute business was under way. On my left, Provost Rougegorgefils of House Archivist, with whom I was now quite familiar thanks to our shared interest in battling the scourge of wine fraud. Opposite and chatting unctuously to Sandra, Provost Jägermeister of House Mercantilist, as vain and preening as ever. And beside me, to my right, the silver hairs shining in her dreadlocks, Provost Jordaan, head of my own House Terroirist and, I hoped, my protector.

One empty chair remained.

"I assume we're waiting for Inspector Ma?" I said to Sandra.

"Inspector Ma is back in Hong Kong," replied Sandra, and returned to her conversation with Jägermeister.

"We're waiting for Provost Slipcote," said Jordaan. "I know," she added, seeing my eyes widen, "the full Quadrumvirate. Gives you an idea how seriously the Institute's taking it."

The issue did indeed appear serious. I'd barely settled down with a group of fellow Minstrels on the rooftop Terraza Asada, preparing to enjoy the mild, light spring evening over a plate of steak barbacoa and a few glasses of superlative Uruguayan Tannat, when a pair of hatchet-faced guards ambushed me and stated, in no uncertain terms, that I'd been summoned. I hadn't even been permitted to finish my kebab. The guards informed me that dinner would be provided in the Salon de Bordeaux and, before my surprised friends' eyes, whisked me away down to the third floor, though they were kind enough to permit me ten seconds to neck my large glass of Tannat.

"Apologies, fellow Provosts, apologies," boomed a voice from the other side of the curtain.

"Well, there's the veil of secrecy ripped aside and torched to a cinder," sighed Jägermeister.

Provost Slipcote tumbled into the room, his purple cloak distinctly asymmetrical.

"Apologies for keeping you all waiting. Been detained by a painful slog in the House of Lords." He rubbed his mop of white hair.

Lord Slipcote of Brighton and Hove, as he was known in non-Institute circles, was Provost of House Hedonist. His arrival meant that the heads of each of the four Extant Houses, otherwise known as the Quadrumvirate, were now present in our tiny, private dining room.

"The special today is Pauillac lamb shoulder," murmured a waiter, slipping through the curtains. "And the lamprey is in season too."

"Never mind the food," said Jägermeister. "We haven't got time for that. In fact, you can remove these." He waved at the olives, through which I had been making decent progress.

"Oh, that's a shame," said Provost Slipcote. "Quite fancied a little *épaule d'agneau de Pauillac*. Never mind, let's get it over with then. Who's taking notes? Should I call for the Italian Hand?"

"No-one's taking notes," said Jägermeister. "It's too sensitive."

"Oh, blimey, right. And who's this?" asked Slipcote, pointing at Sandra. "You're not a Minstrel, are you? Would have remembered, I'm sure."

"Good evening, Provost. No, I regret I am not a member of the Worshipful Institute. I'm Sandra Filton, a former director of Paris-Blois Brands International, now acting CEO of Paris-Blois Beverages. I'm also the executive lead for the wider group's anti-counterfeiting initiative."

"Paris-Blois have recently restructured, and spun off their fine wine business," said Jägermeister, "a divestment not unrelated to the issue we have gathered to discuss tonight. Is that fair to say, Sandra?"

Sandra nodded, briefly. She didn't look at all happy. Not surprising, really, given that she'd just been promoted to a role that could be described as the world's biggest hospital pass. For Paris-Blois Beverages was the new corporate entity into which the world's most powerful luxury goods firm had recently dumped its fine wine and spirits brands. The public excuse for this break-neck restructure was that Paris-Blois believed its drinks brands would be better managed as a stand-alone entity, and that this strategic divorce from its other luxury goods interests would release a soothing balm of cash to Paris-Blois's shareholders. The real reason, of course, known only to the very highest echelons of Paris-Blois International, plus those sitting around this table, was that the entire ecosystem of fine wine was about to be struck by an extinction-level event from which it would never recover, in the shape of Joseph Lee and his fiendish Project Athena. And that Paris-Blois Beverages, with Sandra at its helm, would shortly be the corporate equivalent of a limbless peasant with bubonic plague.

"Ah, Paris-Blois, I see. Very good. And you," said Slipcote, now pointing at me, "you're Minstrel Hart, aren't you? One of Provost Jordaan's irregulars? I'm told you're some sort of marauding bandit. A *voleur sans frontiers*."

"Sounds about right," said Jägermeister.

"Minstrel Hart is the Institute's key operative in our joint anti-fraud investigation with Paris-Blois," said Provost Jordaan. "He has recently returned from a tasting in Macau where he procured a sample of counterfeit wine."

"Ah, was that the tasting hosted by that dreadful Lee character?"

"Yes, Provost," I said. "Though I think that's supposed to be a secret, isn't it?" I glanced at Sandra, but she didn't respond.

"We don't have time for secrets," said Slipcote. "I believe we're here for an update. Who's doing the updating? Is it you, Provost Jägermeister?"

"No, that will be me," said Rougegorgefils, opening a folder. "In my capacity as head of the Institute's wine fraud action committee."

"Very good, Provost. Please, update away."

"Thank you. Five days ago, Minstrel Hart here returned from a tasting in Macau with a sample of unopened wine, purportedly a 1978 Musigny Grand Cru. We have established beyond doubt that the wine is counterfeit. The label was a highly competent facsimile and the bottle, capsule and closure were recycled, their provenance only detectable by skilled, forensic analysis."

"Right," said Slipcote. "But still detectable."

"The packaging, yes. But it is the liquid itself that gives us the most concern."

"Denis Laflamme himself tasted the wine," said Jägermeister. "Phoned me up the same evening, very upset."

"What was he upset about?" said Slipcote.

"The wine was indistinguishable from the real thing," said Rougegorgefils.

"What, taste them side by side, did you?"

"No, a genuine sample wasn't available at the time," said Rougegorgefils.

"Well, there you go. Perhaps old Laflamme was having a bad

day."

"We subsequently carried out chemical and physical analyses of the fake wine obtained by Minstrel Hart and a genuine wine provided by Monsieur Laflamme. Photometry, gas chromatography, stable isotope ratio analysis."

"Yes, I'm sure it was all very rigorous," said Slipcote, waving her on.

"In every test we ran, the counterfeit and the real wine were absolutely indistinguishable."

"This is a disaster," said Jägermeister. "All our worst fears have come true. This Lee character has the technology to create a fake that can fool every test in the laboratory."

"Worse still," added Jordaan, "a fake that can fool the owner of the estate itself."

"Surely you just need to improve your tests, Provost Rougegorgefils," said Slipcote. "This is an arms race. This Lee chappie's clearly doing something very cunning, we just need to concoct a test that will find him out."

"I'm not sure how you can run a test more rigorous than stable isotope ratio analysis," protested Rougegorgefils.

"Well, perhaps you'd better start looking," said Slipcote.

"That's a ridiculous thing to say! Do you even know what stable isotope ratio analysis is?"

"If I may interrupt," said Sandra. All eyes turned to her. "The issue is not that Mr Lee is creating a fake that fools our tests. It's more fundamental than that. He's creating an exact copy of the wine, identical in every way. Quite simply, his version is the same as the original wine. It's like pouring two glasses from the same bottle. One isn't a copy of the other. It's the same wine."

There was a period of silence.

"Hence Paris-Blois International ringfencing its fine wine business as a separate entity," said Jägermeister. "I've already instructed the chairman of the Institute's investment arm to divest ourselves of any exposed stocks before this gets out."

"Christ, I'd better sell my wine industry shares too," said Slipcote. "Starting with Paris-Blois Beverages. Sounds like you're utterly shafted, my dear."

"Well, thank you for the support," said Sandra. "But before we all lose our heads, I want to make a suggestion. It involves Felix. I mean, Minstrel Hart."

"I think my work here is done, to be honest," I said, as an unpleasant feeling began to stir in my bowels.

"What's your suggestion?" said Jordaan.

"I have been informed that Mr Lee is already planning the next *Cercle Chêne* tasting. It will take place in Shanghai, in three weeks' time."

"Sorry," I said. "I'm busy. Work. Holidays. Lots on."

"We understand via Farquhar Fine & Rare that Minstrel Hart has been invited. This time personally, by Joseph Lee himself."

"Really?" said Jägermeister. "Why on earth has he done that?"

"I understand that Minstrel Hart made an excellent impression on Mr Lee and his guests at the Macau tasting. Something to do with a story about a trip to Burgundy with his father?"

"Oh, yes, that. Just a little anecdote. Anyway, sadly, I can't make it. Sorry."

"It would be extremely helpful if you could," said Sandra, glaring at me.

"But why? I've already burgled Joseph Lee's tasting, at huge personal risk. What's the point in nicking yet another bottle? We know he's dodgy."

"Perhaps you could assassinate him," said Slipcote. "Strangle him with your shoelaces."

"Are you drunk, Provost?" said Rougegorgefils.

"I confess I may have indulged in a little light networking in the Peers' Dining Room," said Slipcote, gazing at the ceiling.

"We don't need to steal any more samples," said Sandra. "Inspector Ma tells me that thanks to Minstrel Hart's efforts in Macau, and the Institute's analysis of the bottles, there is enough evidence for the Shanghai authorities to move against Lee. But Lee is very well connected politically, so they want to catch him in the act of serving the fake wine, and they need someone there at the moment of arrest – someone they trust. Someone who can then give a statement to the police that they were attending what they believed to be a legitimate wine tasting. The other attendees will almost certainly be too embarrassed to do such a thing. And, more to the point, they will be the type of person that the authorities do not wish to see embarrassed."

"So, I have to sit around while the police raid the gaff and everyone else escapes through the back door? I seem to remember doing that once before and it ended badly. Forget it. I'm out. I've done my bit. I've fulfilled your contract, too."

At the mention of my contract, Provost Jordaan turned and frowned at me. I cursed silently.

"Tell me, Sandra," said Jordaan. "Why are the Chinese authorities so fixated on punishing Lee for wine counterfeiting? It's not as if China has a big winemaking industry to protect. You're not telling me they're worried about fake *baijiu*, surely? And I don't buy the story about protecting politicians from embarrassment, either. If they were that bothered, they'd just have a stern word with Joseph Lee and warn him to pack it in."

"I think you're right," said Sandra. "There's definitely something else going on. Inspector Ma hinted that the authorities have been unhappy with Lee for some time. Sounds like he's got too big for his boots. I'm told they're particularly upset that he's floating half his company in New York. Inspector Ma won't elaborate further. I doubt he knows himself."

"Sounds like the poppy's grown too tall," said Slipcote. "Choppy-chop time." He made a horizontal karate motion.

Rougegorgefils closed her eyes and clenched her teeth.

"When you were in Macau, did anyone mention Project Athena?" asked Sandra.

"Yes. It came up one or twice."

"Athena," said Slipcote, ruffling his mop of hair. "The goddess of war and wisdom."

"And the goddess of craft," said Rougegorgefils. "Pottery, weaving, the so-called useful arts."

"I recall a conversation about Lee making things using

artificial intelligence or something. Everyone seemed very excited about it. Mainly about manufacturing pharmaceuticals, I think. But I got the impression Project Athena could be applied to anything."

There was a period of silence as the room mulled this over.

"To be honest, Minstrel Hart, I don't think you have much choice," said Jägermeister. "The Worshipful Institute of the Minstrels of Wine needs you. As does the entire global wine trade, frankly. And, may I remind you that you're obliged by the Minstrels' Code to do anything and everything in your power to protect the Institute."

"Minstrel Hart does have a choice, actually," said Jordaan. "I don't think this mission is entirely without risk."

"But he's got the confidence of both Lee and the Chinese authorities," said Jägermeister. "What could possibly go wrong? And, more pertinently, who the hell else is going to do it?"

"Let's allow Minstrel Hart to retire to dinner so the four of us can discuss this ourselves," said Jordaan. "Sandra, thank you for briefing us."

"My pleasure," said Sandra, rising. "I'm sure I can count on your absolute discretion in this matter."

"Of course, of course," said Jägermeister.

I followed Sandra out through the curtains. We crossed the floor of the Salon de Bordeaux, the diners around us feasting on oysters, duck breast, and foie gras. At the door, she stopped and turned. I leaned forward for the first of, I assumed, a pair of air-kisses. But Sandra jabbed a finger into my chest.

"Get your lazy, cowardly arse to Shanghai, Felix, do you understand? You're on the hook for a million dollars. Be in absolutely no doubt – if you attempt to wriggle out of this, I will bankrupt you, I will fillet you and I will leave your corpse strung up beneath London Bridge while the pigeons peck out your eyes. Do you understand?"

I confess I didn't feel much like dinner after that.

# Chapter 27

## Tax Haven

"Mr Hart, hi. James here from your Luxe Premier Banking Team. How are you today?"

"Ah, hello." I glanced around the Gatesave office, checking no-one was within earshot. I needn't have worried, there were barely a dozen people on the entire floor.

"Yes, Mr Hart, just following up on a few things you asked us to take care of."

"Go ahead."

"Ok, great. Firstly, just checking you're happy with our Global Executive Assistant service and that you'd like to continue with it?"

"Definitely," I said.

The Global Executive Assistant service was an absolute delight. All the tiresome administration of bookings, insurance and the rigmarole of hauling bags around on the airport express had been banished. My luggage was now collected from my home or the hotel, there were courtesy cars to and from the airport, and invariably a charming person waiting at check-in to help you jump the queue at security. Restaurant bookings were arranged for me at the most sought-after new openings – whether in London, Paris, or Hong Kong – and on one occasion they even couriered a phone charger to me in Bologna, within the hour, after I left mine on the train. If you have the means, I thoroughly recommend the service.

"Delighted to hear it. We've made the third payment on the ski property in Cervinia, and the agents have confirmed receipt of the funds. The final payment is due next month, on completion."

I'd invested in a rather smart little two-bedroom chalet in the centre of Cervinia, less than two hundred metres from the gondola up to Plan Maison. No more scrabbling around trying to find accommodation for a last-minute ski break. And a nice little earner if I decided to hire it out, too, though if working from home was genuinely here to stay, I'd be basing myself in the Alps for the first three months of every year. Far preferable to dark, drizzly London.

"Our realtor team have confirmed we exchanged on the London property yesterday. We'll transfer the deposit and the funds to cover the stamp duty into our conveyancing account at the end of the week, so it's all ready to go."

A house. Yes, you heard it right. An actual house, with stairs, in fashionable Brixton. Bit of a financial stretch, that one, but a combination of a whacking great cash deposit, selling my tiny flat in Harringay, and an extremely benevolent affordability assessment from the Luxe Premier Banking mortgage team, meant I'd secured a loan large enough to pole-vault my way up the property ladder.

"A few other things. Our legal team is still waiting for some information so they can re-draft your Paris-Blois contract. They've asked me when they might receive that?"

"Actually, don't worry, you can stand them down. I've resolved the issue."

"Oh, I see. If you're sure. Was there an issue with the advice you received from our client legal advisor?"

"No, no, Amrita's advice was excellent, thank you. It's just that events have overtaken, erm, other events and so we can forget all about that contract. Thank you."

"Not a problem. Couple of smaller things. Our pensions team will be in touch shortly regarding a long-term savings plan. You'll receive an invitation to a crypto investment seminar at a spa hotel in Riga, if you're interested. And, finally, our tax team have completed your tax return for last financial year."

The last bit sounded a bit dull, but the sheer quality of my Luxe Premier Banking service had given me a warm glow, and the thought of my elevation to the international property-owning classes had put me in a better mood than I'd felt for months, despite Sandra's malevolent threats.

"Jolly good. Anything else?"

"Yes, you'll need to pay HMRC three hundred and forty-eight thousand pounds."

"Sorry, I beg your pardon?"

"Three hundred and forty-eight thousand pounds. That's your tax liability for last year. You don't have to pay it until the end of January, of course. But you'll want to accrue for it, I imagine."

My throat suddenly felt very dry.

"Why, what? Sorry, I mean, what is that? And why has it happened?"

"It's the income tax on your, well, income, Mr Hart. You may recall that you received nearly eight hundred thousand pounds at the end of the last tax year, in addition to your Gatesave salary. You're liable for the top rate on that, of course."

"I don't actually have to pay that, do I?"

"Well, yes, His Majesty's Revenue tends to insist on it."

"But I can't just be charged a massive amount of money for no reason. Surely tax has been deducted already?"

"The money was transferred in Hong Kong dollars from a company in a different jurisdiction, Mr Hart. It wouldn't have been on PAYE. It's not like your Gatesave salary."

"Can't you put it in a tax haven or something? Jersey or Panama or somewhere like that?"

"I'm sorry, that's not really how it works."

"But that's ridiculous! What's the point of all this Luxe Premier Banking if you can't take care of something as simple as tax?"

"We did offer to set up a limited company for the funds, My Hart. You wouldn't have had to pay income tax on it then."

"There you go, then! Why don't you do that? It's not too late, surely?"

"No, it's not too late to set up an LLC. But you have actually already spent the money, so…"

"So what if I've spent it? Does that matter?"

"Well, you can't just spend a company's money on yourself. You could pay yourself a salary or dividends from the company. But then you'd still have to pay tax."

"Expenses! It's all company expenses! That's tax deductible. I shouldn't have to tell you that, surely?"

"Corporate tax isn't really my speciality, Mr Hart, but I don't think they'll let you buy a house and a ski chalet with company funds. Or have fifty thousand pounds' worth of fine wine delivered to your home. The authorities tend to be quite strict about that kind of thing."

"It feels as though you're presenting me with a lot of problems and no solutions, James. I mean, what do I pay you for?"

"I'm sorry Mr Hart. Maybe some of the travel and meals could be charged as expenses."

"How much money's in my account?"

"After the property transactions, just under eighteen thousand pounds."

"And how much do I owe?"

"Three hundred and forty-eight thousand pounds."

"Right. Good. Goody-good."

I must say, the money did appear to have whittled itself away a little faster than I expected. No wonder all those premier league footballers go bankrupt as soon as they retire.

"I'd like to enquire about an overdraft facility."

"We can certainly consider an overdraft application, Mr Hart. You would need to be confident regarding your ability to repay, of course."

"Yes, of course. I'm extremely confident about that."

There was a somewhat awkward pause.

"Can I help with anything else, Mr Hart?"

"No, I think that's everything. Thanks for the update."

I hung up and put my head in my hands.

\*\*\*

"Thank you for responding so promptly."

Provost Jordaan stepped on to the balcony at the far end of the Top Garden, part of the private realm open only to members of House Terroirist. The guard who had escorted me turned and disappeared into the shadows between the lavender bushes. Jordaan surveyed the constellation of lights illuminating London's West End, the silver hairs that ran through her dreadlocks glittering. I followed her gaze; the floodlights on the Royal Opera House, the winking theatre signs, the red lights atop the developers' cranes. Occasionally, a distant shout or peal of laughter would carry up from the streets of Covent Garden. The evening was mild, but ten storeys up the breeze was persistent and still carried a whisper of spring chill. I buttoned my jacket.

"So, Minstrel Hart. To Shanghai next week."

I wasn't sure if it was a question or a statement.

"Yes, I thought I should, after all."

"You thought you should. Your choice, then, was it?"

I remained silent. Usually, in situations like this, lying is the best policy. But Provost Jordaan was the head of my House and I was under her protection. And, in fairness, she had helped me out on several occasions in the past when I was in a fair degree of peril. So you could say I owed her my loyalty. More pertinently still, she wasn't stupid.

"How is your relationship with Sandra at Paris-Blois, Minstrel Hart?"

"Oh, I try to keep her at arm's length," I said.

"That's your choice again, is it? Difficult to believe, given the way you gaze at her."

I prayed Jordaan couldn't see my cheeks burning in the darkness.

"Actually, I'm more interested in the contract you referred to at our meeting yesterday with the other Provosts."

"Ah, yes. Paris-Blois are paying me to help with the anti-fraud investigation."

"How much are they paying you?"

I paused, feeling a little stupid.

"How much, Minstrel Hart? This is important."

"One million US dollars."

Jordaan gasped and turned to look at me.

"Good Lord. What do they expect you to do for that? Steal a cruise missile?"

"Just attend the tasting, nick the odd bottle, and complete the anti-fraud project to their satisfaction."

"Did you sign anything?"

"Yes. There's a contract."

"I hope you asked a lawyer to look at it."

"Yes, I did," I said, miserably.

"One million dollars. Did it occur to you that that's very generous remuneration for attending a wine tasting? Even if you did have to steal a bottle."

"Yes, it did strike me as a bit toppy. But it's a consortium of multi-national brand owners who've stumped up the cash. I don't think they're short of a bob or two."

"I'm sure they're not. I'm not saying you're naïve, Minstrel Hart, but do you honestly think they're going to pay you?"

"Oh, they've paid me already."

"What? You're telling me there's a million dollars from Paris-Blois sitting in your bank account, right now?"

"Well, a touch under one million now, but yes."

Jordaan turned back to the view over the West End and thought for a while.

"And are you in the habit of being paid millions of dollars by multi-national consortia? I mean, does this sort of thing happen to you often?"

"No, Provost. It's the first time."

"Sounds a bit fishy, doesn't it?"

"Yes. I suppose it does."

"Still, at least you got the money. But then, I don't think you'd have gone if they hadn't paid you, would you?"

"Definitely not."

"So, they're clearly very keen for you to go. But why you, Minstrel Hart? Provost Jägermeister could have sent any one of his well-groomed fine wine experts."

"Well, Sandra and I have a history of working together. I suppose they think I'm the kind of person who'll get the job done."

"I'm sure they're right. The question is, what job?"

I remained silent.

"Minstrel Hart." Jordaan lowered her voice. "This is now a Malherbes operation. Do you understand?"

My bowels gave a twitch of alarm. I did understand, of course. The Malherbes were a secret group within House Terroirist, entrusted with highly sensitive projects. Secret, because those projects frequently involved inquiries into the antics of powerful institutions whose sense of morality was, to put it politely, untroubled by a moral compass. Sensitive, because such enquiries sometimes involved fellow members of the Worshipful Institute of the Minstrels of Wine.

"Yes, Provost, I understand."

I understood better than most. For I was a member of the Malherbes myself. Not through firm-chinned enthusiasm, I hasten to add, but more as a result of devious press-ganging, though that's another story for another time.

Jordaan handed me a purse made of heavy fabric.

"There's a phone in there. The microphone, speakers and cameras have been disconnected so it's harder to compromise the handset and turn it into a bugging device. Obviously, that means you can't use it to make calls, only to send messages or access the internet. The bag is a Faraday pouch, made of woven metal fibres. Keep the phone inside it when you're not using it."

"Why do I need another phone?"

"There's a single contact in the address book. Use the encrypted messaging app to inform us of any important developments. Don't use your own phone, it may not be secure. Make sure you send a message at least once every evening, even if it's just to tell us you're ok. Try not to forget, or we'll think something's happened to you. It may also come in useful if you lose your other phone. So, don't carry it around the whole time.

Keep it in the pouch, locked away and switched off."

"When you say you'll think something's happened to me, what sort of thing did you have in mind?"

Jordaan turned and looked out over the city. She brushed her hand against the lavender bush beside her and the air filled with perfume. "Beautiful," she murmured. "The first lavender of summer."

"Right," I said, putting on a brave face despite the conversation's descent into rather dramatic skulduggery. "I'll set an alarm so I don't forget."

Jordaan turned back to me.

"Minstrel Hart. You have knowledge that could gain or lose people a great deal of money. Be careful. Don't reveal any information that you don't need to. Understand?"

"I shall be extremely careful, Provost."

"I mean it. Hold your tongue. And trust nobody."

# Chapter 28

## Stepping Stone

Direct flights between London and Shanghai had been suspended for some time, on account of war, plague and pestilence. Instead, Sandra instructed me to fly to Hong Kong and travel on to Shanghai a day or so later. She also told me to meet Adam Fromage at Farquhar Fine and Rare as soon as I arrived in town. I was assured that Inspector Ma would make the necessary arrangements with the authorities and, sure enough, after another near-deserted flight I glided through Hong Kong immigration without a hitch. After collecting my lonely bag from the carousel, I linked up with my driver, courtesy of my Luxe Premier Banking's Global Executive Assistant.

The airport express would have halved the journey time into the city, but the wooded hills of Lantau and the view crossing the Tsing Ma bridge were far superior sights to the interior of an MTR carriage. And why forgo a limousine, complete with drinks and nibbles, when it's on the house? I instructed my driver to take the Western Tunnel to Hong Kong Island and straight to Fromage's office in Wan Chai.

It was only as I opened the limousine's door and stepped on to the pavement that the warm fug of traffic fumes and fermenting fish embraced me, and I realised I'd been in an air-conditioned bubble since Heathrow, some fourteen hours ago. I paused for a minute, letting the warmth permeate my bones, then crossed Hennessy Road and entered the frigid reception of Farquhar Fine and Rare.

"Felix, old chap. How are you? How's the jet lag?"

Same strong, dry handshake. Flash of red silk from the

breast pocket.

"Better than last time, Adam, thank you. Trust you're well too?"

"Surviving, though God knows how."

Fromage appeared to be alone. No sign of his beautiful assistant, which was a shame.

"Business a bit tricky, then?" I asked, easing myself into an armchair.

"Tricky's one word for it. It's been up and down like the proverbial whore's drawers for the past few years. At least they've stopped those bloody students smashing the place up."

"What, the democracy ones?"

Fromage rolled his eyes. "Democracy? Spare me. There's never been a shred of democracy in Hong Kong, and it's all the healthier for it. You ever been to Manila?"

"Can't say I have."

"Wouldn't bother. Awful hole. That's what this place would look like if the British had given it democracy. Drug gangs machine-gunning each other on every street corner, a brothel every ten yards, and the locals pissing away every cent betting on the next cockfight."

"I see."

I made a mental note to visit Manila at some point. I suspected that anything Fromage disliked must have something going for it.

"If the British thought democracy was a bad idea for Hong Kong," continued Fromage, "why on earth should the Chinese think any different?"

"It's a generational thing, I suppose."

Fromage scowled.

"No offence. Not suggesting you're old," I said, accompanied by a winning smile.

"No offence taken. You're probably right. Connie left last month, just like that. Didn't even have the decency to give me a month's notice. Her brother was some sort of agitator at the University of Hong Kong. Setting fire to MTR stations, that sort of thing. The pair of them did a runner to London before the authorities could pick him up. Chinese should shut the bloody British consulate down. They're spraying those BNO visas around like confetti. They'll empty the city at this rate."

"Oh. Perhaps I should look her up, check she's ok."

"Wouldn't bother. Silly cow. Who the hell decides to move to London, anyway? Dreadful place. No offence."

"None taken," I said.

"Anyway, enough politics, old chap. You obviously did a good number on Joseph Lee back in Macau. Sounds as though he likes you."

"Yes, so I heard."

"Well, I hope you don't suffer from vertigo. The next *Cercle Chêne* tasting's at the top of the Shanghai Tower. That's double the height of the Empire State Building."

"Do you have a list of what's being tasted?"

"Afraid not. I don't know a thing about it, other than the venue, and I only know that because Lee's people reached out to me to find you. I assume they're not tasting Burgundy. If they are, they're using another importer, which would be extremely irritating. You'll let me know, I'm sure."

"Of course."

"And I hear you managed to pinch a full bottle from Macau. Damn cunning of you. How did you wangle that?"

Feeling a touch smug, I nearly threw in that I'd stolen not one but two bottles, but I recalled Provost Jordaan's warning not to reveal anything unless necessary.

"Wasn't that difficult. I just waited until everyone's back was turned."

"Fancy that. Clever you. Now, sorry to rush you, but it's Wednesday evening and I have a hot tip in the 7:15 at Happy Valley. Look, I'm supposed to give you this."

Fromage handed me a small Samsung phone and charger.

"It's from Joseph Lee's people. In case they need to call you before the tasting. It's a secure device. Apparently, he refuses to call anyone on an unsecured handset, especially a foreign

222

one. You won't be able to use the phone for anything other than receiving calls from Lee or his people, so don't try to watch any porn on it or anything like that. And don't leave it in a taxi or get drunk and drop it off the side of the Star Ferry, will you?"

"I'll try not to."

"And you will remember that the tasting, the venue and the attendees are absolutely confidential, won't you? So far as Lee's people are concerned, I've contacted you directly and no-one else knows. Not that Sandra woman, nor your Minstrel friends, let alone the authorities. So, don't tell a soul, got it? Otherwise I'll be in the doghouse."

"Got it. Oh, and this is yours."

I unzipped my bag and withdrew the 1960s vineyard atlas of the Côte d'Or that Fromage had given me before Macau.

"Ah, thank you. Was going to ask about that. Do you have that leather bag I lent you too?"

"Apologies. I'm afraid I left that in London. Very stupid of me. I'll be back in Hong Kong before too long."

In fact, the bag was so knackered I'd dumped it in my hotel room bin as soon as I'd returned from Macau. God knows what room service had thought. The wretched thing looked like the victim of an amateur voodoo ritual.

"Good stuff. Well, enjoy Shanghai. Make sure you've got a good supply of face masks. They take all that nonsense quite seriously up there."

Exercising an iron will, I limited myself to a single glass of Riesling with my dinner, even though I felt like hitting the town. But I needed to be on top of my game and I'd learned by now that Tsingtao beer and jet lag are unfriendly bedfellows. Back at the hotel, I flicked on the Do Not Disturb light, powered up Provost Jordaan's secret phone and selected Contacts. Sure enough, there was only one entry, named Teasel. I tapped out my message:

*Arrived Hong Kong. Met Fromage. Cercle Chêne tasting Saturday at Shanghai Tower.*

I pressed send. A minute later, the phone replied.

*Acknowledged. Proceed with caution.*

On that brief and barely reassuring note, I decided to turn in for the night.

I slept until midday. After a light dim sum lunch, I strolled through Tsim Sha Tsui to Gatesave's global sourcing office, keeping my pace slow to avoid working up a sweat in the savage humidity. I had arranged a meeting with Tabatha Shunt, in case Gatesave's monitoring systems noticed I'd been failing to clock-in to the London office and decided to grass me up to HR. I ascended to the fourteenth floor and Tabatha waved me into her glass-fronted corner office.

"Breeze on in, sweet cheeks."

I did as I was told. There were no other seats, so I hovered in front of her desk, which was covered with framed pictures of her partying with groups of affluent-looking people in various resorts, restaurants and nightclubs.

"Right, when do our customers get their nice, dry buttocks on those splashback-proof loo seats?" she demanded.

"The containers land in the UK next week, Tabatha. They should be on sale the week after. I know they're slightly late, but we've had a few delays at the Port of Guangzhou."

"They'd better be on sale soon. Otherwise it's spanking time!"

Tabatha Shunt patted her leg and gurned, giving me the impression that she would consider the application of corporal punishment a quite agreeable consolation prize in the event of further supply chain disruption. I glanced at the door, checking it was still open in case I needed to make a sudden dash for the exit.

"I'm confident we're on track. The spider catchers arrive on the same boat. I think they'll sell well too."

"Good. Tell me, have you heard from Charles Fung?"

My heart missed a beat.

"No… I've only dealt with his team recently. Why do you ask? Is he ok?"

"I don't know. He's not been in touch. He cancelled the last Pinot Pimpernels session too. Quite unlike him."

*Perhaps he's dead*, I thought. *Perhaps his heart gave up after all the trauma, poor bugger. Still, at least the murder weapon's done a runner. No way they can pin that on me.*

"Perhaps he's on holiday," I said, brightly.

"Perhaps. Now, remind me again, how is it that you're able to swan in and out of Hong Kong? The only other person I know who can do that is the CEO of Goldman Sachs."

"Oh, it's that wine institute that I represent. The authorities granted me a special waiver when I brought those samples."

"I was talking to a friend who works for Hong Kong Immigration Service. He said there's no way they'd just let in some fancy wine taster, with or without samples."

"I'm not pretending to know how it works," I said, a trickle of sweat running down my back. "The wine institute has a Chapter here in Hong Kong and lots of high-up people are members."

"Can I join, then? I like wine."

"Yes, of course. Though there's an exam. And the tutorials involve drinking a lot of red wine."

"Won't bother, then. Can't bear red wine. And talking of wine, you'd better not have forgotten about our Shenzhen store opening on Monday. You're hosting a little tasting for us as part of the marketing festivities."

"No, of course I hadn't forgotten."

I had forgotten. What an idiot. I'd been hoping to travel to Macau on Monday and visit Kaia, though she hadn't replied to my last couple of messages. Shenzhen would be a chore, but at least it meant I could charge my flights to Gatesave expenses now that I was looking after the pennies again.

"Good. Grand opening is at ten a.m., assuming there's no new lockdown or other disaster, so make sure you're in town the night before. Just stand around and look handsome for the opening, then the PR team have organised your wine tasting for midday. Around thirty attendees, a few tame journos plus a bunch of local influencers. One of them has over a million Weibo followers. Shenzhen Yummy, he calls himself. Apparently, he's a complete arsehole."

"Great, can't wait to meet him."

"That's the spirit. There's a party in the evening too. You should wear a tight-fitting shirt. Any other plans while you're here? Fancy a few Friday evening drinks at Felix, Felix?"

Tabatha gurned again.

"I'm terribly sorry. I'm in Shanghai on a mini-break this weekend."

"Fine, suit yourself. Don't forget to pack your face masks."

# Chapter 29

## Shanghai

As I emerged from arrivals at Shanghai Pudong airport, surgical face mask deployed, I was dismayed to find that my Luxe Premier Banking Global Executive Assistant had let me down. Of the scrum of masked drivers surrounding the exit gate, not one held an iPad bearing my name and, after questioning everyone who looked even vaguely like a chauffeur, it appeared no-one had been issued with instructions to collect me. Eventually, my interrogation of random uniformed flunkies began to attract the attention of the authorities, and I marched briskly to the airport express.

Minutes later I was hurtling towards Shanghai on the Transrapid maglev, the doorway display boasting my 431 km/hour velocity through the lush farmland of Pudong. An impressive feat of engineering, though a Japanese friend later informed me that a much faster service would open soon between Tokyo and Nagoya – which just goes to show that however hard you try, there's always someone just around the corner preparing to piss on your chips.

A short time later, I emerged from the metro into the brown haze of Shanghai. The cooler spring months had by now surrendered to the oppressive mugginess of summer, the yellow, overcast sky trapping the sour air against the ground like an unwashed blanket. The streets were dense with slow-moving traffic. I marched to my hotel, a smart boutique place on the Bund, a little too quickly. By the time I reached it, my shirt was wringing with sweat, the fabric sticking grimly to my back. The hotel doors parted and the air-conditioning hit me like a blast of cold water.

After my limousine let-down, I was pleased to find that my hotel reservation at least was in order. I retired to the restaurant, which boasted a magnificent view of the Bund, and ordered myself a Shanghainese banquet. I fired off a brief note of complaint via my Global Executive Assistant app, ordered a half-bottle of chilled Manzanilla to accompany my dish of drunken crab, then turned my thoughts to tomorrow's tasting. *Le Cercle Chêne* would be taking place in a private dining room at the Heavenly Jin restaurant, on the 120th floor of the Shanghai Tower. The venue was visible from my very seat; a flattened, twisted, aluminium cigar rising from the jumble of mere skyscrapers on the far side of the river, its top storeys swimming in Shanghai's photochemical haze. Nearby stood its two smaller sisters: the Shanghai World Financial Centre, looking for all the world like a half-mile-high beer opener, and the more orientally shaped Jinmao Tower, once China's tallest building but now a distant third.

Unlike my evening at Phantasos, I had no insight into the wines being tasted. I'd dropped a note to Sandra that afternoon, just before my flight, asking whether she'd received any last-minute insight into the line-up, but her only information regarding the tasting had come via Fromage, and she claimed to be as ignorant as me. So, what exactly was my intended role at the Shanghai leg of *Le Cercle Chêne*? Being fabulous company would be part of it, no doubt, but I was suspicious of the idea that I'd been invited to Lee's tasting purely for my wit and wisdom. On the other hand, given the travel restrictions recently re-imposed due to the resurgent wave of infections, it was quite possible that I was the only international wine authority, charming or otherwise, still able to negotiate Chinese immigration. I wondered whether Kaia had been invited. I hoped so. For a moment, I considered messaging her, but I remembered Fromage's plea of confidentiality, not to mention Provost Jordaan's warnings, and thought better of it. I pulled out the phone Fromage had given me, checking for the hundredth time that day whether I'd missed a call from Lee or his minions. So far as I could tell, I had not.

Perhaps I'd be asked to blind taste and identify the wines before the assembled guests, like a performing chimp. Wines, presumably, that Lee had cooked up the night before in one of his high-tech labs. Perhaps I was some kind of perverse quality control, to test the quality of his fakes. At the Phantasos tasting last month, I gained the distinct impression that Lee knew damn well that I knew his wines were counterfeit. But why would Lee invite me if he knew that I was on to him? Perhaps this was how international criminal masterminds behaved. Perhaps Lee was incapable of passing up the opportunity to pit his wits against a worthy rival, despite the risk of exposure. Then again, perhaps it was a trap and his henchmen would simply hurl me from the top of the Shanghai Tower as soon as I showed my face. I gazed across the river at the great tube of metal twisting into the haze. It would take a very long time to fall all that way. Quite enough time to regret having ever got involved in such an idiotic caper.

My thoughts were interrupted by a masked waiter removing the remains of my drunken crab. It was replaced by a bowl of delicious-smelling pork meatballs surrounded by ginger-scented pak choi. I ordered a bottle of Central Otago Pinot Noir and tapped out a message on Jordaan's special phone.

*Arrived in Shanghai. Assume tasting tomorrow evening.*

A minute's pause and Jordaan's phone issued its reply.

*Acknowledged. Proceed with caution.*

I wondered whether the Malherbes were actually reading my messages or whether they'd all headed down the pub and set up an out-of-office reply. I considered my options. There appeared to be just two. First, attend the tasting and pray the police turned up before anyone decided to introduce me to the sport of base-jumping *sans* parachute. Second, run away, immediately. Catch a flight to Hong Kong then another back to London. Refuse to answer any calls from Sandra and pray she'd forgotten about the million dollars and her threat to sue me and string me up.

But the second scenario, or the idea that Sandra would let me off the hook for anything, was inconceivable. And I'd already committed to a rather marvellous house in fashionable south

London, not to mention a sexy little chalet in Cervinia. I've never thought of myself as an avaricious person but, by God, I wanted that house. And I wanted that chalet, too. I imagined myself bumping, by complete chance, into Sandra on the Italian side of the Plateau Rosa next season, her hair bleached blond by the Alpine sun and her legs encased in designer skiwear, and us ending up drinking *Glühwein* in the shadow of the Matterhorn. All of a sudden, we'd realise that the afternoon had disappeared and that she had barely five minutes to catch the final lift back over the pass to Zermatt. It would be touch-and-go whether she'd make it. Then, I'd casually mention that I had a modest little chalet down in the village – with two bedrooms, naturally – and why risk an accident when you could spend the evening in Cervinia and catch the first lift out in the morning?

Now, replace that scenario with one where I'm forced to reveal that I'm sharing a self-catering apartment with four middle-aged Germans who've economised on eating out by carting a suitcase of home-made garlic sausage all the way from Dittersdorf. You'll understand, I'm sure, that despite the danger, I had no choice but to proceed with scenario one.

\*\*\*

I awoke the next morning to the sound of an unfamiliar ringtone. It was Lee's phone, vibrating its way across the glass top of my bedside table. Within a second, I was wide awake.

"Hello?"

"Hello. Is this Mr Hart?"

A Chinese voice, heavily accented. Not Lee.

"Yes. This is Mr Hart speaking."

"You are in Shanghai, Mr Hart?"

"Yes, I'm in a hotel on the Bund."

"*Le Cercle Chêne*, Mr Hart."

"Yes? Is it still on?"

"Please present yourself at the Reception desk for Heavenly Jin restaurant in the Shanghai Tower at five p.m. Seventeen hundred hours."

"Yes, I understand. Five p.m. That's a touch earlier than my previous instructions, but fine, I'll be there. Actually, I was wondering, any chance of an insight into the wines we're tasting? So I can do a little research? You know, add a little context for my fellow guests, for entertainment purposes?"

But there was no response. The line was dead.

Conscious of how I'd ended up slightly tipsy at the Macau tasting, I prepared my stomach for the forthcoming assault with a hearty lunch of fried noodles. I was now a little on edge. The thought of hanging around the hotel killing time for another two hours didn't appeal, so I decided to set out for the Shanghai Tower straight away, despite the likelihood of arriving ludicrously early. I dispatched a message on Jordaan's phone.

*Have been summoned to Cercle Chêne at Heavenly Jin Shanghai Tower 5pm*

*Acknowledged. Proceed with caution.*

Wonderful. How helpful. I tucked Jordaan's handset back into its Faraday pouch, locked it in the safe and headed down to the river. I strolled the length of the Bund in the sticky heat, keeping my pace slow to avoid breaking into a torrential sweat. The air was thick and soupy and I could feel the pollution catching the back of my throat. I paused for a moment and watched the vast freight barges pushing their way down the muddy Huangpu. Then I joined the queue of masked pedestrians waiting to board one of the ferries to the Pudong side.

Even before the vessel reached the opposite bank, I became conscious of the Shanghai Tower's unworldly size. I'm no country bumpkin, but the structure looked plucked from a different planet, one impossibly vaster than our own, and thrust down beside the river without any thought to scale or balance. I still had a fifteen-minute walk ahead of me before I reached the tower's entrance, but the building's height was far greater than my distance from its base. I imagined the tower slowly toppling towards me as I realised I had no chance of outrunning it, even by commandeering a vehicle and driving as fast as possible in the opposite direction. I swallowed my dread and marched grimly towards the entrance.

I found myself in a glass atrium the size of a cathedral. The space was nearly deserted, barely a dozen people visible in the football field-sized reception. A woman in a smart purple suit and cotton face mask approached me, looking slightly alarmed.

"Please, can I help you, sir?"

"Oh, don't worry. I'm here for an appointment. But I'm very early."

"Yes, sir," she replied, nodding.

There was something strange about the woman's manner, as though rather than arriving ridiculously early for my appointment, I was actually late.

"The event is at five p.m., but I didn't want to be late," I said, glancing at my watch. Sure enough, I was nearly two hours early.

"Yes, very early," said the woman. "It is not open."

"What's not open?"

"Yes, the appointment," said the woman, and gave a little laugh behind her hand.

"Heavenly Jin?" I said, attempting to rescue things.

"Yes, Heavenly Jin," agreed the woman. "Very early."

I was led, peculiarly slowly, to the rear of the atrium, where a bank of gold elevators shone brightly from the marble-clad wall. An odd little lectern stood next to the wall beside the nearest elevator. As we approached it, a woman in a paper face mask rushed in on clattering heels and stationed herself behind it.

"Hello," I said. "Now, look. I'm aware that I'm extremely early."

The woman stared at me as if I'd announced I was a stripper about to perform at the opening session of the Communist Party Central Committee.

"I could just hang around in the atrium if you're not ready. It's really no problem."

This suggestion appeared to cause even more confusion. The two women conducted a hurried discussion in Mandarin until the elevator doors beside the concierge's lectern slid open.

You might suggest that it's only with hindsight I realised the entire situation was rather fishy. But I can assure you, even by the intensely polite and awkward standards of Chinese hospitality, both women's behaviour was distinctly strange.

"You can go in the elevator," said the first woman, pointing to the lift.

"Right. Don't you need to check my name or anything?"

The women looked incredulous.

"Don't worry, doesn't matter," I said.

I entered the lift, followed by the first woman. And it is only really with hindsight that all the strange little things that happened next made sense. The fact that as I glanced back at the concierge point, I noticed that the lectern held no screen, tablet, or even a paper diary. The fact that the woman touched the button marked Heavenly Jin, floor 120, but it didn't light up. That a rather stocky man with a wispy beard protruding from beneath his face mask, talking quietly in Mandarin on a mobile phone, stepped into the lift and pressed another button which did light up. That he then positioned himself rather awkwardly behind me when there was still plenty of room in the lift. And that the woman stepped out of the lift just before the doors began to close, and strode away across the atrium without saying another word.

The impressively rapid lift stopped at the thirtieth or fortieth floor, or whatever number the man had pressed. The doors slid open to reveal two even stockier, wispy-bearded men, also wearing face masks. I recall wondering whether there was some kind of Mongolian wrestling convention in town. I stood aside to let the man on the phone out, only to find my arms pinned very firmly to my sides by some kind of vice. One of the men in front of me stepped forward and pressed what looked like a folded-up pocket umbrella into my stomach. I experienced an intense feeling of pins and needles, as though a beehive had erupted inside me, followed by horrible, painful cramps in my legs, arms and neck. I then found myself being carried down a corridor like a shop mannequin, through a doorway, and dumped on a hard sofa that smelled of lemons. I felt something cold against my neck, followed by a sharp hiss, as if a fizzy drink had been opened beside my ear. After that, I remember nothing.

# Chapter 30

## Project Athena

"Most interesting," said the wispy-bearded man. "You have regained consciousness two hours earlier than one would have expected given your anthropometric measurements."

He removed his fingers from the side of my neck and straightened up.

"How do you speak like that without opening your mouth?" I slurred.

"You will experience mild disorientation for the next ten minutes," continued the man, who was clearly some kind of high-end ventriloquist. "Though perhaps a little less. You appear to have an unusually high metabolic rate."

"You haven't even parted your lips," I said. "Are you famous? I recognise your voice."

The man stepped back and vanished from my field of vision.

"Your cognitive function is normalising extremely rapidly," said his voice. "This also perhaps explains your ability to ingest large quantities of alcohol with relatively mild motor impairment."

"Lee," I said. "You're Mr Lee."

"Welcome to my Neural Terror Factory, Mr Hart. The home of Project Athena."

"Terror factory?" I said, my heart rate rising. "That doesn't sound very nice!"

"Terafactory, Mr Hart. Tera. Ten to the power of twelve. Or, more appositely, given the context of Project Athena, two raised to the fortieth power."

I had not the slightest idea what Lee was gabbling on about.

But I was comforted by the clarification that I was not, after all, detained in a terror factory. In fact, I found myself reclining in an extremely comfortable chair, the seat of which was woven from a strange, silver mesh. Before me lay a huge glass table the size of a putting green, perfectly round and just millimetres thick. To my astonishment, the table had no visible legs, appearing to float unsupported above the floor. Then I spotted the slender stem of crystal, no thicker than my wrist, rising from the table's centre into a brightly lit void in the domed glass ceiling.

I turned to my left. Joseph Lee, too, was seated at the table, though some way away; at the nine o'clock position compared to my six o'clock. He wore a tight, silk mask over his nose and mouth. He looked even younger in real life than on the screen in Macau, almost impossibly smooth-skinned, his hair close-cropped and unstyled, like that of a child. He brought his palms together, as if to pray.

"Is this where we're having *Le Cercle Chêne*?"

"*Le Cercle Chêne* took place last night, Mr Hart. You performed most satisfactorily."

My eyes began to focus more clearly. The room, which was only a little wider than the table, was shaped like a bell jar, the walls a seamless curve of glass without any obvious entrance. The floor beneath me was transparent, too, and we appeared to be suspended several hundred feet above the ground. I gazed down. Below us lay a vast expanse of deserted, open-plan office stretching as far as I could see, furnished with what looked like large and precisely spaced white desks. Only a few areas of the floor were lit, creating islands of cold blue light surrounded by an ocean of darkness. I felt a twinge of nausea. Vertigo, I guessed, unless it was a side-effect of my drug-assisted kidnapping.

"I don't remember attending a wine tasting."

"That is because you were not there, Mr Hart."

"I thought you said I performed most satisfactorily."

"You heard correctly."

Behind the silk mask, the outline of a mirthless smile. I licked my lips, which were unpleasantly dry.

"Drink some electrolyte-optimised water, Mr Hart. You will be dehydrated following your muscle spasms."

A filter jug and a glass lay on the table before me. I downed the liquid, which tasted soupy, though not unpleasant. I checked my watch. Just after midnight.

"I don't understand. Did *Le Cercle Chêne* take place or not?"

"*Le Cercle Chêne* took place, Mr Hart, because I wish it to have taken place."

An unpleasant memory flashed up.

"Someone jabbed me with a stun gun!" I said, attempting to struggle to my feet.

I became conscious of a heavy weight on my shoulders. A pair of large, pudgy hands appeared to be forcing me, quite successfully, back into my seat.

"Get off me, you shitehawk!" I shouted. I placed both feet against the glass table edge and pushed backwards, hard. But, other than an irritated hiss as the back of my chair connected with something solid, this only resulted in a pudgy hand placing itself around my throat, which I quickly realised was a discussion-ending move.

"Please refrain from irrational or excitable behaviour, Mr Hart. It is tedious and my assistant is not inclined to indulge it."

"Awk," I croaked.

The Mongolian wrestler released me. I rubbed my neck.

"Everyone knows I'm here," I said, my voice wavering.

"On the contrary," said Lee. "No-one knows you are here. Even you don't know you're here."

"They know I have an appointment at *Le Cercle Chêne*," I shouted, "and that you're at the centre of it! The police will be kicking down the door any second now, and God help you if you touch a hair on my head."

But Lee remained intensely relaxed in the face of my threats. My bowels began to churn, quite vigorously. Other than Fromage and some hapless Malherbes operative sitting in London, no-one else knew I had an appointment at the Shanghai Tower. And I was pretty sure I wasn't in the Shanghai Tower any longer. I gazed down through the glass at the peculiar, deserted office stretching to the horizon. Was I even in Shanghai? Was I even in China?

"What are you going to do with me?"

"I intend to show you Project Athena, Mr Hart. And potentially offer you a very well-remunerated role in my organisation."

"Oh. Really?"

Lee rose and approached the glass wall. He touched an invisible sensor and a panel slid aside. I felt an assertive nudge against the back of my neck that I interpreted as an invitation to join him. Closely accompanied by the Mongolian wrestler, I followed Lee through the doorway and stepped on to an open balcony also made of glass. I gave an involuntary gasp. The building was even more enormous than I had realised; large enough to house a small city. Above us yawned a vast, shallow dome, unsupported by any visible pillars or beams, coated in a glittering spider's web of wires and ducting. A muscular cable rose from the bell jar's roof to the centre of the dome high above and I realised that the three of us, the room and its surrounding balcony were suspended right at the centre of the site. I felt another twinge of nausea.

Lee stopped before the glass balustrade and stared out over the floor. I made to join him, but before I had a chance to move within spitting distance, the Mongolian wrestler grasped my arm, making it clear I was quite close enough. I could see now that the expanse beneath me was not office space but a factory floor, and what I had assumed were large white desks were in fact machines of some kind.

"What do you make here?"

"Anything I choose."

"Wine, perhaps?"

Lee didn't answer. He touched the glass balustrade and, to my astonishment, just a few yards from where we stood a transparent elevator rose noiselessly through a gap in the balcony floor. Lee stepped inside. My Mongolian guide grasped my arm and pulled me in, too, manoeuvring himself so his body remained squarely between mine and that of his boss. We descended, terrifyingly quickly, and within seconds reached the factory floor. We stepped out among the machines. All were identical, so far as I could tell; smooth and rectangular with rounded corners, each around the size of a family car. There must have been hundreds, maybe even thousands, arranged in rows like a frozen army.

"It took humanity two million years to invent printing, Mr Hart. A Chinese invention, of course."

"Isn't everything?" I replied, charitably.

"One thousand years more for moveable type. Again, a Chinese innovation."

"Oh, I thought that was the Germans."

"You are predictably misinformed. Five hundred years passed before Gutenberg and his fellow Europeans were capable of improving, even slightly, upon the original Chinese concept."

I buttoned my jacket. The temperature on the factory floor was distinctly chilly.

"Another four hundred years until the invention of the daguerreotype. One hundred years more for the discovery of xerography."

"I think those ones might have passed me by, to be honest."

"You are claiming to be unaware of both photography and photocopying, Mr Hart?"

"Oh, I see. That's what that is."

Lee stopped before a machine and placed two fingers very gently against it, as if taking its pulse.

"Humanity's desire to replicate is immutable."

He moved his face close to the unit's surface. For a second, I thought he was going to give it a kiss.

"Well, humanity certainly has done a fair bit of multiplying over the years, I'd agree with you there."

Lee turned sharply.

"I do not refer to the pathetic urge to reproduce ourselves, Mr Hart. *That* we have in common with the beasts that slither through the fields and creep along the ocean floor. I am talking of the impetus that drives man to duplicate form and function.

To cast the perfect simulacra."

"Right, sorry, I see what you mean," I said, as convincingly as I could.

"I believe the imperative to replicate is hardwired into our very being. To strive to create the perfect facsimile is fundamental to what it means to be human."

I wasn't quite sure what to say to all this. It all sounded rather earnest and a little too much like hard work, which isn't really my thing at all. But I hadn't forgotten Lee's suggestion that he might be up for bunging me a load of cash for some job or other, so it seemed sensible to play along.

"I couldn't agree more, Mr Lee. Take the world of wine, for example. Many assume winemaking to be a romantic process – simple artisans meandering their way through the seasons, celebrating variation and unreliability as part of their craft. Whereas anyone actually involved in wine, of course, knows it to be a constant struggle for technical precision and consistency."

Lee stared at me in surprise, as if I were a dog that had begun to quote Shakespeare. "A most pertinent analogy, Mr Hart."

Lee stepped away from the machine and strode on. A firm nudge to my back suggested I should follow.

"The process of replication, whether it be woodblock, lithography, or digital printer, consists of two fundamental steps."

Lee's words carried clearly, despite him marching several yards ahead of me. It occurred to me that this was the quietest factory I'd ever seen. Even our footsteps were noiseless, our soles silent against the strange, spongy resin of the factory floor.

"The first step is that of capture. A wood block carved by a Han Dynasty monk. The application of wax to a limestone plate by a Bavarian artisan. The exposure of a photopolymer belt to a thermal laser."

I must have slowed slightly because a fat hand planted itself assertively in the small of my back, urging me on. I picked up my pace.

"Traditionally, this first step is the one requiring the greater craftsmanship."

"Indeed," I said.

"The second step is that of simulation. The pressing of the dye-coated block on silk. The application of the limestone plate to parchment. The transfer of static-charged toner from belt to paper. Relatively speaking, the simpler of the two steps."

I wondered if I was going to have to remember all this as part of my new job. I hoped there wouldn't be a test at the end.

Lee stopped and turned to face me. I was saved the effort of bringing myself to a halt by the pair of vice-like hands that clamped themselves around my upper arms.

"But these techniques are applicable only to two-dimensional images. Or the layering of two-dimensional images in a childish pastiche of the three-dimensional form, of course."

"Of course."

I realised we'd reached a different area of the factory. Instead of further rows of the car-sized units, we were now faced by a single great machine, the length of a metro train, to which were attached dozens of cylindrical tanks bristling with tubes.

"Can you even conceive of the technical challenges involved in replicating a three-dimensional dynamic fluid system, Mr Hart?"

"I imagine it's pretty tricky."

Lee stared at me. In a low light, I swear he could have passed for a thirteen-year-old. He wouldn't have had a hope of being served a shandy at the Pheasant and Ferret, not without some serious ID.

"The machines you have just seen make up the structural capture network of Project Athena. Any substance I wish to replicate is introduced to a networked series of these units. They are compatible with fluid source material of any structure or phase; molecular compounds, ionic solutions, suspended solids, even plasma within certain parameters. The substance is exposed to several hundred individual analytical techniques, principally spectrometric and gravimetric in nature. The output data is then subjected to my neural network of proprietary machine learning algorithms."

My arms were starting to feel a little numb. I considered asking the Mongolian wrestler to loosen his grip. But Lee appeared to be on a roll and I suspected it might be bad form to interrupt him.

"When the molecular structure of the source material has been determined to a satisfactory degree of precision, the data is passed to the fluid facsimile aggregator – the machine you see before you. This device is, by an order of magnitude, the most sophisticated manufacturing unit on the planet. I have christened it *Hǎo Shān*."

Lee waited and I realised I was required to express an interest.

"What does *Hǎo Shān* mean?"

"In English, Mr Hart?" Lee was smirking now behind his mask, though God knew why.

"Well, that's one of my better languages. So, if you wouldn't mind."

"In English, it translates as 'good mountain'."

"Good mountain. Well, it's pretty big. And I'm sure it's very good," I said, tailing off as Lee's smirk faded.

"You will recall my reference to the relative difficulty of the capture versus the simulation step in the duplicative process."

"Yes, I remember it well," I said, wriggling slightly in an attempt to persuade the Mongolian to ease his grip. My attempt met with no measurable success.

"When duplicating a dynamic fluid system, however, it is the simulation, the manufacture, which is by far the more complex step."

Lee paused once more.

"I'm very interested to hear more about how your machine works, Mr Lee, but please could you ask your friend to lighten his grip a little? I think my hands may be developing gangrene. It's not as if I'm a danger to anybody."

"That's not what I've been told," said Lee, but he nodded to my touchy-feely friend. The twin vices relaxed a little and the blood began to return to my lower arms.

"Thank you. I would be fascinated to know how your *Hǎo Shān* machine works, Mr Lee."

*I'd also be fascinated to know how much you're intending to pay me for this new job, whatever it is,* I thought. *Hopefully enough to get me out of the shambles my incompetent bank has caused with the taxman.*

"It is inconceivable that a man of your limited scientific knowledge could understand the principles underlying Project Athena. Nevertheless, I shall attempt an explanation." Lee turned to the *Hǎo Shān* machine. "These tanks here contain precursors, relatively simple organic compounds from which more complex molecules can be built. The precursors are induced to move through thousands of tiny chambers, where they are subject to precisely calibrated electromagnetic field matrices, themselves shaped by the output variables from the machine learning algorithms in the structural capture network. These electromagnetic matrices manipulate individual molecules and ions at the nanoscale, facilitating the iterative fabrication of compounds with an exponentially more complex structure."

"That does sound amazing, Mr Lee."

Lee narrowed his eyes. I wondered if I should ask a couple of follow-up questions, the way they expect you to in job interviews, even though all you really care about is the money and whether your boss is a genuine psychopath or merely a standard-calibre arsehole.

"So, am I right in thinking Project Athena is basically a system for copying substances? Those smaller machines work together to deduce the structure, and the big one churns out the copies."

"A rather facile summary, but yes, you are essentially correct, Mr Hart."

"And you use it to copy fine wines," I said, plunging in at the deep end. Lee's face hardened a little. "Which, incidentally, I think is a wonderfully generous and democratic thing to do."

"Multiplication is a more accurate term than mere copying. And my motives are informed neither by generosity nor democracy. Duplicating a fifty-year-old Domaine de la Romanée-Conti presents an exponentially greater challenge to that of an antiretroviral or a spike protein. Though the molecular sizes are far smaller, at a holistic level an aged wine is many orders of magnitude more complex than a single macromolecule. One must identify and replicate over forty thousand different compounds, many of which are unstable, even ephemeral."

"So, you're creating perfect copies, I mean *multiplications*, of the world's finest Burgundies just to test your machine?"

"Did you think I was doing it for the money, Mr Hart? Selling bottles of DRC to Michelin-starred restaurants to generate a little pocket money while preparing my company's one hundred-billion-dollar float on the New York and Hong Kong Stock Exchanges?"

"No, I suppose that would be rather silly," I mumbled. "So, where does the wine, or whatever else you're multiplying, pop out?"

Lee turned and strode down the walkway beside the giant machine. My Mongolian friend released my arms and shoved me forward.

"The facsimile culmination ports are here, Mr Hart, at the eastern end of *Hǎo Shān*."

The machine ended in a huge, upright cylinder, not dissimilar to a winery fermentation tank, though the upper half of the vessel was covered in a mesh of fine copper tubes like a woven metal pullover. Lee opened a hatch at chest height and withdrew what looked like a white plastic milk crate. He tilted it towards me so I could view the contents. Each of the nine compartments held a glass carafe with a clear membrane stretched across the top. The carafes contained a deep-amber liquid.

"Château d'Yquem 1962, Mr Hart. Would you care to try it?"

"Why not? Don't suppose your machine makes Stilton, too, does it?"

Lee ignored my attempt to lighten the mood. He withdrew one of the carafes and used his thumbs to roll the membrane up to the rim until it snapped aside. He placed the carafe on a trestle table that appeared to have been set up specially for our tour, and used a pipette to transfer a measure of Sauternes into two wine glasses. Lee pulled down his mask, lifted a glass to his nose and smelled the wine. He closed his eyes for a moment in silent approval, then replaced his mask and retreated a few steps. The wrestler nudged me forward. I lifted the remaining glass and inhaled, then allowed the nectar to pour into my mouth.

I had only tried Chateau d'Yquem as venerable as this half a dozen times previously and, on at least two occasions, tragically the wine had been faulty. But there was nothing wrong with this sample. Caramelised oranges, white peach, grilled pineapple, butterscotch; all wrapped in an exquisite, velvet embrace of honey and toasted cream.

"God, that's good," I sighed, trying not to dribble.

"At auction, around three thousand dollars a bottle. If you can find it. Whereas that crate required less than fifty cents in input costs."

"I fear you may not be too popular in the streets of Bordeaux if you start selling d'Yquem at half a dollar a case."

"I intend to purchase the estate next week, Mr Hart. By then, I expect the asking price of the entire district will be rather less than the cost of a London townhouse. Even one in that rather run-down neighbourhood that you aspire to live in."

So, Lee knew I was moving house. Who could have told him that? Though, thinking about it, I had just spent several hours comatose in his presence, so it wouldn't have required a hacking genius to hold my smartphone in front of my face and rifle through my emails. Nosy sod. And why describe Brixton as run-down? It was very much an up-and-coming neighbourhood, semi-gentrified, even; a trend that would only accelerate with my arrival.

"Well, that's all very impressive, Mr Lee. Frankly, I'm amazed you've managed to keep it a secret."

"Oh, but it is not a secret, Mr Hart."

"Isn't it? Who else knows, then?"

"Everybody knows. And it's all thanks to you."

# Chapter 31

## Lunchtime

"What do you mean, it's all thanks to me?" I said, a rather sickly feeling rising in my lower intestines.

But Lee had disappeared around the back of the *Hǎo Shān* machine. I followed and was surprised to discover him sitting at the wheel of a golf cart. The Mongolian wrestler, in his new role as an unpleasantly aggressive caddy, forced me into the back seat and sat half on top of me, presumably to discourage me from leaning forward and slapping Lee on the back of the head.

"As I informed you earlier, you performed most satisfactorily at *Le Cercle Chêne* last night."

Lee steered the golf cart on to the main walkway and accelerated away from the *Hǎo Shān* machine, towards the perimeter of the building where the domed roof met the floor. We glided through acres of the rectangular structural capture machines, the ceiling floodlights blinking on each time we approached a darkened zone of the factory floor. Glancing back, I saw the lights extinguish themselves behind us once we'd passed.

"You are referring to the *Cercle Chêne* tasting at which I was not present?"

"To all intents and purposes, Mr Hart, you were very much present."

"You have me at a slight disadvantage, Mr Lee. Would you be willing to clarify exactly what it is I am supposed to have done at this tasting?"

"You were presented with a series of wines. One half of them original, the other half multiplications courtesy of Project

246

Athena."

"And was I capable of telling the difference?"

"Of course you were not. Because there was no difference. The two bottles of 1985 Vosne-Romanée you tasted were identical. The pair of 1978 Clos de la Roche Grand Cru were also, by definition, indistinguishable."

"And I said as much to the assembled guests, did I?"

"You were most obliging, Mr Hart. The *pièce de résistance* was your incredulity at the similarity of my two bottles of 1921 Richebourg."

"Ah, yes. A wine with which I am already familiar. The real me, that is, not whoever you used as a stand-in. I trust my doppelganger put on a good show? I'd hate to think you compromised on a duplicate Felix Hart when you've put so much effort into your wines."

For a moment, I wondered whether Lee might have birthed a new Felix Hart from his infernal machine, grown from a microscopic flake of skin tweezered from my chair in Macau, or perhaps a careless splash of urine swabbed from the rim of his immaculate toilet.

"A duplicate Felix Hart was unnecessary. If I declare that Felix Hart, Minstrel of Wine, was present at *Le Cercle Chêne* last night, then that is what happened."

"Well, it must be nice to be trusted," I said, wriggling a little. The blood flow to my leg was becoming uncomfortably constricted by the pressure from my Mongolian friend's iron buttock. The wrestler-cum-caddy responded by digging his elbow into my stomach. I stopped wriggling.

"Trust is the resource where demand furthest outpaces supply, Mr Hart."

We were now close to the edge of the factory where the roof, matted with silver ducting and multicoloured wires, reached the floor. To my alarm, Lee didn't reduce his speed, just aimed the cart towards a dark area of the wall free of cables. It looked worryingly as though my billionaire friend had finally lost his marbles and intended to plough us straight into the side of the building.

"Steady on!" I called.

But if anything, Lee speeded up. As we reached the point where collision seemed inevitable, I threw up my free arm and emitted a rather inelegant yelp. The wall pivoted upwards and we hummed beneath into a wide, brightly lit tunnel. After a minute, Lee slowed the cart and nosed it into an alcove. Before us lay a heavy metal door with a wheel at its centre. Lee stepped out of the vehicle and the vicious Mongolian caddy shoved me off the back seat with enough force to propel me into the adjacent wall. Lee spun the metal wheel, eased open the door and stepped through. My assertive friend took hold of the back of my neck and guided me after him. We passed down a narrow passage, three pairs of feet echoing against the metal grille floor, before reaching another airlock-style entrance. Lee spun the wheel and pushed it open.

I'm not sure which sensation was more shocking: the bright sunlight bursting through the doorway or the eye-watering smell, something between an industrial bleach accident and a fish salad that had spent rather too long on the buffet. I checked my watch. Nearly two o'clock. I'd assumed it was the middle of the night, but there hung the fierce Shanghai sun like an open furnace door, baking the whitewashed concrete beyond the doorway. And what was that revolting stench? Someone or something out there in the dazzling light gave an angry shout. The Mongolian wrestler pushed me through the door into the sun. I shaded my eyes and squinted.

We were standing on a balcony that ran around what appeared to be an Olympic-sized, open-air swimming pool. High walls abutted the water's edge on three sides, while at the far end lay a large expanse of concrete poolside. There were no diving boards or steps. As my eyes adjusted to the blazing sunshine, I realised that the water had a distinctly grey hue, quite possibly due to the dead fish and other unspeakable items floating in it. The main discouragement from plunging in for a refreshing dip, however, was the presence of a large family of elephant seals, sunbathing bad-temperedly on the poolside concrete.

"Blimey!" I said, waving away a gang of flies that had begun to torment me.

"The lions of the sea, Mr Hart," called Lee, over the muttering of the elephant seals, which had grown louder following our appearance on the balcony. "Aren't they magnificent?"

I noticed that Lee had slipped on an industrial-grade gas mask and goggles that covered his eyes, nose and mouth. My Mongolian friend, still holding me by the back of the neck, placed his sleeve over his face.

"Beautiful," I lied, as a large, brown specimen ejected a fountain of excrement across the concrete, splattering a couple of its neighbours and triggering a cacophony of angry barks.

"I first encountered these incredible creatures on a visit to Argentina."

Lee's mask must have been fitted with a microphone and amplifier, for his voice had increased in volume and was accompanied by a peculiar echo, as though broadcast from the bottom of a well.

"My company was acquiring some lithium mining assets in Patagonia and my partners suggested a visit to Puerto Madryn. I was immediately bewitched by their majesty."

An enormous, dark-skinned animal the size of a minibus lolloped its way across the concrete, scattering the smaller seals left and right. It bounded over to an unfortunate creature half its size and collapsed on top of it with a roar. The smaller animal screamed, but its shrieks were drowned out by the bellows of the greater beast, which for good measure embedded its teeth in its unfortunate colleague's back.

"They are mating," stated Lee.

"Bit light on the foreplay," I said, removing my fingers from my nose to wave away the rapidly multiplying crowd of flies.

"At five thousand kilograms, the alpha male does not ask, Mr Hart, he takes."

Now, I'm not generally a sensitive soul, but the smell by now was so rich that my throat had begun to spasm involuntarily. I suspected it would only be a matter of minutes before I expelled yesterday's dim sum over the balcony.

"Absolutely fascinating, Mr Lee. I do congratulate you on your spectacular menagerie. Now, I recall you mentioned you might want to employ me within your organisation, in some function or other. Shall we proceed inside to discuss the matter?"

"Later, Mr Hart. It is lunch time. I would be honoured if you would feed my aquatic beauties."

"A very kind offer, Mr Lee, but I don't want to be any trouble. Happy to leave that kind of thing to the experts."

"But I insist."

Lee proceeded along the balcony towards the far end of the pool where the seals were basking. My Mongolian helper, without loosening his grip, directed me after him. The odour increased in violence until the back of my throat began to burn. I was nudged towards a gap in the balcony wall, where a metal spiral staircase led down to a small platform suspended a few feet above the shallow end.

"After you, Mr Hart," said Lee, his eyes expressionless behind his goggles.

I descended the stairs, holding the thin guardrail with one hand and failing to disperse the swarm of flies flocking around my head with the other. My Mongolian friend encouraged me onwards, with a fist nestled firmly in the small of my back, as the grey, oily water shimmered foully beneath me.

"There is a bucket of fish and a pair of gloves on the platform," said Lee, from above. "If you execute the task well, you may even earn their respect."

I reached the bottom of the stairs. The honking increased in volume and aggression. A pair of smaller seals flopped into the pool, sending waves of foetid water slapping against the concrete walls. The stench was quite spectacularly hideous. My eyes were streaming and it was all I could do to keep myself from spontaneously voiding my stomach contents over the side to join the scum of fish entrails and seal poop decorating the water's surface. I stepped on to the platform, a metal grille with no guardrail and barely larger than a manhole cover. Through my tears, I located the metal bucket, which was full to the brim with an unspeakable collection of glassy-eyed fish garnished with a roiling crust of flies.

"I recommend you feed the alpha male first, Mr Hart."

The chorus of seal indignation increased. The alpha male, who had now finished wooing his romantic partner, fixed me with a fist-sized eye from the far end of the concrete. He raised his trunk and bellowed, his throat vibrating like an angry waterbed.

"He is hungry, Mr Hart. If you wish to retain his good favour, do not delay."

I donned the gloves, stupid great gauntlets like something a medieval jouster might have worn. I waved away the mantle of furious flies and attempted to grab the topmost fish, but the slimy little corpse kept slipping from my grasp.

"A question, Mr Hart," boomed Lee, through his amplified mask. "How did you know that Mr Fung would be attending *Le Cercle Chêne* in Macau last month?"

"Can't remember," I called back.

I tipped the pail and somehow cajoled the fish on to my open palm. The nearby seals changed their tune from barks of anger to hoots of excitement and several of them shuffled closer. I straightened up and hurled the fish in the direction of the alpha male, like a clown launching a custard pie. But the horrible thing slipped out of the side of my hand and landed barely a couple of yards away. A largish seal with unpleasantly sharp-looking teeth bounded up and grabbed it in its jaws. The alpha male bellowed in outrage.

"I shall ask you again, Mr Hart. How did you know that my friend Mr Fung would be attending the *Cercle Chêne* tasting in Macau? I would very much like to know."

"Oh, he mentioned it in a meeting, I think. I honestly can't recall the exact conversation. We talk about wine quite often."

I teased another fish into my palm, deciding it might be easier to lob it underarm. I stepped back and gave a mighty upward swing. The fish sailed into the air, stupidly high, before splattering on the concrete between two small seals who subjected it to a short and revoltingly messy tug of war. The alpha male gave another angry bark and began to shuffle aggressively towards me. Despite my elevated position, I suspected the beast would be quite capable of reaching my exposed platform if it reared up on its hindquarters. I spat away a pair of flies that had settled on my lips and focussed my attention on procuring another fish.

"No, Mr Hart. He would not have done that. All aspects of *Le Cercle Chêne* are absolutely confidential. I am very careful to invite guests whose discretion I can rely on. And Charles Fung is one of my oldest friends."

"No, he definitely did. I remember. We were discussing wine and he brought it up."

I scooped up another fish and launched it with a hybrid under-meets-overarm motion towards the alpha male. This time my aim was true and the fish landed barely a yard from the giant seal. But the concrete was slimy with detritus and the fish skittered past him and splashed into the oily water. The alpha male bellowed in frustration and, trunk waving, gave his forward shuffle a more forceful intent. Christ, the creature was absolutely enormous. How did anything that size manage to propel itself across the ground without proper legs? I scooped up a handful of smaller fish, deciding a scattergun tactic might work better.

"But that is quite impossible, Mr Hart. You see, it's not just that I trust Mr Fung implicitly. It's that when you mentioned it to him, he had only received his invitation an hour beforehand. And it is quite impossible for you to have been aware of the identity of the attendees. And yet, you were. So, I ask you a final time, Mr Hart. How exactly did you know?"

"Lucky guess, I suppose," I called.

With a mighty swing, I flung the handful of smaller fish towards the alpha male. But, yet again, the stupid gloves spoiled my aim and the bait scattered far and wide, just a single, pathetically sized specimen landing before my target. The giant seal paused his advance and peered down at the miniscule snack. Then, he fixed me with an expression that suggested lunchtime service had fallen dramatically short of expectations, threw back his trunk and gave an ear-splitting roar. The rest of the harem echoed his displeasure. The beast drew himself up to his full height and a shiver of horror ran through me, for from his stubby back flippers to the tip of his bristly trunk, he measured at least three times my height. For a second, I understood Lee's fascination. There was something undeniably magnificent about the monster. Given his proximity, however, not to mention the fact that the creature had resumed his advance at an even more confident clip, I decided a tactical retreat was in order. But first, one final throw. I eased a large fish on to my glove and prepared to hurl it skywards.

"Most unfortunate," called Lee. "Most infuriating. Just like Mr Farquhar, you have proved a wasted investment. And waste, Mr Hart, makes me extremely angry."

# Chapter 32

## Alpha Male

I had become conscious that Lee sounded rather upset beneath his amplified mask. I was also aware that something had begun nudging my foot, rather assertively. I looked down to find the seal who'd bagged my first fish peering at the lunch balanced on my outstretched hand, a rather entitled, sharp-toothed smile on its face. Something was dreadfully wrong. My platform was now mere inches from the ground rather than several feet and, furthermore, it was still descending. I whipped around and to my horror saw the spiral staircase had retracted upwards, quite out of my reach. My Mongolian friend gazed down at me from the balcony, a control panel in his hand. The grim smile on his face suggested that a hard day's work was nearly done.

"What are you doing?" I screamed. "Bring it back!"

"I asked you a very simple question several times, Mr Hart," called Lee. "But you refused to answer. So be it. The idea that I might never understand how you knew of Mr Fung's invitation I find highly unsatisfactory. My disappointment, however, will be tempered by seeing you torn apart by the world's largest land carnivoran."

"I don't know how I knew!" I shouted. "I can't remember!"

I wasn't lying. My mind had gone completely blank. The chorus from the elephant seals had risen in volume, quite dramatically. It had also become notably more vindictive. With a clang, the platform beneath my feet settled against the poolside concrete. I looked about frantically for an escape route. On one side lay a lake of oily, puke-inducing water entirely enclosed by high walls. On the other a terrace of glistening, turd-strewn concrete, dotted with enormous blubbery mammals in a high degree of agitation.

"What do you want?" I screamed.

The sharp-toothed seal at my feet reared up and lunged at the fish lying in my palm. I swear that if my reactions had been a millisecond slower, I'd have lost a limb. I whipped my arm away and as the creature's jaws snapped, what felt like a sharpened comb raked the back of my hand. The fish and glove remained in the creature's mouth as I tumbled backwards into a slurry of seal crap and discarded fish guts, my other arm still hugging the pail to my chest.

The assembled elephant seals found this an absolutely hilarious development. I attempted to scramble to my feet, but the concrete was coated in a slick of unimaginable foulness. My feet shot out from beneath me and my un-gloved hand plunged into the morass of slime. A squadron of flies settled upon my face, my throat spasmed and I emitted a horrible, dry hurl.

"I know everything about you and why you are here, Mr Hart." Lee had turned up the volume on his face mask so he could be heard above the honking menagerie, and his cruel voice now boomed from the balcony above. "Your pathetic anti-fraud mission on behalf of the Minstrels of Wine. Your fake role at Farquhar Fine and Rare in Hong Kong. Your true role as lavatory seat buyer at Gatesave Superstores. Your inability to remain in a room with a bottle of fine wine or an attractive woman without pawing them into submission."

"Let me out!" I pleaded. "I'll tell you anything! I'm sorry I stole the wine from your tasting!"

"Yes, you took the opportunity to steal a full bottle of my multiplied 1978 Musigny Grand Cru. Your every move was being monitored on ultra-high-definition cameras, Mr Hart. My people reassembled the broken bottles following the disruption you caused and deduced what was missing. I was at the tasting in Macau, Mr Hart, just metres from where you were seated. Most disappointing not to be able to join my guests in person. But then, I already knew you were not what you claimed. That you were a spy. Perhaps even an assassin."

"I'm not a spy! Or an assassin!"

I had just managed to climb to my feet when I became aware of something blocking the sun. A tower of blubber the size of an upended bus stared down at me. He waved his huge, club-shaped trunk, opened his vast mouth and bellowed, letting forth a hot wind so unimaginably foul that I vomited as spontaneously and generously as a babe in arms. The seal harem hooted with glee and I swear several of them actually applauded. Then, the gargantuan seal descended upon me, his livid red mouth agape. I screamed and by pure reflex swung the bucket of fish at the creature's gaping maw. His jaws, studded with thumb-sized teeth, closed on the pail with a sickening metallic crunch and tore it from my grasp. Then, as a follow-through, the beast struck me with the side of his neck. The blow knocked me through the air and I braced myself for what I knew would be a terrible, grazing impact with the ground. But, to my surprise, my landing was cushioned by the inches-thick slurry of skittery dung, festering fish guts and, presumably, elephant seal love-juice, sending me sliding arse-first into the flank of a large, snoozing female.

"Then why can't you tell me the truth, Mr Hart?" called Lee.

The female seal was displeased to have her nap, not to mention her personal space, invaded by a dung-smothered human and communicated her irritation by snapping at me with a mouthful of needle-like teeth. I flung out my arm to protect myself and her jaws closed around the fingertips of my remaining glove, ripping it free. I scrabbled away from the creature, who chewed the glove a few times before spitting it back at me, and managed to clamber to my feet, absolutely astonished all my limbs were still present. I scampered through the maze of angry blubber, my feet slipping and sliding on the cack-encrusted ground, until I reached the back wall. I searched frantically for a protruding stone or a toehold, anything that might help me climb out of reach, but the wall was smooth.

"I have told you the truth!" I pleaded. "I have nothing to hide! Why would I lie?"

"That is what I do not understand, Mr Hart."

And then, like a gift from the gods, I spotted a small gate in the corner where the back and side walls met. I crept towards it, taking a circuitous route to avoid the larger animals and dodging lunges from the more aggressive small ones. A buttock-clenching minute later, I reached the corner and threw myself at the gate. It was constructed of metal bars, just too narrowly spaced to squeeze through, and appeared to lead into some kind of janitor's room. I could see a mop and bucket leaning against the wall just inside. I tried the handle but, sickeningly, it was locked. I fished in my pocket for my phone, thinking I could at least broadcast an SOS to someone – Provost Jordaan, perhaps, or even Sandra – but the battery was dead. Weeping with frustration, I grabbed the bars and shook them, triggering a chorus of barks from the nearby seals.

I turned back to the menagerie and nearly fainted with terror. For the alpha male was making his way, slowly but surely, across the concrete terrace towards me. The crushed metal bucket, impaled on a gigantic molar, protruded from his mouth like a silver tongue.

"There is only space in the harem for one alpha male, Mr Hart. Last chance!"

"I've told you!" I screamed. "I've told you everything!"

I turned back to the gate and thrust my arm between the bars, grabbing the mop and pulling it through. I pointed it at the advancing elephant seal and, despite my stomach-churning fear, laughed wildly, for I may as well have waved a cocktail stick at an approaching tank.

What the hell had I said to Fung all those weeks ago about *Le Cercle Chêne*? I scoured my mind. It had been a video call. Why had I even mentioned wine? Of course, Tabatha Shunt had told me that Charles Fung loved wine! She'd told me to mention my wine background, so I had. We'd talked about the Minstrels of Wine and Fung had asked if he could join. That was it! And where had *Le Cercle Chêne* come in? Why had I mentioned it? Charles Fung had mentioned wine clubs. But it was supposed to be a secret. Sandra has sworn me to it.

But I'd said it anyway. I'd just blurted it out. Like an absolute dick. *Le Cercle Chêne.*

The alpha male had now approached to within a dozen feet. I was cornered. It wasn't even a small corner – I was utterly exposed. Oh, Christ. This was it. Bizarrely, I was overcome by a perverse sense of pride that out of all the world's savage creatures, I would be done in by the world's largest land carnivore. More impressive, even, than being savaged by a grizzly bear, and certainly better than being torn apart by a pack of rabid dogs. Or being bitten on the arse by a spider in an Aussie outdoor toilet.

The colossal seal reared up and bellowed. His family, girlfriends and hangers-on joined in, goading him to finish the job. He roared again, basking in the adulation. Hell, I'd show off, too, if I weighed five metric tonnes. The monster dropped to his front flippers and looked round, just to check he had all their attention. I saw my chance. Holding the mop at forty-five degrees, I ran at him and as he turned back, I thrust the soft end as hard as I could up the creature's trunk. To my astonishment, it went right up the nostril, leaving barely a foot of shaft protruding. The beast screamed and reared up, then swiped his neck at me. But this was our second fight and I anticipated his move, throwing myself backwards so his great head passed harmlessly in front of me. The monster turned and lolloped away, moaning, the mop handle still protruding from his trunk. A couple of the smaller male seals laughed. The alpha paused, embarrassed, and turned. I shrank into the corner, the gate's bars pressing into my back.

"It was a guess, Mr Lee!" I shouted. "It was a guess!"

Lee stared down at me from the balcony, calmly observing my imminent death from behind his goggles.

"I'd just been briefed about *Le Cercle Chêne* by Sandra," I shouted. "She's my contact at Paris-Blois. They pay me to investigate wine fraud for them. And Inspector Ma. He's an inspector in the Hong Kong Police. He's investigating you."

The elephant seal lay down and banged his trunk against the floor, attempting to dislodge the mop handle. The crushed metal bucket clanged and scraped against the concrete as he swiped his colossal head back and forth.

"Everyone swore me to secrecy," I shouted. "Everyone made a massive fuss about it, as if it was the most terrible secret in the world. They paid me a ridiculous amount of money. And they told me Owen Farquhar had been killed, or fell off the ferry, or something. And that I had to come to Hong Kong and investigate it anyway. Even though I didn't want to."

The alpha male pressed his trunk against the ground and the end of the shaft suddenly snapped. The creature snorted. A wad of blood and mop end shot out of his trunk and splattered on the ground. The alpha male stared at the mess for a second, then looked at me. He appeared extraordinarily displeased. Slowly, and determinedly, he began to lollop towards me.

"*Cercle Chêne* was all I could think about!" I shouted, panicking. "I even dreamt about it. So when Charles Fung mentioned the Minstrels of Wine, and whether it was just like joining a wine club, I just said it."

The alpha male was nearly upon me. He reared up, blocking the sky, and swayed from side to side. He bared his teeth, the crushed bucket still impaled upon a triangular tooth the size of a metalworker's vice. He gave a great, roaring moan, like a dreadful fairytale giant about to consume an entire village-worth of hapless peasants.

"I just said it!" I screamed. "*Le Cercle Chêne! Le Cercle Chêne!* Stupid bloody *Cercle Chêne!* I'm sick of it! I didn't know Fung was invited to your stupid bloody tasting. And I didn't care! Do what you bloody well want. Fake your own piss if it turns you on! Who cares! It's only bloody wine!"

Behind me, a metallic click. I spun round and yanked the handle. Like the gates of heaven themselves, the door swung open and I fell into the room. I felt a tremendous gust of wind at my back, like a lorry roaring by on a busy road. Then, the most terrible sound I ever hope to hear: a skull-rattling roar of rage, pain, and frustration. I didn't look, I just ran, and that creature's bellow still haunts my nightmares to this very day.

# Chapter 33

## Deepfake

I don't know whether you've ever managed to hail a Shanghai taxi in the baking afternoon sun while slathered in foetid fish guts and elephant seal crap, but if you have, you're a better negotiator than me. It took me four hours to walk back to the city centre, and I swear I'd have been eaten alive by the swarms of carnivorous flies that accompanied my every step if I hadn't stumbled across a toothless monk cleaning the side of a Buddhist temple on the city outskirts and persuaded him to hose me down with his pressure washer.

Upon arrival at my hotel, I dashed through Reception, discarded my clothing outside my bedroom door and spent most of the rest of the day in the shower, on full monsoon setting, attempting to remove the unspeakable crust that had adhered itself to every surface of my body. Then I retrieved Jordaan's phone from the safe and dispatched a message.

*Kidnapped, drugged and given tour of Terafactory by Lee. Thrown into giant seal enclosure, nearly eaten. Now back at hotel. Not happy.*

It took me a couple of attempts to type the message, partly because of my shaking hands, partly because the autocorrect kept attempting to change Terafactory to the more appropriate 'tear factory'. I wondered whether the Malherbes would still advise me to proceed with caution. I tucked Jordaan's phone into its pouch, plugged the charger into my own dead mobile and collapsed on the bed.

I was woken a minute later by my phone chirruping its way across the bedside table.

"Minstrel Hart?"

"Yes, that is me. Can I call you back please? I'm off-duty."

"Hold for Provost Jägermeister, please."

That puffed-up trollop. What the hell was he calling me for? He wasn't even my Provost.

"Hart? Minstrel Hart?"

"Yes, Provost, this is Minstrel Hart speaking. How are you?"

"Hart! You absolutely appalling bastard!"

"Oh. Have I done something wrong?"

"Wrong! You're about to collapse the entire bloody global wine trade single-handed! We've been trying to get hold of you for the past two days. What the hell were you doing at that tasting last night?"

"Tasting?"

"At *Le Cercle Chêne!* Good God, man. Are you deranged?"

"Ah, yes. That is probably fake news, I'm afraid. I wasn't actually there."

"What do you mean you weren't there? Of course you were bloody well there! Ten million people have already watched your catastrophic tasting video. Everyone can see full well you were there!"

"Oh. I haven't seen it. I've been having some local difficulties."

"Local difficulties? We're having global difficulties, you imbecile, thanks to your little stunt! What the hell are you playing at?"

"I don't know. I honestly don't know what I'm playing at."

"Good grief! I knew it was a mistake sending you to China, right from the start. What on earth were we doing trusting such a sensitive issue to an idiot like you? Right, just answer me this. What's the truth about Lee's factory? Project Athena."

"Oh, you know about that, do you?"

"The entire bloody world knows about it, you nincompoop! There's a video of you, with Joseph Lee smirking in the background, declaring that you can't tell the difference between Richebourg and some grape juice farted out of his God-forsaken machine."

"I don't think that happened."

"Are you on drugs, Hart? It happened, man, I can assure you. Now, tell me, this is extremely important – I need to know the truth about Lee's project. The share price of every major wine company is forecast to collapse when the stock markets open tomorrow morning. A lot of people stand to lose a great deal of money. We need to get ahead of this."

"Mr Lee took me to his Terafactory. It's enormous. He showed me the machines where they can copy any liquid, anything at all. It's supposed to be for pharmaceuticals. He just copies wine for fun."

A strange gurgling sound emanated from the phone. I wondered whether Provost Jägermeister was conducting his own comparative tasting.

"Copies wine for fun?" he spluttered. "For bloody fun?"

"That's not all, Provost. After Lee showed me his machines, he attempted to feed me to his walruses. No, not walruses, elephant seals."

There was a period of silence.

"So, you are on drugs, Minstrel Hart."

"No, I'm definitely not, Provost! Although I may have been injected with something on Saturday evening, now you mention it."

"Don't bother coming home, Hart. You're expelled from the Worshipful Company of the Minstrels of Wine. And from any role in the wine trade, anywhere on Earth. Blackballed. Cancelled. Good day."

The call ended. A text message informed me that I had eighty-three new voicemails. I opened Twitter and checked what was trending. With a sickening feeling, I realised it was me, along with the hashtags #RIPWine and #FineWhine.

The thirty-second video, which now had over twelve million views, showed me (looking rather dapper, if I may say so) sniffing and slurping a pair of wines, Shanghai's evening skyline in the background. I watched myself declare several pairs of wines completely indistinguishable, then assure the audience that as a

Minstrel of Wine, my tasting prowess was second to none. My performance ended with my statement that this was an epoch-defining moment in the history of wine, bigger even than the Judgment of Paris. Then, someone off-camera asked me what the future held for the fine wine trade. I responded by stating, 'Rest in Peace'; a comment followed by a roar of audience hilarity.

I put my head in my hands, trying to work out exactly when the video had been filmed. I assumed I'd been forced to perform under the influence of some fiendish narcotic before I remembered that the video was a deepfake. A deeply unsettling and unpleasant sensation came over me; a feeling that I had been simultaneously mugged, burgled, and aggressively fondled.

My phone rang again.

"Hello? Minstrel Hart?"

"Yes, hello, speaking. Who's this?"

"It's me. Minstrel Shuttlewort. I'm on a video call. I can only see your ear."

I peered at the phone. Sure enough, Shuttlewort's face and enormous round glasses filled the screen.

"Oh, yes. Hello."

"Minstrel Hart, are you not wearing any clothes?"

I tilted the phone so I could only be seen from the chin up.

"Of course I am. It's very warm here. I've been beside the pool."

"Pleased to hear you're not over-exerting yourself following your exhibition in Shanghai, Minstrel Hart."

A second voice, not Shuttlewort's. Shuttlewort angled the phone to reveal Provost Rougegorgefils perched beside her like a highly displeased hawk.

"Ah, hello, Provost Rougegorgefils. Yes, there's a lot to explain."

"It would appear you have gone native, Minstrel Hart. Do we understand that you are now working for Joseph Lee?"

"No, Provost, I can categorically declare that I am not working for Mr Lee. That video is a fake. A deepfake. I wasn't at the tasting. I'm not even sure any tasting happened. Instead of the police raiding the place, I was kidnapped and taken to his factory."

"That is a rather extraordinary story, Minstrel Hart. The video looks very authentic."

"I expect that's why they call them deepfakes, Provost."

Rougegorgefils and Shuttlewort muted the call and exchanged a few words.

"Minstrel Hart," said Shuttlewort, unmuting herself. "You say Joseph Lee took you to his factory. Can you describe what you saw?"

"Lots of machines."

"Yes, and what did they look like?"

"Most of them white and rectangular. About the size of a car."

"That's not terribly helpful. Did you see any centrifuges?"

"I'm not sure I'd know one if I saw one. There was one enormous machine, the length of several railway carriages, with all sorts of pipes and things attached to it. I got the impression that was the replication machine. Lee called it *Hǎo Shān*. It translates as good mountain."

"Better in German," said Shuttlewort, after a few seconds.

"*Guter Berg*," said Rougegorgefils.

"Even better in the dative," said Shuttlewort. "*Auf dem guten Berg*. Gutenberg. Johannes Gutenberg."

"Ah, the medieval printing fellow," I said, pleased I could contribute to such a highbrow conversation.

"Yes, Minstrel Hart," said Shuttlewort, blinking happily. "It appears our Mr Lee isn't above a knowing pun or two."

"He is a bit full of himself," I said.

"Back to the subject of equipment, Minstrel Hart," said Rougegorgefils. "Are you sure you didn't see any centrifuge columns? They would have been quite noticeable. Probably at least as tall as you, might have been double your height. Somewhere between the diameter of a large paint pot and an oil drum."

"No, I don't think so. But I didn't see the whole factory."

"That's a shame. And, one other detail, Minstrel. The Richebourg that you're drinking in that video of the Shanghai tasting. Did you see the bottle?"

"The deepfake video, you mean, Provost?"

"Ah, yes. You're claiming you didn't attend the tasting."

"Correct. I didn't see the bottle because I wasn't at the tasting. I was being abducted by Mr Lee's goons and forced to tour his factory."

"It's just that we've received the background radiation results from the '21 Richebourg bottle you stole in Macau," said Shuttlewort. "The glass and the sediment emitted no trace of radioactivity. So, they're definitely pre-1945."

"There appear to be a lot of these '21 Richebourgs around," said Rougegorgefils. "The late Owen Farquhar claims to have drunk one with a client a few years ago. I think we can assume the client was Mr Lee. And then there are the two you tasted in Shanghai."

"The two I didn't taste, Provost. Because I wasn't at the tasting."

"Minstrel Hart. I'm sure the reaction of the Worshipful Institute to the video will be weighing heavily on your mind."

"Well, it is weighing a little. Provost Jägermeister told me I was to be expelled, blackballed and cancelled."

"Yes. Well, that does sound like jumping the gun a touch, but a formal investigation is almost certain. And should one occur, I would advise you to tell the truth and cooperate fully with the Institute authorities. Have you spoken to your own Provost Jordaan?"

"No, not yet. I've been a bit tied up."

"I recommend you do so. I assume it's late in Shanghai so I will bid you goodnight."

"Good night, Provost. And to you, Minstrel Shuttlewort."

"Good night, Minstrel Hart," said Shuttlewort. And a couple of seconds later, a whispered, "And good luck!"

I'd no sooner swiped up the control centre, ready to engage Do Not Disturb mode, when my phone vibrated into life yet again. A French number.

"Felix Hart speaking."

"Whatever Mr Lee is paying you, Felix, I hope it's more than one million dollars."

"Ah, Sandra, hello. Look, there's been a bit of an incident."

"You see, the contract you've signed allows us to claw back the money we've paid you in the event you fail to deliver on your obligations. And it's fair to say you've failed to deliver in an absolutely spectacular and quite fundamental way."

"That's not entirely fair, actually. Let me explain."

"No, Felix, I'm not interested in hearing another word from you. Ever again. Our house bankers have advised us that market sentiment is so negative against Paris-Blois Beverages that our shares will be suspended when the stock market opens tomorrow morning. My business is effectively worthless. There's little we can do about that now, but our Group CEO has made it absolutely clear that he wants you bankrupted and driven into extreme poverty."

"There's a bit of a problem with paying the money back, to be honest. I've had to put down a couple of fairly hefty deposits and I don't actually have the liquidity available, as such."

"I'm so glad. That means you'll definitely be driven into bankruptcy. And I'm sure Provost Jägermeister will ensure you're unable to earn a penny in the wine trade ever again. I do hope the toilet seat industry holds up. Though I must warn you that for good measure I'll be reporting you to Gatesave for having secondary employment, which I'm pretty sure is a breach of your contract."

"This is extremely unfair!" I said. "I've been through hell this weekend for you! All I was asked to do was attend a wine tasting and wait for the police to arrive. Instead, I was electrocuted and nearly eaten alive by elephant seals!"

"You're an idiot, Felix. Go away."

Sandra ended the call. To my immense frustration, before I could trigger Do Not Disturb mode my phone lit up once more. This time, the number was in my contacts. With a sense of foreboding, I answered.

"Evening, Tabatha."

"Evening, sweet cheeks. Hope I haven't interrupted you doing something I wouldn't?"

"No, just got out of the shower."

"Too much information, pert pecs! Or maybe not enough." Tabatha gurgled with amusement. "Anyway, I'm calling because you've been ignoring my messages all weekend. I'm checking you'll be at our new store opening in Shenzhen tomorrow morning. For the influencer tasting."

"Oh, yes."

I'd forgotten, of course. My brain was so scrambled I barely knew what day it was.

"I hope you're in Shenzhen already?"

"Yes."

"Good. I can't go, the border's still closed to ordinary punters. But for some reason you appear to be able to swan about China like some Ming Dynasty princess. Anyway, be on your best behaviour, understood? The retail team want some good mentions for our wine range from local influencers."

"Actually, I am feeling a little unwell. Do I really have to–"

"Shut up. Yes, you do. And are those toilet seats still on schedule?"

"Due to dock in the UK on Tuesday. Should be in store by next weekend."

"They'd bloody better be. And don't you dare pretend to be unwell, or you're fired, understand?"

Tabatha hung up.

Clearly, I was not in Shenzhen. I'd disregarded Tabatha's instructions to arrive the evening before and booked the early Monday morning flight instead. After my evening in Macau, there had seemed a reasonable chance that the Shanghai leg of *Le Cercle Chêne* might also be a big night. I'd been hoping Kaia might be there, of course. Not that she'd returned a single message.

The thought of attending a store opening in Shenzhen after

the past twenty-four hours did not fill me with joy. I'd had it with wine tastings, kidnappings and carnivorous wildlife, I wanted to go home. I checked for Shanghai departures to Europe, but there was nothing until the following evening and even then I'd need to change flights twice. Given that my Minstrel days and any chance of working in wine ever again sounded numbered, it probably wasn't a good move to let down Tabatha Shunt and be exiled from the world of bathroom accessories, too. I would fly to Shenzhen tomorrow, get the tasting out of the way, then take the train over the border to Hong Kong and instruct my Global Executive Assistant to bring forward my return flight home.

I finally managed to engage flight-safe mode, gave a groan of self-pity, and allowed my head to sink into the pillow. I wondered whether I was still in danger. I vaguely considered grabbing my passport and spending the night at the airport. But a blanket of exhaustion had descended upon me, and even the thought of an elephant seal bursting through my hotel door in the middle of the night couldn't convince me to lift myself from my gorgeous marshmallow of a bed. It occurred to me that I should probably call Provost Jordaan and ask her advice, but I decided that could wait until the morning. I set my alarm for a filthily early hour and passed out.

# Chapter 34

## Shenzhen Yummy

It was still dark as my alarm hauled me from the abyss of sleep. My head was swimming with fatigue and my body felt like tepid death. My soiled clothing had been removed from outside the door and probably incinerated, so I had barely anything to pack. I removed my passport and spare cash from the safe and gathered up my little pile of belongings from the bedside table. Watch, wallet, charger, and no fewer than three phones: my own, Jordaan's, in its Faraday pouch, plus I still had Lee's stupid little Samsung. I tossed them into my bag, bought a horrible, packaged croissant from the vending machine in Reception, and slipped into an airport-bound taxi.

I used the journey to check through the weekend's missed voicemails. Half were from the apoplectic Provost Jägermeister or his slimy minions, commanding me to call him on pain of crucifixion. A few were from various Minstrels and wine trade acquaintances, keen to get the inside track on my Shanghai video. Sandra had left several, each angrier (and dare I say, sexier) than the last, describing the ravages her company's legal team intended to inflict on me. Three were from my bank, fussing about something dull, and one was from Zak at Fulmination Tech, almost screaming with excitement at my transformation into the wine trade's foremost disruptive influencer.

I checked Jordaan's mobile, just in case the Malherbes had sent a message. They had. In fact, it was timed at just a minute after the one I'd sent on my return from my zoological adventure.

*Leave China immediately. Do not delay. First available flight regardless of destination.*

Wonderful. Nice to see someone was looking out for me. Just a shame they were several hours too late. Given that it was only ten p.m. in London, I risked a call to Provost Jordaan, but she didn't pick up. I left a message saying I had toured Lee's factory, seen his machines, and that I appeared to have been horribly set up. I didn't mention the elephant seals.

I landed in Shenzhen just before nine a.m. and spent an hour in heavy traffic, thankfully avoiding the boredom of the grand opening. I made my way to the shiny new wine department and located Laura, Gatesave China's fearsomely organised head of PR.

"Disappointing that you weren't at the opening ceremony," said Laura, without looking up from her iPad. "Was about to call Tabatha Shunt and tell her we had a no-show."

"Apologies. Bit of unfinished business in Shanghai."

"So I understand. Quite a sensation on wine Twitter, I believe."

"Oh, you've seen the video, have you?"

"Yes, Felix. I'm the Head of Comms for Gatesave China. It's kind of my job to see when someone's trending on social media. Particularly when they're a Gatesave employee. I assume you had clearance from the executive board in London to speak at that wine event?"

"Yes, of course."

"I very much doubt that. But, so long as you haven't brought Gatesave into disrepute, it's not my problem. Right, the tasting's all set up in the bar, over there. Put that Gatesave sweatshirt on and go and check the wines. The influencers will be here in half an hour."

"Since when did branches of Gatesave have their own wine bar? You don't see many of those in Stoke-on-Trent."

"It's a China flagship store, Felix. They all have wine bars."

I did as I was told. My job would be to stand behind the counter, holding forth on the glories of the Gatesave wine range, while the influencers perched on designer bar stools and generated inspirational digital assets. I sniffed my way through the tasting line-up. A Prosecco, a Pinot Grigio, a couple of Sauvignons, a Picpoul de Pinet, a Provencal rosé, something pink and unspeakable from California, and the grand climax of the whites, a generic Chablis. Then the reds. A Chilean Merlot, a red from southern Spain festooned with gold wire, a brand from an unspecified region of Italy with a flying cherub on it, and an anonymous Bordeaux. Finally, a sweet red from South Africa that tasted like a half-sucked prune.

"The range has definitely gone downhill since I was in charge," I said.

"I'm sure it has. To be honest, Felix, you're just the warm-up act. We have Shenzhen's top mixologist joining us at one p.m. to create some Cantonese-inspired cocktails. That's when we expect the seats to fill up."

"The warm-up act. Right."

"Sorry. Anyway, I thought you'd just declared wine dead on arrival, or something."

"I said rest in peace, not dead on arrival. Actually, I didn't even say that. The video was a deepfake."

"Whatever. Now, listen. The seat in the middle is for Shenzhen Yummy, he's our big fish. One-point-two million followers on Weibo. We pay him a fortune, but he can be a little volatile. I doubt he'll turn up for your bit, but you never know. If he does, don't let him wind you up. He's kind of a prick."

"I'll bear that in mind."

By midday, just eight of the bar stools were occupied. Six young women, slim and beautiful, and two well-moisturised young men, all of whom smiled indulgently at my nǐ hǎo. The middle seat remained unfilled. Laura welcomed the group in Mandarin, then introduced me as a Minstrel of Wine, at which point I beamed like a film star and began dispensing Gatesave's entry point Prosecco. I was just getting into my stride extolling the virtues of cheap, tank-fermented sparkling wine, when a rather tubby young man marched into the bar.

"Shenzhen Yummy reporting for duty!" he called, saluting the room.

The other influencers turned and applauded.

"*Nǐ hǎo,*" I called, with a welcoming smile.

"*Nǐ hǎo!*" replied Shenzhen Yummy, delightedly. "*Nǐ hǎo!*"

He marched to the bar and held out his hand. I reached out to shake it but Shenzhen Yummy snatched it back.

"*Nǐ bù hǎo!*" he squealed, pointing at my hands. "Germy, germy, make diseases!"

The other influencers laughed.

"I have washed them," I said. "Never mind. Please, do take a seat. It's been thoroughly sprayed with alcohol."

Laura shot me a warning glare.

"Allow me to pour you a glass of Italian sunshine," I said, holding the bottle by the base, sommelier-style, and preparing to pour.

"Is this Champagne?" asked Shenzhen Yummy.

"No, not Champagne, but similar. It's Prosecco, which is–"

"Which is pee-pee," said Shenzhen Yummy, knocking the bottle away with the back of his hand. "Pee-pee!"

The influencers giggled into their glasses. One raised her phone but Shenzhen Yummy waggled his finger. "No pictures, bitches! Unless you pay!" Everyone laughed again.

"Actually, Mister Gatesave Guy, I only drink Champagne," said Shenzhen Yummy. "Real Champagne, from Champagne region, made by the *Méthode Champenoise.*"

"Well, I salute your good taste, Mr Yummy. I'm pretty much Champagne all the way myself."

"So, then, Mister Gatesave Guy, why must Shenzhen Yummy be served pee-pee?"

"I'm sure we could find some Champagne," I said, glancing hopefully at Laura.

"Discount store Champagne," said Shenzhen Yummy. "Don't bother. Probably also pee-pee."

"Well, then, perhaps we should move on to this mouth-watering Pinot Grigio," I said, sliding the bottle from the ice bucket.

"Pee-pee Grigio, you mean," said Shenzhen Yummy.

The influencers laughed.

"Yes, very good," I replied. "This blend contains wines from Alto Adige, giving it a real twist of sophistication."

"Why is this tasting so boring?" said Shenzhen Yummy. "Maybe I should post that Gatesave has the most boring wine range in China."

Laura advanced briskly on Shenzhen Yummy. She murmured into his ear and he pouted.

"Oh, you are so contractual, Miss Laura. Very well, Shenzhen Yummy will behave."

"We're delighted to hear it," I said. "Now, how about some crisp, summery Sauvignon? We have two – one from the Loire and one from New Zealand."

"I bet they taste the same," said Shenzhen Yummy.

"No, they're actually very different," I said, through gritted teeth. "Different altitude, different climate. Different diurnal temperature variation."

"Ooh, fancy words, Mister Gatesave Guy. But, can *you* tell the difference?"

"You know he is a big Minstrel of Wine?" said the influencer beside him, tittering behind her hand.

"What, this guy? I did not know that." Shenzhen Yummy turned to Laura. "Was that in the information you sent?"

Laura smiled icily.

"Oh. I never read that. Too boring!"

Suddenly, his jaw dropped.

"Wait, no! You are the guy from the video! The Shanghai tasting! Oh, my God. Did everyone see that?"

Some of the influencers nodded. One woman gave a little gasp. "Oh, I did not recognise you. You looked very handsome in the video. But, sorry, now you wear a very ugly shirt!"

The influencers laughed and my eyes dropped to my blue Gatesave sweatshirt, which might indeed have better suited a medium-sized elephant seal.

"Ok, then, Mister Famous Minstrel Guy, we will have some fun. A blind tasting!"

Before I could stop him, he grabbed both bottles of Sauvignon and placed them on the floor. Laura dived in like a sparrowhawk but Shenzhen Yummy held up a hand.

"Just for fun, Miss Laura! To see if Mister Minstrel can taste the difference. Everybody, hide your eyes! And you, Mister Minstrel Guy, you turn around."

I glanced at Laura.

"Can you tell the difference?" she mouthed.

"Of course!" I whispered.

She rolled her eyes and waved us on.

"Ok, no peeping!" called Shenzhen Yummy.

The influencers placed their hands over their eyes. I turned around. The bar had a mirrored back but Shenzhen Yummy took care to pour the wine at his feet, out of view. He straightened up and placed a pair of glasses on the bar top.

"Ok, Mister Minstrel Guy, you ready?"

I turned back and Shenzhen Yummy pushed the glasses towards me.

"I do apologise, Mr Minstrel Guy, I thought you were just some store guy. You will be able to tell, easy, I am sure."

I lifted the first glass, swirled it and smelled. Pretty bland, lime fruit, touch of grapefruit. The vaguest hint of herbaceous grassiness.

"This is the French, I think."

"Wow, confident! He hasn't even smelled the other yet!"

I lifted the second glass and repeated my actions. A more prominent fruit character, a little more grassy, a touch of green pepper, too.

"And this one's the Kiwi."

"Are you sure?" said Shenzhen Yummy, grinning.

I returned to the first glass, just to be certain. But now this one seemed more vibrant too. Christ, was this the New Zealander? I tasted it. One dimensional fruit, fairly prominent acidity. Cooler climate, I was sure of it.

"Yes, I think this is the French one. It's from Touraine, you can tell."

I tasted the second. But, damn it, this one now tasted blander than before – none of the capsicum or hints of tarragon I'm sure I'd picked up a minute earlier. Was this the French one, after all? I wiped my brow. Perhaps after the weekend's trauma my perception was off.

"Actually, give me a second."

"Oh, no, Mister Minstrel. You cannot tell the difference! You must send back your Minstrel hat!"

The influencers laughed and I felt a flush of anger. What was this, some kind of trick? I tasted the first wine again. Dumb, stupid, flat, lemon and unripe peach, awful acidity, lean and sour. Then the second. Stingy, pinched, stale herbs and over-ripe pear, supermarket lime juice in a plastic squeezy bottle. Revolting.

"Actually, that's the New Zealander," I said, pointing to the first one, "and that's the French."

"You changed your mind! Are you sure? Final answer!"

I lifted both glasses and moved my nose between the two. They were clearly different. Crap, but different.

"Well, it's actually quite tricky," I said, going redder still. "The French one is made in a very ripe style. While the New Zealand is quite restrained and a deliberately old-world expression."

Shenzhen Yummy giggled.

Smell again. Think, damn it! Pyrazine. Wet flint. Fresh-grated nutmeg.

"No!" I declared. "That's the French one. And that's the Kiwi. There. Now, tell me."

"You are right!" said Shenzhen Yummy.

"Yes!" I shouted, making the nearest influencer jump.

"And you are also wrong!" he laughed.

"What? What do you mean?"

"Both wines are the same!"

Shenzhen Yummy let out a shriek of laughter. The other influencers tittered at me from behind their hands.

"The same?" I said.

I looked at the glass in my right hand, then the one in my left, then stared at Shenzhen Yummy until his laughter stuttered and faded to a nervous smirk.

"The same," I repeated. "Oh, my God."

I banged the two glasses down on the counter. Laura skipped behind the bar and placed a hand on my arm.

"Now, Felix. Calm down. He's only having a little fun."

"Oh. Bad loser," whispered Shenzhen Yummy.

I stepped out from behind the bar and Laura launched herself after me, grabbing my oversize sweatshirt with both hands.

"No, Felix, don't!"

But I had no intention of causing trouble. A wave of euphoria was rising inside me, a moment of clarity that made the back of my neck tingle and my head pound.

"Shenzhen Yummy, thank you!" I called. "I shall post you my Minstrel hat the moment I'm home!"

# Chapter 35

## Enlightenment

"It began with a viral video clip from a Saturday night Shanghai wine tasting," said the presenter, striding across the studio, "and by Monday morning it had become fully fledged stock market rout."

She waved her hand at the vast screen behind her; a sea of red figures, downward-pointing triangles and multicoloured line graphs plummeting like streamers from a party popper.

I glanced up and down the deserted carriage for the hundredth time, but the Shenzhen–Hong Kong bullet train was as empty as when I'd departed. I offered a prayer of thanks for the latest border restrictions and my eyes returned to the screen above the seat opposite. In the bottom right corner, a rectangle of silent video played above the caption 'RIP Wine?' The star of the video? Felix Hart, of course, Minstrel of Wine, global tasting supremo and victim of the most horrendous deepfake since the invention of Photoshop. I watched Fake Felix for the hundredth time, a glass held delicately in each of his fake hands, expounding on the genius of Joseph Lee and his wine reproduction machine.

"Project Athena is the phrase on every stock picker's lips," continued the presenter, "as Joseph Lee, CEO of Greater China Pharmco, reveals the secret at the heart of his AI-driven Neural Terafactory. Premium drinks companies and pharmaceutical stocks are the biggest fallers, as short sellers pile in and investors take fright at the implications for their business models. Paris-Blois Beverages, the newly created vehicle for that company's drinks brands, is the biggest faller, losing forty per cent of its value in just ten minutes' trade, its Paris listing now suspended until tomorrow morning."

I wondered how many Paris-Blois Beverages share options Sandra had. Quite a few, I guessed. I strongly suspected that I'd properly blown it with her this time. Maybe I was never in with a chance. But it's nice to dream. The bullet train glided into West Kowloon's gleaming, deserted railway station. I sailed through immigration and jumped into a cab for the short ride to the Shangri-La hotel. Despite my excitement, I'd reckoned it safer to wait until I was back in Hong Kong before sharing my news. With trembling fingers, I brought up Provost Jordaan's number. But an incoming call beat me to it.

"Felix! Adam Fromage speaking. How are you, old chap?"

"Ah, hello, Adam. Extremely glad to be back in Hong Kong, that's for sure."

"Yes, you've been causing a bit of trouble up-country, I believe?"

"I've had a pretty rough time, to be honest. That *Cercle Chêne* tasting turned out to be a complete hoax."

"Didn't look like a hoax, old chap. I've seen the video. Looks like you had a hell of a time. Going by social media views, you're the only thing the wine trade's talking about right now."

"Look, I'm sure you're as upset as the rest of the trade about that video, but I can explain."

"What's to explain, old chap? That clever devil Lee has invented a wine machine, or whatever the hell it is. Sure, it's a bloody disaster for winemakers. And I wouldn't want to be a wine trade shareholder right now. But you can't just un-invent something like that. We'll have to adapt. Looks like I'll be buying fine Burgundy from Joseph Lee in future rather than selling it to him."

I could hardly bear to let Fromage finish. If you've ever unearthed a wonderful, terrible secret, you'll know just how I was feeling right then. The frothing, boiling pressure that threatens to burst through your chest. The giddy, childlike excitement that makes you want to dance like a Dervish. I'd bottled it up all the way from Shenzhen, across the border and into Hong Kong. But the euphoria was now so overwhelming that I feared it would blow the top of my head off.

"You have nothing to worry about!" I said. "I've worked it out!"

"Worked what out, old chap?"

"It's all a big fraud," I shouted, the blood rushing to my head. "The whole thing!"

"What's a fraud? I don't understand. Are you sure the Shanghai sun hasn't got to you?"

"Joseph Lee's machine."

"You're gabbling, old chap. I don't follow."

"Joseph Lee is pretending. He's been pretending all along! His wines are genuine!"

"You've really lost me, I'm afraid. Your Minstrel of Wine friends analysed that bottle. They're fakes. Dodgy as a nine-dong note."

"Joseph Lee is a billion-dollar bullshitter!"

"It sounds like you've had a hell of a weekend, old chap. Why don't we go for a drink? I can ask my driver to collect you. You're at the Shangri-La, yes?"

I don't know what it was that turned my hot-headed euphoria to an icy chill. A slight change of tone in Fromage's voice? The fact that he suddenly wanted to socialise, when it was pretty clear from our earlier meetings he couldn't bear me? Or was it my recollection of his ex-boss, the late Owen Farquhar, and the thought of his shark-nibbled corpse bobbing around the South China Sea? Whatever it was, I realised I should have kept my stupid mouth zipped instead of blabbing like a teenage drunk.

"To be honest, Adam, I might just turn in. It's been a long weekend, and a pretty long Monday, too."

"Nonsense, old chap. I won't hear of it. I've just left Wan Chai, I'll get my driver to circle round and pick you up. Stay put, ok?"

"Ok," I said and hung up. I leaned forward and placed my nose against the plastic safety screen.

"Airport, driver," I said. "Change of plan. Very quickly, please."

"Wa? You go back West Kowloon?"

"No, no, not West Kowloon station. The airport. Chek Lap Kok. Quickly, please."

Muttering in Cantonese, the driver continued past the hotel turn-off, taking us north and then west along Austin Road. I'd left my spare clothes and laptop at the Shangri-La, but I didn't dare retrieve them. I had my passport and my phone, everything else was expendable.

Incoming call. A Macau number.

"Hey, handsome. What are you up to?"

It was Kaia. My mood immediately lifted.

"Heading home, actually. Had a pretty hectic few days. You?"

"I'm in Hong Kong. Wondered if you wanted to drop by this evening. I don't have any plans."

"I would, but... damn, I'm supposed to be flying home tonight."

"So, change your flight. I'm bored. I need entertaining. I'm staying at the InterContinental."

"My God, which billionaire paid for that?"

"Tell me about it. The bathroom's absolutely enormous. Way too big for me alone. I was about to take a shower, actually. But I could wait, if you're quick. When can you be here?"

I thought back to our night together after the Macau tasting. And the next morning, when the chief flunky from Phantasos had dropped off those empty bottles, including the Musigny '78, the very one I'd been tasked with stealing. Even then, it had seemed too ridiculously good to be true.

"The InterContinental it is. See you in ten minutes."

"You go InterContinental now?" asked the driver, changing lanes for the Western Tunnel turn-off.

"No!" I shouted. "The airport! Chek Lap Kok! Chek Lap Kok!"

Muttering rather louder now, the driver changed lanes again, just in time. My phoned pinged with a message.

*Room 805. No bathrobe required. X*

Absolutely shameless. You had to hand it to her. Was she

even in Hong Kong? Seemed unlikely. I wondered what awaited me in the bathroom of room 805. A naked hitman with a garotte and a bone-saw, no doubt.

My phone rang again. The same number that Fromage had used earlier.

"We've just arrived at the Shangri-La. Where are you? Can't see you in Reception."

"I'm feeling a little off-colour, Adam. Do you mind if we take a rain check?"

"Come on, old chap," said Fromage. "Don't be a bloody woman. Get yourself down here. I want to hear about your adventures."

"Ok, ok. I'll be right with you. Give me a few minutes to get changed."

I hung up. Could he tell that I was in a vehicle, racing along the motorway? Would he guess that I was heading for the airport? More importantly, could he stop me? I scrolled through Skyscanner to find the next London flight. Back in the days before pestilence, recession and war, there had been several Hong Kong to London connections each day. But right now there was only a single flight each evening, and the departure wasn't for another five hours. Not ideal when the hunt's picked up your scent.

The driver pulled up at the drop-off zone and tutted at the deserted taxi queue. Once I'd paid, he didn't waste a moment, accelerating into the dusk the moment I'd shut the door. I strode into the terminal, swapping the warm evening air for the frigid air-con. After the noise and speed of the motorway the airport was ghostly still. Most of the check-in desks were deserted, though I spotted a sad, silent queue at one of the Cathay counters yet to open. I glanced at the screen and realised it was the London flight. I thought of Fromage's assistant, Connie, and her brother, leaving Hong Kong's comfortable climate for the cold drizzle of my home city.

But I didn't dare hang around for five hours. Both Fromage and the duplicitous Kaia would have guessed by now that I was doing a runner. Both, it was safe to assume, would be reporting their suspicions to Lee or his minions. Where the hell could I flee to? I checked the main departures screen. The next flight was to Singapore. That would have been absolutely perfect. But agonisingly, as I watched, the indicator flicked from Final Call to Gate Closed. The next two flights were to Chengdu and Hangzhou. Not a good idea. No doubt Lee had a private army, not to mention a zoo full of carnivorous aquatic animals, in each city. But the departure after that, just ninety minutes away, was Toronto. Perfect. I marched up to the Cathay ticket desk, my tiny, near-empty cabin bag under my arm, trying not to appear suspiciously desperate. The clerk looked up from her phone.

"Can I buy a ticket to Toronto, please?"

"Why don't you buy online, sir?"

"I did, but my secretary booked the wrong flight. Wrong day."

"Ok, so, I can change the ticket."

"Sorry, no. She booked the wrong airline. Wrong city. As well as the wrong day. All completely wrong. Not her fault of course. She's new. Badly trained. My fault. Can I just buy a ticket for that flight, please? The one at seven p.m.?"

"This one tonight?" The woman gave a little laugh. "That is very soon!"

"Yes, I know. That's why I like it. Can't wait to go and see the, erm, that very tall tower."

"They have taller towers in Shanghai."

"Yes, I've seen them. Loved them. Can't wait to see more. Hence my enthusiasm for Toronto. Can I buy a ticket, please?"

"It may be too late, sir. Let me check."

The woman made a phone call, which I suspected, though I do not speak Cantonese, included rather more social chit-chat than necessary for a straightforward booking enquiry. After five rather agonising minutes, she replaced the handset.

"Yes, that should be ok. Your passport, please?"

I handed it over and my heart rate slowed a little. An hour and a half. Hopefully, that was enough to evade Lee's pursuers, especially once I was through security.

"You have Canada visa?" asked the woman, flicking through the pages.

"A visa? For Canada? I'm British. Can't I just fly there?" I said.

"You need eTA authorisation. You can apply online."

"Oh, God. How long will that take?"

"I don't know. Maybe a few hours, or one day, something like that."

"Jesus! That's no good, then, is it! What else do you have?"

I turned back to the departures screen. The next flight after Toronto was to Hanoi.

"You need a visa for Vietnam, don't you?"

"Yes, I think so," said the woman, now looking a little alarmed.

The following flight was to Beijing. The next to Manila. After that, a Qatar flight to Doha, but that was four hours away.

"How about Manila?"

"You want to buy now?"

"Yes, please."

*Quick as you can please, madam*, I thought. *I simply can't wait to hang out with a bunch of machine-gunning gangsters. My idea of heaven. Perhaps I'll bet on a few cockfights as I wait my turn in the nearest brothel.*

"Return flight?"

I nearly asked which was cheaper, but I suspected that a mildly desperate-looking man with no luggage requesting an immediate one-way flight to Manila might raise the suspicions of even the sleepiest travel agent, so I opted for a return.

Fifteen colon-churning minutes later, I had a return ticket to the Philippines in my sweaty hand. I obtained my boarding card from the Manila check-in desk, passed through security, with little more than a pair of underpants and three mobile phones to convey through the X-ray machine, then headed to the line of immigration exit cubicles guarding the departures hall. Only one booth was staffed. I handed over my passport. The officer examined it as if it was something that had adhered itself to the sole of his boot.

"You go Manila on holiday?" he frowned.

"Yes," I croaked. "Nice beaches."

The officer stared at me as sweat cascaded down my back. Then, he pushed my documents back beneath the window. Heart thumping, I crept through into departures and installed myself at a deserted caviar and Champagne bar. I tried calling Provost Jordaan again, but her phone went straight to voicemail. I tapped out a message on her special handset:

*At HK airport leaving China now*

I placed my own phone on the bar and eyed the glass-fronted fridge full of frosted Champagne. I was desperate for a palate cleanser. I wondered whether they'd mind a little self-service. I still had a wad of US dollars; I could leave cash on the counter, surely? I slid off my stool, checked to see whether anyone was watching, and slipped behind the bar. As I reached innocently for the fridge door, my phone erupted into the silence like an air-raid siren. I spun round, snatched it up and dropped to a crouch behind the counter. A withheld number. Fromage again, trying to disguise himself? Should I ignore it? It might be Provost Jordaan, finally calling back.

"Hello?" I whispered.

"Felix Hart. This is Inspector Ma."

# Chapter 36

## Final Call

Inspector Ma! What the hell did he want? It must have been two months since I last saw him, when he and Sandra first briefed the Provosts about *Le Cercle Chêne*. God, that seemed like years ago now, and I'd sincerely hoped I'd seen the last of him.

"I'm just here, having a drink," I said, sweating freely despite the aggressive air-con.

"And where is here, please, Mr Hart?"

"Oh, sorry! Yes, I'm here in the bar. At the Shangri-La, Kowloon. Is everything all right?"

Why had I lied? The inspector was allegedly on my side, wasn't he? We were all trying to bring down Joseph Lee, a crook who had just attempted to feed me to his harem of elephant seals. I had no reason not to trust the extremely creepy Hong Kong detective inspector, a man who looked as though he collected insects and pulled their legs off for fun.

"I think you are at the airport, Mr Hart."

My blood turned to ice.

"Well, it doesn't look much like an airport from where I'm sitting, Inspector," I said, feeling sick. "Unless they've just converted Victoria Harbour to a seaplane runway!"

"You are in the departures lounge at Hong Kong airport."

How they hell did he know that? Was I being tailed? I slowly lifted my head and peeped over the bar. The only person visible was a cleaner in the distance, pushing a V-shaped mop along the gleaming floor. I watched him for a few seconds, but I was damned if I could tell whether he was a spy brilliantly impersonating a cleaner, or the real thing.

"I'm not going to argue with you, Inspector. If you don't mind, I'm a little busy with work right now. Perhaps we can speak tomorrow?"

"But I insist on speaking to you now, Mr Hart."

"Sorry, I really can't, right now. But I'll definitely call you back."

"I will be arriving at the airport, in person, very shortly. The authorities have been instructed not to permit you to board that flight."

I sank back to a crouch. A horrible, dry lump crept slowly down my throat, like a wad of coarse sawdust.

"Why... why not?"

"I wish to ask you some questions. Then you will be free to go. Where are you, exactly, in the departures lounge?"

"I'm heading to the business-class lounge," I said, eyeing a plastic tub of cocktail olives to which someone had attached a sticker saying, 'short life'. Call it intuition, but lying definitely struck me as the safest policy.

"Turn around and return to passport control. One of my officers will be there presently. He will escort you back through security."

"Right," I said. "I'll still have time to catch my London flight, will I?"

A short pause.

"That should not be a problem, Mr Hart, provided you follow my instructions."

The inspector hung up. I remained crouched behind the bar, staring at my phone. It looked pretty damn clear that Inspector Ma was not on my side. Was he even a real policeman? Perhaps he was something worse. After all, his special letter had sped me through Hong Kong and mainland China immigration all those times with suspicious ease. And there was something else that had been nagging at me. When Lee was showing me around his factory, before he decided to feed me to his psychotic menagerie, I'd requested whether his bodyguard might treat me a little more gently. Lee had seemed unsure and suggested someone had told him I was dangerous. But who would have done that? I'd behaved immaculately, relatively speaking, at the Macau tasting, so it can't have been Kaia or any of his flunkies. Fromage had never seen me misbehave. Nor had Charles Fung. But Ma had witnessed the rough and tumble at the Magnum Club Platine tasting, right at the start of the whole jolly adventure. It looked unpleasantly likely that Inspector Ma was Lee's man.

As was dear Sandra, let's face it. Not nice to realise the whole world's conspiring against you, but Sandra did have form. You might even describe her as serially duplicitous when it came to my wellbeing, so it would have been naïve to be overly surprised. All the same, a bit of a shame. I thought this time might have been different. Then, as I stared at my phone, a more urgent thought occurred to me. I was still carrying Lee's little Samsung handset. What an idiot. Of course, that's how they'd intercepted me at the Shanghai Tower. Those strangely behaved women at the Heavenly Jin desk beside the elevator, half-panicking as they realised I was incoming two hours early. It was almost funny imagining them scrambling to set up the phoney restaurant desk and assembling the heavies. Almost funny, but not quite, considering the nightmare I'd been subjected to by Mr Lee and his circus of carnivorous blubber.

Time for action. Fifty minutes until my Manila departure, but four whole hours until the London flight. When I failed to turn up at security, Ma would assume I was laying low in the business-class lounge, or perhaps hiding in the toilets. Frustratingly, due to the collapse in passenger demand, only one Cathay lounge was currently operating. In happier times, there would have been half a dozen. This, obviously, counted against me. So, where was the lounge? Near gate 65, according to the terminal map. Gate 65 was the London gate, which was ideal. Whereas my Manila flight departed from gate 45, a pleasing distance away in a different wing of the terminal. Might that be far enough away to buy me some time?

I snatched up my bag and began jogging in the direction of the lounge. No doubt this would attract the attention of Inspector

Ma's spies, but I was pretty sure I was the only non-Chinese person in the entire terminal, so it barely seemed to matter. I passed gate 63, then 64, then neared gate 65. There was the lounge, just beyond. I slowed and caught my breath. A lone woman was seated behind a concierge desk a few yards inside the lounge entrance. Keeping close to the wall, I sidled up to one of the giant pot plants straddling the entrance, extracted Lee's little Samsung phone, and shoved it into the clay pebbles covering the soil. I retreated and marched swiftly back the way I'd come, towards the Manila gate.

Forty minutes to departure. There was the aircraft, looming outside the window, the jet bridge already attached to the gate. A couple of dozen passengers sat silently, waiting for boarding. No sign of any staff. I glanced at the screen. Departure time five minutes later than scheduled. My heart sank. I ducked into the gents' toilets opposite the gate and locked myself in a cubicle. I closed the toilet seat and sat on it. My phone rang. A withheld number.

"You are not at passport control, Mr Hart. I thought my instructions were clear."

"I headed there straight away, Inspector," I said. "There was no-one there to escort me through."

"I told you an officer would be there presently. You must return immediately."

"I asked the officer in the booth, but he told me to go away. He was quite abrupt, actually."

"Return to the passport control area now, Mr Hart."

"I did tell the officer in the booth that Inspector Ma wanted to see me, but he didn't seem to care. I'm rather concerned that if I return, he'll arrest me."

"You are currently in the Cathay lounge, is that correct?"

Well, that answered that little conundrum. I wondered how accurate the tracking app in Lee's phone was. Hopefully, no less than a couple of dozen metres. That would include the adjacent gates, toilets and various other hiding places, making a search just that little more time-consuming.

"Yes, I'm back in the lounge now. Would you mind sending one of your men to collect me, please? I really don't want to have to deal with that other chap again."

"Proceed to the passport control area immediately, Mr Hart. I'm not requesting–"

"Sorry, Inspector," I shouted, "I have another call! It's the office, must be important. Hold on, please!"

I hung up. For now, it sounded like the good inspector's jurisdiction didn't extend beyond the immigration exit booths, though I suspected it would not take long for Ma to make the necessary calls to the Hong Kong Immigration Service.

I listened for a second, checking no-one was outside the cubicle, then stepped out and eased open the main bathroom door, just an inch. I peered through. The passengers were now queuing at the gate. Best to take cover for a few more minutes, I reasoned, rather than find myself exposed in the open. My mobile rang. I switched it to silent before answering.

"Is that you, Inspector?"

"If you don't proceed to passport control immediately, Mr Hart, you will be arrested. And you will not make your flight. Not today, not next week, probably not even next month. Do you understand?"

"I'm on my way already, inspector. I don't see why you have to be so rude."

"I hope you are not lying to me, Mr Hart."

"I'm nearly at passport control now! I've left my bag in the lounge."

"You should not have left your bag unattended."

"Apologies, Inspector, you're right. I'll go back and get it."

"No, do not–"

I hung up. There were only so many times I was going to get away with that trick. I opened the gents' door a crack and took another peep. To my relief, passengers were now trickling past the desk and on to the ramp. But slowly, oh-so slowly. Still a queue of twenty or so, and only a single member of staff processing the boarding passes. Given his harassed expression, I guessed he was some kind of trainee. My phone started vibrating in my sweating hand. I let it play through to voicemail. *Come on, man*, I urged, through the crack in the door, as the trainee held a boarding pass in front of the reader, frowned, then with a smile turned it and presented the other side. One more passenger through. Good God, what was that, one every two minutes? At this rate it would be another hour before everyone was boarded.

It was warm in the gents' bathroom. I moved away from the door and grabbed a handful of toilet tissue to mop my brow. I wondered how annoyed the inspector was getting. I tossed the ball of sodden tissue into the bin and stepped up to the door again. I moved my eye close to the crack, preparing to take another peek at the gate, and pulled slowly at the handle.

The door exploded open, as if booby trapped. The corner cracked against my head and my phone was sent spinning across the floor. I staggered backwards, clutching my forehead, and groaned. Not in pain, despite the grievous assault upon my skull, but in despair. For standing in the doorway, in starched white shirts and neatly ironed trousers, were two officers of the Hong Kong Immigration Department.

I looked from one officer to the other, wondering which one intended to hurl himself upon me first. A persistent buzzing filled the air. I assumed it must be concussion. Then I realised my phone was vibrating against the floor tiles in a nearby cubicle.

"Do you mind if I get that?" I said.

The officers appeared nonplussed. I staggered into the cubicle, retrieved my phone from the floor and answered it.

"Mr Hart. I have run out of patience. I have sent officers to collect you."

"There was no need for that!" I moaned, stepping out of the cubicle to meet my fate. "I told you I was on my way!"

"You all right?" said one of the officers, peering at my forehead.

"Yes, I suppose," I squeaked, utterly defeated.

"Be more careful in future."

The men stepped around me. Two cubicle doors banged shut

and the tinkle of emptying bladders filled the air. I nearly fainted with relief.

"I'm... I'm heading back to passport control right now," I said to Ma, slipping swiftly out of the gents and checking left and right for lurking authority figures. "The staff at the lounge confiscated my bag because I left it unattended. They've locked it away. The person with the key has gone for a cigarette break."

"Where are you, Mr Hart? Right now, what is your location?"

"I've just passed gate 63. Nearly at gate 62. Going past gate 62 now. Gate 61 just ahead of me. I'll be passing gate 61 in a minute or so. There are a lot of gates."

As casually as possible, I joined the back of the queue snaking from the Manila gate. The attendant now appeared to have familiarised himself with the workings of the boarding-pass machine but was determined to protect himself from any suggestion of over-productivity by leaning over the desk, arms folded, and chatting with a rather infirm-looking elderly couple. I bit my lip and supressed the urge to march to the front of the queue and start processing passengers myself.

"I'm expecting you at passport control in one minute, Mr Hart," said Ma's voice.

"Make it two, Inspector. Just nipping to the gents for a pee. I'm a bit desperate."

I hung up.

The elderly couple moved past the desk and began tottering their way down the gangway, the gate attendant watching their progress. The elderly woman paused and glanced back. The attendant gave her a little wave. For a terrible second, I thought he was going to sing a song to accompany them all the way to the aircraft. But, finally, he turned back to the queue and smiled at the next passenger. I clenched my teeth and tried to take deep breaths. My phone was vibrating. I ignored it. A boarding pass was presented, the machine gave a burp, another passenger stepped past the desk and disappeared down the ramp. Then a pause. I craned my neck to see what was happening. The desk appeared to be surrounded by a semicircle of passengers and

I could swear the attendant was attempting to perform some kind of card trick with his fistful of boarding passes. Behind me, I heard the gents' toilet door opening. A crackle of radio and a short burst of Cantonese. I stood completely still, armpits dripping, imagining the officers drawing their weapons and taking aim at my back. I could hear their voices approaching. I began to shake. I didn't dare turn round. My phone vibrated again and, for want of anything better to do, I answered it.

"Mr Hart."

"Yes, Inspector," I said, quietly. "I'm here, at security. Where are you?"

"Are you playing games, Mr Hart? I hope, for your sake, that you are not."

The two officers were right behind me. I could hear them breathing. I tensed my shoulders, expecting the iron hand of the authoritarian police state to seize the back of my neck.

"I'm not playing games!" I whispered. "I'm here, at security!"

"Where? Where exactly?" shouted Ma.

"Erm. I'm near Jenki Korean Kitchen."

I heard Inspector Ma bark something in Cantonese.

"Where is that? You should be next to the immigration exit kiosks."

"There are definitely kiosks here. I'm next to Cha Cha Bubblicious Bubble Tea. Does that help?"

Again, I heard Ma shout. The officers strolled slowly past me. The nearer one turned and stared. I gave a friendly rictus grin that was not reciprocated. The men walked to the front of the queue and exchanged a brief greeting with the attendant, then turned and sauntered on to the next gate. There was movement at the front of the queue and a large party began filing their way down the ramp, shortening the line to half a dozen.

"Describe your position more clearly!" shouted Inspector Ma.

"I've told you," I said. "I'm between Jenki Korean Kitchen and Cha Cha Bubblicious Bubble Tea. On level four."

"Not level four!" shouted Ma. "Level seven! Passport control is on level seven!"

"Oh, goodness!" I said. "I'm sorry. Hang on, I'll be right there."

I hung up.

A young woman held her smartphone against the gate attendant's scanner, they exchanged friendly smiles, and she proceeded down the gangway. Just four passengers to go. Then, in the distance, rapid, heavy footsteps. Two men running. My heart quickened. I lowered my head. Another passenger cleared the desk and descended the ramp. Out of the corner of my eye, I could see the two white-shirted officers jogging towards us, one of them with his hand to his ear. I shuffled a little closer to the man in front, hoping by some miracle I might be overlooked. Another passenger passed through the doorway. But it was too late. The officers were upon us. I closed my eyes. I felt the waft of air as they thundered past, the pounding of their boots growing quieter as they hurried back to the main departure hall.

My phone was vibrating. But I was at the front of the queue, the last to board. The gate attendant smiled and held out his hand. I gave him my boarding pass. He held it to the scanner and the machine thought for a second. Then a second more. Then it gave an angry beep. The attendant shook his head.

"Sir," he said. "No space."

"I will very happily lie in the aisle," I said, tears welling in my eyes. "Or curl up in an overhead locker. Or stand on my head in the toilet. Or cling to the undercarriage. Anywhere. Please. Please."

"No space in economy, sir," he beamed. "You are upgraded. Business class!"

With a flourish, the attendant defaced my boarding pass with his pen.

"Oh, oh, good," I said, the tears now cascading down my cheeks.

"You ok, sir?" said the attendant, looking concerned. He peered at my forehead. "Ah, you are hurt. I call for medical assistance?"

"No, no need," I said.

"But perhaps you are not ok to fly," he said. "Let me call for help."

"It's a birthmark," I said, snatching the boarding pass from his hand. "And I'm allergic to nurses. I forbid you from taking any further action!"

I leapt through the doorway and sprinted down the gently sloping gangway. As I sped around the corner, I nearly collided with the line of passengers still queueing to enter the aircraft. I could see the elderly couple making heavy weather of stepping through the aircraft door, despite the pathetic assistance of the flight crew. I considered barging to the front and giving them a helpful shove.

My phone was vibrating. Three missed calls. Too dangerous to ignore.

"Before you start shouting, Inspector, I can inform you that I have now returned to the business-class lounge. I could not find the passport control booths. They must look completely different from the other side."

"But I am in the business-class lounge, Mr Hart. As are six members of the Hong Kong Immigration Service. The lounge is empty. It is quite clear that you are not here."

"This is a little embarrassing, Inspector."

"Where are you, Mr Hart? I assure you the consequences of wasting any more of my time will be extremely unpleasant."

"I'm in the gents. Not feeling too good, actually. I had a fish supper in Tai O last night and I think I've eaten something funny. I wouldn't come in if I were you."

Ma gave a shout. I heard the sound of boots running and doors being barged open. The elderly couple finally negotiated the aircraft door and wobbled their way on board. I was relieved to see them guided left into business class, allowing the remaining passengers to file into economy.

"Where? Where are you?" shouted Ma.

"I'm not in the lounge toilets. I'm in the other ones, opposite the lounge entrance. I told you, I'm not in a good way. I didn't want to cause any awkwardness with my fellow business-class passengers."

Further shouting and more thumping of boots. I stepped on to the aircraft. The attendant showed me to my seat and pressed a glass of Champagne into my hand.

"If you do not reveal your location in the next few seconds, Mr Hart, you will be taken to the police facility at Tsing Yi. You will find their techniques differ quite markedly from the gentlemanly approach of your own Scotland Yard."

I didn't doubt it for a second. I muted the phone as the safety announcement played from the video screens. The aircraft door swung closed with a thump. Back in economy class, I could hear the cabin attendants slamming shut the overhead lockers. When it was quiet, I unmuted my phone.

"I'm finishing up, Inspector. Oh, just a second. I've run out of paper."

"You were in Shenzhen last night, Mr Hart. Not Tai O."

The aircraft's engines increased in volume and the plane began to trundle away from the gate. The flight attendant leaned over and directed me to switch my device to flight-safe mode. I nodded and fiddled with the handset, pretending to do what she asked. Just another minute, to be sure.

"Ok, Inspector, I'm done," I said, ducking so the attendant couldn't see me speaking. "I'm over here."

"Where?"

"I can see you, Inspector. Next to the water fountain."

"Where? Where?" shouted Ma.

"No, the other direction. Over here. I'm waving at you!"

"WHERE?" screamed Ma.

I switched the phone to flight-safe mode as the engines built to a roar. The aircraft accelerated down the runway, lifted slowly from the ground, and within seconds the rush of grey tarmac was replaced by the blue South China Sea.

# Chapter 37

## Eastward Bound

I confess the flight was perhaps the least relaxing of my life, despite the regular Champagne refills. Every little nudge and lurch of the plane had me fearing that the pilot had been ordered to turn around and return to Hong Kong, where I pictured a reception committee of the People's Liberation Army lining the tarmac, weapons drawn. I kept my face pressed to the window, watching the portion of sky visible from my seat, expecting a pair of fighter aircraft to drift lazily into view at any moment, the pilots' mirrored faces scanning the airliner's fuselage, then a gloved hand suddenly stabbing a finger towards my little window. Or I would stare down at the sea, watching for the tell-tale flash signalling the launch of a surface-to-air missile, then the terrifying few seconds as the missile streaked towards its prey, my futile escape ending in an inferno of aviation fuel and a screaming, flaming, ten-thousand-foot plummet into the shark-infested ocean.

But it appeared that Inspector Ma's authority didn't extend to the People's Liberation Army Air Force, nor the missile batteries perched upon the atolls of the South China Sea, so my nerve-shredding terror only persisted for ninety minutes, until the flight path tracker on my seat screen suggested we were firmly in Philippine airspace. Even then, I remained on edge as I emerged from the aircraft, fearing the inspector might have rounded up a joint Philippine–Chinese reception committee.

Then again, perhaps Inspector Ma's goons were still busy kicking in every toilet cubicle door in Hong Kong airport. Even if they were, I decided it was still wise to put as much distance between me and the People's Republic of China as possible. I called my Global Executive Assistant and instructed them to book a night at Manila's Peninsula Hotel and a morning flight to Los Angeles, followed by one to London. Definitely the long way round, but I felt I should avoid Chinese airspace for the foreseeable future, possibly for the remainder of my life. Conscious of my promise to Provost Jordaan to stay in touch, I texted the Malherbes.

*Arrived in Manila. Fromage and Ma hostile, working for Lee. In danger. Help.*

A couple of minutes later came the reply.

*Return to London asap. Assume everyone hostile. Do not reveal location on unsecured channels.*

This rather unhelpfully broad advice did nothing for my peace of mind. Worse still, upon arrival at the Peninsula Hotel, I was frustrated to find no record of my reservation. My credit cards appeared not to work either, so I was obliged to pay cash in advance. Thankfully, I still had a reasonable wad of US and Hong Kong Dollars from my Macau bribery fund and was able to cover the cost of a small, sweaty room with a view of the car park. I locked the door, called room service and ordered a bottle of Champagne and a plate of dim sum to calm my nerves. When the concierge arrived, he refused to release my food and beverage until I had paid in full, in cash. Beginning to feel rather like a Serbian scrap metal dealer, I called James, my Luxe Premier Banking account manager, intending to point out that the Luxe Premier Banking service was showing signs of relegation to a decidedly inferior league. To my utter outrage, James informed me that my balance was residing in an 'unapproved, negative status position' and my Global Executive Assistant privileges had been suspended.

"Then I suggest you move my balance back to a positive status position, pretty sharpish," I said. "I'm in the Philippines and I have to return to London within the next twenty-four hours to close a multi-million-pound deal."

"I'm afraid you are at your agreed thirty-thousand-pound

overdraft limit, Mr Hart."

"Thirty thousand pounds!" I gasped. Where in God's name had the money gone?

"You seem surprised, Mr Hart."

"I am surprised, James. How am I supposed to manage day-to-day expenses with such a small overdraft? I demand you extend it immediately, please."

"We can arrange a loan of up to fifty thousand pounds. But it will need to be secured against your assets."

"Fine," I said. "But I need my credit cards unfreezing now. Otherwise, I can't get home."

"Given that you have been such a loyal customer, Mr Hart, I am able to extend your limit by another five thousand pounds and reinstate your Global Executive Assistant service. But it will take two working days to arrange the secured loan."

"Do what you need to do. And I have further instructions for you. Once you have arranged the loan."

"Yes, Mr Hart?"

I explained what needed to be done.

"Right. Actually, Mr Hart, can I suggest you speak to one of our wealth planning specialists first? Or an independent financial advisor?"

"You can suggest what you like, James, but that's what I want you to do."

"I'm not permitted to give financial advice, but your instructions do strike me as uncomfortably bold, Mr Hart. I do advise you, most very strongly, to wait until I can arrange an appointment with one of our wealth planning specialists."

"For a man who is not permitted to give financial advice, you do appear to be advising me rather a lot, James. Do I need to report you to the financial ombudsman?"

"No, definitely not. That's not what I meant, Mr Hart."

"Then can I assume you will proceed with my instructions as soon as the funds are available? And not persist in attempting to advise me, a man at the very pinnacle of the global financial system, on how to handle his money?"

"Very well, Mr Hart. The loan will be arranged and secured against your recent property purchase. The funds will be available in forty-eight hours."

"Jolly good. I'll be in touch. Please ensure my cards are unfrozen immediately, otherwise you'll be hearing from my lawyers."

My dim sum had gone cold. I finished the Champagne and fell asleep in my clothes.

In the morning, I found I was able to purchase breakfast without counting out a wad of Macanese patacas, which suggested James had at least made some effort to unclog my cash flow. At checkout I was handed an envelope containing my Los Angeles boarding passes and informed that my driver was waiting to take me to the airport. I was directed towards a smart young man with a neat moustache, standing beside the concierge desk. As I accompanied him to the door, another young moustachioed man jumped to his feet.

"Mr Hart, sir? Global Executive Assistant service. I am your driver."

"Goodness," I said. "Looks like I've been double-booked. From famine to feast."

"I will be taking sir to the airport," said the first man, giving the interloper a rather unfriendly stare.

"No, this is a mistake," insisted the second man. "I am the driver. Please, sir. Come with me."

The first driver stepped forward and snarled something in, I assume, Tagalog. It struck me Philippine chauffeur culture might be a little rough around the edges, before a rather more alarming implication dawned on me.

"If you'll give me a second, gentlemen, I'll just pop to the gents while you resolve this amicably."

I strode back to the buffet restaurant and headed for the fire exit. Ignoring the shout of, "No exit, sir!" from a nearby waiter, I barged open the door and charged outside, the annoyed squeal of the alarm fading behind me as I sprinted for the taxi rank. I dived into a cab and ordered my third driver of the morning, who was pleasingly ancient and didn't appear the type to turn and plunge a commando knife into my guts, to take me to the airport as fast as possible. *Assume everyone hostile*, the message had said. Damn right.

Four feature films and several fitful dozes later, my plane descended into Honolulu for refuelling. A few passengers disembarked and I checked my messages. I had three: an unpleasant one from a nasal-toned lawyer employed by Paris-Blois, demanding an address so he could serve me with some spiteful documents, one from Provost Jordaan telling me to contact her as soon as I'd left China, and finally a short message from Tabatha Shunt, consisting of her shouting "Call me, sweet cheeks, and I mean NOW!"

It was six a.m. in London, but I called Provost Jordaan anyway, apologising for the early hour.

"It doesn't matter, Minstrel Hart. You didn't send a message last night. Where are you?"

"Sorry, Provost. I've been on a flight. I'm in Hawaii."

"That's not quite the answer I expected. Dare I enquire whether this is a long holiday, or just a mini-break?"

"I'm passing through. Should be back in London tomorrow evening."

"Don't tell me anything else, particularly regarding your travel itinerary. You should assume your personal phone has been compromised. I'm sending Bittercress to collect you from the airport and bring you straight to Minstrels Hall."

Bittercress. That was a *naturae nominee*. A codename for an operative of the Malherbes. The back of my neck prickled.

"Did you book your flights using your personal phone?"

"Yes, but not online. I instructed my Global Executive Assistant to book them. It's a service my bank offers."

"That's not ideal. Listen, Minstrel Hart. Message us on the secure phone when you've landed in London. That will give Bittercress enough time to meet you at the airport. And, most importantly–"

I waited for Jordaan to continue.

"Sorry, Provost, most importantly what?"

But there was no response. My mobile was dead. Damn peculiar, I'd charged it overnight in Manila and had kept the handset on flight-safe mode for the past ten hours. I tried restarting it. Nothing, just a stubbornly blank screen. I plugged it into the USB charger and watched the Honolulu passengers as they settled into their seats. Might one of my fellow travellers be an assassin, preparing to strangle me on the evening leg into Los Angeles? I shelved my plans for a pleasant doze and felt beneath my seat for the fork I'd dropped at lunchtime. There it was, four inches of blunt metal, carefully designed to be of absolutely no use to a violent attacker. I ran my thumb over the rounded prongs. Not an ideal weapon when faced by a fanatical secret service agent wielding a can of neurotoxin, but better than nothing. I slipped it into the seat pocket in front of me, the handle protruding for quick deployment.

But I was not assaulted on the flight to Los Angeles, and the world's least-sharp eating utensil remained safely nestled in its holster. On arrival, I leapt from my seat, grabbed my near-empty hand luggage, and was the first to exit the plane. As I emerged from the ramp, I was surprised to discover a tall woman in an airline uniform holding a tablet displaying my name. Her long, dark hair spilled gorgeously from her cap.

"Mr Hart?" she smiled. "Please follow me."

Los Angeles airport was an astonishing contrast to the morgue-like terminals of China. I'd almost forgotten that airports were supposed to be busy, frantic highways, the arteries of commerce and freedom. The place was heaving with travellers of every shape and colour; lean business folk with ear buds, fractious family groups herding garish wheelie cases, everyone rushing, bustling, and generally doing their thing.

"Do you have your passport ready, Mr Hart?"

The woman's name badge said Julieta. I made a mental note to congratulate my Global Executive Assistant team on the dramatic rebound in their customer service.

"Right here, Julieta."

I noticed that the sign for transit was pointing in the opposite direction. We appeared to be heading for immigration.

"Why are we going this way? I'm in transit, catching a flight to London. It's the same terminal."

"New rules, Mr Hart. Just a quick security check, then we'll show you to the lounge. It's a fast-track service."

"The sign there says I need a visa, or an ESTA visa waiver to pass through immigration," I said, joining the back of the queue.

"We've arranged that for you, Mr Hart."

"Very efficient," I said. "Are you going to accompany me all the way?"

"Would you like me to?" She smiled.

"Yes, please," I said. "But do you mind if I pop to the bathroom first? Long flight."

"Of course not. It's just over there. Let me show you."

The woman accompanied me to the door of the gents.

"You're coming in, are you?" I pushed the door, stepped inside and held it open. I raised my eyebrows and smirked like the worst kind of slimeball.

"No, Mr Hart." A glimpse of irritation. She turned her back and folded her arms. I allowed the door to swing shut, but not before springing through the closing gap like a gazelle and fleeing on tiptoes back the way we'd come, hunching and ducking behind groups of passengers in an attempt to conceal myself. I leapt onto a moving walkway and kept running, weaving between the slower moving travellers, following the signs for transit. Only as I neared security did I glance back. So far as I could tell, no assassins were on my tail, whether long-legged brunettes or otherwise. I switched on Provost Jordaan's phone. A message flashed up from the Malherbes.

*Your other phones and devices likely compromised. Dispose of asap.*

My stomach gave a lurch. What did compromised mean? Could they still track my movements? Were they listening in? Watching? As I joined the queue for screening, I tore a couple of corners from the envelope holding my boarding passes, licked them and stuck them over my smartphone's front and back cameras. The woman in front had a straw beach bag slung over her shoulder, emblazoned with the word *Mykonos*. The top was wide open. I moved closer. Then thought better of it. Not a good move if I was being monitored by some beady-eyed Sherlock in the security control room.

I cleared screening and, rather than retiring to a premium lounge, remained among the crowds thronging the main departures hall. Having abandoned most of my clothes in Hong Kong, I spent a few minutes perusing the apparel in a casual menswear outlet. I tried on a few jackets, made my choice and returned the others to the rail, the inside pocket of one now the new home for my compromised mobile phone. I whiled away my final two hours at Los Angeles International Airport at a bar, keeping my back to the wall and sinking several fortifying glasses of Napa Cabernet. I waited until the departures screen declared that the London flight was boarding before draining my glass and striding to the gate.

# Chapter 38

## The Scourging of Verus

*Just landed Heathrow.*

The reply arrived seconds later, the plane still trundling along the taxiway to the gate.

*Clear immigration soonest. Familiar operatives will meet you at arrivals.*

Familiar operatives. Nice ones, I hoped. Might my Malherbes phone have been compromised too? Had it been merrily feeding me disinformation all week? But no, as I emerged from immigration, there were the rather serious, but reliable faces of Bittercress and Speedwell. Those were their *naturae nominee*, of course, their Malherbes codenames. For Bittercress was none other than Lily, my close and wasp-tongued sommelier friend with whom I had shared a number of unacceptably hair-raising adventures over the past decade. Speedwell, real name Marjatta, was a six-foot tall wine buyer for the Finnish alcohol monopoly, who I had personally witnessed half-drown a sexual harasser in a barrel of fermenting Carignan in a winery in the Languedoc. Both sound lasses to have your back when being hunted by international brigands, that's for sure.

"No chatting, no kissing," said Lily. "Plenty of time for that later. Let's move."

Lily filled me in on what to expect on arrival at Minstrels Hall. Provost Jägermeister, the malevolent snake, had invoked a procedure known as the Scourging of Verus, the most serious disciplinary hearing in the entire Minstrels code. The procedure was reserved for the most heinous crimes possible, namely those that threatened the very existence of the Worshipful Institute itself. The Scourging of Verus was considered so draconian a process it had been invoked only seven times in the past two thousand years. The first time, and the incident that gave the procedure its name, was the attempt in 193 A.D. by Provost Clodius Verus, a drunken poet who headed the ancient House Dionysian, to secede from the Institute and set up a rival version of the Minstrels. As every Minstrel of Wine knows, that incident ended with the drowning of Provost Verus in a barrel of Falernian wine, after which the Institute's guards obliged Verus's followers to drink the barrel's contents as the Provost's lifeless body bobbed and macerated within it.

The last invocation of the Scourging of Verus, and the only occasion in the modern era, was against a character called Minstrel Snipes, a Hitler-worshipping wine merchant from the Isle of Wight, who in 1940 invited a Nazi spy into Minstrels Hall and showed him the secret passage to Covent Garden Tube station. The spy had subsequently attempted to smuggle a wheelbarrow of explosives into the building in an attempt to send Minstrels Hall and much of the surrounding neighbourhood into orbit, a plot foiled only when the spy was detected and accosted by Minstrel Bauhaus, the Institute's house terrier. The German spy was hauled away by the authorities and shot, while ex-Minstrel Snipes was put on trial for treason, found guilty and promptly hung. Even poor Minstrel Bauhaus came to a sticky end after developing a taste for German blood and savaging a perfectly innocent Rhineland winemaker a few months after the armistice; a crime for which he, too, was put down. A cautionary tale against consorting with the far right if ever I heard one.

Frankly, as a selfless servant of the Minstrels, I was extremely aggrieved to find myself in the same boat as a lunatic Roman poet and a Nazi-sympathising terrorist. Nevertheless, it was within the power of any Provost to invoke the Scourging of Verus, and if a majority of the remaining Provosts agreed with the invocation, the Institute was obliged to proceed with the disciplinary process. Apparently, both Provost Rougegorgefils and Provost Lord Slipcote had agreed that there was a case to answer, with only Provost Jordaan demurring.

And so, just minutes after arriving at Minstrels Hall, I was marched by four staff-wielding guards into the Johan Sanz Terre Grand Boardroom, the heart of House Mercantilist, to be tried for grievous crimes against the Institute. Around the boardroom's perimeter sat forty-eight observers, twelve from each House, resplendent in their purple cloaks. As I made my entrance, a babble of excitement rose from the benches and I even discerned a couple of cowardly boos. I recognised faces I'd previously drunk and caroused with, including a few from my own House Terroirist. I wondered if any of them were still my friends.

An ancient wooden table dominated the centre of the Grand Boardroom, its surface pitted with scars. On each of its four sides lay a throne-sized seat. My guards escorted me to one corner of the table, into which a man-sized niche had been cut, where I was obliged to stand and await judgement. The guards positioned themselves behind me and, as one, thumped their staffs four times against the boards. The Provosts entered, their ceremonial gowns a more plummy purple than those of the common Minstrels. The babble quietened. Jordaan took the seat to my left, giving me a nod and a brief smile. Provost Rougegorgefils sat to my right and stared at me like a livid heron. Provost Slipcote took a seat on the opposite side to Jordaan and beamed at the assembled observers from beneath his mop of blond hair. Finally, Provost Jägermeister, the instigator and host of the proceedings, took the remaining chair. I noticed his was slightly higher than those of the other Provosts. Beside him, on a low stool, sat the bespectacled Italian Hand, the note-taker for all official Institute proceedings.

Four more guards filed into the room. But rather than wielding staffs, each carried a decanter of wine and a golden goblet. Each then strode to a particular Provost, placed their goblet reverentially on the table before them and, after a quick glance at one another to ensure they were in concert, filled their respective goblets to the rim.

The Italian Hand then withdrew a wooden flute from the folds of his cloak. He placed it to his lips and brought forth a most startling tune, best described as fire alarm test meets demented song thrush. Provost Jägermeister, an expression of discomfort briefly flitting across his face, placed his middle finger in the ear most exposed to the instrument's trilling. Thankfully, the melody lasted just seconds and the flute vanished back into the Italian Hand's cloak as smoothly as it had appeared. But the music had done its work. The room was now silent. Without thinking, I raised my hands to give a short round of applause, but a filthy look from Jägermeister suggested that clapping at the Scourging of Verus, particularly when one was the subject of the proceedings, was not the done thing.

"Let it be recorded that the Scourging of Verus is now spirituous," snarled Jägermeister. He lifted his golden goblet and took a malevolent sip.

Provosts Rougegorgefils and Slipcote did the same, the latter taking a rather larger sip than the former. Jordaan left her goblet untouched. The Italian Hand observed each Provost, lifted a quill, dipped it in a silver ink-pot, and began scratching upon a roll of parchment.

"Minstrel Hart," boomed Jägermeister, replacing his goblet. "You have been summoned to this place to answer the most heinous charge that it is possible to level against a Minstrel of Wine. You are accused of no lesser crime than plotting the destruction of the Worshipful Institute itself. The evidence of your plot is incontrovertible and has been flaunted before an audience of millions. It is clear that you did blatantly conspire with a hostile polity, led by the Chinese billionaire counterfeiter known as Joseph Lee, to evangelise the benefits of an infernal machine that claims to replicate the bounty of the vineyard in all its myriad facets. And that, therefore, you have committed grievous heresy against the intellectual property, financial sustainability, corporeal body and ethereal soul of the Worshipful Institute in particular and the viticultural world in general."

Jägermeister paused. He looked very pleased with himself.

The Italian Hand dipped his quill and continued to scratch at the parchment.

"Provost Rougegorgefils, do you concur?" said Jägermeister.

"I do," replied Rougegorgefils, fixing me with the look a buzzard might give a baby rabbit as it grasps it in its talons. "Minstrel Hart, to our great disappointment, appears to have thrown in his lot with this Lee character and is clearly acting, quite shamelessly, as his agent."

"Provost Slipcote, do you concur?" said Jägermeister, turning to the Provost opposite.

"Yes, I should say so!" declared Slipcote, taking a hearty swig of wine. "It's one thing reporting back on the end of the wine industry as we know it, but it's quite another becoming a bloody cheerleader for it. Talk about spraying petrol on the barbeque. I know at least a hundred blameless investors who've been reduced to penury this week thanks to the share price collapse this ne'er-do-well has precipitated. Hanging's too good for him!"

"Thank you, Provost Rougegorgefils and Provost Slipcote. We have a majority verdict."

At this, a hubbub rose from the observers. The guards behind me stepped closer. Jägermeister lifted his wine and took a magisterial gulp before banging the goblet down upon the table.

"Minstrel Hart, you are guilty! The penalty, as specified in Dionysian law, is death!"

The hubbub grew louder. Jägermeister raised his voice.

"Unfortunately, in order to retain harmony with local laws and customs, I am obliged to commute your sentence to expulsion from the Worshipful Institute of the Minstrels of Wine. Once you have been escorted from this room, you shall be regarded by the Institute and all its Members, Chapters and Houses as an ex-Minstrel. Let all who have witnessed this judgment be reminded that it is the sacred duty of all loyal Minstrels to confound any attempt by an ex-Minstrel to find employment, realise profit, or enjoy succour of any form in the worlds of viticulture, vinification, cooperage, or the arts and industries deriving from those crafts. Guards, take Minstrel Hart from this place and prevent his return by all means necessary!"

Students of jurisprudence may have spotted that the Scourging of Verus deviates quite significantly from what might be described as legal best practice. In fairness, I had been warned that the procedure dated back to a simpler, more straightforward time, before the widespread implementation of such novelties as legal representation, witnesses, juries, appeals, or even allowing the defendant to speak. Thankfully, not all was lost.

As the guards grasped my arms, Provost Jordaan rose to her feet.

"I invoke the right to Violent Advocacy," she called.

Jordaan lifted her goblet, held it high in the air, then hurled the contents across the table. Immediately, half a dozen of the observers who had been sitting peacefully around the room sprang to their feet, each withdrawing a large wooden truncheon from their cloaks. The guards released me and spun to face their assailants, pinecone-topped staffs at the ready.

"Splendid!" declared Provost Slipcote. "This is proper medieval stuff. When was the last time a Provost demanded Violent Advocacy? Must have been the twelfth century, when we had all those problems with Bernard of Clairvaux. Though, now I think of it, the Portuguese Inquisition was a bit raucous too."

"What nonsense is this?" roared Jägermeister. "Observers, return to your seats at once!"

The Italian Hand, eyes wide behind his spectacles, dabbed a piece of blotting paper delicately against his parchment where Jordaan's wine had contributed a spray of illumination. He unrolled another length of paper, dipped his quill and continued scribbling.

"Interesting," mused Provost Rougegorgefils. "A Provost holding a dissenting opinion regarding the verdict of the Scourging of Verus on a member of their own House is, in theory, permitted to challenge that verdict in armed combat. Provided, of course, that the weapons used are not bladed and are fashioned solely from the wood of the vine."

"This is absolutely ridiculous," shouted Jägermeister. "You can't just trot out some obsolete old nonsense like that and expect us to go along with it. This is the Grand Boardroom of Johan Sanz Terre, not the bloody Colosseum!"

"I beg to differ, Provost Jägermeister," said Slipcote, rubbing his hands. "Provost Jordaan is entirely within her rights. And those House Terroirist boys and girls look like a tasty bunch. Wouldn't bet on your lot if it comes to fisticuffs, my dear Provost."

Provost Slipcote had a point, for Jägermeister had filled his allocation of observers with a distinctly gerontocratic bunch. A useful team to have on your side if the contest was to be argued on the finer points of commercial law, perhaps, but not much use in a proper dust-up.

"Well, Provost Jordaan," sneered Jägermeister. "Now that you have introduced thuggery to this hallowed boardroom, pray tell us how you propose to proceed."

"House Terroirist is in possession of intelligence that contradicts the entire premise of this hearing," declared Jordaan, eyes glittering. "By preventing Minstrel Hart from sharing his findings, the foundations of the Worshipful Institute face an even greater peril than the vicissitudes triggered by his alleged crimes. Not least, the foundations underpinning the Institute's funding, Provost Jägermeister, which I understand you are honour bound to protect on pain of your own expulsion!"

At this, many of the seated observers gasped. Jägermeister avoided Jordaan's eye, scowling instead at the spray of wine, shaped like a flying scimitar, soaking slowly into the boardroom table. He waved a hand at the guards, who returned their staffs to the vertical. Jordaan's club-wielding militia, in turn, lowered their weapons.

All eyes slowly turned to me. The Italian Hand waited, quill poised over his parchment. I cleared my throat.

"Provosts, fellow Minstrels. Thank you for allowing me to update you on this most alarming saga. I understand that many

310

of you fear for your livelihoods. You may even, in part, hold me responsible for the fever currently gripping the financial markets."

"Damn right we do," muttered Jägermeister.

"As you are aware, I have recently returned from Shanghai, where I was a guest of Joseph Lee, the CEO of Greater China Pharmco and one of the world's richest men. Mr Lee is reputed to have built a top-secret facility on the outskirts of Shanghai, which he calls his Neural Terafactory. This facility is the venue for Project Athena, an attempt to create a network of machines that can reproduce the world's most complex materials at high speed and in great quantity. The principal aim of Project Athena is to replicate pharmaceutical products, such as vaccines. But, such is the versatility of these machines, they can allegedly reproduce any organic compound, however complex. Fine wine, for example."

"We know all this, Hart," spat Jägermeister. "And we know you're Lee's emissary on Earth too, damn you."

"On the contrary, Provost. Three days ago, while in China, I deduced the truth about Joseph Lee and Project Athena. As a result, I was obliged to flee the country. As I made my escape back to London, I was subjected to no fewer than five attempted abductions by Lee's agents, including one by an inspector of the Hong Kong Police Service."

"Found you in bed with his wife, did he?" sniffed Jägermeister.

"Decorum please, Provost," said Rougegorgefils. "These proceedings are being recorded."

I glanced at the Italian Hand, scribbling furiously at his parchment.

"I imagine there are several hundred thousand people who'd like a pop at you, Minstrel Hart," said Slipcote. "What makes you think it was Lee?"

"Because I know he's a liar," I said.

The observers stirred and muttered to one another.

"For goodness sake, Minstrel Hart! We know he's a liar," said Rougegorgefils. "He's been faking fine wine and pretending it's genuine at his *Cercle Chêne* tastings for the past year."

"No, Provost. Joseph Lee is a liar because he is *not* faking wine."

The room quietened. I glanced at Jordaan. She gave an encouraging nod.

"Minstrel Hart," said Rougegorgefils. "You stole a bottle of 1978 Musigny Grand Cru from the *Cercle Chêne* tasting in Macau two months ago and brought it to us yourself for analysis. You were in the room when we examined it. The wine was a fake!"

"The packaging was fake, Provost. The screen-printed label with its colour separation. The clumsy attempt to age the label with heat and wire wool. Your very capable assistant, Minstrel Shuttlewort, spotted that in seconds. All very amateurish. But deliberately so. Lee wanted me to steal the empty bottle. We were supposed to think it was a fake."

"But the wine *was* a fake, Minstrel Hart, for goodness sake!" said Rougegorgefils.

"No, Provost! The wine inside the bottle was genuine! Didn't your isotope analysis show a perfect match between the supposedly fake wine and the genuine article from Monsieur Laflamme's estate?"

"Our stable isotope ratio analysis did indeed indicate a precise match," said Rougegorgefils. "That was rather surprising."

"So I understand, Provost. I confess I am not well versed in nuclear physics, but Minstrel Shuttlewort certainly is. She explained to me, very patiently, that even if one is able to precisely reproduce the chemical composition of a compound, which itself is a mind-blowingly complicated feat of chemical engineering, it would be a different level of challenge altogether to replicate its isotope signature."

"It would," said Rougegorgefils.

"Good grief!" exclaimed Slipcote. "If I never hear about isotope ratio analysis again, it will be too bloody soon. So, tell me this, Minstrel Hart. Joseph Lee is alleged to be one of the cleverest men on the planet. A science prodigy. A mathematical genius. Data science, machine learning, all that jazz. So, who's to say he can't replicate the isotope thingies too?"

"Very well. Let us assume he can," I said.

"There we go, then," said Slipcote. "Good at wine, terrible at labels. Wouldn't be the first winemaker to have trodden that route. Not sure your theory holds water, Minstrel Hart."

"But that doesn't explain the other bottle I retrieved from *Le Cercle Chêne*. The unicorn."

"You refer to the empty bottle of Richebourg '21," said Rougegorgefils.

"I do, Provost. The one that you locked in your German battleship safe and analysed for background radioactivity."

"For the love of Bacchus," groaned Slipcote. "One diversion into the realm of nuclear physics is unfortunate. A second is quite *de trop!*"

"Forgive me, Provost Slipcote. But this is rather important. You see, the bottle of Richebourg and the sediment inside it was dated by Provost Rougegorgefils and her team as pre-World War Two. That means it's probably genuine."

"We've covered this already," sighed Jägermeister. "This Lee is a clever devil. Who's to say he can't fake a radiation-free, pre-Second World War wine bottle?"

"It's theoretically possible," said Rougegorgefils, tapping her lips with her forefinger. "But it would be an awfully inconvenient thing to do. You'd have to manufacture the glass in a blast furnace surrounded by an atmosphere stripped of background radiation."

"And you tested the label, too, I believe, Provost Rougegorgefils?" I said.

"We did, yes. The paper stock was also free of background radioactivity. It definitely dates to before the nuclear age. Minstrel Shuttlewort also tested the glue and examined the ink under a high-powered microscope. I would swear that it's genuine."

"At the risk of repeating myself, we're dealing with the world's most cunning billionaire!" shouted Jägermeister, banging on the table. "If he wants to fake a bottle of 1921 Richebourg, he has the means to do it!"

"Then why did he do such an amateur job with the Musigny bottle?" I said.

"I have no bloody idea!" spluttered Jägermeister.

"No. But I do," I replied.

# Chapter 39

## Fake News

The room was silent, all eyes on me.

"Provosts, with hindsight it's clear that Lee was absolutely desperate for me to steal an empty bottle of Musigny '78. The empty bottles were lined up beside me throughout the *Cercle Chêne* tasting. Then, the following morning, a selection of the same empty bottles, including the Musigny, were delivered to the room in which I was staying. They were not aware, you see, that I had already obtained a full bottle."

"What? They sent a bottle to your room?" said Slipcote. "Couldn't they just have posted it to London? Would have saved a hell of a lot of trouble."

"It wasn't exactly my room, Provost. It was another guest of Lee's."

"A guest whose room you were occupying the night of the tasting, Minstrel?" Slipcote raised his eyebrows.

"Good grief," muttered Jägermeister. "The man's a complete moral vacuum."

The Italian Hand peered at me over his glasses and dipped his quill in the ink-pot.

"Indeed," I said, reddening a little. "Lee's staff were aware of my location and pretended the empty bottles were a gift for the other guest. I was then, most conveniently, left alone with them. By contrast, I was not expected to steal the lone bottle of Richebourg '21. Nevertheless, I managed to obtain both bottles and conceal them, undetected, while beneath the table."

"You were with another guest, presumably?" said Slipcote.

A light tittering rose from the room's perimeter.

"I was not, Provost. My point is that the ancient Richebourg was entirely genuine, both the wine and its packaging. Whereas the Musigny was a genuine wine in a fake bottle. A deliberately poorly executed fake, at that."

"It's a creative scenario, Minstrel," said Slipcote, running his hand through his blond mop. "But it's also highly speculative. We'll need more than your vague intuition if you expect us to believe you."

"Provosts, I ask you to recall how this investigation started. We were told that at a *Cercle Chêne* tasting in Dubai, the line-up featured a Burgundy from 1947 – from a domaine that had not resumed its post-war production until 1948."

"We all make mistakes," shrugged Jägermeister.

"A simple enough mistake if you're a mere fraudster. But I've met Joseph Lee. He's an obsessive, whether it's wine or anything else he turns his mind to. Not the type to make a rookie error like that. I believe the dodgy vintage in Dubai was a false flag, created to raise our suspicions and kick-start an investigation."

"Are you suggesting the suspect tasting card from Dubai was created especially for us?" said Rougegorgefils.

"Exactly, Provost. We haven't been investigating Joseph Lee. We've been tricked into thinking we're investigating him. But it's all at his behest."

"Intriguing," said Slipcote. "But still terribly circumstantial, Minstrel."

"Who informed us of *Le Cercle Chêne* in the first place?" I said.

"It was Sandra Filton, that smart young woman from Paris-Blois," replied Jägermeister. "Paris-Blois have been loyal corporate benefactors to the Institute for many years. Their entire wine business has been torpedoed by this scandal. A scandal facilitated by you, in case we'd all forgotten! Are you seriously suggesting she's part of your topsy-turvy conspiracy too?"

I would be lying if I said I hadn't experienced a rush of euphoria as I deduced Sandra's role in the whole deceitful affair. For there was no doubt about it. That spiteful, callous, duplicitous, indecently radiant beauty had been suckered just like the rest of us. The giveaway had been her anger. The volume and frequency of those apoplectic phone messages, culminating in the raw, visceral hatred in her final call just after I'd staggered back to my Shanghai hotel room, the scent of elephant seal dung from my ragged clothes still choking the air. If she'd been in on it, there would have been no need for all those blood-curdling threats. After all, so far as Lee was concerned, everything was going to plan. Poor Sandra. After everything we'd been through together, she now stood to be humbled and humiliated, her company and career destroyed. A victory of sorts, given the way she'd treated me, I supposed.

"It was Inspector Ma who informed us," I said. "Inspector Ma works for Joseph Lee."

"And what do you base that on?" said Jägermeister. "Because he wanted to question you in Hong Kong? He's a detective inspector, for goodness sake. It's his job to ask questions."

"Because while I was being held hostage in Shanghai last weekend, Lee revealed that he knew I'd stolen the full bottle of Musigny '78. That information could only have come from the meeting that you, I, and the other Provosts had with Sandra in the Salon de Bordeaux a month ago. Sandra would have passed that information in good faith to Inspector Ma, who would, of course, then have informed Lee."

"Are you sure?" said Slipcote. "Maybe you were spotted stealing it from his tasting, after all."

"No, Provost. Because while he was interrogating me in Shanghai, Joseph Lee didn't mention the unicorn – the empty bottle of Richebourg '21 I stole at the same time – despite claiming that his people had reassembled and counted all the bottles at the end of the tasting. He didn't mention it because the theft of the Richebourg '21 wasn't raised in our Salon de Bordeaux meeting. Lee had no reason to reassemble and count his bottles, because despite his team's best efforts to tempt me into thieving one, they assumed I hadn't done so. And even if Lee had reviewed the

CCTV footage, I doubt it covered the space beneath his marble-topped table, which is where I performed my cunning sleight of hand. By the time Sandra passed on the news of the full bottle's theft to Inspector Ma, nearly a week later, all the broken bottles would have been long disposed of. You see, if Lee had realised I'd stolen that unicorn, he'd certainly have asked me about it. He would have suspected that Provost Rougegorgefils and her team were highly likely to establish its authenticity."

"That is very interesting," said Rougegorgefils, tapping her lips. "We didn't discuss the Richebourg '21 at that Salon de Bordeaux meeting, of course, because we hadn't yet received the results of the radiation analysis. And there's something else unsatisfactory about that unicorn. We were informed, quite categorically, that a similar bottle had been sourced by the late Minstrel Farquhar on behalf of a wealthy client several years earlier. More pertinently, that the wine had then been consumed by that client with Minstrel Farquhar in attendance. It was the prospect of a 1921 vintage Richebourg in the Macau line-up that convinced us Joseph Lee was up to no good."

"Thank you, Provost," I said. "And I'm sure you recall the identity of the character who furnished us with this tale of the resurrected Richebourg?"

"We received the information from Sandra at Paris-Blois," said Rougegorgefils. "But I believe she in turn was informed by Adam Fromage, the replacement managing director of Farquhar Fine and Rare."

"Correct. And Fromage also works for Joseph Lee."

"Another one?" spat Jägermeister. "How on earth do you come to that conclusion?"

"Because Adam Fromage has fed us nonsense every step of the way. As well as spinning us the tale of the supposedly fake Richebourg '21, Fromage was the one who suggested stealing an empty bottle of Musigny '78. He also informed me that last Saturday's *Cercle Chêne* tasting would take place at the Heavenly Jin restaurant on the 120th floor of the Shanghai Tower. Instead, I was intercepted, kidnapped, and interrogated by Joseph Lee.

And when Fromage realised I'd cracked the conspiracy, he tried to persuade me to remain at my hotel while they sent the goons round to pick me up. Fromage even supplied me with a phone from Lee's people, which was used to track my movements, not least by Inspector Ma as I attempted to flee Hong Kong."

"I suppose," said Rougegorgefils, "that if Joseph Lee wanted to decant genuine Burgundy into fake bottles as part of a conspiracy, Fromage would be a useful little helper."

"I'm sorry, I'm calling time on this absurd charade," said Jägermeister. "Pray tell us, Minstrel Hart, why did you allow yourself to be filmed in Shanghai declaring Lee and his machine to be the Second bloody Coming?"

"I didn't, Provost. The video was a deepfake. Lee's people had enough footage of me speaking at the tasting in Macau to engineer a perfectly convincing video. The Shanghai recording was supposedly filmed on Saturday night. But I was unconscious all evening, following my kidnapping at the Shanghai Tower."

"How enormously convenient. I suggest there's only one deepfake round here, Minstrel Hart, and I'm looking at him."

"On that issue, Provosts, I realise I'm asking you to take my word for it."

"You're asking us to take your word on a very great deal!" snorted Jägermeister. "And I don't believe your word is worth much around here, Minstrel Hart. Time to bring this pantomime to an end."

"Provosts, please. I beg your indulgence for just two more minutes. If you will allow me to summarise?"

"Two minutes, Minstrel Hart," said Slipcote, taking a swig of wine. "That's your lot." He thumped his goblet down.

Jägermeister scowled and folded his arms. Rougegorgefils stared at me, motionless. Jordaan clenched her hand into a fist and nodded.

"Thank you, Provosts. I ask you to choose between two scenarios. The first scenario is the one fed to you by Joseph Lee and his agents. It asks you to believe that a billionaire scientist and wine obsessive has invented a fluid facsimile machine, codename Project Athena, intended to reproduce complex pharmaceuticals. It is also capable of counterfeiting wine, even the finest and most ancient vintages. You are asked to believe that the billionaire has been serving these manufactured wines to potential investors at his ultra-exclusive tasting events, known as *Le Cercle Chêne*. The attendees, of course, are unaware the wines are fake. The billionaire's plan, as part of a headline-grabbing PR strategy, is to reveal the truth of their manufacture just before his company's multi-billion-dollar float."

Jägermeister continued to scowl at me.

"You are then asked to believe that the billionaire wine obsessive makes a careless but honest mistake. At his Dubai tasting, he presents a wine vintage that never existed. This is brought to the attention of the Worshipful Institute, who dispatch an undercover Minstrel to attend the next tasting, in Macau, and procure a bottle for analysis. At this tasting, our undercover Minstrel judges the wines – an apparently superb line-up of Burgundies indistinguishable from the genuine article. His suspicions are raised, however, by the fact none of the wines are opened in his presence and that, furthermore, his own wines, which he has been invited to present, are mysteriously decanted before the tasting."

Rougegorgefils tilted her head to one side, like a stork spotting a glittering fish among the weeds.

"Our Minstrel manages to procure a full bottle of Musigny '78 plus, as a bonus, an empty bottle of Richebourg '21. The samples are subjected to analysis back at Minstrels Hall, where the Musigny '78 label is revealed as a moderately sophisticated fake. But when the wine itself is analysed, not to mention tasted by the domaine's owner, it is found to be indistinguishable from a genuine sample. This is proof the billionaire has indeed cracked the challenge of perfectly replicating fine wine. So precise, in fact, is his technique, that not only are the molecular compositions of the fake and genuine wines identical, but the ratio of isotopes, too – a feat of engineering that would make an Iranian nuclear scientist wail with envy. Our undercover Minstrel is then asked to attend the next *Cercle Chêne* tasting, in Shanghai. He does so and the billionaire's PR strategy is executed. The artificial origin of the wines is revealed, and our Minstrel publicly declares them indistinguishable from the real thing. Understandably, investors react enthusiastically to the billionaire's imminent stock market float, and bearishly to companies in exposed sectors, particularly pharmaceuticals and fine wine."

I paused. My mouth was dry. But I had their attention.

"Well, yes," said Jägermeister, after a few seconds. "That's our understanding."

"Bring the condemned Minstrel some wine," ordered Slipcote, making a circular gesture in the direction of one of the decanter bearers. "He's put on a good show and if he's to be marched off the premises in the next sixty seconds, he deserves a final drink. You agree, Provost Jägermeister?"

Jägermeister closed his eyes and gave a dismissive wave. A glass tumbler was placed before me and filled with red wine.

"Thank you, Provost," I croaked.

I took a healthy swig. Claret, Left Bank. A damn good one. I felt my stage voice return.

"And the second scenario, Minstrel Hart?" said Rougegorgefils.

"Yes, Provosts. The alternative scenario begins the same way but unfolds rather differently. Our billionaire wine obsessive invents a fluid facsimile machine, under the codename Project Athena, intended to reproduce complex pharmaceuticals. Unfortunately for the billionaire, whether by intention or incompetence, the machine doesn't work. Undeterred, he presses on with his stock market floatation and hatches a headline-grabbing PR strategy to make it appear that his machine does, in fact, function as advertised. He serves genuine fine wines to potential investors at his ultra-exclusive tasting events, intending to announce, at a suitably strategic moment, that these wines are in truth the output of his machine. To provide further credibility, he seeks the endorsement of certain world-renowned wine experts. He is perceptive enough to realise that he must publicly fool these experts, too."

The room was silent. I took another generous sip of wine, for lubrication purposes.

"And so, the trap is sprung. The billionaire makes a deliberate vintage mistake at his Dubai tasting, designed to raise the suspicions of a Minstrel of Wine. Not the Minstrel you see before you, Provosts, but a member of our Hong Kong Chapter, by the name of Owen Farquhar."

"The late Owen Farquhar," murmured Slipcote.

"Unfortunately for the billionaire once more, Minstrel Farquhar spots the conspiracy, takes a dim view and decides he wants no part in it. More unfortunately still, the billionaire then arranges Minstrel Farquhar's night-time ejection from the Cheung Chau ferry as it is traversing the South China Sea.

Provost Rougegorgefils gave a sharp intake of breath.

"The deliberate vintage error is then drawn to the attention of the Worshipful Institute itself by a corrupt Hong Kong police inspector in the pay of the billionaire. An undercover Minstrel – Yours Truly – is duly recruited to attend the next *Cercle Chêne* tasting, in Macau. He is tasked with stealing an empty bottle of Musigny '78, an idea proposed by a crooked wine merchant by the name of Fromage, who is also in the pay of the billionaire. Said wine merchant helpfully points out that another of the featured wines, an incredibly rare Richebourg '21, is almost certainly a fake, given that a similar bottle was known to have been consumed by his colleague, the conveniently deceased Owen Farquhar, at an event some time ago."

Provost Slipcote rubbed his head thoughtfully.

"Our Minstrel attends the tasting in Macau, as instructed. He finds the wines indistinguishable from the genuine article because they are, of course, the genuine article. After engineering a brilliant diversion, and unbeknown to the billionaire, our Minstrel returns home with a full Musigny '78, rather than the empty one the billionaire intended him to steal, and the empty Richebourg '21 he was not supposed to have stolen at all. Back at Minstrels Hall, the empty Richebourg bottle is analysed for background radiation. The results of the tests show that the bottle, the label, and the sediment inside are the best part of a century old, implying the sample could not have been manufactured recently. Which it wasn't, of course, because it is a genuine 1921 Richebourg. The dinner at which the wine was supposedly consumed by the late Owen Farquhar never happened."

Provost Jägermeister stared at me, eyes bulging.

"The Musigny '78 label is an obvious fake, designed to fool an amateur but not an expert such as Minstrel Shuttlewort. The wine inside, however, is analysed and found to be indistinguishable in every way to the genuine article. Because, of course, it is the genuine article! At the request of the corrupt Hong Kong police inspector, our undercover Minstrel is dispatched to the next *Cercle Chêne* tasting, in Shanghai, supposedly to aid the authorities in their take-down of the billionaire. Unsurprisingly, the police are nowhere to be seen. Instead, our Minstrel is kidnapped by the billionaire and interrogated as to how he had advance knowledge of an attendee of the Macau tasting. The explanation is an innocent coincidence, but understandably the billionaire finds this difficult to believe. He then attempts to feed our Minstrel to his menagerie of giant carnivorous seals."

"Good Lord!" said Slipcote, banging down his goblet.

"Our Minstrel, through the application of calm, logical argument, convinces the billionaire of the innocent coincidence. The relieved billionaire releases our Minstrel, allowing the plan B version of his headline-grabbing PR campaign to be executed. A deepfake video is released, purporting to show our Minstrel declaring the billionaire's manufactured wines indistinguishable from the genuine article. Investors react enthusiastically to the billionaire's imminent stock market float, and bearishly to companies in exposed sectors, such as pharmaceuticals and fine wine."

I took a victory swig of wine and turned to Provost Jordaan. She winked back.

"Hell's bells!" said Slipcote. "We've all been royally had! This Project Athena thing is a house of cards!"

323

"Yes, Provost," I said. "Lee's entire set up is a fraud. Project Athena. The Neural Terafactory. His multi-billion-dollar float. The only question is, when will his investors find out?"

"May I also add," said Provost Jordaan, "that following his expulsion, with the entire Worshipful Institute denouncing him, Minstrel Hart would have found it near-impossible to gain a fair hearing regarding his misrepresentation."

I thrust out my chin in a humble, yet defiant pose. Jägermeister, I could see, had turned distinctly pale.

"Furthermore," continued Jordaan, "I suspect that we would be waking to the news, a day or so from now, that a dog walker had found Minstrel Hart's lifeless body on some muddy bank of the Thames Estuary. The verdict of the inquest, I'm sure, would be suicide, brought on by the humiliation of this very day. But I have no doubt that the hand of Joseph Lee, tying up loose ends, would be behind it."

I also turned pale. I made a solemn vow to myself never to volunteer for any task, ever again, that implied even the faintest whiff of self-sacrifice, altruism, or gallantry.

"Sounds like you'll need to throw a protective ring around Minstrel Hart for the time being," said Slipcote. "I suggest you deploy some of these athletic young men and women you've brought with you today."

"Arrangements will be made," said Jordaan.

"And poor Monsieur Laflamme," said Rougegorgefils. "He was mortified at the idea that anyone could produce such a perfect fake. He hasn't been the same since. I must call him at once and give him the good news."

"I have a question for you, Minstrel Hart," said Slipcote.

I was in the midst of swallowing a very large gulp of wine in an attempt to bring some colour back to my cheeks. I lowered my empty glass. "Provost?"

"How big were these carnivorous seals?"

"The smaller ones, around the size of a three-seater sofa. The largest, which I was obliged to subdue with a home-made spear, the size of a bus."

"By the beard of Bacchus!" shouted Slipcote. "What an adventure! Refill this Minstrel's glass immediately!"

"If you'll excuse me," said Jägermeister, rising from his seat, "I must speak to the Institute's investment team, quite urgently."

"Aren't you forgetting something, Provost?" said Jordaan.

"No, I don't think so," said Jägermeister, striding to the door.

"The Scourging of Verus is still spirituous."

Jägermeister looked over his shoulder, his hand already on the doorknob.

"Oh, that. Yes. Well, under the circumstances, I declare the Scourging of Verus rescinded. Do we concur, Provost Rougegorgefils? Provost Slipcote?"

"Yes, rescinded," said Rougegorgefils, bowing her head towards me.

"Yes, yes, bit of a shame, was looking forward to a proper exiling, but deservedly rescinded," said Slipcote, nodding to me.

The Italian Hand signed off the parchment with an elaborate flourish and laid down his quill. My glass was replenished and I felt my strength return. The room erupted into applause and, as I raised my wine high above my head, the observers leapt to their feet. I bowed to the three remaining Provosts, and to cries of "Bravo, Minstrel!" I dispatched my claret with the joy of a man reborn.

# Chapter 40

## Market Volatility

"You never call, you never write! What have I done to deserve this treatment, sweet cheeks?"

Tabatha Shunt's face gurned from my workstation in the small, but comfortable tenth-floor safe house nestling deep in the heart of Minstrels Hall.

"I do apologise, Tabatha. I ran into a few problems at Chinese immigration."

"Finally busted for your dodgy visa, were you? Still can't figure how you were able to sashay through immigration like some buff little catwalk model for so long."

"I told you. I had special dispensation from the authorities to chaperone consignments of high-value fine wine."

"Whatever. Now, what about the sales of our splashback-proof toilet seat?"

"I was just about to check the figures, Tabatha. I've been slightly detained over the past few days."

"What?" shouted Tabatha. "You mean you don't know? You haven't seen the stats?"

"I'm sorry, I was about to run the report. Give me a couple of minutes. They've only been on sale three days, so I doubt–"

"Babes, they're a goddam sphincter-busting sensation!"

"I'm sorry, they're what?"

"They're the fastest selling bathroom accessory in general merchandise history! An absolute triumph! You've sold over ninety thousand units since launch."

"Oh, blimey. That is good."

"Good? It's orgasmic! God, I could kiss you."

I thanked the gods that I was eight thousand miles from Tabatha's enveloping limbs.

"And that press release you wrote! I have to hand it to you, sweet cheeks, that was genius. All that stuff about researching monks' toilets in the monasteries of Qinghai. Was that true?"

"Of course. The design was inspired by my visit to the Tibetan Shatuo Monastery. The monks there are legendary for their bodily cleanliness. They fit membranes fashioned from yaks' stomachs over their lavatories to prevent unholy splashback on their prayer robes. It's humbling, actually, to see such attention to bathroom hygiene in a supposedly backward region. It genuinely makes you reassess your cultural assumptions."

"Yeah, I know, I read your press release – as did every wellness blog on the planet. The Gatesave website's already out of stock. The police had to be called to Dudley store to deal with a punch-up over the last seat. They're popping up on eBay for five hundred quid. We've had queries come through from the US, Australia, even Argentina."

"Well, that's splendid news."

"Sure is. And Brad, our CEO, messaged me yesterday. He's well impressed. I told him it was partly down to you, of course. My little protégé. You should drop him a note. I'm sure he'll want to schedule a call to congratulate you."

"Will do."

"But before you do that, before you do anything, make sure you order a ton more seats, got it? We need a million, with an option on double that. I've been trying to get hold of Charles Fung myself, but he's still not responding to messages. Any idea where he is?"

"I believe he's convalescing. He had a little health scare."

"Did he? What's the matter with him?"

"I think something disagreed with him at dinner."

"Oh dear. Well, contact the factory and don't stop until you get a commitment. Every retailer on the planet will be copying that design. Remember, sweet cheeks, you're only as good as your last gig. Don't let me down."

Tabatha blew me an obscene kiss and ended the call. I'd barely typed out a message to Fung's export manager before my laptop began trilling enthusiastically. An incoming call from Brad the Impaler, no less. I arranged my features into an expression I hoped was both innovative and disruptive.

"Good morning, Brad."

"Felix Hart! The man! The legend!"

"Oh, well, that's very kind of you to say so. The entire Homeware division is delighted with the sales of our splashback-proof toilet seat, of course. I'm working on the re-order right now."

"Hell, I'm not calling about splashback, Felix! I'm calling about fine wine. Or, should I say, the death of fine wine?"

"Ah, yes. Sorry about all that. I know I should have got clearance before a public-speaking event. I didn't realise it was being filmed."

"Never mind that. You're a true disrupter! The guys from Fultech told me all about your wine tasting in Shanghai with Joseph Lee. I mean, that's insane, man. I have so many questions. Firstly, how the hell did you manage to travel to Shanghai? Even I can't get to Shanghai!"

"Well, Joseph Lee helped a little. And, to be honest, stories of fine wine's death might be a touch premature."

"It's dead, Felix! Hell, you called it. You know, Joseph Lee is one of my mentors. Met him back in my Goldman days. A real hero of mine. How come you know him?"

"Oh, I kind of do a little consulting for him, in the wine sphere."

"A little consulting, huh? You're part of Joseph's Project Athena team, aren't you? That is super-insane. You realise you are disrupting at the absolute quantum level?"

"Yes, I suppose I am really."

"I'll let you into a secret, Felix. Gatesave is investing some serious cash in Joseph Lee's IPO. Makes complete sense as a stand-alone investment, of course, because basically the guy makes King Midas look like a crypto day-trader. But, more importantly, the association gets us serious, serious clout in China. It'll supercharge our expansion into the tier-three cities."

"Makes perfect sense," I said, my heart sinking.

"Certainly does," beamed Brad. "And Felix, you can probably guess what I want you to do."

I attempted to hold my enthusiastic expression in place, but my face had begun to strain with the effort. And my bowels were already churning in a way they hadn't since my escape from Lee's aquatic amusement park of death.

"Basically," continued Brad, "I need someone I can trust on the ground in China. Someone to help manage the tier-three city roll-out. Thanks to your relationship with Joseph Lee, you're the perfect candidate."

"But surely you have people far more qualified," I wailed. "I'm just a bathroom accessories buyer!"

"Loving the self-deprecation, Felix! You do make me laugh. Anyway, need you in Beijing next week. Congratulations on the promotion. Ciao."

Brad's face vanished. With a depressed sigh, I closed my laptop and headed down to the Salon de Dijon for a fortifying lunch.

\*\*\*

Given the sudden, unwelcome improvement in my career prospects, I decided to award myself Friday off. Due to the threat presented by Joseph Lee, Provost Jordaan had expressly forbidden me from returning home, hence the safe house at Minstrels Hall. But Jordaan hadn't explicitly banned me from staying with friends. And so, I decided to slip out of my friendly prison and instead spend a long, lively weekend with Marissa, Gatesave's Head of Product Integrity for canned and packaged goods, who regaled me with tales of malfeasance in the tuna canneries of the Maldives. The distraction relegated all thoughts of Joseph Lee, Project Athena and fine wine mischief to the back of my mind and it wasn't until Monday afternoon, once I'd returned to my temporary base in the heart of House Terrorist's realm, that I received a text from Provost Jordaan.

*First cracks...*

Jordaan had pasted a link to a social media post by an Australian investment hotshot called The Shares Bloke.

*More froth than a warm Prosecco*, opined The Shares Bloke, who in turn had provided a link to a blog article he'd written entitled, *If You Like Your Cappuccino Cold and Decaffeinated, You'll Love this IPO.*

The replies beneath The Shares Bloke's post alternated between gifs of deflating balloons and cartoon characters running off cliff tops, sprinkled with a few angry accusations of anti-Chinese racism. I texted a thumbs-up to Provost Jordaan and applied myself to the task of negotiating a better cost price for one million faecal splashback-busting toilet seats, while ignoring the increasingly frequent voicemails from Brad the Impaler's PA demanding to know when I planned to fly to Beijing.

*\*\*\**

The following evening, I found myself in the Salon de Dijon with Valentina and Hugo, giving them the inside track on my triumph at the Scourging of Verus. My inspired performance during that medieval ordeal, not to mention my hair-raising adventures in the Far East, had elevated me to an A-list celebrity within the walls of the Worshipful Institute. Barely a minute passed without admiring Minstrels asking my advice on Shanghai stock market opportunities or demanding to be regaled with tales of unarmed combat against sabre-toothed sea mammals. So, it was no surprise, as I nodded my approval of a very pleasant biodynamic Poulsard, to feel a hearty slap on my shoulder. It was a surprise, however, to hear the sneering tones of Provost Jägermeister transformed to jolly bonhomie.

"Minstrel Hart, you young buck, guessed I'd find you here," he brayed. "Drinking the Salon de Dijon out of Côtes du Jura, as usual?"

I turned and smiled warmly, for in victory I am relentlessly benevolent. Jägermeister was accompanied by an older Minstrel I only vaguely recognised.

"I assume you know Minstrel Hollensen, Chairman of the Institute's investment arm? And a senior member of House Mercantilist, too, of course."

"Yes, a pleasure to meet you again," I said, rising from my seat.

I spotted Valentina rolling her eyes at Hugo.

"On behalf of the Institute," said Minstrel Hollensen, shaking my hand enthusiastically, "I wanted to thank you personally for your insights regarding our strategic investment portfolio."

"Delighted to be of service," I replied, wondering what the hell he was talking about.

"Quite a close shave," Hollensen continued, showing no intention of releasing his grip on my fingers.

"Well, there've been a few recently," I said.

"I'm sure you've seen today's South China Morning Post?"

"Actually, I hadn't quite got round to it," I said.

"Oh, I assumed you would have, given your expertise in the region." Hollensen lowered his voice. "Just the latest ripple caused by our own little Operation Drip-Drip. I suspect this may the last day we'll retain any privileged insights vis-à-vis the wider market." He winked at Provost Jägermeister.

"I'll be sure to take a look."

Hollensen finally released my hand.

"I also bring some rather special news, Minstrel Hart," said Jägermeister. "House Mercantilist has voted to offer you the Freedom of Johan Sanz Terre. Henceforth, you will be granted permission to attend every major House Mercantilist function. Quite a singular honour. Only three Minstrels have received it in my entire time at the Institute."

"That is indeed an honour, Provost, thank you very much."

"You'll need Provost Jordaan's permission before you accept," piped up Valentina from behind her goblet of Poulsard.

"Anyway," said Jägermeister, scowling at Valentina,

"anything I can do for you in the meantime, don't hesitate to drop my secretary a note."

"Actually, there is something, Provost."

"Oh, is there?" said Jägermeister, his face falling a little.

"I wonder if you might tip off Sandra at Paris-Blois Beverages and advise her not to give up on her employer just yet? From a financial perspective."

"I don't know about that, Minstrel Hart. Don't get me wrong, I'm an admirer of that formidable young woman, but careless talk and all that."

"I agree!" whispered Minstrel Hollensen. "Operation Drip-Drip is a meticulously engineered plan. We cannot compromise such privileged knowledge. Who knows what she might do with it?"

"But, Provost, might it not help the Institute cement its future relationship with Paris-Blois? No need to mention me. Much better if it came from an authoritative source such as yourself."

Jägermeister and Hollensen looked at one another. Neither spoke aloud, but through an impenetrable exchange of forehead furrowing and eyebrow twitching, I sensed a parsing of risk and reward culminating in a consensus on future return on investment.

"On second thoughts, that might not be such a bad idea at all, Minstrel," said Jägermeister, smirking like a landlord announcing a rent increase. "All about the timing, of course. I'll consider it."

He and Hollensen departed.

"*South China Morning Post*," said Hugo, handing me his phone. "I'm guessing that's the article you want, right at the top."

'Investors Challenge Efficacy of Lee's Flagship Project,' stated the headline. Not the snappiest of titles, but I read on. A large and usually discreet Singaporean fund had gone public with their concerns regarding Greater China Pharmco, not least that Joseph Lee was resisting independent verification of his Terafactory's pharmaceutical output. A couple of American hedge funds were being rather more forthright, mocking the fact that Lee appeared more interested in manufacturing fine Burgundy than lentiviral vectors, whatever the hell they were. The article highlighted the awkwardness of such concerns, given that Greater China Pharmco's IPO date was just one week away and that allaying investor concerns was likely to be a priority for Mr Lee.

"God, I'm so jealous that you'll get to attend all those exciting House Mercantilist dinners," said Valentina. "Geopolitics and high finance surrounded by old clarets and old farts. I guess you won't have time for the little people like me and Hugo anymore."

"Don't worry, it won't change me," I said.

***

I awoke to the sound of my mobile trilling helplessly beneath a pile of discarded clothing. A couple of confused seconds passed as I realised I wasn't in my usual bed. Then, a poke to the ribs and Marissa's voice from under the duvet telling me to switch it off. I slipped out of bed, unearthed my phone and padded to the bathroom.

"Felix Hart speaking."

"Yes, Mr Hart. How are you this fine morning? It's James from your Luxe Premier Banking Team."

"I'm rich in spirit, James. Don't tell me you're calling to complain about my overdraft's negative status position again?"

"Oh, no, no, nothing like that Mr Hart, ho, ho."

"Just a social call, then, is it?" I wondered whether James could hear me tinkling into the toilet bowl. I redirected my aim against the porcelain to muffle the sound.

"It's a courtesy call, really, Mr Hart. To advise you that you might wish to optimise your portfolio. You are still incurring overdraft charges on your current account and interest on the secured loan you requested."

"It appears you are indeed calling to complain about my overdraft."

"No, no. No complaints. No complaints at all, Mr Hart. After all, the Private Wealth Unit exists to help you optimise your assets."

"So, optimise away, James. What do you suggest?"

"Well, the most obvious step would be to liquidate some of the Paris-Blois Beverages shares you purchased two weeks ago. Don't get me wrong, Mr Hart, we don't mind charging you interest, but it is our duty to point out scenarios where you might enjoy improved overall portfolio performance."

"Ah, yes, the Paris-Blois shares," I said. "Would those be the ones you tried to discourage me from buying, James?"

"Oh, ha, ha, yes. Sorry about that. But as part of our rigorous due diligence procedures, we are obliged to warn clients that assets can depreciate as well as appreciate. On this occasion, the assets have appreciated, of course."

"Oh, the shares went up, did they? Good. Thought they might. How much?"

"They did, Mr Hart. Seventy-six point two euros, as of ten minutes ago."

"Seventy-six euros? Is that all? Fine, stick it against the overdraft. Is there anything else?"

"That's each, Mr Hart. Seventy-six point two euros each."

"Each?"

"Yes, each. A very shrewd investment, if I may say so. I've never seen volatility quite like it. All connected to that Chinese pharmaceutical scandal that broke yesterday. Of course, as an expert investor I'm sure you know much more about it than me."

"How many?"

"How many shares? Well, we invested your entire fifty thousand-pound loan in the share purchase, as instructed. So, in total, we purchased ninety-eight thousand, three hundred and four units once the Paris Bourse lifted the suspension. After fees and stamp duty."

It struck me that I should probably put a call in to Berry Bros., so I didn't miss out on next year's en primeur allocations.

"The shares were at rock bottom, absolute junk, when you bought them, of course. Right now, they're worth around, let's see… Seven and a half million euros."

And did you need planning permission to excavate a wine cellar beneath your house? Or was that just loft conversions? And were you allowed to do both?

"Oh, my mistake. They're now seven-point-six million. And rising. They're still around ten per cent off their original level, so you might want to hold on for a bit. You'll have to pay capital gains on anything you sell, of course."

And what was the going rate for a private chef in Cervinia? Not all year round, that would be decadent. Just for January and February. Maybe March, too.

"Mr Hart? Are you there, Mr Hart?"

To my embarrassment, I realised I was peeing on the bathroom floor.

# Chapter 41

## Reconciliation

"Well, I'm absolutely delighted that we've finally put this unpleasant business behind us," said Jägermeister, swirling his Lafite. "Such tribulations, of course, are mere background noise compared with the longstanding symphony of cooperation between Paris-Blois and the Worshipful Institute."

"And we, in turn, consider it an honour to extend Paris-Blois's sponsorship of the Nathaniel Jägermeister scholarship in perpetuity," replied Sandra.

Jägermeister beamed.

If you'd told me a week ago that I would be invited to an intimate dinner with Provost Jägermeister and Sandra, I'd have been confident the agenda would begin with my decapitation, followed by my burial in a shallow grave. But a week is a long time in politics and here I was, much to my surprise, surrounded by warm words and plump smiles.

My eyes drifted to the headline on Jägermeister's copy of the *Financial Times*.

*Joseph Lee humiliated as Greater China Pharmco IPO withdrawn. Billionaire under house arrest.*

"I'd like to propose a toast," declared Jägermeister. "To truth, authenticity, and decency!"

The three of us touched glasses.

"And may I say once again, congratulations to you, Sandra, on your promotion to permanent CEO of Paris-Blois Beverages International. I'm told your company is now the star performer across the entire international group."

"Thank you, Nathaniel. It's been a baptism of fire but, as our

International Group CEO said to me yesterday, that heat has forged us into a diamond-hard asset."

"No doubt, no doubt," said Jägermeister. "And Minstrel Hart here is back in the beverages saddle, too, I understand?"

"Yes Provost, we've had a little restructure at Gatesave following the rather abrupt departure of our own CEO."

Brad the Impaler, it transpired, had utilised a fiendishly innovative and disruptive financial vehicle to hose an eye-watering sum of Gatesave's money over Greater China Pharmo's Hong Kong listing, presumably in an effort to endear himself to Joseph Lee. Following the IPO's collapse, however, Gatesave's funds had gone awkwardly absent without leave and were last seen waving plaintively from the website of a distressed Chongqing bank, the principal shareholder of which was one Joseph Lee. Given that Joseph Lee was not currently returning calls, presumably due to him being given the piñata treatment by the Chinese People's Financial Shenanigans Department, the likelihood of Gatesave recovering its funds appeared remote. The episode had been declared 'a disappointing lapse in governance' by Gatesave's chairman, and Brad the Impaler had been ejected from the company as ceremoniously as a cat expelling a hairball. By way of a cleansing exercise, all Brad's recent decisions were being reversed at pace, and given my splashback-proof toilet seat triumph, my request to be reinstated as head of the wine department was speedily fulfilled.

"Delighted to hear it," said Jägermeister. "Now, please accept my apologies but duty calls. I am obliged to chair an action committee in response to the government's disgraceful attempts to tax Vintage Port out of existence. I shall leave you two with the remainder of this magnificent Lafite." He rose to his feet and wafted his hand over the bottle. "Minstrel Hart, will you...?"

"Not a problem, Provost. I'll take care of it."

"Very good, thank you. *À bientôt*."

Jägermeister disappeared through the curtains, leaving Sandra and me alone.

"There were a couple of things I wanted to clear up," I said.

"Oh? And what might they be, Felix? Your aspiration to be the wine trade's preeminent lord of chaos? Your world record as the greatest individual destroyer of value in the history of the stock market? Your self-appointed role as international bull in a china shop?"

Harsh words, but I fancied I detected more than a hint of playfulness in Sandra's tone.

"Bull in a china shop. Very good. I didn't have you down as the punning type."

"That's an idiom, not a pun."

"I'm perfectly happy to be thought of as a bull. That's almost a compliment, from you."

"Well, I certainly think you're full of it, Felix, if that's what you mean."

"How terribly rude. And, just to be clear, I think of myself more as a creator of value than a destroyer. I assume you received my investment advice last week via our favourite Provost, before all this news broke?"

Sandra pursed her lips and studied her Lafite.

"Is that a new Chanel suit you're wearing? Looks rather fabulous on you, by the way."

Sandra took a sip of wine.

"My point," I continued, "was that I hoped we could bring a certain contractual matter to an amicable conclusion."

"That would be the contractual matter that states you're obliged to complete a certain project to Paris-Blois's satisfaction?"

"That's the one. Are you suggesting you're not satisfied?"

"For me, the jury's still out on whether you caused the near-collapse of Paris-Blois Beverages and half the stock exchange or saved it."

"Looking at your current share price, I'd call it a firm save. If Paris-Blois or Provost Jägermeister had sent anyone else to China, I think Joseph Lee would have played them like a fiddle. They might even have ended up dead. Either way, there'd be no Paris-Blois Beverages."

"I think you fluked it, Felix. Like you fluke everything."

"It might look like a fluke to you, Sandra. But it's skill. Pure, unadulterated skill."

Sandra finished her Lafite, rose, and moved behind my chair. She put her hands on my shoulders.

"I'll instruct Paris-Blois's lawyers to draw up a letter stating that you have discharged your obligations, in full, to our satisfaction. Happy?"

"I would be most grateful, thank you."

"Though I'm tempted to add a clause that obliges you to wear a sign around your neck, permanently, saying *Danger, Bull*."

She leaned over and kissed me on the cheek.

"And thank you. I do look good in Chanel, don't I?"

## The End

# About the Author

Peter Stafford-Bow was born into a drinking family in the north of England in the mid-1970s. A precocious, self-taught imbiber, he dropped out of university to pursue a career in alcohol. After managing several downmarket London wine merchants, he became a supermarket buyer, a role which kindled his life-long love of food, other people's hospitality, and general gadding about. After periods living in East Asia and South Africa, Stafford-Bow returned to the UK to pursue a literary career. He has written four novels which form the successful Felix Hart series; *Corkscrew, Brut Force, Firing Blancs* and *Eastern Promise*. He lives in London with a wealthy heiress, an extensive wine collection and his pet ferrets, Brett and Corky.

# Corkscrew
## Volume One of the Felix Hart Novels

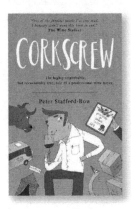

Felix Hart, a tragic orphan, is expelled from school, cast onto the British high street, and forced to make his way in the cut-throat world of wine retail. Thanks to a positive mental attitude, he is soon forging a promising career, his sensual adventures taking him to the vineyards of Italy, South Africa, Bulgaria and Kent.

Felix's path to the summit is littered with obstacles, from psychotic managers to the British Board of Wine & Liquor. But when he negotiates the world's biggest Asti Spumante deal, Felix is plunged into a vicious world of Mafiosi, people smuggling and ruthless multinationals.

Part thriller, part self-help manual and part drinking companion, Corkscrew is a coruscating critique of neo-liberal capitalism, religious intolerance and the perils of blind tasting.

*"...one of the funniest novels I've ever read. I honestly didn't want this book to end."*
Joey Casco, *The Wine Stalker*

*"This book gets a big thumbs up from me... this is not for youngsters."*
Dave Nershi, *Vino-Sphere.com*

# Brut Force
## Volume Two of the Felix Hart Novels

Felix Hart, a wine buyer at the top of his game, finds himself compromised by a ruthless multinational drinks corporation. Forced to participate in a corrupt, high stakes wine tasting, Felix is drawn into a terrifying game of cat-and-mouse, pursued by blackmailers, assassins and organic wine fanatics.

The action moves from the Byzantine intrigue of the Minstrels of Wine to France's most glamorous chateaux, Felix relying on his quick wits, fine palate and a touch of muscle to stay ahead of his enemies. But he meets his match in Lily Tremaine, a beautiful and passionate sommelier, who disrupts his easy, pleasure-seeking life and turns his world upside down.

*"It's an insane novel. It's clever... and brilliantly conceived."*
Tamlyn Currin, *JancisRobinson.com*

*"...a very enjoyable romp... the entertainment value is super."*
Peter Donnelly, *The Reading Desk*

# Firing Blancs

## Volume Three of the Felix Hart Novels

Felix Hart, Head of Wine at Gatesave Supermarkets, is in a highly problematic spot. Choking his CEO to death during a boardroom presentation was embarrassing enough. But evidence that Gatesave's biggest wine supplier is brutalising its workers threatens a far greater scandal. Felix is dispatched to Cape Town and finds himself stranded, penniless, at a highly entrepreneurial township guesthouse.

Persecuted by his bosses, blackmailed by his suppliers, and terrorised by politicians, policemen and other criminals, Felix is obliged to fling himself on the mercy of his hosts. But the forces ranged against Felix and his new allies are as powerful as they are ruthless, and our hero soon finds that he is very much expendable.

> *"...this is his best. Shades of Evelyn Waugh*
> *here in its humour and satirical thrust."*
> Tony Aspler

> *"Just like its two predecessors, Firing*
> *Blancs rattles along as fast as a bullet."*
> Simon Woolf, *The Morning Claret*